MW00851201

BY XHENET ALIU

Brass

Domesticated Wild Things, and Other Stories

EVERYBODY
SAYS IT'S
EVERYTHING

EVERYBODY SAYS IT'S EVERYTHING

A Novel

XHENET ALIU

RANDOM HOUSE

NEW YORK

Copyright © 2025 by Xhenet Aliu

Penguin Random House values and supports copyright. Copyright fuels creativity, encourages diverse voices, promotes free speech and creates a vibrant culture. Thank you for buying an authorized edition of this book and for complying with copyright laws by not reproducing, scanning, or distributing any part of it in any form without permission. You are supporting writers and allowing Penguin Random House to continue to publish books for every reader. Please note that no part of this book may be used or reproduced in any manner for the purpose of training artificial intelligence technologies or systems.

All rights reserved.

Published in the United States by Random House,
an imprint and division of Penguin Random House LLC, New York.

RANDOM HOUSE and the HOUSE colophon are registered trademarks of Penguin Random House LLC.

LIBRARY OF CONGRESS CATALOGING-IN-PUBLICATION DATA
NAMES: Aliu, Xhenet, 1978- author.
TITLE: Everybody says it's everything : a novel / Xhenet Aliu.
DESCRIPTION: First edition. | New York, NY : Random House, 2025.
IDENTIFIERS: LCCN 2024016236 (print) | LCCN 2024016237 (ebook) |
ISBN 9780593732274 (hardcover ; acid-free paper) | ISBN 9780593732281 (ebook)
SUBJECTS: LCGFT: Novels.
CLASSIFICATION: LCC PS3601.L3967 E94 2025 (print) |
LCC PS3601.L3967 (ebook) | DDC 813/.6—dc23/eng/20240423
LC record available at https://lccn.loc.gov/2024016236
LC ebook record available at https://lccn.loc.gov/2024016237

Printed in the United States of America on acid-free paper

randomhousebooks.com

1st Printing

First Edition

Book design by Sara Bereta

To TOK: No, *you're* the phenomenology.

EVERYBODY
SAYS IT'S
EVERYTHING

1

ON HER NINTH BIRTHDAY, DRITA FINALLY HELD IN HER HANDS THE thing she'd asked for seven months before, at Christmas: Parisian Barbie, the one in the hot pink cancan dress and the kind of lacy black stockings she'd only ever seen on women in the sorts of magazines dads—even ones that barely qualified, like Dom—kept at the bottom of their toolboxes.

"Oh my god," Drita said.

Her brother, Pete, had handed it to her, then punched his right fist into his left palm like he was waiting for something in return. He should have been; it was his ninth birthday, too, but all Drita could offer him was a face struck dumb by the box she held and some words that meant nothing to him, because Pete was only interested in things that went boom.

"That's the one you wanted, right?" Pete asked. He knew very well that it was, a present so good there was no need to wrap it. At Christmas she'd received, naturally, Italian Barbie, not just because Mattel didn't make an Albanian version but because their mother, Jackie, was always trying to impart a cultural legacy that her adopted children would never truly share. The doll Drita had really wanted—the one staring at her at that moment from beneath the cellophane——was beautiful and a little slutty, not dressed like a peasant about to milk cows the way her Italian Barbie cousin was.

Drita thought of the little box she planned to give Pete later that night, covered in a page from the Sunday comics. The key chain inside that she'd crafted for him out of a tumbled rock and airplane glue was objectively hideous, and stupid to boot—they were nine, they were years away from possessing keys to anything.

A tear slipped over Drita's eyelid, something she knew she was going to have to learn how to control soon, before the kids at school got meaner, which Pete had warned her was coming.

"But that's the one you said you wanted," Pete said, immediately defensive.

"It is the one I wanted," Drita said. "It's just that I don't have anything for you."

She'd been planning to present him the key chain over cake, after the song, when Jackie and Dom would give him the handheld Space Invaders game everybody already knew he was getting. It wouldn't have mattered then how stupid her gift was, because handheld Space Invaders was the kind of present grown-ups were expected to deliver for birthdays. Kids were supposed to give each other some trinket made out of the better things grown-ups got them, like a preshrunk Shrinky Dink, or a chewy brownie baked for an hour under an Easy-Bake lightbulb, or a key chain made from a rock tumbler kit. Nine-year-olds didn't have the money for real presents. She didn't have money. How did Pete have money?

Pete shrugged. "It's okay if you just made me something."

"Wait, how were you able to get this?" Drita asked, turning the box over in her hands. On the side of the box, Barbie explained what life was like in France. The part of Paris on the right side of the Seine River was where French fashions came from. The cities that weren't Paris grew grapes to make into wine.

Drita knew from the way Pete smiled that he was desperate to tell her, despite shrugging and saying only "I have my ways."

School is free and children work very hard, the box said. School was also free in America, but Barbies weren't, which made the box in Drita's hand take on a different weight when she looked down on it again.

"Pete, how'd you get this?" Drita asked again.

"I pulled it from a hat," Pete said, pantomiming a magician's flourish.

"But really," Drita said.

"I delivered newspapers."

"You did not."

"I rode to Bradlees and stole it," Pete said, giddy, finally, with the truth of it.

"Pete," Drita gasped.

"What? I did it for you."

Drita wasn't sure how to respond to that, except to stop crying. She recognized that her gut reaction was even more childish than holding a doll was: stealing is bad, lying is bad, those were lessons they were supposed to have taken from those Little Golden Books Jackie read to them when they were small. But those lessons seemed too simple now that they were nine; they didn't allow for all the not-that-bad choices in between. Pete had ridden his bike all the way to Bradlees, for example, which must have taken over an hour, meaning he technically spent more time on Drita's present than she did on his, the six unattended weeks the rock tumbler ran in the basement notwithstanding. And he had at least paid more attention to Drita's wish list than Jackie had, which was touching and which, despite what people believed about twins, hadn't previously proven to be based on some innate biological bond.

But still, she knew by the smile on his face that he didn't do it just for her. Even if the booty was for Drita, he'd gotten something for himself out of it. He'd gotten to graduate from Dennis the Menace mischievous to at least a middle school level of dangerous, trouble being the only subject in which Pete was ever ahead of the curve.

Meanwhile Drita was still playing with dolls and making toys for her brother's birthday out of toys she'd received from her last one.

Drita looked at Parisian Barbie again. She shouldn't have been playing with dolls anymore, not when her brother had already moved on
from Cops and Robbers to flat-out robbery. But around Barbie's neck
was a choker with a cameo, so alluring even in satin and plastic instead
of velvet and ivory. She did want the doll. She wanted a portal to the
kind of life that could only be lived in far-off places, and in exchange
she had to give Pete something, even if it was just the suggestion of
respect.

Cool, she wanted to say, because it was the word he'd most appreciate, but she'd feel like a fraud using it, and it seemed inadequate besides, so she hunted for something better. On the side of the Parisian
Barbie box was some French vocabulary, and she looked there for help.
There was the word for mother, there was the word for father, the one
for house, dog, I, but no thank you, and no brother.

The only words left on the box translated to goodbye, and so that
was what she said to him.

"Au revoir, Petrit!" she said, using his real name because it was foreign, if not French. "Au revoir!"

1999

Au revoir indeed.

Drita remembered every exquisite detail of that Barbie seventeen
years later, between the third and fourth rings of the phone call coming in at 6:34 A.M., when she was certain that whoever was on the other
end of the line would be calling to tell her that Pete had au revoired for
good. That was the only reason for calls at that hour, something she
understood despite never having taken any previous middle-of-the-
night phone calls about the deaths of various loved ones, the sole fortunate by-product of what had become, since returning to Waterbury
to nurse both the strangers who provided her paychecks and her own
mother, an otherwise excruciating loneliness. The aunts and uncles

and grandparents she and Pete had acquired through Jackie and Dom
had lived like they were supposed to—within blocks of the places of
their birth, taking all the time-and-a-half a human body could with-
stand at Chase Manufacturing so their children could attend St.
Margaret's–McTernan, despite its obvious affiliation with some goddamn Mick or another—and they died like they were supposed to, in
hospice from aggressive lung cancers no one would dare suggest had
anything to do with lifelong exposure to asbestos or Merit Golds. Even
the phone call about Dom had come at a reasonable afternoon hour,
and his left anterior descending artery blockage seemed inevitable
enough that she hardly remembered the details of the message.

Drita's hand hovered over the receiver until the ringing stopped,
when she let herself take a breath and indulge the possibility that it
was just a wrong number. That gave her a minute to excavate some
good memories of Pete, just in case.

Like the way they used to steal church wafers together at all those
funerals despite Dom's occasional reminders that, underneath their
Reeboks and Lees, they were still born Moslems taking what they
shouldn't from the body of Christ.

Like the way they'd slip away from their adopted Catholic great-
aunts and cousins, who'd grieved for every corpse like pros, wearing
something from the Dress Barn Burial Collection and using the phrase
"God's will" about everything from the final comatose hours to the
catered potato salad.

Like the secret twin language they used to pretend they shared, each
of them blurping out a consonant-heavy dialect that made no more
sense to them than it did to anyone around them. *Let's make a fort in
the woods,* Drita would attempt to say, and Pete would shake out some
pellets from the purple side of a box of Nerds, and they'd laugh know-
ingly despite not knowing the intent behind the other's sounds at all.

Then the ringing began again, and she remembered that they hadn't
laughed together in a long, long time, those days ending even before
Pete and his girlfriend, Shanda, had taken off three years before with

their toddler in a van destined for who knows where, other than doom. And now it would never happen again, not after she answered the phone to learn of his inevitable overdose, or the drug dealer dead set on vengeance, like the one Drita couldn't protect her brother from before he skipped town.

Wouldn't. If Pete was alive, he would have said she wouldn't protect him, not that she couldn't.

In which case she deserved what was coming, which meant she had to answer that phone.

"Yeah?" she said, breathless, like she'd been running. She had been, a few minutes before, in her dream—running from a falling airplane, as usual, that being the theme of her recurrent nightmares of late. She dropped onto the futon in preparation for her legs giving out. Surely they would. Her fingers and toes had already gone numb, her heart failing to pump oxygen all the way to the ends of her.

"Drita," Jackie said. She was crying. "Oh, honey."

Drita didn't answer. If she didn't answer, then Jackie wouldn't continue, and whatever news she was set to deliver couldn't be received.

"Drita? Are you there?" Jackie asked.

She had to be brave. Just enough to be competent, which shouldn't really even require bravery. She couldn't leave this work to Jackie, already paraplegic, a widow, and now a grieving mother, still not quite back to herself after the stroke a couple of years back, no matter how fine she insisted she felt. Drita would have to take over, make the arrangements, call in the death notice, and demand a closed service. In order to do these things, she would need to be able to speak.

She tried once and failed. She tried again, after clearing her throat. "Yeah," she said. "Yes, Ma, I'm here. What's going on?"

"Did you read it?"

"No," Drita said.

"Oh, it's just so awful."

That *it* again. Was she supposed to know what noun *it* was replacing, or was it too awful to be spoken?

"I just can't believe it," Jackie said. "We never even got a chance to meet her."

Her. The *it* was feminine. The blood that had been dammed in Drita's core rushed out and found its way to her limbs again. Her was not Pete. Pete was not Her. Drita could think of no Hers, aside from the one on the other end of her telephone line, whom she would even mourn.

"I can't believe it," Jackie said again.

"Can't believe what, Ma? What are you talking about?"

"It's in the paper. Haven't you seen it?"

"It's six-thirty in the morning. No, I haven't seen the paper. Just tell me what's going on."

"It's Nadia. She died. I just can't believe it," Jackie said.

Nadia. Nadia. The name rang no bells, aside from the Romanian gymnast she aspired to be when she was a kid.

"Who?" Drita asked.

"Shanda's mother, Dakota's grandmother. It's just so awful."

Now Drita felt something familiar: irritation, and it brought with it an odd kind of relief, in the sense that anything that wasn't the grief she was expecting would serve as relief. Nadia, the mother of her brother's junkie girlfriend? Nadia, a woman she'd never even met, and in fact would've avoided if the opportunity to meet had presented itself? *That* Nadia was worth all of this—Drita having to momentarily mourn her already long-gone brother, missing the last few minutes of her snooze, which was now over, according to the shrill alarm coming from the bedroom? God, she could kill Jackie. And then, to clarify: God, don't take that literally. But, God, that woman needed some friends.

Like Drita should talk, but still. She'd had a life once. She'd had a partner. It wasn't like she'd wanted to ditch it all to spend most of her Friday evenings alone, exactly the way she had her prom night back in high school.

"Ma, Jesus, why would you do this to me?" Drita said.

"Do what to you?"

"You don't even know the woman. She was probably as messed up as her daughter."

"Drita, how could you talk like that? She's a human being. She's family."

"She's not family. She's someone who gave birth to someone we kind of know who's also not family."

Jackie was back to crying. Either her sleeve or the phone muffled it, but she was obviously crying.

Drita sighed. "I'm sorry, Ma. I'm sorry. I feel bad. I'm sorry Nadia died."

"I just thought you'd want to know," Jackie said. "Didn't you say she was your patient?"

"She was *a* patient, not *my* patient. I work for the VNA, we have lots of patients that aren't mine."

"Well, she probably died alone. I thought you might care about that," Jackie said.

Drita let it slide. For once, it probably wasn't meant to provoke Drita into agreeing to dinner at Bocco's with the neighbor's cousin, or to responding to Isaac's last birthday message, not like he sent her a third after the first two went unanswered. Jackie was just worried about losing the last of her tenuous connections to her son. Drita could understand that. It was time to wake up anyway. At least she got to wake to a human voice for the first time in—well, however long it had been.

"I have to go get ready for work now, okay? I'm sorry I snapped," Drita said.

"I just thought you'd want to know," Jackie said.

"I did. I do. I just have to get ready now. Thank you for calling, Ma. I'll see you later today, all right?"

Jackie didn't respond, but Drita knew she was nodding. Jackie was quick to forgive, and good thing, because Drita found herself quicker to be an asshole to her these days. Something she should work on. Unlike Pete, the woman couldn't help the situation she was in.

The *Republican-American* lay scattered across the table in the break room at the VNA building, which employees, including Drita, seldom used as anything more than an office supply depot and a place to use the bathroom on the rare occasions when a McDonald's was less convenient. Drita double-checked the date to confirm it was that morning's edition—March 2, 1999—and, dusting the last visitor's powdered sugar from the newsprint onto the floor, sat down with the local section, the end pages of which were always dedicated to the region's newly departed.

There she was, as Jackie had said: Nadia Zapatka, an elvish blond woman described in the accompanying heading as a Loving Mother and Grandmother:

> Nadia Zapatka, 56, of Waterbury, died peacefully at St. Mary's Hospital after a brief illness.
>
> Ms. Zapatka was born on November 13, 1942, in Waterbury to the late Humbert and Ethel (Jankowski) Zapatka. A graduate of Wilby High School, Nadia was for many years a supervisor in the injection molding department of Waterbury Buckle, one of only two women to hold this post. Before beginning her professional career, Nadia traveled widely and counted Perth, Australia, and Crete among her favorite destinations.
>
> Nadia was a communicant of St. Joseph Catholic Church and enjoyed baking, traveling, and was an accomplished quilter. An avid reader, Nadia had been working on writing a mystery novel under a pseudonym, Blake Ashfield, at the time of her death. Nadia's greatest passion, however, was for her daughter, Shanda, of Waterbury, and her beloved grandson, Dakota DiMeo, the light of her life. The burial will be private. In lieu of flowers, donations can be made to a trust established for Dakota.

More than a few of Drita's elderly patients had died alone, and the sadness of that usually lasted only as long as their names lived on in her patient rolls. Nadia wasn't even her patient. Drita tried not to think of Nadia baking birthday cakes and sewing quilts for a grandson she probably hadn't seen in years. Drita tried, in fact, to forget about the obituary altogether, thinking instead of the hamster whose cage that morning's paper would be lining by the time she finished her shift.

She wondered, then, at the end of the day, what she was doing sitting outside of Nadia's apartment, staring at the building's concrete siding from her driver's side window.

She'd volunteered to pick up the medical detritus left behind in Nadia's apartment, stupidly telling Nadia's usual nurse that she'd be in the neighborhood anyway, which wasn't even remotely true. By the time Drita realized it was both a bad idea and a pointless one—what was she planning to do, commiserate with a dead woman about their mutual abandonment?—it was too late to take it back. Her co-worker had swiftly accepted Drita's offer and headed off to happy hour at the Brass Pony, telling her she owed her one without specifying what the one would be, both of them knowing a return favor would never actually happen.

Now Drita understood why her co-worker had suggested that she walk to and from her car with the keys at the ready between her knuckles. The buildings all along that street, both the boarded up and the inhabited, were the kind that managed to endure after the ones that produced brass shut down, if only because they manufactured and distributed pure ruin instead of pipes and bathroom fixtures. It was worse than she'd been warned, something that could have been Drita's thesis if she was still studying Public Health at Columbia, working on a paper with a title like "Wealth Disparity as Predictor of Adverse Outcomes in Connecticut's Naugatuck Valley: A Statistical Analysis." But she wasn't a Columbia student anymore. She was a Columbia dropout and a VNA nurse, and it was—at least until she'd accepted this fool's errand—just another Tuesday, one that wouldn't officially end until

Nadia's oxygen tanks had been returned to whatever medical supply company would promptly allocate them to another lost cause.

Drita flicked the limp, bleached air freshener that hung from her rearview mirror, readied her keys, sighed as if on camera, and exited the car, only bothering to lock it because of the Medicaid-funded pharmaceuticals stashed in the trunk. The punky wooden steps she climbed astonishingly still held weight, though the railing was now gone, removed, according to her colleague, to gurney the impressively huge Nadia days before in a feat that likely required both engineers and EMTs. The drop from the third floor to the ground was significant, with enough rusted metal below for the tetanus to finish you off if the drop didn't, and looking straight down made Drita woozy.

She held the key to the door in her hand, steering it toward the lock. Why was she doing this again? She could have been home already, picking the crusted cheese from a Bacco's take-out container, waiting for *Jeopardy!* to come on so she could get just enough answers correct to remind herself that she wasn't a genius but wasn't a complete idiot, either. What she actually was, however, remained a question, and maybe that's why she was there, because Nadia's death served as at least an interruption to the routine that Drita's life had fallen into since she landed back in Waterbury, and it would take some kind of disruption to get her moving toward an answer again. That explanation sounded good enough to Drita—better than simply being bored and not opposed to a little time-and-a-half—to convince herself to insert the key in the dead bolt and turn it to the left.

It met no resistance, no click of the bolt releasing from the strike plate. Drita hesitated for a moment, but then told herself that of course the door was unlocked—the EMTs or whoever managed to free Nadia last week would have had greater concerns than remembering to lock the door behind them. From the outside, nobody would assume there was anything inside worth taking. Nobody could possibly be inside an apartment that looked as if its last occupant had died years, not days, before.

Drita turned the knob and stepped inside. Somebody was, in fact, inside that apartment. A child, a boy, five or so years old, looking up at her from the floor, no surprise at all on his face, eyes that suggested he was bored with her already.

"Hey," he said, like they were buds, the greeting of a man but in a high, thin voice that made Drita think she may have gotten the sex of this child wrong. But no, he wore Spider-Man jammies and a buzz cut, two signifiers given to otherwise androgynous children to assign them a gender. He held a fistful of green plastic military figures, but he wasn't playing, just grasping, as if the men were engaged in some magnificent orgy.

The shock at the sight kept Drita's scream from emerging, though it wasn't the child's blasé stare that caused it so much as the fact that he was there at all, camped in a cleared-out circle of a kitchen floor otherwise littered with literal inches of trash.

"Ha," Drita managed to get out, not a laugh but simply a sound, a weak attempt to place herself back in her body.

She noticed then that someone else stood at the threshold, this kid perhaps part of a group of some postindustrial Boxcar Children. Drita could feel the presence before she moved her eyes to it, and when she found the courage to turn her head, she saw someone far too tall to be a child, though the person had the same bored eyes as the boy on the floor, the same immunity to shock.

Drita knew that face. It took a moment to register it, but it came to her in seconds.

"Shanda?" Drita said.

"She's dead," Shanda answered.

"Jesus fucking Christ," Drita said.

"She's dead," Shanda said again. "My mother, I mean."

"I know," Drita said. "You scared the living shit out of me."

Shanda went back to what she'd been doing in the next room, which gave Drita time to collect herself and wonder what Shanda was doing there at all. Or Dakota.

Fuck, that boy was Dakota.

She looked back down at him, the fear replaced by a dyspeptic burn in the vicinity of her heart when she realized that she had failed to recognize her own nephew, whose cheeks had only grown in scale since she'd last seen him as a toddler. Dakota, in turn, seemed to feel nothing toward Drita, judging by the blankness of his expression.

"Mom, who's that lady?" he asked, without looking up.

"That's your aunt, baby. Your daddy's sister," Shanda told him.

He streamed the army men to the floor, one by one, and looked back up to her when his hand was empty. It seemed like he was waiting for Drita to fill it with something else, and when she made no move toward him, he swept the men up again and pressed them so hard together that Drita could see his little fingers shaking, the skin on his hands and his face turning red.

Drita was starting to come to, though she still felt dizzy, the way one does in the moments after narrowly avoiding a car wreck. But she was beginning to correct, beginning to be able to form coherent thoughts again. Nadia had died, and Shanda, of course, had come to collect. Collect what, was the question. As far as Drita could tell, none of the piles of trash in that room had any monetary value, but then again, Drita didn't think like a scavenger, the way Shanda and Pete did.

Pete. Fuck. The nausea struck deeper.

"Pete?" Drita asked.

Finally, for just a moment, Shanda's eyes flickered with something like life. "What about him?" she asked.

"Is he here?"

The brief flicker of light went out. "No," she said. And then, hesitating, almost nervous, she asked, "Have you seen him?"

"Last time I saw him was with you, three years ago," Drita said.

Shanda nodded.

"Yeah, what? You don't know where he is, either?"

"I haven't seen him since Arizona," Shanda said, as if Arizona were a marker of time instead of a desert state Drita had never cared to see.

"What happened in Arizona?" Drita asked.

Shanda shrugged. "I don't know, he left. We broke up."

"And that's it? That's the last you heard of him?"

"Yup."

Or the last thing you remember, Drita thought.

Shanda stepped away from the door and walked back into the living room. She spoke, as if directly responding to what Drita managed to not ask, "Just a note, not a word. And I threw away the note."

Shanda's posture seemed to suggest it was the end of her story, and Drita needed to find a way back in. She couldn't let Shanda walk away like that, not when Pete's flesh and blood—her *own* flesh and blood, a condition she shared with exactly two people in her world—was sitting there on the kitchen floor. She followed Shanda into the living room but stopped in her tracks as soon as she entered. Mounds of garbage had been shoved into black lawn bags, and Shanda, on her hands and knees, shoveled yet more debris in, looking ironically less animal than she ever had before among all that trash. Now she just seemed broken, though Drita wondered why people always talked about that as a pejorative, as if it wasn't what was done to horses to make them able to live proximate to humans.

"You should be wearing a respirator for that," Drita said.

"You think I'm exposing myself to anything worse than I've already had?" Shanda asked. Sarcastically, Drita assumed, though her tone—or lack thereof—made it impossible to tell. It was maybe too late anyway. The place was still a horror, but progress had been made, enough trash transferred into plastic bags that Drita could see bits of carpet that likely hadn't been exposed to air in decades. It was almost impressive, the effort, especially for a task so obviously futile.

Drita stood and watched Shanda for another little while, and then she asked, "Why are you doing this?"

Shanda looked at the wall, at some stained voodoo-looking macramé that had likely come prestained from the Salvation Army, and shook her head in disgust, though it was hard to tell if it was directed at Drita or at something she had just touched.

"I'm here to pick up the oxygen tanks," Drita said, to remind Shanda that she was there.

"So pick them up," Shanda said.

Drita didn't move.

Shanda sighed. "How did you know I was here?" she asked.

"I didn't know you were here," Drita said. "I heard about your mother, but I'm just doing my job."

"I don't know where your brother is, if that's what you're after."

"I'm not a cop," Drita said. "You don't have to protect him from me."

Finally Shanda straightened up, rested her contaminated hands on her hips, and looked Drita straight in the eyes for what Drita realized may have been the first time ever. "I have no idea where that motherfucker is," she said.

The motherfucker clinched it: Drita knew then that Shanda was telling the truth, because that was a word that could only be spoken about Pete in earnest. What a motherfucker. He was the guy who could tell the best jokes, and make indolence into a lifestyle choice. She silently did the breathing exercises she'd been taught on the job so that she wouldn't lose it in front of Dakota, who had scooted his way to the threshold of the living room, waiting to be invited in. He was no doubt his father's child, with enormous round cheeks that would eventually be chiseled into angles in puberty. She nearly cried recognizing how much he looked like his father, and her fury at Pete had never been so strong as when she looked at that moment at his son.

"No, baby, you can't come in here, okay? It's caca," Shanda told Dakota, who remained slack in the doorframe.

Drita turned her head from the kid, the only way she could keep some kind of composure. "How long have you been back in town?"

"Couple months," Shanda answered.

"A couple months?" Drita cried. "Like, a chunk of a year?"

"Yeah, couple months."

"You didn't think to call somebody in two months?" What she meant, of course, was You never thought to call me? "You know Jackie spends all day alone. She would love to see her grandson."

"Pete said Dakota's not her grandson, because she's not his mother."

"She's the woman who raised us our whole lives. He doesn't even remember anything else," Drita said.

"He says he does. He said you and him used to talk about going back and finding the people you belonged with."

"We also used to talk about finding leprechaun dens in the woods. He wanted to belong to whatever group won the most fights in the parking lot at the mall. He had a Puerto Rican accent for a month, for Christ's sake. I don't know what he told you, but Jackie's not the one to blame for whatever went wrong in Pete's life."

"I mean, at least one of you didn't turn out all messed up," Shanda said.

"Yeah, exactly," Drita said.

"I'm just telling you what Pete told me," Shanda said. "I always thought Jackie was okay."

"She was okay. She is okay. I mean, not like in health so much these days, but she raised us fine."

"I always told him he was lucky."

Drita would've agreed, but Shanda didn't need to hear anything about luck, not while she was kneeling in a wading pool of filth, in the apartment of her dead mother, her silent child staring in at her from the doorway.

"Your mom was fine, too," Drita told Shanda, by way of consolation.

Shanda flung the trash bag she was holding away from her hand and expertly flipped Drita off.

"She was fine. I read her obit." Drita eyed a family-sized plastic junk-food barrel that had been repurposed as an ashtray, stubby butts now filling up the space that cheese puffs once had. "She sounded, you know, a little different than I would've thought."

"I made that shit up," Shanda said.

"What shit?"

"All the shit," Shanda said. "Everything but her name."

Drita looked for some sign that Shanda was lying, but there was nothing to see. Then she looked for signs that Shanda had lost the last of her mind, because if what she just said was true, that was some wacko business—making up your mother's biography, as if there were anybody out there to impress with it. Drita stared, and Shanda stared back, and finally, in the context of the insane late afternoon, it all just felt so perfectly reasonable that she found herself suddenly on the verge of something close to laughter, as if all of what had transpired was standard watercooler talk.

"Crete? Where the hell did you come up with Crete?" Drita asked.

"A book," Shanda said.

"A book, like the one your mother was writing?"

"No, a real one," Shanda said.

Man, the girl was weird. It explained a little about what Pete must have seen in her in the first place.

"Well, in any case, I'm sorry your mom died," Drita said.

"I was almost ready to see her again," Shanda said. "I had to get myself ready to see this place again, you know?"

Drita nodded, but she didn't know. Until that morning, she never stopped to wonder what had made Shanda, Shanda.

"Where you been living all this time anyway?" Drita asked.

"On Baldwin. Halfway house. I'm clean," Shanda said.

"How long?"

"Long enough that I'm about to get booted. I guess it's good that I got somewhere else to go now," Shanda said, eyes skittering around the grim room they had somehow all found themselves standing in.

"So you really don't know where Pete is?" Drita asked.

Shanda looked at Dakota. She told him, "Dakota, baby, I need you to go play in the kitchen, okay? Don't touch the things I told you not to touch."

"What can I touch?" he asked.

"You got your army guys, that book, your blanket. That's it right now. Don't open the cabinets. And don't go outside."

"K," Dakota said and slid away, and Drita wondered how Pete and Shanda had produced such a compliant offspring.

"He's cute," Drita said.

"He was almost dead. We almost killed him," Shanda said.

"What?" Drita asked. "What do you mean?"

"He got sick. We fucked up and he almost died."

"But how?" Drita asked again. "That's, like, a serious thing to say."

Shanda shrugged. "He was regular sick, like little-kid sick, and then he got into the children's Tylenol. He ate the whole frigging bottle like they were Tic Tacs. He liked his medicine a little too much. What can I say, like mother, like son."

"Oh," Drita said and unclenched her core. For a moment she'd worried about malice, one of a few defects she wasn't prepared to attribute to Pete. "You made it sound like you almost murdered him. Christ. And anyway, he's his father's son, too."

"At least Pete wasn't a junkie," Shanda said.

Drita stared at Shanda, as if the clarity needed would come from a moment of eye contact Shanda wouldn't make. "What do you mean, Pete wasn't a junkie?" she finally asked.

"He wasn't a junkie. He didn't use junk. You assumed he did because he was with me?"

Before she could answer that, Drita had to process it. Her brother was not a junkie: he associated with junkies and fought with junkies and disappeared in a Vanagon and abandoned the tiny bit of family he had and he was not a junkie. This was information that, at first, brought an even greater sense of relief to Drita. Junkie? Of course my brother's not a *junkie*. She was almost proud, as if, in his absence, Pete had accomplished something. He had gotten clean, gotten his act together, might think about enrolling in the community college and becoming a certified welder, because he liked to see sparks fly and because it was a decent way to provide for your family.

"I did," Drita said. "I did assume he was a junkie because he was with you, among other reasons." She waited for Shanda to be offended by that, but Shanda seemed to accept it.

"I went off on his ass when I found Dakota. I told him to get out, I never wanted to see him again, that kind of stuff." She shrugged. "And he did. I didn't expect that, but, I guess, like, the things you say have consequences. They don't let you forget that in rehab."

Whatever relief Drita briefly felt upon learning that Pete wasn't an addict fell away. The man ditched his sick baby because the sick baby's distraught mother told him to—that was the sole time in his life he actually listened to someone telling him what to do? At least a junkie could stop being a junkie by getting off drugs, whereas who knew what kind of rehab would fix whatever was wrong with Pete.

"That," Drita said, "that is not your fault."

Shanda stared at Drita.

"What? It's not. Nobody should ditch their own kid because someone else tells them to." She said nobody, and that was true enough, but what she meant was Pete specifically. He was the one always so hung up on loyalty, as if he couldn't imagine a life in which one earns love and commitment through action and not simply the obligation embedded into bloodlines.

"Anyway, he's better now," Shanda said.

"Pete?"

"No, Dakota," Shanda said. "It was scary," she added, after she had fully turned away. "It was fucked up. That's why I came back here, so he can get all the way better."

Drita looked around at the walls that had penned Shanda in. She was skinny and scrappy, her bones probably calcified on Top Ramen and Little Debbie. Not exactly the kind of environment that produced hale little children.

"What Dakota needs is an actual father," Drita said. "Someone who'll pull his weight. You have no idea where he is?"

"I tried his beeper for months," Shanda said. "I just, like, called and called, and I assumed it was pointless, like the thing wasn't even turned on anymore, but it was all I could think to do."

Drita glanced again at Dakota and exhaled deeply, the room cold enough for her sigh to be a vaporized, visible presence.

"Well," Drita said. "If you ever need, like, any help with him, I could maybe like babysit or something."

"Why would you do that?" Shanda asked.

"Because he's my family."

"So? So's Pete, and he clearly doesn't give a shit."

"Well," she said, "not everyone in this family is negligent. Anyway, nephew or not, it's just common decency."

"You never wanted to help us before," Shanda said.

Those words hit her like a slap, one that Drita was expecting but not braced for.

"I just didn't want to enable Pete, that's all," she said. She used the language of the 12-step programs she'd absorbed from some of her harder-luck clients, now that Shanda presumably spoke it, too.

Shanda shrugged.

"Do you want my help or not?" Drita asked.

Shanda blinked, picked up the plastic bag she'd dropped, and began gathering trash again. "Maybe," she said, without looking up. "Thanks."

She said it so quietly that it could've been something Drita just imagined. Because of all the crazy things that had transpired that morning, gratitude was maybe the hardest to wrap her head around.

Drita had to set the three-liter orb of Riunite on Jackie's front step in order to jiggle the key in the lock, open the door, and punch in the code to the security system, which Jackie had apparently remembered to arm for once. She used the extra seconds to refasten her hair tie, zip her fleece to cover the spot of mustard crusted on the left boob of her scrubs, and hope the thing that had shot that day's nerves didn't present too differently from the things that usually did it, like driving home on a section of highway designed by nihilists, or knocking on the doors of Alzheimer's patients who had vanished without a trace.

"Hi, honey. I'm in the living room," Jackie shouted, as if Drita needed directions, as if Jackie weren't always in the living room with a glass of iced Lambrusco and the day's crossword puzzle already completed on her lap.

"You're later than usual," Jackie said when Drita dropped onto the sofa. "Is everything okay?"

How much bigger would Jackie's smile be if she knew her grandson was a seven-minute drive away.

And how it might disappear forever if she'd learned what her son had done to the kid.

Anyway, Shanda had asked Drita not to tell Jackie that she and Dakota were back until she got her shit fully together, and, not convinced that that condition would ever be met, Drita thought it kinder to everyone to oblige.

"Yeah, Ma," Drita said, "just a little extra work today."

"Well, don't work too hard. I don't want you dropping dead of a heart attack," Jackie said.

She wondered if Jackie would invoke Dom as a cautionary tale, but Jackie just sipped from her wine and reviewed her crossword squares. Dom had spent most of his time at the fabrication shop, true, but if he had been working himself to death, the fruits of his labor weren't reflected materially in their house. Not much had changed in it after he dropped dead, in fact, save for the La-Z-Boy that Jackie had replaced with a newer model that had been scotchgarded for no reason, because no one ever sat in it.

"Sorry to abandon you as soon as you get here," Jackie said, "but nature calls."

"You need some help?"

"Oh, come on, Drita, you think I don't pee when you're not here?" she answered as she rolled herself down the hall.

Jackie had come a long way in the two years since her stroke, that was true. No thanks to Pete, of course, who practiced being a deadbeat dad by being the same kind of son. He didn't even know about Dom's heart attack until two months after it happened, when he finally deigned to call home, probably for money, though Drita hadn't let him get far enough to ask for any.

You motherfucker, Drita had seethed when she answered Jackie's phone that day, before getting herself back under control so she could point out to Pete very clearly all the things that made him so. That Dom was already buried. That Jackie had ignored the swelling in her right thigh until two weeks after Dom's funeral, when the blood clot that had been silently growing there hitched a ride up to her lung and nearly took her down with a pulmonary embolism. That Drita had been stuck at Jackie's taking care of things that somebody on a perpetual leave of absence from life would have had plenty of time to help out with.

I'm paying New York City rent on a New York City apartment that I'm not even living in, she'd said.

Isaac's still there, Pete said.

He shouldn't have to swing the rent alone. He's hardly ever even there.

Like he can't afford it. He's a doctor.

He's in med school, asshole. He has to pay for that. We already have to figure out what to do when I start my fieldwork in South America.

South America? South America? What business do you even have going to South America?

My job is literally helping people, Pete, something you obviously don't know anything about.

I got a kid, all I do is help someone. I can't give up my own life to take care of someone else's. I learned that from you, remember?

That's not the same. Jackie didn't choose this for herself. She didn't decide to almost kill herself.

Yeah, Drita, I get it, everybody else in the world deserves help except for me. Sorry, but I can't. I just can't.

I leave in a month, Pete. One month. Ma's still going to need help by then.

Things will work out for you. They always do.

Things don't work out for me, I work for things. Don't act like I got lucky somehow. We grew up in the same exact house with the same exact parents.

They're not our parents, he'd said, after a pause long enough to come up with at least several better things to say.

Then what about me? Aren't I your sister?

Drita didn't remember how he'd responded to that, exactly, just that the absence of any phone call after that served as an answer nonetheless.

It was true that Dom never earned even a gag version of a World's Greatest Dad coffee mug for Father's Day, but Jackie had always done right by them, which—someone like Nadia made clear—wasn't a given with all mothers. The fact that Jackie had managed it all in the wheelchair she'd been bound to since her run-in with a semi at age nineteen didn't even strike Drita as remarkable until she was an adult, because it had seemed so natural to Jackie, at least until the past few years, when Jackie somehow seemed to keep the Riunite more stocked than her warfarin prescription, citing some *Prevention* article she'd scanned in a checkout line that told her a glass of wine helped naturally thin the blood. And if one helped, imagine what three or four could do.

Jackie was just sad these days, and who could blame her, with her dead husband and her good-as-dead son.

But she still came back smiling to the living room, handing Drita a cup of wine from the bottle she'd purchased herself earlier that week.

"Here, help me finish this up. It's getting vinegary," Jackie told Drita. "You want to stay for dinner?"

Drita felt bad saying no, knowing that she and the kid from down the block who collected payment for the *Waterbury Republican-American* were Jackie's primary conversation partners, but the day had been too much, starting with Jackie's phone call that morning and ending with her having to keep her mouth shut about all the rest of it. She had plenty more nights ahead of her to resent spending alone, but for once Drita was looking forward to the emptiness of her apartment.

"I can't, Ma, I'm beat. I gotta get going soon," Drita said.

"Yeah, yeah," Jackie said. "You gonna eat before you conk out? You gotta eat, honey. Look how skinny."

"Not that skinny, Ma. Just regular skinny. You know I'm on my feet a lot," Drita said.

"That's why you gotta eat more. Get fat with me."

"You're not fat, Ma."

"I ain't skinny, either. Course I'm not on my feet a lot."

"Ma, come on."

"I'm joking, Drita, lighten up. But you want something to take with you? I got half a grinder left from yesterday."

"I can feed myself, Ma," Drita said.

"I know you can, Drita. That's not the same as having to do it by yourself all the time."

Here it comes, Drita thought.

"It might be nice to go to dinner with that Annunziata kid. He seems nice."

"He's a cop," Drita said.

"What's that mean? That's a good job."

"I'm just not interested."

"I'm not saying you have to marry him. I'm just saying it's nice to eat out sometimes with someone your own age."

"I'm not trying to start something up with anyone around here. I'm not going to be here forever, remember?"

"Oh?" Jackie said. "Got something in the works?"

"Not, like, firm plans," Drita said. "I just mean once you're better."

"Drita, honey, I am better," Jackie said.

"Not all the way better."

"I've never been all the way better and I've always gotten by just fine. Anyway, there are people that get paid to help other people out. You should know that."

"And there are people who get paid to help people who I would never trust with my own family," Drita said. "I know you're not helpless, Ma, but your cousins aren't knocking down the door to lend a hand, and it's not like you have much family left beyond that."

"And you want to end up like me?" Jackie asked into the bowl of her wineglass, taking one last, long pull.

Drita looked at her own glass. She hadn't even gotten enough down to fuel the furnace in her belly and already felt a hangover.

"Listen, I'm really tired. I'm going to go," Drita said.

"I didn't mean to push, Drita."

"It's fine. I'm not mad, I promise, I'm just tired."

"You shouldn't always be so tired, is all I'm trying to say. You're only twenty-six."

"I'll figure it out, okay?"

"I know you will, honey," Jackie said. She said it kindly, which made it more infuriating, which made Drita decide—unambiguously this time—to somehow make it true.

2

IT WASN'T CLEAR WHAT WOKE PETE: THE LURCH OF THE SUDDEN braking; the protracted screech of it; the alcohol wearing off and the residual sugars kicking in; the smell. God, the smell. It was shit. Literally, unmistakably, human shit. Dakota had often smelled of it, something that people accepted in babies—lying in bubbles of their own squishy waste, which was always soft, often green, usually enough volume of it to overflow from their diapers and spread up their backs and down their chubby thighs, which strangers liked to grab on to and squeal with delight over. The filth was the part of babies that people failed to mention, and which horrified Pete the most, which meant that correcting it was also the part of parenting that Pete was most successful at. He changed diapers at regular intervals, plus whenever actually needed. He woke in the middle of the night to change them so that Dakota wouldn't have to lie for hours in his own filth, though without fail, no matter if there were two or three changes in the night, there would be a fresh pancake of waste filling the entire cavity between Dakota's tiny little ass and the breached dam of superabsorbent polymer. In the first months, Dakota would cry when he soiled himself, and then he got used to it, and that was the second most horrifying thing about babies to Pete: their willingness to adapt to anything, including living in their own filth. It reminded Pete too much of himself, and he wished Dakota would cry about it. Pete could take the crying, though that seemed to be the most horrifying part of babies to Shanda. For a while, they convinced each other it worked out that way. They each had things they could manage about Dakota, and each had things they couldn't. At some point Pete realized that you were supposed to be able to manage everything, because all that stuck were the failures. He realized that when he smacked Dakota's bottom after finding him, that last night in the apartment in Arizona when he was supposed to have been potty-trained for almost two years, lying in not just an Underoo of shit but an entire mattress of it. Pete knew immediately that he had done something unforgivable to Dakota with that one little smack, and that he'd better start thinking about an exit strategy from this new little family he had created and that, he was certain, he could just as easily and accidentally ruin.

How rad would it be now for Dakota to tug on Pete's sleeve and tell him in human words he had to go to the bathroom and for Pete's job to be simply to accompany him. He'd willingly wipe the boy's ass, and he'd make sure that ass was good and clean. That ass would gleam.

And what a piece of shit Pete would be to show up now, after what he'd done to the kid.

Piece of shit. That reminded him that there was definitely some of that close by. Pete opened his eyes and, once the light stopped razoring them, looked around. It took a minute to decipher where he was. It was a distinctive setting, and he knew that he should know it. Orange seats. Yellow seats. Rows of seats, shallow scooped ass slings. A poster of a guy named Zizmor, rainbows shooting from his head.

Subway. Subway, New York City, broken-down van in Mt. Vernon, Metro-North ticket the conductor didn't collect, some Irish joint in Midtown that Pete recognized as a place of doom even before ordering his first drink. The file cabinet in his brain that stored this information was wide open now. He was in New York, but the wrong New York. He was supposed to be making his way to Ronkonkoma, where his buddy Dave had a cousin with a construction business that hired laborers at Dave's word, no matter how worthless Dave's word consistently turned out to be. He wanted to help Dave make good—but the van. If he ever managed to find where he'd parked that metric ton of junk again, it'd be a goddamned miracle.

But the first miracle of the day would have to be not retching, and in order to perform that, Pete had to get away from the smell.

He looked around. It was a crowded car, but no one sat in the seats surrounding him. He must have looked dangerous, in that way he generally both encouraged and found hilarious. Pissed off, dark-skinned white boy with only the borders of his tattoos peeking out from his collar and sleeves, little black em dashes that surely spelled out, in various ways, trouble. In reality his tattoos were mostly random flash from the walls of various strip mall tattoo studios. The only text his body bore was the name of his son in heavy black script across his chest, and even that was a cop-out; he'd wanted it tattooed across his abdomen, but Shanda thought it was too weird, because babies go in mamas' bellies, not daddies? As if that girl were any more maternal than he was.

Nah. He shouldn't think like that about Shanda. She was actually good with Dakota when she was clean, and at least she stuck around when she wasn't. Unlike himself, she wasn't the kind of loser to skip town just to not have to face the things that freaked him out.

What he mostly couldn't face now was the stench. Lucky for him, that's when the MTA conductor came through and handed Pete his first real win of the day: turns out he'd camped himself out on the uptown D train, which stopped on Fordham Road, a neighborhood Pete actually knew from back in those few months he had that job delivering Snapple to vending machines and bodegas, before he sampled too much of the merchandise and got himself pink-slipped. A bunch of Albanians out there, including that pizza joint where he used to stop in for garlic knots and Hawaiian Punch from the fountain. He'd requested to work that route specifically, knowing that there were only two places outside of Albania itself where the double-headed Albanian eagle he'd tattooed on his chest on yet another night he had very little memory of counted for anything: Waterbury and the Bronx, and he'd effectively exiled himself from the former. For a moment he was impressed that his drunken self had the wherewithal to board the right train at some early morning hour that was now lost to him, even if he suspected that a tattoo and a smile wouldn't get him as far as it used to, not that it had ever gotten him that far with the off-the-boat Shqiptars in Belmont.

In any case, it wasn't Ronkonkoma, but it was a destination. He covered his nose and listened to the indecipherable voice on the loudspeaker until he heard something with the right number of syllables, and when the car slowed enough for him to make out tiles that spelled Fordham Road, he prepped himself to stand, grabbing on to the railing and launching himself up quickly. Too quickly. His legs were as bad off as his head and his stomach, resistant to gravity and not quite ready for solid ground, never mind the surfing one had to do to stay afoot on this train, which seemed to be steered by somebody who'd drunk as heavily as Pete had the night before. He rose and closed his eyes and grasped the strap by his head with both hands. The train was slowing hard, releasing, slowing again. Finally it stopped, the doors opened, and people began streaming in before the bing-bong even finished. Pete released the strap and plowed through them, motivated anew by the promise of fresh air.

But even on the platform, he found he was still miles from fresh air. The stench had followed him. He looked at the faces around him, but the current of passengers streamed by too quickly for him to pick out the culprit. He stopped in his tracks and waited for the platform to clear, then leaned against the wall and checked the bottom of his sneakers. Clean, or if not clean, not shitty. Did the whole city just stink like this? He tried to think of the afternoon before, emerging from the Metro-North into Grand Central, but he couldn't discern if the memory was from yesterday or from any of the other trips he'd taken into the city in years past. He couldn't remember a reason for any of the trips, other than getting messed up in different scenery that would, at some point, devolve into no scenery his eyes could discern. If only his sense of smell could fail as epically as his memory, but in fact it seemed heightened, like a blind man overcompensating. He walked, then almost jogged down the length of the platform toward the stairs. Outside would be better. Outside was where again? Fordham, Fordham Road. Close enough to the zoo to sometimes catch a whiff of ape piss, as if he needed that to complete his scatological sensory ride.

Fordham Road was bright, but not fresh. The smell was still pungent, if more diffuse. Pete was feeling more confident about being upright than he had a few minutes before, but something about his movement was still off. It was the weight of his steps—too heavy, like he was wading instead of walking. Wetness, that was it. His jeans felt soggy, and not just because he wore them four inches too big in the waist and cinched mid-crack. Had he sat in something? He strained to see behind him, and then shifted his pants around so that the back right pocket twisted over to his hip. A little wet spot, nothing too bad, could have been gum residue or grease or something. He backed into some shrubs outside of an apartment building and pressed a little harder. It was definitely moist when he pressed his jeans against his skin, more so than that little outward spot would indicate. It was almost like it was wet inside his pants. It was almost as if . . .

Oh no. No no no no no no no.

When he pressed, it released a fresh puff of stench, like hitting the nozzle on a gag air freshener. Pete retched. Passersby turned their heads when he emptied the contents of his stomach into the grass, heaving and gasping like he was both performing and receiving an exorcism. A brave soul even called out from the sidewalk, "Hey, man, you okay?" and Pete raised a hand and nodded toward the ground, universal code for: Yes, sir, now get the fuck away.

The puking did clear Pete's head a little. The problem with clarity was the shame that went with it, but the shame would have to wait until after he rinsed out his drawers, something he wasn't going to do in a driveway in the Bronx if he could help it. He wiped his mouth and moved away from the spot, back onto the street, and looked around. Where was that pizza place? Everything around there looked the same, mostly residential, squat redbrick single-families or duplexes, the occasional travel agency or karate studio, the kinds of small businesses that didn't even have to advertise their lack of public restrooms. That far north was a city by virtue of its density, but there didn't seem to be much going on, no landmarks to give him some bearings. A hospital, but there was always a hospital; a mattress store, but there was always a mattress store.

Then the White Castle. A beacon. He used to throw his parking tickets in the mailbox outside of it and wonder how desperate someone had to be to willingly eat in that place.

Pete's desperation dwarfed those White Castle patrons' at that moment, but now he had something else, and it wasn't a fistful of disgusting little mini-burgers. It was hope. He waddled faster until he could make out the pizza joint, one of those generic white-and-red exteriors with an equally generic name that he couldn't remember, Roma or Little Italy or Mario's By the Slice. Halle-freaking-lujah, man. He sped up until he got to the façade, and then he slowed down, back to casual, so he wouldn't draw the kinds of stares that speed-walking grown men in saggy jeans and Raiders beanies tended to attract.

He got stares anyway. Small as it was, the place wasn't filled, only a single guy at a table with an empty paper plate and a full waxed paper cup in front of him, spread out over the bench like he was in it for the long haul, and two guys behind the counter.

"Hey, bros, what's up? You guys remember me?" Pete said.

He didn't remember them, either, not these guys in particular, but their indifference to his presence seemed familiar.

"I used to deliver your drinks." Pete pointed at the cooler, which appeared untouched since he'd last stocked it, it had to be—what, two, three years ago?

One of the men shook his head. "No need drinks," he said.

"Nah, I don't do that anymore, I'm just saying I used to do it. And you used to let me use your bathroom, so listen—I got a long day ahead of me, it's kind of an emergency, can I use your bathroom again?"

"Toilet is for customers," the guy at the table said, in an accent that was an amalgam of foreign and New York, something found exclusively in the boroughs.

"Yeah, I'm gonna get something on my way out. I gotta piss first," Pete said.

"Gotta pay first," the guy said.

"You even work here?" Pete asked.

"A friend," the guy said.

Pete looked at the guys behind the counter, who looked right back. The guys were tough, that much was clear just by looking at them, even the one employee who couldn't have been more than five-five. They had done much more scowling in their lives than anything else, judging by where the lines on their faces had settled. But Pete really needed that bathroom. The garlic and the sausage were covering up his stench from a distance, but that wouldn't work for long.

Pete shoved his hands in his pockets and smiled, drawing from the well of charm that seemed to have been drying up over the past couple of years. "Dude, you're Shqip, right? Shqiptare. I am, too." Pete crossed his hands in front of him, linking his thumbs and flaying his fingers like wings, the way the Albanian kids back at school used to do in the hallways and at the lunch table when they let him sit with them. "Albanian eagle, right? That's why I remembered this place, that's why you used to let me piss here."

"You were working for them then. You're not now," the guy at the table said.

"Why are you answering for them if you don't even work here?" Pete said.

The guy shrugged. "Like I said, I'm a friend."

If Pete was in a position to risk someone getting closer to him, he'd have called the guy what he really was, which was a dick. A pretty enough dick, a dick who might've actually packed some muscle inside that Wilsons leather he was wearing, but a dick Pete was pretty sure he would, under ordinary circumstances, not have to worry too much about.

But these weren't ordinary circumstances. Pete sighed.

"Put in a slice of pepperoni for me, I'll get it on the way out," Pete said. "Now can I use the bathroom?"

The employees moved their eyes from Pete to the guy at the table, who, after an excruciating half a minute, released a syllable that Pete didn't recognize and shrugged. The short guy behind the counter reached behind him, grabbed a twelve-inch wooden baton with a single key dangling from it, and threw it toward Pete. He missed it, of course, and bent down to retrieve it, which released a bit of stink. But it was almost over now, and he didn't have to fake his gratitude. "You guys are awesome," Pete said.

Inside the stall, Pete's eyes watered as soon as he dropped his trousers, not from the stench, which was no longer a surprise to him, but from the disgust, which, were he to think about it, should also not have been a surprise to him. Until seeing it with his own eyes, he could still hold out some hope that he hadn't actually shat himself, that he had instead allowed some form of shit—say, dog or baby—to enter his pants, and while he couldn't think of the logistics of how something like that would happen, it still seemed more likely than he, a grown man, shitting himself on the subway train he temporarily called home. But he wasn't any grown man, he was Pete, who was always coming up with new ways to suck and fail and suck and . . .

Never mind that now, Pete told himself. Just get out of these goddamned shorts. He kicked his sneakers off, stepped out of his jeans, and pushed his boxers down like he was playing Operation, keeping his hand steady so as to avoid touching the cotton to his flesh. He wrapped up the boxers in a paper towel and disposed of them in the trash, then pulled more paper towels from the roll, dampened them, and set off to cleaning himself up. After several passes, he was sure that this was as good as it would get until he got himself to a hot shower, wherever the hell he managed to find one of those. He dabbed the crotch of his jeans with a bit more soap and water, just enough for him to convince himself that the bacteria and stink were neutralized, but not so much that the water would bleed through the denim and make it look as if he'd pissed himself, too. Finally, he was feeling a little better, and finally, he felt ready to emerge.

Before leaving, Pete stopped to take a look at himself in the mirror, and immediately the disgust came rushing back.

You dumb, worthless waste of flesh.

The guys out there were probably getting suspicious, thinking Pete was in there hitting the pipe or something. He slapped himself in the face a couple of times, cleared his throat, and stepped back into the pizzeria. It looked as if nobody had moved the entire time he'd been in the bathroom, except now there was a slice on a paper plate waiting on the counter.

"Pepperoni," one of the employees said, in such a way that Pete understood it was one of the few English words he spoke.

The last thing Pete desired in the world at that moment was food, but the grease might be good for him. It was always getting the first bite down that was the hardest, but it was a challenge he was ready to take on. He nodded and reached for his wallet, which wasn't in the designated right front pocket, so he checked the left, and then the ones in back. Nothing. He reached into the front pouch of his sweatshirt, and of course it was empty, because what kind of idiot stores anything in there.

"Shit," Pete said. "Hold on."

He went back to the bathroom and checked the floor, the toilet, even the trash can, but all he came up with was his own soiled boxers. He began to panic: without that wallet he had no ticket back to Mt. Vernon, no gas money to Ronkonkoma, no way to start the rest of the life he told himself was coming once he got settled out on Long Island.

That life was dead before it was even begun. It was the abortion he probably should have let Shanda have all those years ago.

Don't look at that mirror, Pete thought. Don't do it, boy.

He did it. The face staring back was his, but red and a little blurry. It was shaking. He was quaking, the little Etna in his gut erupting once again.

"Fuck!" he yelled and punched the mirror. It was reflective stainless steel and didn't shatter, so Pete's only option was to turn away. He flung open the bathroom door and marched toward the exit, but the guy from the table finally rose and blocked the path.

"Where are you going?" the guy asked. "Your slice is up."

"I lost my wallet," Pete said.

"Then how are you going to pay for this pizza?" the guy asked. He didn't really ask, not in the way where he expected an answer. Pete knew the guy was messing with him, and that these words were just part of the ritual before the guy tried to get physical. The guy was a good three or four inches shorter than Pete, but clearly held a membership at Gold's or some other local meathead place, where you lifted deadweight over your head in a maneuver that would prepare you for exactly nothing in the world outside the gym.

"I can't pay for the pizza, so I'm not going to eat the pizza," Pete said.

"You're not going to pay for the pizza? And what do you think they're going to do with the slice? They can't put it back on the pie, can they?" It was less clear how much experience the guy had with targets that fought back, though Pete had to imagine the guy wouldn't be stepping up unless he was prepared to follow through. Maybe he'd depend on the other guys behind the counter to step in, and those guys wore their past battles on their faces. They weren't making any moves, though, just staring from where they stood, slabs of raw dough lined up on the counter behind them like pasty mounds of flesh.

There was a small, pathetic part of Pete that still believed he should not obliterate everything right there. There was still some chance that his wallet was waiting for him at the crappy Irish pub that started this mess the night before. There was still some chance he could make it to Dave's cousin's place and show the man he could frame out a house with the rest of the young, strapping dudes whose bodies did not yet wear the effects from booze or drugs or whatever it was that would eventually make them too weak to hoist two-by-fours and pneumatic nail guns. This could not happen if he was arrested, especially not with his priors, most of which came from fights very much like this potential one and a few petty thefts, including the time he got nabbed at CVS with two jugs of Similac for Dakota. He still couldn't believe the police got involved in that one. Wasn't that some biblical shit, it being okay to steal to feed your family?

Pete didn't need to eat. He didn't want that slice of pepperoni to begin with. And he didn't want to fight, not with his head pounding and his future dependent on some good karma he knew he'd have to earn somehow.

"Man, I'm sorry," Pete said. He looked at the guys behind the counter. "I lost my wallet and I'm pretty freaking screwed right now. I wasn't trying to mess with anybody."

"You come in here and shit in the bathroom that these people have to clean, and then you make them throw away their profits, and you're saying you're not trying to mess with anybody?"

"Yeah, that's what I'm saying. I'm sorry. Can't you tell those guys I'm sorry?"

"You're really Shqip, you tell them yourself."

"I am Shqip," Pete said. "I don't speak it, though. I grew up over here."

The guy laughed and shook his head slowly. He looked over at the employees and spoke some gibberish to them, and then swung his head back to face Pete.

"Let's go outside," the guy said.

Pete couldn't tell if this was an invitation to walk away, or if these were fighting words as classic as they were universal. Then the guy pushed Pete's shoulder, rammed him right toward the door, and Pete had his answer.

So this was how it was going to be. Pete still said, one last time, "Man, I'm not trying to start anything. I'm having a really bad freaking day."

"It's about to get worse," the guy said. He opened the door and pushed Pete through it, and then pushed Pete again, this time against the wall outside.

"Dude, you don't want to start this shit," Pete said, as much to himself as to the meathead.

The guy squinted like he was genuinely confused. "I didn't start this shit. You messed with them, which means you messed with me. That's all you, bro." What was Pete supposed to say to that? He knew that was the score with these guys; it was why he sat at that lunch table back in high school even if he couldn't understand a word they were saying. Albanians—even the kids like they all were back then—they were tough and they were loyal, and it didn't matter to them if Pete could say hello or not, because to them it was all about blood and loyalty. No, wait: blood, *honor,* and loyalty, which he knew was the creed for just about any loosely organized group of pissed off young men, but these guys meant it, and wouldn't hesitate to prove it. Honor—it sounded so good to him, it was another word he would've tattooed on himself that day if he had any real honor of his own or the couple hundred bucks to pay for the ink. And loyalty was something his own sister didn't seem to understand, even if she came off the same boat as he had, and this is why they never could really see eye to eye. And this was why Pete knew that a blow from this guy was coming no matter how much he tried to bargain his way out of it, and that he deserved a punch to the face.

So he took it, and before his jaw had a chance to register the sting, he gave it right back.

Pete didn't work for the strength he had, other than a few random pull-ups mostly meant to show off to whoever happened to be around to impress at the time, and the cardio workouts he got from having to bike around town when his cars crapped out, or from running away from whoever was chasing him for whatever it was he'd done. The guy from the pizzeria wouldn't have been able to tell what was under that double-XL New York Giants sweatshirt Pete frequently wore, but it was the kind of elastic, wiry muscle that was ready to snap in an instant. His waist was stupid, a solid slab carved into something like bas relief, with two snaking divots that began at his obliques and ended at his groin. The universe had bestowed this body upon Pete, and it was the last gift he'd been given by it. He'd used his gift the way most males of the species tended to, as peacock feathers and as a hammer, the latter of which seemed to be on display more frequently of late. His plumage was fading, perhaps, but the carbon steel beneath was hanging on.

There were no witnesses. The employees of the pizza place didn't leave their posts to see what was going down outside their door. There was no reason for Pete to keep standing there, hovering over the knocked-out tough guy splayed on the pavement, other than feeling kind of bad about how all of this went down.

"I told you, man," Pete said, when the guy's eyes began to flutter open, though Pete wasn't sure exactly what he'd told him. He watched the guy watch Pete come back into focus, recall the events of the past few minutes, and shake his head as the playback ended.

"That hurt, man," the guy said.

"You hurt me, too, man," Pete said.

The guy slowly rose to his feet, using the wall behind him as support. He brushed off his pants and rubbed his hands together, particles of grit dropping to the ground where he'd just lain.

"And now I gotta go change my clothes," the guy said.

"I told you I didn't want trouble," Pete said.

The guy stared at Pete. "I thought you said you were Albanian."

"I am," Pete answered.

"Then why don't you know this isn't about trouble?"

"I told you, I lost my wallet. That's not bullshit."

"It doesn't matter, man. You know the rules, don't you?"

He didn't. He vaguely liked the idea of these rules, the only rules he'd ever encountered that he didn't live to flaunt, but he didn't really know them. It seemed like some cool samurai shit, something he promised himself right there and then he was going to work on when the next part of his life started the following day. Once his pants were clean, and he had his photo ID back.

"I'll come back and pay those guys later, man. I'll buy a whole damn pie," Pete said.

The guy looked at Pete sideways again. "Yeah, no shit," he said. After a pause, he added, "Are you really Albanian or what?"

Honor. If that was the thing that did it, then no, he shouldn't claim it.

But he did.

"I am," Pete said. "Me and my twin sister. But our mom died so we grew up with some Italians in Connecticut."

"Waterbury?" the guy asked.

"Yeah, how'd you know?"

"Because that's where Albanians live. I know a bunch of guys there."

"I haven't been in a while," Pete said.

"Where you been?" the guy asked.

"Nowhere. Everywhere. Just traveling around."

"You a hobo or something?"

Pete looked down at himself. He wanted to deny it, but his sweatshirt was filthy. He had no identification, a savage hangover, and now a bloody lip. He shrugged.

"You smell like a hobo, bro," the guy said.

Oh yeah, and shitty pants. The guy was right. Pete was a goddamned hobo.

"Listen, you're kind of an embarrassment right now. I'm just saying. You gotta pull yourself together," the guy said.

"I gotta find my wallet before I can do anything," Pete answered.

"You have to shower before you do anything. For real. It's bad. Like, real bad."

Pete sighed. His breath wasn't smelling much better than the rest of him, which made him want to stop breathing altogether.

"What's your name?" the guy asked.

"Pete," Pete said.

The guy raised his brows.

"Petrit," Pete said.

"Valon," the guy said. "I'm not shaking your hand until you clean yourself up. I can't believe I even had to touch you with my fist."

"You didn't have to."

"The fuck I didn't. You want a shower, you can come with me. I got one at the shop."

Pete hesitated. Who the hell was this guy, coming out swinging and five minutes later acting like his best friend?

"The way I see it, bro, you have one thing going for you right now, and that's that you can throw a punch. You clean yourself up, maybe you can have two things going for you. I'm trying to do you a favor," Valon said.

That's why Pete had to trust him: Valon was, at that moment, not his best but his only friend.

3

DRITA OPENED TO THE HAPPENINGS PAGES OF THE *NEW HAVEN AD-vocate* first: rock shows, reggae shows, DJ nights, comedy open mics, self-defense classes, country western dance classes, Harugari folk dance classes, poetry workshops, Green Party meetings, Intro to Shamatha Meditation, GLBT Pentecostal study, bowling for veterans, bowling for singles, past life regression, current life progression, some children's events that she skipped right over. She read restaurant reviews for Ethiopian and Peruvian places that would close down long before she ever made it to the Route 1 strip malls where only take-out Chinese joints, urban street wear boutiques, and Western Unions thrived. It all reminded her that she'd picked up a copy of the local alt weekly in order to find an alternative to being a local, so she moved on to what she was really there for, the classifieds. There she found perpetual telemarketing opportunities, medical researchers seeking the HIV-positive, heavy metal cover bands seeking drummers, and only ever drummers.

It was pointless. The *New Haven Advocate* wasn't going to be the portal to what Drita sought, whatever it was she sought. The employment ads recruited exclusively for jobs that paid poorly and by the hour, the real estate listings were for by-the-week motels, and the personals were for by-the-hour encounters in those same motels, the dates discreetly arranged by an agency with a name like Le French Connection. Drita would probably make more working for Le French Connection than the VNA of Southern Connecticut, but money wasn't really the thing she was looking for. She paid her student loans on an automatic debit plan and had enough money left over at the end of the month to plug some into an interest-bearing savings account and to buy satiny bras from Victoria's Secret that fit so poorly they must not have been designed for natural breasts. What she wanted was something that wouldn't drive her to spend her weekends at the mall buying stuff she didn't need just to not be in her apartment being gassed out by the Yankee candles she'd gotten on the last trip.

Christ, even Pete had found something alluring enough in the great wide open to abandon his entire family for it.

She used to be the one who knew what she wanted. She was the one who took the PSATs, the SATs, and AP bio, chemistry, and U.S. history, even if she didn't pass the last of those. Watching *St. Elsewhere* in high school had convinced Drita to get a nursing degree, and a college adviser in the nursing program convinced her to look into public health, since she was, as her adviser put it, more *big-picture oriented* than people oriented. She attended UConn for the in-state tuition and Columbia for—she could admit—what would be printed on the degree, not just because it was what Dom called name-brand but because it would matter to the people who do the hiring at the kinds of places she planned to work for, for whom she was otherwise too plebeian to matter. Maybe she'd work for an NGO; *maybe*, someday, the UN. She'd never admitted the extent of her aspirations to Pete, who already thought she rode a horse too high, or even to Jackie, who just wouldn't get it, but she built a blueprint in her head and, after meeting Isaac in a way-uptown bar that medical residents were known to frequent, she finally managed to begin saying it aloud.

She had said it aloud. God. Remembering that made her current situation more embarrassing.

In any case, it was an analog world the last time Drita had mapped her way out of Waterbury, but things had changed since then. Now the world was connected by a digital web, one she used occasionally for work but otherwise ignored, since she sucked at Super Mario Bros. and, after visiting an internet café and logging off after twelve minutes of reading the rules to *X-Files* drinking games, deduced that she also sucked at the internet. But even the escort services were printing web addresses in their *Advocate* ads. Even the med school graduation party invitation Isaac had sent included an email address that Drita didn't bother to respond to, since the kinds of regrets she had to express weren't the kinds the invitation asked for.

Drita supposed it was time to cash in on all those shiny CD-ROMs that AOL somehow managed to slip into her mailbox every two hours and get herself a personal computer.

Anyway, it was a Saturday, and until then she had dreaded waking up, having to figure out how to fill the span of the next sixteen hours. It was good to have an objective—it meant going to the mall again, but for something substantive this time. She brushed her teeth and pulled her hair back and got herself so excited on the way out the door that she had to run back inside to use the bathroom. She tried it again, and this time, she flung open the door and found herself face-to-face with Shanda.

"Holy crap, you scared the hell out of me," Drita said, once she'd recovered enough to make out the face.

"I need a favor," Shanda said, stepping into Drita's apartment. "Can you watch Dakota for a while?"

Drita looked at Dakota, crouched down at Shanda's knees, hovering a toy car over the floor but not letting the wheels make contact. He clearly wasn't good at being a kid, and Drita didn't know if that made her more or less qualified to look after him.

"I was just on my way out. You saw me about to run out of here," Drita said.

"You said you would help. And I have to do something important."

She did say she would help, but that was when the idea was theoretical. Standing at knee height was a child whose survival required actual earthly things: sustenance, air, stimulation. "I know, but, like, maybe some advance notice? It's not really kid's stuff, what I have to do today," Drita said. "Wait, how do you even know where I live?"

Shanda looked at Drita the way Drita might look at Dakota. "I looked it up on the internet," she said.

"You have a computer?"

"At the library."

Jesus, even Shanda was one up on her.

"Drita, I have a job interview and I really, really need to get there and I really, really can't bring a five-year-old with me."

"A job interview? Where?"

"Does it matter?"

"Yes."

"Family Dollar. It's close and it's a job."

"I didn't say anything."

"You were thinking it or you wouldn't have asked in the first place."

"I wasn't thinking anything," Drita said, though she had, for a moment, imagined Shanda responding to one of Le French Connection's open calls, knowing that those kinds of places recruited exclusively women without options.

"I don't care what you do as long as it's an honest living," Drita added.

"It's honest. We both know it's not a living," Shanda said. "But I need it. And the Women's League daycare isn't open on Saturdays."

Drita eyed the two of them and sighed. "How long are you going to be?"

"I don't know, a couple of hours? I have to get ready and then there's like a test to take and then I have to maybe stop at the store on the way back."

It all seemed premeditated. There was no reason she couldn't have called first, or stopped by ahead of time if she didn't have a phone. But what was Drita supposed to do, turn her only nephew out on the street? Again, as Pete might say?

"Fine," Drita said. "Sure."

"Thank you, Drita," Shanda said. Drita could see that it was work for Shanda to get those words out, but she got them out and that was what mattered. She even made eye contact, which seemed to be a brand-new experience for her, a new trick that she'd hopefully show off to the Family Dollar manager on duty.

"You're welcome," Drita answered. "Oh, and good luck." Shanda was on her way down the stairs when Drita called it out, and Shanda paused for a second, threw a hand up in acknowledgment, and trotted off to live her new sober Shanda life, whatever that entailed.

Drita looked down at her nephew.

"Want to go to the mall?" she asked him.

He stopped staring at the car in his hand and looked up at Drita for the first time since stepping inside. "What's the mall?" he asked.

"It's a place that's filled with stuff that's supposed to make your life better," Drita said. "Clothes, toys, Orange Juliuses, that kind of thing."

"Okay," Dakota said.

"Okay," Drita said. He was out the door before Drita even grabbed her purse, and she was about to call to him to wait for her, but he seemed to know to stop at the door downstairs and, when she opened it for him, to stop at the end of the sidewalk before it became street. The kid might've been weird, but he was docile, so she wasn't about to complain. At least that part of him didn't take after his father.

Drita parked at the Penney's, near the entrance by the jewelry counters, not because she wanted to browse through any of that crap but because nobody did, and there was thus always plenty of room in the Penney's lot. She'd held Dakota's hand to the entrance but forgot to pick it back up after she let go to open the door, and by the time she remembered, it was evident that Dakota didn't need any hand-holding.

He didn't reach to jangle any gaudy tennis bracelets, and when they passed a kiosk of remote-control helicopters outside Penney's great glass entrance doors, he didn't reach out for those, either. He seemed not to care that he was among other humans or the junk they sold that other kids found wondrous. The boy was going to be a regular old friend machine in kindergarten, and the thought of it made Drita feel a kind of ache that resembled affection.

Pete had been nothing but want for meaningless things, for as far back as Drita could remember. Toys, then wheels, then girls, then the kinds of boys that traveled in packs to get girls, which was mostly unsuccessful unless the girls were too young to know better. Even then, Drita thought Pete always wanted the wrong things, the easy things, the wrong people who facilitated access to the easy things. But a total absence of desire wasn't healthy, either, and she worried about that in Dakota. So when she caught him staring at the Bungee Bounce attraction, empty except for the bored middle-aged operator waiting for teenagers to harass or be harassed by, she said, "Cool, huh?"

"Yes," he replied. He spoke how she imagined the Terminator would speak if cyborgs were developed as children. It was unnerving, and while Drita acknowledged that she was no natural around children, it was even harder when the child seemed so unnatural to begin with.

He was too young to goad into taking a jump, but she wanted to get more out of him. She realized she'd made a mistake by setting his expectations low on this trip, telling him he was going to see a lot of things that he couldn't touch. His expectations had been set low in the rest of his life, so maybe it was time to instill some desire in him, some want for something more than what he already had, which seemed to be a Matchbox car and the ability to recite the twelve steps the way that she, as a kid, had recited Double Dutch chants, hoping for Double Dutch partners to appear.

She asked him, "Are you hungry?"

"Yes," he said again, and this was good. This was evidence of attentiveness.

"Do you have to use the bathroom?" she asked.

"No," he answered, and this was also good. This meant he understood the difference between affirmatives and negatives.

"Okay, and will you tell me when you have to go to the bathroom?"

"Yes," he said.

"Thank you. And, you know, you can also tell me when you're hungry. You don't have to wait for me to ask."

The boy finally looked up at Drita, and his face registered some confusion. Drita felt bad for that, but it passed quickly enough, and she was pleased to see, clearly, how this process of information acquisition happened in children: confusion, processing, acceptance. It was a beautiful thing, especially considering how most of the adults she dealt with managed information, which was instant and outright rejection.

"Do you know what to call me when you want to tell me something?" she asked.

"No," he said.

"You say, 'Aunt Drita,' and then you say it. Do you understand that?"

"Aunt Drita, yes," he answered.

"You don't have to say Aunt Drita every single time you talk to me, only when you want to get my attention. If we're already talking, you don't have to say it. Does that make sense?"

He hesitated, then stored this information in the appropriate compartment.

"Yes," he said.

"Good. Now what should we get to eat?"

Dakota stared up at her, a look of vague panic on his face. It was good to see eye contact, and some modicum of emotion, but she understood that she had asked too open a question, and that this type of freedom was overwhelming to a kid like Dakota.

"How about I name something and you say yes or no?" she said.

"Yes," he said.

"Okay. Pretzel?"

"No."

"Pizza?"

"No."

"Chinese food?"

"No."

"Have you ever had Chinese food?"

"No."

"Do you know what Chinese food is?"

"No."

"Well, I'll show you, because I'm not going to the mall without a stop at Panda Express. How about McDonald's?"

"Yes," he said.

"McDonald's it is," she said. "Happy Meal?"

He nodded, and it was great, a conversational exchange that bordered on normal.

"You're really lucky, kid, you know that?" Drita said and instantly realized what a dumb statement that would be if he understood the wider world. She added, quickly, "You're really lucky to be going to McDonald's today of all days. You know why?"

"No," Dakota said.

"I'll tell you why: Furbies." And when it was clear she was the only one who'd seen the commercials advertising McDonald's current Happy Meal giveaway, she added, "They're pretty much the best things ever. Wait till you see."

The way he looked at her, like she was something that had never been seen before, made Drita feel like a wizard.

Dakota was a regular kid in some ways. For example, he walked excruciatingly slowly. Drita understood that his stride was truncated by the length of his legs and that he had only been at this walking thing for a few years, but it stressed her out to take so long to do something so essentially human. Drita was someone who walked with purpose, even when there wasn't any, or when the purpose was an oversized plate of mushy General Tso's served up by a sixteen-year-old Puerto

Rican boy at the Panda Express. She was in no position to pick and choose her friends, but slow walkers were nonetheless ruled out, because slow walking suggested to her some kind of character defect, sloth or even arrogance, like the world was expected to wait for this single person who couldn't be bothered to bring their heart rate over eighty beats per minute. Dakota, though, was next-level slow. He stared down at his legs while he walked, as if amazed he was able to do it. It would take a patience that Drita couldn't conjure to make it the few hundred yards to the food court, so Drita took Dakota's hand, thinking it would speed him up by proxy. It didn't. Drita considered just snatching the boy up and carrying him like a toddler, but he wasn't a toddler, and she worried that he'd shriek and flail and Drita would look like one of the shitty mothers she herself judged every time she witnessed a similar scene.

"Dakota," Drita called down to him. He stopped walking altogether when he looked back at her, not having mastered doing those two things at once.

She wasn't sure what she was going to say. Hurry it up? Pick up the pace? Quit your goddamn dillydallying, which had been Dom's preferred motivator for her and Pete as kids, despite the fact that Jackie was usually lagging behind all of them in her wheelchair? It never worked anyway. They'd speed up for twenty seconds and then fall right back into their old pattern, until Dom would just pull away and go missing for the next hour or two.

"Wanna race?" she asked.

The kid had no idea what she meant by that; his furrowed little brow made that clear.

"Here are the rules: no running. You can't run. We just have to walk as fast as we can to the food court and whoever gets there first gets a Mrs. Fields as a prize. You know what a Mrs. Fields is? It's a cookie. A really, really, really good cookie. Get it?"

"Yes," he answered.

"Good. On the count of three: one, two, three," Drita said and started at a pace that was still half her usual one. Even then, she had made it a good twenty feet ahead of Dakota by the time she checked back to see his progress. Progress was perhaps too strong a word. Dakota stood right where she had left him, looking horrified both that he'd failed at a task and that Aunt Drita had abandoned him for it.

Drita stopped and called back to him. "Dakota, what's wrong?"

She was too far ahead to hear his response, and so she trotted back to him. "I don't understand it," he was saying. He looked on the verge of tears, and that was an awful thing, but it was also a normal thing, and so Drita thought that maybe this experiment had not been a total failure.

"What don't you understand?" she asked him.

"To walk fast," he said.

"You don't understand how to walk fast?"

"No," he said.

"It's just walking but faster. That's it. I don't know how else to say it." His face began to crumple, just as Drita's patience did. "You understand run, right?" she said.

His head, still held low, bobbed slightly up and down.

Kids were not supposed to run indoors, was the thing. She could tell him to run now and then confuse him later by telling him it's not a thing he should be doing, or they could move in quarter-speed and get to the food court sometime next Tuesday. She decided to go with the former, thinking back to all the contradictions the adults in her life had made when she was a kid, how it was supposed to all add up not to logic but to authority, and that was the thing kids responded most to.

"Okay then, never mind fast walk. We're going to run, okay?"

Dakota did not appear convinced.

"Dakota, okay? Listen, this is a special treat. You don't usually get to run in the mall and then end up with a cookie at the end of it all. Don't you want a special treat?"

He looked at her, waiting for her to feed him the answer.

"Of course you do. We all want a special treat all the time, but we only get them some of the time. This is the time. Don't blow it. All you have to do is make it right to that food court"—she pointed—"and then all your Saturday dreams come true. Okay? Can you nod your head or say yes?"

"Yes," he said.

"Awesome. Okay, then, on the count of three: one, two, three."

And he was off, not like he was in pursuit of something but like he was being pursued, his wide eyes cartoonish in fear. Drita speed-walked backwards, keeping an eye on him, until he reached and then overtook her, when she pivoted and speed-walked on his tail. The bugger could actually move when he wanted to, just as Drita suspected. All he needed was some motivation, and if positive reinforcement wasn't it then fear seemed just as legitimate. But when they landed in the food court, Dakota running straight through the legs of the people in line at the McDonald's, she saw that the fear was gone, replaced by something nearly unrecognizable on him: joy. He peered up at her from beneath the counter, and Drita ignored the dirty looks of the moms and teenagers around them and laughed at Dakota's exaggerated panting.

"Man, you creamed me," she said.

"Aunt Drita, I creamed you," he echoed.

"Yeah, yeah, no gloating. Come on out now and get in line so we can get that cookie."

He ate the cookie—he wanted oatmeal raisin, because the kid was off—and he ate the Happy Meal, after he scraped the onions and the mustard from the bun, and he ate a single bite of Drita's orange chicken without complaint, though his face upon swallowing made it clear that it was the last bite he'd be taking of it until at least adolescence.

"What kind of stuff do you eat at home?" Drita asked him.

"Hot dogs," he said.

"Just hot dogs?"

"Hot dogs, cereal, spaghetti, bread . . ."

"You ever try a vegetable?"

". . . macaroni and cheese, animal crackers, McDonald's."

"So ketchup is a vegetable to you?"

He looked blankly at her.

"Want to try a piece of broccoli?" she asked.

"No," he said.

"Didn't think so. What about school?"

The boy shrugged.

"Do you go to school?"

"No."

"I guess you'll be going in the fall."

"Why?" he asked.

"So you can learn stuff and make friends. Do you know the alphabet yet?"

"Yes," he said, and he recited it in its entirety, not in the song form that most kids use because they understand letters only as sounds, but in a dry, determined way that sounded like a dramatic monologue.

"That's good, Dakota. Do you know what letter this is?" she asked.

"H," he said.

"And this?"

"Y."

"You know what it spells?"

"Happy," he said.

It could have been a guess—it was a Happy Meal, after all, one of American children's primary forms of sustenance—but he had studied the word for a moment before pronouncing it, so maybe he was reading after all. Drita herself remembered reading at his age, at least rudimentarily, and being baffled by Pete's inability, at the time, to do so. He was never what they called book smart, though nobody offered what kind of smart he was instead. He wasn't really street-smart, since he was always getting caught for stupid offenses, like petty theft, or tagging the post office, or pissing in a bus shelter. He had instead physical tal-

ents that were largely unearned and untrained. He could scale anything, from spindly trees that didn't look like they could support the
weight of a robin to flat brick walls with just enough texture to the
mortar for Pete's hands to grip. He probably could have been a track
star if joining a team wasn't for dorks, and he definitely could have
been a BMX star, based on the stupid air he could get on the neighborhood bikes he stole and subsequently trashed on the bank of the Mad
River. He'd just needed to find his thing was what everybody thought,
until his thing turned out to be forties of St. Ides and the skinny, fa-
therless girls who were attracted to him when he held them.

"Hey, Dakota, can you do this?" Drita asked, pulling the right side of
her top lip into an Elvis curl. "But without your finger, just using your
face?"

It took a moment for Dakota to register the question, but in that
input-process-output cycle so obvious on him, he did, and proceeded
to wiggle his lips until he found the muscle he needed to complete the
task.

"Okay, hold that," Drita said, "and try to bring your bottom lip down
on the other side, like this." She pulled her bottom lip down in the opposite direction from the top, again with her finger.

He didn't really need to process the directive this time. He just
dropped his lip down in the opposite direction, so that the top and
bottom corners of his lips looked like they were trying to escape each
other.

"You look like a madman," Drita said, and Dakota seemed to like
that, holding his face in that eerie position until he laughed and broke
both the pose and the spell. It was the first laugh Drita had heard from
him, and the sound of it made him seem even more like a lunatic than
the face did. He was, in this way at least, his father's son, with the elastic face and the clownish snort, which Pete had used alternately to
make her laugh and make her cry.

"Who taught you how to read?" Drita asked.

"Mom."

"Huh," Drita said. She didn't want to reveal that she was surprised by that. "Did your father teach you how to do all that stuff with your face?"

"No."

"Who did you learn it from, then?"

"You," he said, looking confused. "Just now."

Drita flushed. It felt like an unexpected compliment, that she had managed to do something for this boy stranger.

"Do you remember your father?" Drita asked him.

"Yes," Dakota said.

"What do you remember?"

Dakota thought for a second: input-process-output. He answered, "The bird."

"The bird?"

"Yes."

"He had a bird?"

"Here," Dakota said, pounding his belly like a pro wrestler.

"A tattoo," Drita said.

Dakota shrugged and went back to his French fries, now cold as well as soggy, and none the worse off for it.

"Was he nice to you?" Drita asked.

Dakota nodded. "He's nice. He's funny. He plays with my toys in funny voices."

Present tense. The poor kid.

"All right, kiddo," Drita said. No point in making the kid think about the things he didn't have when he was in an entire building designed to make him do just that. "You're going to have to hurry it up now. We have to skedaddle to a boring electronics store."

Dakota looked at her and chewed even more deliberately on his fry, his eyes gone devilish. An hour with his aunt Drita and the boy was already getting contrary, and that kind of thing would make Shanda's life a little harder than it already was. Still, it was exactly the kind of temperament he needed if he was going to have a shot at the kind of life that life itself seemed determined to keep from him.

4

IN CARTOONS, MICE LIVED IN THEIR OWN LITTLE PLACES BUILT INTO the walls of human homes, little meta-houses where they cross-stitched and raised mice children and the lady mice wore funny puffy hats as they sat knitting stockings in their mouse rocking chairs. The mouse doorways in Nadia's apartment weren't decoratively arched like they were in the cartoons, just crude trapezoidal cutouts near the refrigerator and in the cabinet under the sink, but as a kid Shanda would peer into them anyway, wanting to see the mouse living rooms, the mouse family portraits, the twin mouse beds where husband and wife mouse lay side by side in the old-timey days before husband and wife were allowed to share beds. Even with the flashlight she'd taken from the porch, left by a careless neighbor after a power outage or too many unpaid electric bills, it was too dark to really see inside the holes. She could make out only wood slats and crumbling plaster and, off to the sides, long dark channels of pure, aching mystery. The channels looked like corridors, which to Shanda meant she was seeing a big fancy mouse building, like the old folks' home her kindergarten class visited to make the old people weep, or the hospital her mother went to sometimes, like when she drank instead of her usual Popov the entire bottle of Shanda's yellow Listerine, which a teacher had secretly dropped into her backpack and which Shanda had deemed too precious to ever touch.

Shanda had reached her arms into the hollow, feeling for doors or mouse elevators. She'd found some old newspaper clippings and rusty nails, but no signs of mouse civilization. But she knew it was in there somewhere, because in the mornings there would be fresh mouse poop on the kitchen floor and counters, on the table, once even inside Shanda's backpack, despite it having been securely zipped shut. The mice clearly were third shifters, working and living their mouse lives in the overnight hours, and so Shanda decided that she would stay up overnight, too, wanting some mouse friends, wanting to convince them that she was not like the shrieking human housewives of the cartoons, though she did desire the housewives' beautiful puffy-skirted dresses and the blueberry pies they baked. She sat beside the trapezoid holes for hours and took to bringing her pillow and blanket into the kitchen in case she fell asleep while she waited. She always did, and she always missed them, and this was Shanda's first lesson in determination leading absolutely nowhere.

It was only after she stopped trying that she began to see the mice emerge. First there was the one stuck inside the plastic bag of Wonder bread, having burrowed its way inside but too fat and drunk on white flour to find its way back out. Shanda zipped that one into her backpack, but when she checked on him several hours later he was dead, his tiny mouse toes capped with perfectly manicured mouse nails. Shanda disposed of that body discreetly, wrapping it in several layers of KFC napkins and ejecting it from the window. She couldn't have the other mice discover what she had done, lest they believe her to be murderous rather than someone who, as humans sometimes did, had just made some careless mistakes.

Then there were more: in the cupboards, snacking on errant puffs of Rice Krispies, and when those ran out, on the wood of the cabinets themselves. A mouse couple on top of the refrigerator, poking through the rubble like rescuers after an earthquake. On the arm of the sofa, watching television beside Nadia, who was oblivious until the mouse grazed her forearm. Nadia responded by flinging the rodent halfway across the room. The mouse ran a few compact circles, then convulsed a few minutes before lying perfectly still except for a few quick twitches of its feet. Shanda was horrified at what her mother had done, and Nadia was horrified in turn when Shanda picked the corpse up and began stroking it.

"Shanda, no! That's a bad thing," Nadia said. "Just flush it. Flush it down the toilet."

It was so soft, though, and it was Shanda's only chance to know that, because the mice otherwise ran from her touch. Even though they had scuttled across her feet as she made herself a peanut butter and fluff, they fled when she made any move to reciprocate. That was what made her realize, eventually, that this was because the mice weren't offering affection at all, nor would they ever. They, like the humans she was hoping the mice would substitute for, rejected her. The mice were just like Cassandra, Cristal, and Shamika, who had pretended to befriend Shanda only to tell her, days later, *Psych!* and to bring the entire second-grade class onboard, every single one of them at recess surrounding her and chanting Shanda has body lice, Shanda has body lice.

So Shanda sought vengeance. The girls at school were too powerful to take on, but these mice were weaklings. Weaklings and thieves, eating Nadia and Shanda's scraps, living rent-free in their home, which, in truth, Nadia and Shanda also lived in rent-free, thanks be to the good state of Connecticut. One stomp and their mouse guts erupted from their sides, though Shanda tried this only once, seeing as how it just about ruined her shoes and made the floor dangerously slick for days. Mostly she trapped them underneath bowls or boxes and let them suffocate or starve, which took anywhere from several hours to several days, depending on the mouse's constitution, the time since their last meal, and the airtightness of the container. Nadia insisted Shanda flush each mouse corpse down the toilet, so she did, until eventually the toilet clogged, overflowed, and caused a flood in the downstairs apartment. This had caused the downstairs neighbor to bang on Nadia and Shanda's door, screaming and looking to fight, until the neighbor got a peek inside and decided the better recourse would be to call the Department of Children and Families and have someone snatch Shanda away. They did, citing health concerns and general neglect, and it seemed for a while that the mice would indeed have the last laugh.

But Shanda had more tricks up her sleeve, too. She knew that the social workers responded to any perceived improvements in behavior as miraculous, and that a simple smile or turned-in homework assignment could be presented as evidence of having made significant enough improvement to be recommended another chance to live as a normal child. And while it was the landlord who was responsible for the cleanup, extermination, and plumbing repair the state demanded after the neighbor's call to the housing department, and while he performed his duties extremely reluctantly under threat of very expensive penalties, fines, and possible criminal charges, DCF also used the improved condition in Nadia's home as evidence of her renewed fitness as a mother.

Upon her return, Shanda planned a mouse genocide as revenge, and she was only slightly disappointed that it had already been executed in her absence. The mice had been cleared out, along with nearly all the papers, wrappers, boxes, knickknacks, outgrown clothing, toenail clippings, used Band-Aids, and various precious things that her mother had spent years collecting and that had coated the interior of their home like a padded cell.

Shanda had been sad when she saw the apartment. She tried to remember what the sadness stemmed from: the loss of the precious things or the realization that none of it had been precious at all.

She wasn't a child when she returned, was how she remembered it. Whatever it was that made children children, she no longer had it. She didn't play, she didn't smile, she learned to flirt with grown men to get things she wanted, like packages of gum and jelly bracelets. The landlord, though still resentful of Nadia, came to appreciate Shanda. She had sass and street-smarts. She didn't recoil when he took out his dick and squeezed it to show how big it could get. She rolled her eyes when he suggested she touch it, but she'd do it if he dangled a shiny enough prize before her. The landlord had lost interest when Shanda began sprouting breasts, but he didn't go so far as to evict Nadia and Shanda, knowing that she was not a girl who would tattle to anyone. She didn't have anyone to tattle to, and anyway, she would never even realize there was anything worth telling.

Even when the apartment reverted to its previous state, it was never the same. When the mice returned a year or so later, Shanda didn't have interest in avenging anything. Vengeance suggested a belief in justice, that some kind of balance existed in the world. By age nine, Shanda had abandoned that belief. By age twelve, she'd forgotten she ever held it.

Shanda was just remembering it now, at age twenty-four, staring down at her son, who was attempting to fetch the Hot Wheels he'd flung down a mouse alley. The wall was swallowing his arm, and she knew he wasn't anywhere near the little metal chassis he was chasing. She alternated between cursing the mice and using this as a lesson for Dakota: you send anything out into this world, it's going to damn well keep what you give it.

"Mom, I can't get my toy," Dakota said, in his little-man diction that people often found weird.

"Why'd you throw it in there?" Shanda asked him.

"I didn't," he said.

"Then how'd it get in there?"

"I flung it."

"I thought you just said you didn't do that."

"I didn't throw it, I flung it."

Shanda was about to ask him the difference, but the difference didn't matter and she knew it. And she was about to tell him too bad, and to repeat the stuff about consequences she'd learned in rehab, but instead she said, "Just leave it, baby. We'll get you another one. That one's for the mice now."

"Mice don't play with toys," Dakota said.

The kid was smarter than she was at his age, that was for sure. Knowing this brought her no relief. This would be hard to manage as he got older and kept getting smarter than her. She thought it a miracle that she'd kept him alive this long, and she knew better than to believe her luck would last forever.

Shanda's counselor would tell her that she was only sabotaging herself with that kind of thinking. Her sponsor would tell her that the purpose of taking that fearless moral inventory was not to feed the fire of self-hatred but to free herself from those very combustibles. Officially, Shanda was on Step 6 of the Big Book, but she knew she was lying to herself and others if she suggested she'd purged her defects of character instead of sweeping them inside some holy NA-sanctioned closet. And she sure as hell hadn't completed Step 5, admitting to God, herself, and another human being the exact nature of her wrongs, but she didn't consider that one entirely her fault, as she didn't much believe in God, and she wasn't sure what human being would be interested in hearing the exact nature of her wrongs. Lying to herself and to her home group meant she wasn't really clean and sober, her sponsor would tell her, because lying was addictive behavior, and addicts are as addicted to excuses as they are to the needle, but she knew for a fact that everyone in her group lied constantly, most of them about more important stuff than she did. At least she wasn't using. At least she didn't go right back into the arms of her captor/trigger/lover, like most of the other women in her group had. Of course she hadn't had much of a choice in that, since Pete had Houdinied himself out of her life. And she did end up right back here, in the apartment on Pine Street, which wasn't just a storage room for her demons but the actual hell-mouth.

And she'd brought her son. Why had she done that? The place was literally dangerous.

Not as dangerous as the street. They needed a place to stay, was why. Nadia had been the only tenant left in the triplex, and the landlord would probably try to burn the place to the ground once the Section 8 vouchers stopped being sent. This was why Shanda had to hang on to those combustibles from Step 4—she needed to stay as dangerous as the things she and Dakota would surely face. When the junkies came around looking to loot whatever copper and working appliances were left in the building, she'd be ready with a shiv and the Big Book. When the landlord came, she'd have a lighter.

Also, practically speaking, the apartment on Pine Street was free for now, and it had to be kismet that Drita showed up there before Shanda even had a chance to look for her. Their only chance at real escape was Drita, even if Drita had always acted too good for her and Pete, even if she'd already turned them away the last time they were out of options. Then again, Shanda and Pete were total pieces of shit by the time that happened, so that was fair enough. Everybody *was* better than them.

That's dangerous water you're treading, her sponsor's voice said.

Fearless moral inventory, Shanda silently responded.

She wasn't fearless in dragging Dakota back to where she'd sprung from; she was terrified of stepping into that space again herself, never mind exposing her child to it. But it was moral, because it had led her to Drita. Drita was the only person Shanda knew who couldn't fathom the kind of life Shanda had lived, the kind of life Shanda refused to pass on to Dakota.

5

AFTER WHAT FELT LIKE HOURS TALKING TO THE STAPLES SALESPER-
son, who made Drita feel like she were choosing a new life partner
instead of a machine; after Shanda retrieved Dakota following what
must have been the world's longest dollar store job interview; after
cussing and losing her cool on account of the box of plastic now sitting on her kitchen table, where she had never once eaten dinner; after
a neighborhood high school kid had coaxed the box of plastic from
something inert into something that blinked and bleeped and showed
some sign of digital life, and he accepted the ten-dollar bill Drita offered him without a word of gratitude; after all of that, Drita was finally ready to use an hour or two of the thousands of free AOL hours
that had been sitting in her junk drawer, literally wasting time. She
plopped a disk in the tray and pushed the button to close it, listened to
the machine whir, pause, and whir again, and minutes or days later—
long enough for Drita to consider tracking down the neighborhood
kid again, or just returning the expensive piece of junk to the Staples
guy who'd assured her she was getting the best bang for the consider-
able buck—a box appeared on the screen, asked her a series of questions, and demanded she have a credit card number so that she could
blow more money in the most extravagant Saturday of her life. The

modem, which until that point had been another expensive but much smaller table decoration, began initializing, according to the message on the screen, and while Drita didn't know what that meant, it looked like something she had paid a lot of money for it to be doing.

But it was doing it, whatever it was. The little running man had started out at Connecting and made his way to Connected! A voice announced that she had mail, sounding as astonished about that as she was. But when she navigated to the mailbox, it was simply another welcome message from AOL, and the familiar disappointing Saturday loneliness came right back.

She reminded herself that the PC was a tool to construct a bridge to a new life, and that new life did not exist in the machine itself. She had to tell the machine what she wanted, and she was embarrassed in front of the soulless thing to have to think so hard about it. She typed *masters public health* and was brought to Columbia University's virtual front door, which served to remind her of the debt she'd already accrued and her last pleading phone call to the registrar, which had converted her leave of absence to a permanent withdrawal after her third semester away. She typed *masters public health connecticut*, thinking she could continue working at the VNA to pay off her old debts while accruing her new ones, but the prospect of beginning the coursework all over again, this time after eight to ten daily hours of tending to actual patients before converting them into theoretical statistics and pie charts, made her lift her glass and swallow enough burgundy in one gulp for her body to reject it and have to spit into a nearby tea towel. She stared at the embroidered tea towel, the threads that formed the image of a little babushkaed farm girl under the word Hungary, and though it had come not from Eastern Europe but a neighbor's tag sale, it made her think bigger, of all the places on the globe still uncharted to her, and this made her type in *peace corps*. She could finally make that trip to French Guiana she'd never gotten to take, or since French Guiana was as arbitrary then as it was now, to Lesotho or Vanuatu or, if she was feeling relatively cosmopolitan, Mongolia. All of it reminded her that Jackie's blood clot and ensuing physical decline was the reason she'd been derailed from her original plans in the first place, so she typed in *home health aides*, and this reminded Drita that working for the healthcare system was what made her unable to trust her mother to fend for herself with it.

It was a long, circuitous trip right back to where she was sitting at that very moment, now cast in an unearthly digital glow.

She sighed and steered back to the home page, where she hovered the mouse over what must have been the family of AOL's Running Man, four faceless icons that somehow struck Drita as midwestern, huddled together and waving as if seeing their beloved oldest son off for his freshman year at the University of Iowa. Chat was written below them, nonsensically—why be online at all when you've got an intact nuclear family with whom to play Scattergories on a Saturday night? If AOL was being honest, the picture would have been of a lone figure with bad posture and a glass of worse wine in their non-mouse hand. It would have been of Drita at that moment, hesitating before clicking on the link, then doing it before she could talk herself out of it, though she had plenty of time to bail while waiting for the next page to load. When it did, she was faced with the kind of anxiety that usually struck at office Christmas parties, when her co-workers segregated themselves by race or job rank or religion or political affiliation or some combination of any or all: too many groups all at once, none of which seemed quite the right fit for her to join. That wasn't completely true; there was one chat room simply titled Lonely, but she knew enough to avoid people who readily identified as such. She scanned some other options. Biker Bar? Saturday Brunch and Sunday Brunch, with no explanation as to how they were different? Pagan Tea House? Elvis Sightings? Hartford?

Okay, Hartford. That was concrete, a literal place thirty minutes away from where she sat. At the very least, she'd have geography in common with whoever she might find there. They could talk, what—insurance? The Mark Twain house?

Or nothing. She entered the room and the conversations were already under way.

BillyWilly: no the tacos there suxxx

CamelToe21: lolololol

KixStand.99: not worth the drive if u ask me

candy chameleon: i heard they're on tour again w new drummer this time

It was hard to decipher who was addressing whom, which made jumping in even more impossible than it was to her in real life. Then a smaller window appeared on her screen:

FoolsballChamp69: a/s/l

The cursor blinked before her. She downed more than what could be called a sip from her juice glass and set it on the table before typing.

DDiMeo73$: American Sign Language?

FoolsballChamp69: lolololololol

So obviously this person wasn't asking her to speak ASL, which, come to think of it, wouldn't make any sense in this medium. Still, there was clearly some kind of a language barrier, because she had no idea what the person was trying to say.

DDiMeo73$: What do you mean by a/s/l? I've never done this before.

FoolsballChamp69: you 4 real? A virgin? ;^)

DDiMeo73$: Only at this.

FoolsballChamp69: i'm asking age/sex/location

FoolsballChamp69: and hoping the answer is 18/f/my lap

Drita quickly x'd out of the box, not simply because she wasn't eighteen but because she was embarrassed about not understanding more than she did about how to proceed. Was that all there was to it—log in to a chat room ostensibly on the topic of Connecticut's capital city and immediately find yourself lap-bound? It explained the popularity of the internet, for sure, but the endgame was still fuzzy. Was it all fantasy, like XXX videos and party lines, or was it supposed to be a conduit for a real-life meeting, like the kinds of personal ads she always talked herself out of responding to?

She tipped a glass she'd already mostly emptied onto her lips, a tiny bead of cabernet slowly making its way to her tongue. It was a quarter to ten, the earliest she'd let herself call it a night on a Saturday. Fifteen minutes. Only fifteen minutes to kill before she could go to sleep at an hour she could convince herself was respectable for someone who, as Jackie always told her, was in the prime of her life.

A menu on the homepage offered some suggestions to pass the time. She clicked on the News option, so she could go to bed feeling at least a little smarter instead of frustrated and a little drunk. Oscars predictions for the following night. Jack Kevorkian on trial again. A surge of donations for Bill Clinton following his acquittal in his impeachment trial. All the same stuff she could read about in the *Republican-American,* not even the fringy take on current events that the *New Haven Advocate* offered. She typed *isaac robinson columbia* into the search bar and found him not at Columbia but at Tufts, and she felt some relief knowing he'd landed a residency in a city she hated, because it meant it probably wouldn't have worked out between them even if he had waited for her while she tended to Jackie and her brother did fuck all.

Her brother. Now there was a real mystery, one that even the all-knowing internet surely couldn't solve.

Still, she entered *pete dimeo* into the search bar. Plenty of hits, but none on her brother, and lots of noise to boot—Pete something-or-others and something-or-other DiMeos. She tried again, this time using his full name, Petrit, and waited for the next screen to disappoint her as well, but to her surprise, she found herself staring at a page full of news sites.

The hits weren't related to her brother, but some other Petrit DiMeo.

They must have been, because the guy they referred to was some kind of a guerrilla soldier, somebody who'd signed up for something called the Kosovo Liberation Army. The articles were essentially duplicates of each other, reprints from a single wire service, but Drita clicked through them all, not because she thought she'd found her brother but because each tap killed a few more seconds, and it was novel to think of a parallel Petrit DiMeo out there in the world, one with convictions and a sense of purpose beyond scoring his next pack of Kools. Kosovo had been popping up in the news lately, but Drita assumed it was mostly because the news had to come up with something to fill the airwaves after Bill Clinton's impeachment trial, not because anyone actually knew or cared what was going on in a part of the world that not even the Peace Corps got involved with.

But there was a human interest angle for the news to pick up on: a bunch of exiles and immigrant kids in the U.S. had volunteered to fight for the independence of their homeland, or their parents' homeland, a place they maybe visited once or twice or, for some, never at all. One of the pieces had a photo to accompany it, and strangely, the photo showed a guy who looked a lot like her brother, if she could imagine her brother clean-shaven and wearing camouflage. And stranger still, the caption called this doppelgänger Petrit DiMeo, which at first amused Drita, and then, after she clicked on the photo to expand it in her screen, made her swat her empty wineglass to the floor.

This was no doppelgänger. That was Drita's brother, Petrit DiMeo, staring back at her in black and white, his thick hair buzzed the way he wore it for the three months he played Pop Warner football in middle school.

Petrit DiMeo, 26, stands at attention between the American and Albanian flags in the nondescript office of a construction company in the Bronx. "I can't just stand by and watch my people get slaughtered," said DiMeo, an Albanian-born roofer now living and working in New York. "The Serbs know the Albanians there don't have weapons, they know they can't fight back. But we have weapons. We can fight."

The last sips of wine threatened to join the glass it had come from on the floor, but Drita swallowed the bile and read over from the beginning.

The men are truck drivers, waiters, construction workers, college students. Some are quiet, perhaps self-conscious of their accents or imperfect English, others brash, speaking in thick New York accents. Some are parents, others young enough to still need parenting themselves. What they have in common is their Albanian heritage and, now, their uniforms, pulled together from American Army-Navy surplus stores. These are America's foot soldiers in the Kosovo Liberation Army, or KLA.

Drita tried to figure out the connection between what she was reading and the brother she knew. The Pete she'd shared a bathroom with had gotten suspended for aiming spitballs at the Marine recruiter who parked out daily in their high school cafeteria, and believed anybody who willingly signed up for any organization that made you rise before dawn and told you what to do and when to do it deserved what they got. The Pete she knew couldn't put in an honest day's work to buy Pampers for his own kid. He hadn't shown up for his father's funeral and couldn't be bothered to pick up a prescription for his mother unless it was something worth ciphering for himself, and now he was going to sacrifice himself for strangers he didn't have the language to introduce himself to because they were his "people"? No. No. No. No way. Pete didn't have "people," or at least, a caravan of fleeing Kosovar Albanians weren't his people. She and Pete didn't even come from Kosovo, as far as she knew. Neither one of them spoke the language. They ate baccalà on Christmas Eve and went to funerals at Our Lady of Mt. Carmel like all the other goombahs in town. They'd stopped talking about returning to their homeland years ago, right around the time that Pete found more accessible surrogates and Drita decided it'd be easier to try to fix the world than to convince people she belonged in it, right around the time they'd diverged enough to stop talking about much of anything at all.

It didn't matter how long it had been since they spoke; she knew Pete wasn't doing this for his people. He didn't do anything for anybody without wanting something in return, starting with Parisian Barbie back on their ninth birthdays. He wasn't even doing it for his own offspring. Pete's MO was fucking lives up, not fixing them.

Drita's fury settled the nausea in her belly the way a ginger ale would with normal people. She reread the article, picking out what might be called clues. The Bronx, roofing, some American faction of the KLA. She wrote them down on the closest paper she could find, a calendar that she no longer used to keep track of days that, until very recently, had all felt the same.

It wasn't exactly the direction she was seeking when she'd laid down all that money, but the internet did succeed in giving her at least a new short-term objective. Dakota needed food to eat and Jackie might get her precious son back, even if it meant finally seeing that Pete wasn't content screwing with just his own life or his family's lives, but was apparently determined to spread his havoc all over the world. The truth might hurt Jackie, but the truth was always the best policy, according to those Little Golden Books Jackie had read to them. And anyway, Jackie could probably stand to be a little less naïve.

6

MAY 1970

JACQUELINE SANTOPIETRO WAILED ON CONTACT WHEN PA'S PALM met her cheek, partly because that was the response he'd want from her and partly because Pa aiming above the neck meant he made the choice to protect the baby she'd just confessed was in her belly, and a howl was the only sound she could release that could adequately express her joy. It's not that she enjoyed other people's displeasure, and God knows she was surrounded by the displeased. Pa had that spittle that collected in the corner of his mouth when his anger couldn't be expressed in human language, and Ma was convulsing silently, hands clasped to her chest to convey in gesture what she would say to Jackie in words for years to come, right down to when her heart broke for its final time in a St. Mary's hospital bed a dozen years later. Dom stood red-faced and shrunken by the doorframe, where he'd positioned himself in case he had to run from Pa.

"Next month, you marry," Pa told him, calmly, after he wiped his mouth, and Dom didn't even nod. There was no agreement to be had; it wasn't a negotiation. Afterwards Dom would remind Jackie how lucky she was that he respected her father enough to accede to his wishes, but Jackie knew honor had nothing to do with it, and she didn't even hold it against him. There were some growing pains when boys become men, they never went willingly—she had brothers and neighbor boys and they all worked exactly the same way, content to suckle until pushed off the teat.

So it's not that she enjoyed everyone's displeasure so much as she knew that their displeasure would eventually give way to acceptance, and down the road, some kind of happiness akin to what she had the foresight to already feel. Dom wouldn't have to put up a fight to get Jackie into the potato cellar at his uncle's house anymore, because he could just roll her over lazily in their own marital bed. Her parents would have one less mouth to feed on weekdays and two more to feed on Sundays, when everybody was expected to come together over a dinner table so loud that there was no burden on anyone to engage in any meaningful talk. And she would have her own place with her own baby instead of her mother's place with her brothers' babies, all of them as fat and ungrateful as their fathers.

Our Lady of Mt. Carmel kept its Thursdays open for the kinds of weddings that couldn't be scheduled months in advance, and since Thursdays were workdays for all of the Santopietros on the left side of the pond, and since Thursday weddings were implicitly shameful for all involved, the celebration would be as small and austere as such occasions could be. This was intended as a kind of punishment for Jackie, but she wouldn't have asked for anything different if she'd been able to plan it all herself. She either didn't much care about or actively disliked most of her cousins, who'd normally comprise the vast majority of the pews and seats at the reception at the Ponte Club, and her parents didn't like Jackie's real friends, hippies who might as well have been practicing pagans, despite their fathers all belonging to the same Knights of Columbus chapter as Pa. She'd always secretly flipped right past the wedding and bridesmaid dresses in the Sears catalog straight to the lingerie section anyway; at least the garments there could be worn more than once, even if so much of what they were made of was fascinatingly purposeless—dozens of clasps and hooks designed to make both parties have to work harder than necessary to get to the reward underneath. The models were such pretty little towheads, with hair that formed the kinds of perfect coils nobody had ever approached in real life, and they smiled wholesomely despite the iniquity suggested by their corsets and garter belts.

Only the hippie friends deigned to be happy for Jackie in the short term. They were girls who freely talked about sex, though they weren't as free with their own as the *Life* magazine articles about their kind would have led people to believe. They were, at heart, still as much their fathers' daughters as they were their own liberated women, aligned with Jackie in spirit if not in dress. They still mostly wanted a single man they couldn't have, and they ultimately wanted families of their own. They didn't pretend they were scandalized when Jackie told them she was getting married in a few weeks, which they understood as code for the unsaid message.

"To Dom?" Denise squealed. "Didn't you say his pecker leaned so hard to the right you thought it was gonna rupture your appendix?"

"All the better aim to hit that fallopian tube, huh, Jackie?" Antonella said. But they were happy for her, they told her so with the hugs and the baby blankets they began crocheting in the proceeding days, using one of the few skills their mothers taught them that transferred directly to the commune life they aspired to but hadn't managed to embark on. And soon Jackie's ma started making and freezing batches of food for the wedding and five or so months after that, when Jackie would be too tired from feeding and changing a newborn to cook for herself and her husband. Even Pa never brought up the subject again, which meant things in general were going better than she ever could have hoped for. It was only Dom who seemed to hang on to a grudge, not even bothering to thank Jackie for talking her father into getting him a job at the fabrication shop, which he'd previously been hitting her up to do for months, or bothering to kiss her before he pushed her into a corner and tried to slide a few fingers inside.

"Ow, what are you doing, Dominic?" Jackie yelled and slapped his hand away, as if he were a child reaching into a forbidden box of cookies.

"What, you want me to use my prick so you can force me to marry you again?" he said.

"I didn't force anything," she said, and it was true: she wasn't really one of those girls who got pregnant on purpose, she just wanted to try screwing out to see if it was something she could look forward to someday when she found somebody truly special to do it with. But then what happened happened and she looked around at all the boys she'd ever known and realized her chance at plucking somebody special from among them was slim, that her best chance of having somebody special in her life would be making one of her own. She was pleased with herself for learning such a valuable lesson at only nineteen, so she wouldn't grow into one of those bitter old ladies who only realized it after they'd spent all of their good years trying to make their default husbands into good ones.

Dom would come around after the wedding. Then he'd go back the other way after a few years married. Jackie knew how these things went, which meant she might as well do what she could to make herself happy, since there was no point in wasting so much energy trying to do it for someone else. The wedding itself didn't get her too excited—Ma told her it was bad luck to wear a stranger's dress, told her the lady was probably murdered in it or divorced or else why would it have ended up at the Salvation Army, but Jackie found one that fit well enough and didn't poof too much at the wrong places and only cost eight dollars, and that was good enough for her. All the money she saved on the silly stuff would be reallocated to the important things, like the Peg Perego stroller she already had on layaway at Howland-Hughes. One benefit of Dom's indifference to everything related to Jackie and their incubating baby was that Jackie was utterly unsupervised day to day; she continued working her job at the courthouse, spent her lunch hours browsing and sometimes buying baby wares that a husband who paid attention would've considered frivolous, and spent her evenings enjoying the secondhand smoke exhaled by Antonella and Denise.

Sometimes Jackie wished she could fast-forward to the part where she and Dom lived separate lives surrounded by people of their choosing. Jackie would've chosen Antonella and Denise, as she always had. Antonella especially—she was one of those fair-skinned girls whose family must've come from somewhere in the northern part of the old country, with pale amber eyes framed by dark brows that didn't match the rest of the hair on her head. She could've been a popular girl, and the fact that she'd never given a damn about that made her even more desirable to the neighborhood boys, none of whom she'd ever wanted anything to do with. When Jackie first mentioned that Dom had asked her out, Antonella laughed, thinking Jackie was looking to commiserate.

"Oh god," Antonella said. "Where'd he want to take you?"

Jackie herself hadn't realized how pathetic it sounded until the words were about to leave her lips. "Frankie's, for footlong hot dogs."

They both laughed. Jackie didn't tell Antonella that she'd agreed to it, but when it became obvious that they were going steady, Antonella never made fun, and not because she was too nice to make fun—that was one of Jackie's favorite things about her, her open disdain for the little world from which they'd all sprung. "It's like a satire of that Mario Puzo novel everybody's talking about," she'd say. "It's like we're all supposed to be walking around in communion dresses all the time."

Jackie could still recall Antonella in her communion dress—she'd been the only one among them who managed to keep it white all day. She was pretty in it. She'd be pretty in a bridesmaid dress if Jackie would've been allowed to invite her to the bridal party. She'd certainly be pretty in the lingerie those Sears models wore in the catalogs she used to look at. She was pretty even now in the hideous patchwork muumuu she wore that somehow called attention to her bralessness.

Antonella made smoking look both as natural as breathing and as sensual as the Renaissance paintings the Sisters at Mt. Carmel tried to

convince them were about religious ecstasy. The doctors were all saying nowadays that smoking was bad for pregnant women, and all the
older ladies in the neighborhood had always said that smoking was for
whores, but Jackie accepted the cigarette that Antonella passed to her
as they sat on the concrete patio outside the complex where Antonella
and Denise had recently moved in together, an act that was so contro-
versial in the neighborhood it made Jackie and Dom's upcoming sudden nuptials comparatively tame enough to get into the church
bulletin. Antonella's lip balm rimmed the filter, or maybe it was pure
spit—in any case, it didn't add to the flavor of the Winston but still
enhanced the pull Jackie took from it before handing it back.

"Keep it, I'll light another," Antonella said.

"I'm not supposed to smoke," Jackie said.

"Says who, your mother? Didn't she also tell you not to screw?"

"The doctors say it's bad for the baby."

"You believe doctors, like they're not just a part of the medical-
industrial complex?" Antonella said. She liked to parrot the crazy
things she heard at Southern Connecticut State, where she was enrolled half-time and halfheartedly, but mostly she said New Haven was
only good for catching the train to the real city, New York, where she
smoked marijuana openly in a park filled with people so wild that
Antonella looked like the Catholic schoolgirl she once had been next
to them. She rolled closer to Jackie then and placed her hand on her
stomach, which made Jackie embarrassed and thrilled.

"It kicking yet?" Antonella asked.

"Nah, it's too soon for that," Jackie said, but Denise joined in anyway, their hands on Jackie's belly like it was some kind of crystal ball.
It didn't take the black arts to see into Jackie's future: a brick ranch and
an ever-fattening husband and maybe two or three more kids to join
the one she was baking up now, and the only thing truly depressing
about that picture to Jackie was the certainty that these girls would
meet and marry the kinds of husbands they didn't grow in their city,
which would mean eventually moving somewhere at least on the other
end of Route 8, maybe even farther.

"So's that little bump the baby or is that just the grinders you been putting back at lunch?" Denise asked.

"It's the baby," Jackie said, not even bothering to act offended. She was the opposite of offended; she was grateful for every hour she got to spend with these two, sensing that those days were dwindling, now that they weren't kids anymore. On days like this, Jackie didn't think the commune idea was so nuts—why not incorporate some free will into your living situation instead of just depending on fate to dump you into a family that you could tolerate?

"Did the doctor say you can't drink when you're pregnant, too, or are you gonna at least get to have some fun on your honeymoon?" Antonella asked.

Jackie had let Antonella's cigarette burn down another half inch before she ashed it and considered taking a second drag. Wasn't worth it, she decided. She stubbed it out in the grass and just breathed in Antonella's exhale.

"We're not taking a honeymoon," Jackie said. "Pa said Dom can't take the time off from the shop since he just started there, and anyway, we're gonna need the money."

Antonella pulled her hand from Jackie's stomach and sprung upright. "No honeymoon? He expects to saddle you down with all the conventional marriage bullshit without letting you have any of the conventional marriage fun stuff?"

"The fun stuff's what got her knocked up in the first place," Denise reminded them.

"I don't really mind. I'm not feeling up to traveling anyway," Jackie said. The truth was, hanging out in a Howard Johnson's in Lake George didn't really strike her as worth the drive, and heading south to Atlantic City would mean she'd be left to entertain herself while Dom burned through the down payment on their house on a craps table he only thought he knew how to run.

"Well, I mind," Antonella said. "I want you to get in some last good times before you're pushing a stroller around. I mean, I bet he's having a stag, right?"

"Yeah, he's having a stag," Jackie said.

"And I bet you're not having a, a girl stag," Antonella said.

"I'm having a shower," Jackie said.

"Showers are for old ladies to give you things," Denise said. "She's talking about something for fun."

"I'm having fun now. I couldn't take more fun than this," Jackie said. It was supposed to sound facetious but she half meant it. She got flustered when they paid too much direct attention to her instead of just letting her hang around them.

"We'll take you on a honeymoon, how about that?" Antonella said.

"We will? I don't have the money to go to Bridgeport, never mind Niagara Falls," Denise said.

"It'll be a one-night honeymoon. You know, since we're not invited to the wedding anyway. It'll be our chance to get to celebrate with you. We'll go somewhere nice, we can take the train into the city, go see a show or something," Antonella said.

"No, I can't do that," Jackie said, flustered. What she meant was she didn't deserve that, it made her nervous to even dream of so much.

"Why not? I'll drive us down to New Haven and we'll take the train. We'll do it on a weekday so Dom'll be at work anyway. You can take the day off. You're quitting that job anyway, right?"

"It's too much," Jackie protested, but really, she'd decided at that very moment that the only thing she wanted in life more than the baby was a day in New York City with Antonella and Denise. Antonella had casually offered Jackie more than anyone she'd ever known had offered, including Dom when he slid his dead grandma's quarter-carat diamond ring to her over supper a few weeks before. It was an invitation to the world outside her door. What kind of mother was she even going to be if she didn't know a thing about the world?

"It's settled, then. I'm not giving you a choice in the matter," Antonella said.

Finally there was a choice Jackie didn't have that somehow didn't feel oppressive.

"I like this idea. And I gotta pee," Denise said.

"I like it, too," Jackie said, though Denise had already hopped up and run inside.

"You're too pretty to stay here forever," Antonella said to Jackie. She lay down and dropped her head on Jackie's belly. "Does that hurt?"

"No," Jackie said. It didn't hurt, not the pressure of Antonella's head against her stomach anyway. "I'm not too pretty for anything."

"You're too pretty for most of this," Antonella said.

"Most of what?"

"This."

"Dom?"

Antonella shrugged, which made her shoulders undulate in Jackie's lap. Jackie was so happy in that moment. She had everything she could ever think to want and then some, including, now, a honeymoon she actually wanted to take, and she didn't understand why she was so close to tears.

"You want to be the godmother?" Jackie asked.

"Ha, yeah, your mother's never gonna let that happen," Antonella said.

"The secret godmother, not the church godmother. I'll write it down somewhere so nobody'll find it beforehand. I don't want my cousin Marie to end up with this kid if I die. She's a cow," Jackie said.

"And what am I?"

Jackie blushed. Why was she blushing? "You're a pretty, fun girl who'll turn my kid into someone more interesting than anybody else around here," she said.

Antonella smiled. "Sure, I'll be the secret godmother, but you gotta promise me one thing."

"What's that?"

"You gotta promise not to die."

Jackie didn't know which of the sins promising something out of her control might've been, but it was surely one of them.

"I promise," she said.

The ceremony went exactly as it was meant to. All the parties said yes on cue, and Dom's unhappiness read as solemnity, and there was even a little moment right after the exchange of rings where the corners of Dom's lips raised up a little, which Jackie liked to think of as the moment when he accepted that he could've done worse and was now free to devote his spare time to pursuits other than convincing Jackie to maybe give it a little suck before he stuck it in her. The idiot was probably certain he was getting a son, and that was fine, Jackie'd be happy with a son who she could raise up to be nothing like Dom, who'd instead want to join the Navy or go to college and bring back souvenir sweatshirts for them at Christmas. Ma cried, and Pa did, too, a little, during their dance together. Jackie snuck sips of burgundy at the reception, but not so much that it would explain why she later had so little other memory of it. The snapshots would show her smiling, and later, when she'd show them to Drita and Pete as kids, she'd cite them as evidence of how it had been the best day of her life, at least until they came along.

But that was a kind of forensic reconstruction. She didn't even remember the buffet; she just assumed it was a buffet because all the receptions she'd ever attended at the Ponte Club had been, so she inserted a blue Sterno glow into her re-creation, and kids being chastised not to play with it. People were more practical in those days, she'd tell herself later, you didn't make such a to-do about a wedding, but in truth, weddings were among the only to-dos to be had in her world. The rest of it was made up of a humility that was fully earned.

She remembered the honeymoon, though—not the night in the downtown Holiday Inn that followed the reception, but the one that came the next Friday, when Antonella and Denise swung by in Denise's Corvair, which she pulled up right in front of Jackie's apartment instead of having to park it down the street, where Jackie's parents couldn't see. "Have fun with your lezzie friends," Dom called out, and she politely ignored him. She was a grown woman now, heading into a grown city she'd lived her whole life on the periphery of without ever having stepped inside. Grown women didn't get upset about the stupid little digs stupid little men threw their way, and they didn't awe over being on a commuter rail that other people rode daily, so Jackie didn't awe over it, either—she sat in a middle seat that faced backwards and didn't complain about the motion sickness, which wasn't even that bad compared to the morning sickness she'd only recently gotten over. When they all got out of their seats to make their way to the bar car, she didn't express the momentary terror she felt when passing through the glass doors and over the speeding tracks. She didn't order her own Manhattan but accepted sips from Antonella's and Denise's glasses. She looked up at and vocally appreciated the constellations on the ceiling at Grand Central, but only after Antonella and Denise pointed them out and did the same.

They did the tourist stuff that Jackie would not have recognized as such had Antonella and Denise not called it that: sandwiches at the Carnegie Deli; a huddled walk through the strobing crosstown streets of Times Square, where Jackie was propositioned not in spite of but because of her little bulging tummy; passing the velvet ropes outside Broadway's theaters, where Jackie had secretly hoped to take in a show but didn't want to press Antonella and Denise's generosity. Without them, she'd have thought this was how New Yorkers lived all the time, in an exhausting loop of food and smut and shows described as *splendiferous!*

"Did you ever see that *Hair*?" Jackie asked them.

"Nah," Denise said, "that's just so the bridge-and-tunnel crowd can see some pseudo-hippie boobs onstage."

"You want to see some real dropouts? We should go to Washington Square Park," Antonella said.

"With Jackie? Pregnant, married Jackie? No way," Denise said.

"Pregnant first, married second," Jackie reminded them. "I'm not some Catholic schoolgirl."

"Well, you were," Denise said.

"So were you," Jackie said.

"So was I, until I wasn't. Jackie can handle it. You should know she's tougher than she lets on," Antonella said, and Jackie spent the entire subway alternating between wondering what Antonella meant by that and wondering if it was true.

But it was true that Jackie could handle it. After a few minutes of weaving through bodies in various states of consciousness, it was actually kind of boring. It wasn't exactly novel to see a bunch of young men doing not much of anything and a bunch of young women paying more attention to the young men than was reasonably justified. They were all doing, in public and in stranger clothes, exactly the kind of thing she suspected was happening in suburban rec rooms everywhere.

"What do you think?" Denise asked. "Not exactly like back at home, is it?"

"Nope," Jackie said, but it didn't seem so different, just people looking to pass some time. The night might end up for these people in the same act that she'd been engaged in with Dom for months now, and after all the dance and performance leading up to it, it just seemed a little disappointing.

Antonella looked at Jackie. "You look tired," she said.

"I am, a little," Jackie admitted, and felt like she was as disappointing to them as sex had turned out to be for her.

But it was Denise who fell asleep on the ride home, and then in the rear seat of her own car while Antonella drove them back from New Haven. Jackie sat in the passenger seat beside Antonella, whom she'd promised to not let nod off.

"Just keep talking. Tell me stories," Antonella had said.

"I don't have stories. You know all my stories," Jackie said.

"Then sing," Antonella said.

That's what they both did for most of the drive through the Naugatuck Valley, Jackie retuning the dial every time a commercial hit so they'd never be without a backing track, and the fact that neither one of them possessed what anyone would call a singing voice just made it better, especially when "Gimme Dat Ding" came on and they took turns alternating between the bass and falsetto lines.

"What the hell does that even mean?" Antonella asked. "What's even a ding?"

"Probably a wiener. Every stupid-sounding made-up word is just a code for wiener," Jackie said.

"You would know," Antonella said.

By the time Three Dog Night came on for the third time just outside of the city limits, though, they'd gotten quiet, too tired to sing. It was later than Jackie told Dom she'd be home, and she hadn't bothered to call him from the train station with an updated ETA, thinking she'd just be bothering him anyway and not feeling the need to spend the dime. Jackie was looking forward to bed, her feet were killing her, she was hungry again despite the pastrami she'd put back earlier that day, but she wanted to stretch out these next ten minutes anyway, understanding them as among the dwindling moments she'd get to be alone with Antonella. She was grateful to these girls for finally getting her to the city and grateful that the day had confirmed for her that what she mostly wanted was quiet times like this, when they didn't feel the need to perform for each other or anyone else.

"You're not singing," Antonella said.

"Sorry," Jackie said.

"It's okay. Let's just talk instead. Did you have fun today?"

"I did, I really did. Thanks for letting me come along."

"Come along? Honey, the whole day was for you. Sorry if we kept you out too late?"

"Dom won't care," Jackie said.

"I mean sorry if it was hard on your body. It's a lot of walking, especially for a pregnant lady."

"It was fine," Jackie said.

"What's it feel like?" Antonella asked. "Being pregnant."

Jackie reached down to her stomach. It was a habit now, despite a bulge barely bigger than what would follow a Sunday dinner.

"It doesn't really feel like anything right now," she said.

"Really?" Antonella said. "That's not how I would imagine it."

"It's not how I imagined it, either," Jackie said. "I thought it would always feel like something. At first it was nausea, and then I thought it'd feel tight in my stomach, like there's a little person in there. Which there is. But it doesn't feel like it."

Antonella paused. "Do you feel like you're not alone?"

Jackie stared at Antonella's profile. She didn't have a nose like the rest of them, either. It was slender and upturned, like she was pressed against the glass at a restaurant, looking in at the people feasting.

"No, it's just still nothing," she said.

"I feel alone most of the time," Antonella said.

"But you're hardly ever alone. You're always around people, you have so many friends. You live with Denise," Jackie said.

"I didn't say I *was* alone, I said I *feel* alone. I always figured you for somebody who understood that. I remember even thinking that way back in grade school, when I first noticed you. You were standing by yourself and you seemed so okay with being alone."

"I don't like it," Jackie said. "I guess I'm just particular about my company."

"So you end up with Dom?" Antonella said. Then, "Jesus, I'm sorry. That came out bad."

"But that's it exactly. With Dom, it's kind of like the pressure's off. He doesn't care who I spend my time with, as long as I don't bother him about his. So I get to have a kid who I get to make into somebody I want to be with, and I get to, you know." The highway lights shone too bright, suddenly. They were making Jackie's face burn up.

"Know what?" Antonella said.

"I still get to be with you," Jackie said.

"It's not the same as real being together," Antonella said.

"I don't know how you grew up in the same neighborhood as me and never learned how to take what you can get," Jackie said.

"That's why you're going to get to be happy and I'm never going to be."

"You'll be happy, Nella. You'll get yourself accidentally knocked up by some jamoke someday, too."

Antonella didn't seem to hear the joke. She bit her lip, almost as if she were about to cry.

"Wouldn't it be nicer if we could just leave the jamokes out of it and do it together?" she asked.

Jackie felt something move in her belly. Maybe the shift finally happened, the stage where she felt the presence of another. But then the quiver moved into her heart, which was confusing.

"You say the funniest things," Jackie said softly. But that's what Jackie loved about her.

Those were the words that lolled around Jackie's brain just before she dozed off: this is what I love about you, Antonella. They were the same words that were there several days later when she woke up. The doctors said she'd never recall anything that happened in between, the moments that seemed to Jackie's parents and to Dom to be the ones that changed her life forever, but to Jackie it was the words, not the wreck, that had broken her and rebuilt her into someone entirely different.

7

FOR TWO YEARS DRITA'S CO-WORKER LINDITA HAD GREETED HER AT staff meetings by calling out *Përshëndetje!*, despite knowing that Drita didn't speak a word of her mother tongue. Drita had routinely dismissed Lindita's invitations to come to one of the endless dinners or dances or festivals at the Albanian Social Club, not because there wasn't room on her social calendar but because she sensed they would be even more awkward than those New Haven internet cafés she'd tried out in desperation. There'd been a diaspora in Waterbury for a couple of decades, poor souls who hadn't heard that the factories there had collapsed long before the Communist government in their home country had, and there were even more now that Kosovar refugees were evacuating to wherever there were Albanian enclaves waiting for them in the U.S. But Drita couldn't claim membership with the old-guard Albanian wave that came in the seventies or the newfangled Yugoslavian one arriving in the last couple of years. She was simply there by chance, probably because some adoption agency thought there might be an Albanian family in town willing to take some foundlings like her and Pete in, before they realized the market was cool enough that they had to hand them over to an Italian-American with a wheelchair and some substantial lawsuit money.

But Lindita didn't seem to take Drita's previous rejections to heart. She was too excited that Drita expressed any curiosity about her people to be suspicious now about the sudden interest.

"I've been reading a little about what's going on in Kosovo," Drita said casually, over slices of a ShopRite sheet cake someone had brought in to celebrate someone's supposed birthday, though the cakes seemed to outnumber the personnel. "I mean, it seems like the UN should step in or something."

Lindita grasped Drita's forearm, as if the mere mention of Kosovo could bring her to her knees.

"It's Kosova, not Kosovo. Kosovo is the Serb name for it; you should use the Albanian one. But my god, yes, it's a nightmare," she said. "Our mosque has been fundraising nonstop."

"Fundraising? Fundraising for what?"

"The things money buys—food, medicine, that kind of thing. And bribes, of course."

"Bribes?"

Lindita shrugged. "That's what it costs to make sure those other things get where they should go."

"I heard something about people forming an army?" Drita asked, in an inflated timbre she hoped didn't sound as artificial as it felt. "Like, an army of American Albanians signing up for the KLA?"

"Oh, it's not just Americans," Lindita said. "It's Albanians everywhere. Switzerland, Austria, Germany, Turkey. You know us, we get around. And by the way, we call it UÇK, not KLA." She pronounced each letter distinctly and phonetically, *ooh chay kay*, and Drita found it a little obnoxious how eager Lindita was to school her on all the things she didn't know about her own people.

But Drita smiled and nodded as if grateful for the correction, and really, she should've been, considering how ignorant she actually was. "Do you know anyone who's joined the ooh chay kay?" Drita asked, mimicking the sounds she'd just heard. "From the mosque or anything?"

"Oh, they all talk about it," Lindita said. "But I bet most of them will never go. Do you think most of their mothers will let their sons go back to a place they risked their own lives to get out of? And you know men, they mostly want to show off for each other. It's a shame, because the UÇK needs good men, brave men." She shook her head. "And they're going to have to be brave because they're going to be slaughtered unless the U.S. or NATO steps in."

"How do they even enlist?" Drita asked. "I mean, it can't be like the Marines, where you sign up at the mall."

Lindita raised her impressively groomed brows. "No, it's even easier than that. The Marines want paperwork. The UÇK wants any willing human. There's a call in every week's newsletter at the mosque."

"Huh," Drita said. "That reminds me, would you bring me in a newsletter? I've been thinking maybe I should check out the calendar, maybe go to a dinner or something."

Lindita jumped up and down and clapped her hands, as if Drita were a pup that had finally peed in the right place. "Oh, of course! There's so much coming up that would be so much fun for you, and I can introduce you to so many people, like my cousin Bujar, the one who owns the car stereo shop I talked about, or my other cousin Haxhi, who's only working at a diner now but is such a good cook, I know he'll have his own place someday."

Lindita followed through with the newsletter a few days later, and in return Drita committed to a concert at the social club the following week, which gave her plenty of time to think of an excuse for bailing. Drita suddenly had an agenda, which sometimes, when she disassociated what she was doing from why she was doing it, felt almost good, certainly more purposeful than rifling through the newspaper or lurking in random chat rooms inhabited exclusively by the indiscriminately horny. The content of the newsletter wasn't by itself inherently more interesting than her typical reading, or different than what she imagined any place of worship's newsletter to be, just calls for money, assistance, and prayers printed on cheap goldenrod paper. But buried in there, on the penultimate page, was exactly what Drita was looking for: an ad for the Eagle Calling Fund, imploring in English and Albanian: *Support an Independent Kosova*. The ad gave no instructions on how to express support, only a P.O. box in the Bronx and the email address eaglecalling@aol.com. She had only days of experience on the World Wide Web, but it was enough for her to know that it was a medium that would allow her to take advantage of something the internet made stupidly easy to do, which was cloak oneself in absolute horseshit, the kind she smelled on all those pretend barely legals in all those AOL chat rooms.

What the KLA would be looking for wasn't a healthcare worker who'd never been in so much as a fistfight but good, strong men, as Lindita had said—men like Jetmir Kushta, a persona Drita invented and whose first name came from a guy she sat behind in a high school biology class and whose last was copied from a random countryman she encountered in the phone book. Jetmir was nineteen and worked construction. Jetmir was sickened over what he heard from his family and saw on the news. Jetmir might have been American born but would always be Albanian first, and he didn't care how his mother begged him to keep his head down and not cause trouble, he just had to help somehow.

> I don't have money to send, but I need to help. I won't sleep again if I just stand by and let the Serbs kill my people. Please tell me how I can get involved.

Jetmir, by way of Drita, proofread the message. Not too sophisticated; desperate, but hopefully not as desperate as the posers in the chat rooms. She hit send and heard the satisfying whoosh of the message lifting off into cyberspace, and she momentarily didn't feel as pathetic as she usually did on a Friday night. She poured herself another cup of wine, and, to keep herself from checking her inbox every few seconds for a response from eaglecalling@aol.com, she thumbed through the mosque newsletter. Printed in ten-point font at the top of each page was a running head that Drita surmised was an excerpt from the Quran:

> Allah commands justice, the doing of good, and the liberality to kith and kin, and He forbids all shameful deeds, and injustice and rebellion: He instructs you that ye may receive admonition.

Drita could read that passage as either permission to do what she was doing or a rebuke of the same. She thought about it, and then she chose a third option, which was to fold the newsletter and go back to staring at the screen, refreshing her inbox, and waiting.

Eagle Calling hadn't written back overnight, which meant Drita was already crabby when Shanda showed up at her door twelve minutes before the time that Drita had agreed to babysit Dakota.

"Hi, Aunt Drita," Dakota called from waist height.

"Hi, Dakota," Drita said. "Come on in."

Shanda was wearing her work uniform, khakis and a black polo shirt, the standard issue for both minimum-wage service workers and the rich golfy douchebags they had to serve, only the latter didn't have to wear name tags that read Shawnda.

"They spelled your name wrong," Drita pointed out.

"So I should tell you that Dakota's sick," Shanda said.

Drita looked over at Dakota, who'd taken a seat on the futon. He didn't seem sick, or at least not any different than usual. He was still awkward and pale and quiet, but not paler or quieter than he ever was.

"Sick? What kind of sick?" Drita asked.

"I don't know," Shanda said, "some kind of rash. Or maybe chicken pox? What do chicken pox look like?"

Drita walked to Dakota and knelt beside him.

"What's up, kid? Where's this rash?" she asked him. She noticed a few bumps on his neck and face before he pulled up his sleeves to show her more.

"Jesus Christ," Drita said. Dakota's skin looked like a topographic map, dotted with dried blood and ooze. She lifted his shirt and saw that his trunk was worse, so many raised welts that they became a singular thing, a swollen pink vest over Dakota's paltry frame.

Drita looked at Shanda first in horror, and then in revelation. "You have them, too?" she asked. The same marks covered Shanda's arms, what Drita might have assumed a few weeks before were abscesses from recycled needles.

"I didn't think you could get chicken pox twice," Shanda said. "I already had them as a kid."

"Oh my god, those are bedbug bites, Shanda. Jesus Christ, that place must be infested." Drita managed to keep her shit together about bedbugs and cockroaches and other horrifying things when she was on the clock, but this was a day off, and she could feel her shit quickly coming apart. She looked at Dakota and knew the futon he sat on was a goner, soon to be set out on the sidewalk or, even better, aflame.

"Dakota, can you stand up for me, please?" Drita said. She didn't want to tell him why, but because he was Dakota she didn't have to. He stood beside the futon, close enough that his bulky denim still brushed the fabric, and Drita imagined all the tiny insects climbing that bridge back over to the upholstery.

"Oh god," she said, involuntarily.

"Anyway, can you still watch him?" Shanda asked. "I figure he's in good hands with you anyway, since you're a nurse and all."

"Shanda, do you understand what's happening here? You guys are being eaten alive. You can't go back there."

"I cleaned the place up," Shanda said.

"You can't just clean this up," Drita said. "Comet doesn't fix this. Napalm fixes this. Gasoline and a match fix this."

"Well, where are we supposed to go on my dollar-store salary, the Ritz?"

"There's a whole lot of places in between a bedbug-infested crack den and the Ritz, Shanda." Drita was thinking of the beige-sided complexes with neglected handball courts that lined the interstate, the kind of place Pete-the-apparent-roofer could put a deposit down on when he stopped being Pete-the-wannabe-rebel.

It was premature to invoke Pete's name, though, so she said, "I don't understand why you won't just go see my mother. She'd gladly take care of Dakota every damn day. She'd die happy if she could do it."

"I have the church daycare on weekdays," Shanda said.

"But you wouldn't have to pay anything for my mom. And she'd fatten him up, too."

"I'm just not ready yet."

"Ready for what? It's just as easy to take the bus there as it is here."

"I'm too embarrassed for her to see us like this," Shanda said.

Drita wasn't used to hearing Shanda's voice inflect the way it did when she said it. It made Drita go briefly silent.

"Fine, go to work," she finally said. "But he's not going back to that shithole. Ever. Not even for his things. It's all cockroach food now."

"Aunt Drita, can I get my Furby?" Dakota asked in his little, flat voice.

"No, sweetie, that's gone now. We'll get you another one. We'll get you some new clothes and stuff, too. And don't you go back there, either," Drita said to Shanda. "And change before you leave work and don't bring those clothes back here until they've been washed and dried at the laundromat. And don't bring any of your other things back here, either. My god, it's disgusting."

"I'm sorry," Shanda said, facing the door she'd paused in front of. "I didn't know."

Damn. Why did she say disgusting? It was disgusting, but she didn't mean to say it. It wasn't Shanda's fault. It was, somehow, she believed, Pete's. She sighed. "I know you didn't know," she said. "It's just it's kind of serious. Dakota shouldn't be around that stuff. He'll be better off here. Right, Dakota?"

Drita looked down at Dakota but, seeing his rashes, couldn't bear to take his hand. He was using it anyway, waving at Shanda as she opened the door and loped down the stairs.

"Bye, Mom," he called out, and she echoed it back to him without turning to face them.

Drita looked down at her nephew, wiped her hands clean to let the bedbugs know that she was an inhospitable host, and, with one final exhale, clasped his little shoulders.

"Let's get you cleaned up, kiddo," she said.

Drita had intended to use the spare room as an office, but not long after moving in she'd confronted the dual problems of having nothing to officiate and a dud radiator that made merely existing in there unbearable from late September through May. The Compaq therefore lived on the dining table, and the houseguests would have to live in the unlivable space. Drita felt bad about that, even if it was probably still the most habitable four walls Shanda and Dakota had ever slept among.

"You having fun in there?" Drita asked Dakota, who'd disappeared into his sleeping bag as soon as they returned home with it. It was a discount model from a discount store, printed with Day-Glo pirated Power Rangers that Dakota didn't seem particularly stimulated by. Instead, he was amazed at the dark cavern inside, even occasionally gurgling something that Drita now recognized as a laugh.

"Yes, Aunt Drita," he said.

"You planning on ever coming out?" she asked.

His wiggling stopped for a moment. Drita remembered the kid was the most literal human she'd ever encountered, and was likely considering an earnest response.

"It's fine by me if you want to hang out in a sleeping bag all night, dude," Drita said. He must have at least ingested the chicken nuggets and Capri-Sun she'd passed to him in there, since their empty receptacles had been placed on the floor outside the bag, and anyway, it would make getting the work Drita had to do easier if she weren't si-multaneously entertaining a child whose turn-ons were more unpre-dictable than those of any adult she'd ever known.

"You sure you can breathe in there?" she asked.

"Yes," he answered.

"Okay. Don't pee."

"I won't, Aunt Drita."

Drita pulled a fleece anorak over the sweatshirt she was already wearing and opened the door to the spare room. It had been weeks since she'd stepped inside it, and in that time, the cold seemed to have accumulated, despite the plastic film she'd sealed over the windows. New Englanders had managed to survive here long before oil furnaces were standard fixtures, and anyway, maybe the cold would incapacitate the bedbugs that would be left behind after Drita removed the futon cover, double-bagged it, and dropped it into a dumpster behind the Stop & Shop when nobody was watching. She couldn't purge the bare futon mattress, because Dakota and his mother would have to sleep somewhere, so she dragged it into the spare room and wondered what else she could do to make the place feel like somewhere a child might belong. Was she supposed to paint a mural on the walls, something with clouds or clowns or GoBots? It was a rental, and besides, Dakota had apparently decided to live submerged in polyfill, and besides that, this was all a temporary arrangement anyway, just a crash pad for the two of them until Shanda earned enough at the Family Dollar to get herself a place of her own. Which, now that Drita thought about it, might mean they'd be crashing there forever.

She pushed the rest of her stored belongings—a laughably large family pack of toilet paper, a tote of summer clothing that the endless Connecticut winter had convinced her she'd never get to wear again—into a corner and threw her arms up. This arrangement wouldn't work forever. Not even for very long. She didn't know how to be a guardian. She might've accidentally killed Dakota already, because his form lay perfectly still in the sleeping bag, and for a brief moment she panicked that he'd been lying about being able to breathe in there, but when she pulled the flap open she found him inhaling and exhaling in the steady rhythm of sleep. But the kid had lied about something: he'd told her he wouldn't pee in there, when the smell that escaped told her that clearly he had. She sighed the way she never got to do with her patients, but unlike them, at least Dakota was featherweight and compliant. He didn't object, or even wake, when she pulled him from his cocoon, stripped him of his damp clothes, patted him down with a wet towel, and re-dressed him in the clean briefs she'd also bought him at the discount store.

It was too cold in the spare room to lay Dakota down there, so she brought him to her room and dropped him on the side of the queen-sized bed she rarely touched. It was sad how she'd instinctively still saved room for a person who wasn't there, in an apartment that was always supposed to be temporary. Now the bed didn't feel like her own, and she was reluctant to lie in it. She wasn't really tired anyway, so she did what had, in alarmingly short order, become a reflexive way to kill time. She plugged in the modem, impatiently waited for it to gurgle to life, and braced herself for the disappointment of the nothing she assumed she'd find in her inbox. She audibly and embarrassingly gasped when she saw, amidst the three pages of spam, an actual message from a presumably actual human.

Mirëdita, Jetmir.

It makes my heart swell with pride to learn of young Albanians such as yourself who are moved to act for Kosova in this time of crisis.

It is an unfortunate fact that the greatest assistance we can offer our brothers and sisters at this time is cash. Our fighters need weapons and the families who lost everything need food, clothing, and shelter. However, you say that you do not have money. If you live in an area with an Albanian mosque or community center, there may be fundraisers that you can start or become involved with.

There are also ways to become involved overseas, but this requires deep commitment and is very dangerous. If you are interested to know more about this possibility, perhaps we can arrange a phone call and I can tell you more.

Të fala,

Ramadan

The pores on Drita's palm opened and greased the plastic mouse she gripped while she read. She had a first name, which was useless on its own. She had an offer of a phone call, which she couldn't take up because she couldn't disguise her voice to become a Jetmir. She stood from the table and walked a lap around the living room, then remembered she had company whom the squeaking floorboards might wake, so she sat down again.

Drita thought, cracked her knuckles like a private eye in a movie, and began typing.

Mirëdita, Ramadan, she wrote, mimicking the salutation he'd used and hoping she wasn't screwing up something grammatically essential. **I can't talk on the phone, because I live with my parents and I don't want them to hear me or find the charges on their bill. But I would like to know more. Please email me, or if you use Messenger I can chat.**

Whoosh. Off the message went, bringing her, maybe, one step closer to the many miles between her and Pete. There couldn't have been so many Americans signing up for the KLA that this Ramadan guy didn't know him, or know someone who knew him, or know someone who could find him. Then once she found the guy who knew a guy who knew Pete, all there'd be left to do was retrieve him from wherever he was, which could be anywhere from the Bronx to the Balkans, and convince him to take care of the son he had once seemed so happy to have, that the kid wasn't like the handheld Space Invaders game he could discard once he grew tired of it.

Fuck.

There was no equilibrium with the internet, Drita was learning. From crippling insecurity to triumph to despair in the span of three minutes, and the mean average of all of those extremes never landed anywhere close to just plain old okay.

Airplanes again, crash-landing. Drita recognized her dream as a dream and was disappointed that even her subconscious had become so predictable.

"Aunt Drita," a voice called. There was a siren behind it. Of course there was—a plane crash was an emergency, even in a banal dream.

"Aunt Drita, wake up," the voice said. She opened her eyes to a dwarf figure, not the shadowy kind that recurred in her night terrors but a short one made of saturated color.

"What is it?" she said. Her words were raspy and quiet, but she knew she said them aloud, because the feel of them passing through her throat began to rouse her.

"It's beeping in your room," the figure said.

She sat up. The figure was Dakota, of course, and the beeping was her alarm. It was morning, a workday. She was watching Dakota. What was she doing still watching Dakota? She sprung into the bedroom to slap off the alarm and only then felt the searing pain in her neck, no doubt the effect of having slept head down at the kitchen table all night. She was usually a light sleeper and was surprised that she hadn't woken when Shanda came home.

Shanda.

Drita walked to the spare room and looked inside. The bare futon mattress lay right where she'd left it the evening before, with no skinny girl atop.

"Hey, Dakota?" Drita said, but then she reconsidered. If she expressed uncertainty about his mother's whereabouts, it might rightfully freak the kid out.

"Yes, Aunt Drita?"

"Just wondering if you like toast for breakfast," she said.

"I don't know," he answered.

"Okay, maybe we'll just try it. Why don't you go use the potty now?"

He did as he was told, and he didn't seem to register or react to the fact that he was waking up in a new place, in the care of a woman who was a virtual stranger until a couple of weeks before. Adaptability was perhaps a benefit of having been reared in chaos, because Dakota seemed not at all distressed, while Drita felt herself grow shaky with a rage she knew she couldn't express. Where the hell was Shanda? Probably Drita didn't want to know. If Shanda wanted to fall back into her old habits, fine, Drita wasn't going to stop her, or rather, Drita knew she couldn't stop her, but what about this child, who was currently her de facto responsibility? If she didn't show up to work, she could be responsible for pretty much killing people. She'd learned that the hard way after calling in with a bout of acute food poisoning from a take-out joint she still reluctantly frequented, after which one of her clients ended up hospitalized on account of cellulitis that Drita otherwise would have caught before it became septic.

Goddammit, Drita knew it would end up this way. She told Pete that explicitly six years before, when Pete told her Shanda was pregnant.

"Shanda's pregnant," Pete had told her that day. He was four Bud Lights in to Drita's two, and struggling to get the charcoal to light in the backyard grill at Jackie and Dom's, where they'd gathered for Independence Day hot dogs and black market fireworks their neighbor had smuggled back from Myrtle Beach.

At first, Drita had felt nothing, until she felt the literal heat of the match she'd struck to light a citronella candle lap against her finger.

"That's why she's not here today. She got the morning sickness," Pete said, but Drita knew it was a lie. Shanda wasn't there because she didn't show her face around Pete's family much, since people trying to make good first impressions tended to bring flowers with them and not bags of junk.

At Columbia, Drita could identify the risk factors for addiction—genetics, environment, behavior types, problems with impulse control, et cetera. She could begin with the biological boxes in two adults' Punnett squares, add to them poverty and neglect and abuse, could predict with some confidence the consequences of what the literature would call adverse conditions. She could propose interventions to minimize negative outcomes and advocate against the criminalization of what was clearly a disease. She could see Shanda as a walking case study and be ashamed of herself for thinking of any human as a case study.

But in her parents' backyard, all she could say was "Pete, what the fuck is wrong with you?"

She only noticed that Pete had been smiling when she watched the smile dissolve from his face.

"What?" he asked, as if he hadn't heard what she said.

"Do you need money?"

He shook his head, still confused. "We got jobs. You're the one living off of loans."

"I can take out another one if you need to pay for, like, you know."

"No, I don't. Pay for what?"

Drita stared at him. She was trying her hardest to be measured and compassionate. It wasn't just an opportunity to practice what she'd been learning; it also had been months since they'd seen each other, and she was trying to gracefully age into the part of adulthood where you see family occasionally and engage with them respectfully, as you would with colleagues. But Pete was still the same Pete, living in the same place and doing the same things, which made her revert to the previous version of herself, the asshole one who had no problem stating the hard, obvious truth.

"I mean, you're obviously not going to have a baby," she said, finally.

"Obviously we are," he said. "That's what I just told you."

"You told me she's pregnant."

Pete was finally, it seemed, beginning to understand, and the knowledge rendered him silent, the way knowledge often did.

"What?" Drita said. "Why are you looking at me like that? You know you're not ready to be a father. Shanda's not ready to be a mother. I mean, Christ, is she still using? Do you know what that will do to a fetus? Do you know what that will do to a kid if they even make it out of the womb alive?"

"She's not using anymore," Pete said. The lighter he'd been flicking to coax the charcoal to burn he now lit beneath his open palm. It was a habit he'd picked up in middle school, holding a flame to his flesh to see how long he could bear it.

"See, that's the kind of childish shit people with babies can't do," Drita said, pointing to his hands. "And how long has Shanda been clean? How long is it going to last this time? How long is your money going to last, the way you blow through it?"

Pete shoved the lighter in his pocket. "I know you think I'm stupid, and you know what, you're right. I'm stupid because I thought you might be happy for me. Or I guess I hoped you would be. We were the only two of us in the world and now there's gonna be another."

"I don't need another," Drita said.

"No shit, Drita, you don't even need me."

"Why would I need you? You're my brother, need's got nothing to do with it."

"Normal people need other people."

"And you're going to create another human just to meet your needs? That's so selfish, Pete. They're going to have needs, too, and if you're not prepared to meet them that can really fuck a person up. Look at your girlfriend, for Christ's sake."

"What's wrong with Shanda?"

"Are you serious? Uh, I'd say someone who ODs at a family dinner might be trying to fill a few voids."

"Oh my god, Drita, yeah she's got voids. Yeah, I have voids. You have voids, too, you just dress them up so it doesn't look like it. It's not like we're not capable of loving a kid. If people who fuck up weren't allowed to have babies, there wouldn't be any babies in the world."

"Loving a kid doesn't feed them. It doesn't put a roof over their heads. Yeah, everybody fucks up, but you fuck up enough and that becomes what you are. You have two fuckups having babies and guess what you get?"

Pete whipped the lighter at the grill, and later, upon reflection, Drita would come to see that as a small piece of evidence of the kind of growth Pete was trying to argue he was capable of, because clearly he wanted to aim for her face. He had that natural arm, he surely could've hit her.

"You don't want anything to do with our fucked-up kid, then stay the hell away," he said. He crumpled the drained can he held in his hand and whipped it perfectly, as expected, into the trash.

"We'll see how long it takes for you to come back begging for help," Drita yelled at her brother's back. He'd already reached the end of the driveway, and—again, in retrospect—she gave him some credit for not flicking her off as he walked away.

"Help for what? Where's he going?" Jackie asked. She wheeled herself to the bottom of the ramp, gripping a Tupperware bowl of potato salad, and looked between her two children, one fleeing, one anchored to a spot on the lawn. "Drita, what did you say to him?"

Drita looked back at Jackie. "Nothing I didn't mean," she said. She didn't say sorry, because she wouldn't have meant that—not then anyway. He was already long gone.

Shit. She wished she were back asleep, dreaming of something she knew how to manage, like smoking ephemeral fuselage.

"Dakota?" Drita called out.

"Yes, Aunt Drita?" He appeared from the bathroom pulling his new underpants up, staring at them as if he didn't know where they came from, because, in fact, he didn't.

"Do you," she started. She almost asked, Do you know where your mother is? but of course he didn't. If Shanda was doing what Drita suspected she was, Shanda probably didn't even know where she was herself. "Do you know where your daycare place is?" she asked instead.

Dakota shook his head, his befuddled look suggesting that he didn't really even understand the question.

"Do you know the name of your daycare place?"

"There's a lady named Nancy and a lady named Latoya," Dakota answered.

Drita exhaled deeply to expel the rage she'd come dangerously close to directing at her nephew. There would be time for rage later, and a more appropriate target. She let out one short huff and began putting herself together, pulling off yesterday's denim and tugging on a clean pair of scrubs.

"Okay, dude, you gotta put on some clothes for me, okay?" Drita pulled the sweatsuit she'd bought for him from the plastic shopping bag and ripped the tags off with her teeth. She figured yesterday's underwear should be fine for another day, even if she hadn't properly bathed the pee off him the night before.

"Did your mom ever tell you about Grandma?" Drita asked.

"She told me that Grandma Nadia is dead," he answered.

"Not that grandma, another grandma. Do you remember Grandma Jackie?"

"No."

"That's because you were so little when you last saw her. Well, let me remind you about Grandma Jackie," Drita said. "Grandma Jackie's in a wheelchair because her legs don't work. Do you know what a wheelchair is?"

"Yes. I got to be in a wheelchair at the hospital except that my legs worked."

"Cool. Well, Grandma Jackie can't walk but she can get around pretty good. She cooks like really really really good food, better than my stupid chicken nuggets or any McDonald's Happy Meal you ever had."

Dakota looked at Drita skeptically.

"Keep putting those socks on, kid, pick up the pace a little bit. And listen, you know how you get toys with Happy Meals? I bet Grandma

Jackie would get you some toys that would make your little Furby look like an old banana peel. Sounds good, right?"

Dakota nodded, pausing his dressing to do so. Multitasking was going to have to be another thing Drita taught him, along with bladder control.

"Well today's your lucky day, because you get to meet Grandma Jackie and hang out with her while I'm at work." It's not like Drita had a choice about it—she had to work, and if it was so important to Shanda to keep him hidden for no good reason whatsoever, then she should've considered the fact that Drita also had a job before she jammed a needle in her arm.

"But you gotta hurry, kid. You've got until I'm done brushing my teeth to get the rest of those clothes and your shoes on," she said.

Dakota stopped moving altogether and instead dropped his sweatshirt to the floor.

"What? What's the matter?" Drita asked. Here it comes, she thought: the recognition that he's been abandoned by the last parent he had left in the world.

"You said we would try toast," he said.

Drita breathed a sigh of relief, which dribbled a mouthful of Colgate onto the floor. The boy was just learning how to be a regular brat, and it made Drita feel momentarily and inexplicably happy.

"You will, I promise, Jackie will give you as much toast and butter and jelly as you can possibly hold in that Buddha-belly of yours, okay? I'm so bad at this cooking stuff I can even screw up toast. She's the best, okay? The best."

Dakota nodded, and Drita pointed to his sweatshirt, which he pulled on awkwardly and backwards.

It was going to be okay. Jackie at least was a natural with kids, even if fate hadn't allowed her her own.

It was still dark when Drita pulled into Jackie's driveway, but she knew her mother would be awake. Drita didn't call before coming, because this wasn't something she would've been able to explain over the phone and because she thought her mother might reconsider if she gave herself any extra steps before following through. Somewhere during the six-minute drive over the anger Drita had felt toward Shanda had given way to nerves, which she didn't understand. It was going to be a joyful reunion, something that would make Jackie happier than Drita on her own would ever be able to. Seeing Dakota might actually be enough to stop Jackie's heart if all that red wine hadn't kept her cardiovascular system good and hale.

Drita parked the car but kept it running while she unbuckled Dakota and walked him up the driveway to the front door. St. Patrick's Day had passed, but Jackie still had her leprechaun flag up, in honor of a holiday celebrating a saint from a culture her own people had been trained to detest since landing on these shores and being pitted against them for jobs at the mill.

"I'm coming, I'm coming," Drita heard Jackie's voice call out. In another half minute Jackie flung open the door, coming eye-to-eye with a grandson she barely had the chance to recognize.

"Hey, Ma, I'm glad you're sitting down," Drita said. "This is your grandson."

8

THE WORK WAS NO JOKE, AND NEITHER WAS THE RAKI WITH WHICH
Valon had supplied Pete the night before. The work involved buckets
of black noxious tar, and the raki seemed composed of a transparent
version of the same. Pete was not a virgin to most kinds of drink, including the types distilled exclusively for boxcar winos, and while the
taste of raki wasn't quite as hateful as some of the other things he'd
tossed down in various backwoods places just off America's highways,
the aftertaste he was getting now was enough to make him consider
walking off the edge of the roof of the uptown building on which he
was standing. Four stories tall, this one was, and the hard landing
would take care of all his problems, from the liquid burps he could
barely keep down, to the lost wallet he was up there working to replace, to the little family he'd left that he'd been drinking to forget
about to begin with.

But it was possible that the raki didn't just taste of diesel but actually fueled like it, because he was miraculously still moving, and so was
Valon, and so were the other guys that Pete was pretty sure had drank
just as much as he had the night before. Valon wasn't the kind of foreman who stood back and yelled shit that grunts like Pete were supposed to take as orders. He yelled the shit, and then he picked up a

broom handle and got down to the shit himself, and that was something Pete respected about the guy. The guy was pretty respectable all around, actually. Not much Pete could find to not like about him. Even the fistfight a couple of weeks back came from a noble enough place, Valon defending the honor of his people, and if someone could equate honor with what Pete now knew to be pretty bad pizza, then obviously honor was a concept that person took very seriously.

As bad as Pete's body felt, it was good to recognize respectability on someone. It'd been so long since he'd considered what that even meant. It'd been even longer since he'd partaken in anything approaching it himself. Or maybe he never had. Every job he'd ever taken before, he felt like he was pulling one over on the boss, not putting in anywhere near his capacity for physical labor, just clocking in and moving stuff around in a pantomime of work, then collecting a few paychecks before splitting with no notice given. For some reason he was really getting his back into it now. Roofing was the dirtiest, hardest, smelliest job he'd ever taken, and there he was, if not enjoying it then at least respecting the concept—if buildings were composed of walls, floors, and roofs, he was now responsible for a good portion of what constituted a shelter. It was respectable. R-E-S-P-E-C-T-able. The Aretha song was getting stuck in his head, and it wasn't a bad thing. Better, at least, than the crazy gypsy-sounding Albanian shit blasting out of the boom box that teetered dangerously close to the edge of the building.

The hours were long and they started early, so by 10:30 Valon was yelling that it was time to break for lunch. This was the part where the other guys grabbed their Igloo Playmates, all slapped with different stickers so they could tell them apart, and pulled out sandwiches and Snapples, the contents of their coolers as identical as their outsides. Pete had meant to stop at a bodega and grab an Italian combo to go, but he was still drunk enough when he walked into one on the way to work that he ordered up an egg and cheese on a hard roll and ate it before he made it to the exit, washed down with the jug of Gatorade he'd also meant to save for the job site.

"Fuck," Pete said. One side effect of the job was that it made him hungry all the time, even when he was nursing the kinds of hangovers that normally would keep him off food for twelve hours. "Man, I gotta run down and hit up a sandwich place."

"I told you to bring lunch," Valon said.

"Yeah, I didn't have time this morning."

Valon shook his head and laughed to himself, but for the benefit of everyone there. "Man, you're such a fuckup," he said. "Don't you have a woman to keep you straight?"

Pete had never told Valon anything about Shanda or Dakota, even at his drunkest, which was when he thought of her and Dakota the most. And anyway, Pete had been staying in a back room of the Tristate Roofing shop, and Valon damn well knew there was nobody sharing his cot.

"I don't need a woman. I just need a sandwich," Pete answered.

"Nah, you need a woman," Valon said. "I'll take you to meet somebody later if you can keep your shit together."

No shit would be kept together without a sandwich and a bottle of something cold and saccharine hitting his belly real soon. "Dude, I gotta run. Be back in ten."

"I got a cousin," Valon yelled at Pete's back as he headed toward the stairwell. "I got a dozen cousins. Good girls. A grown man can't rely on his sister forever."

Pete paused and looked back at Valon. He must've at least mentioned Drita, after a few glasses of raki, which was when he was most likely to get confessional, between the shots that made him happy and the ones that made him weepy.

"All my sister ever did for me was remind me how much I suck," Pete said.

"Oh, you suck, then? Don't worry, I got guy cousins, too, if that's your thing," Valon said. He was laughing, the only one aside from Pete to do so, likely because they were the sole English speakers among the crew.

That Valon was all right. A ballbuster, but that was something Pete could deal with. It was something, frankly, he needed and deserved.

Valon had cousins for sure. Every guy that came around the shop or into the social club was a cousin, every guy that Valon slapped hands with on the street as they passed by, no words spoken, was a cousin. They'd slap Pete's hand, too, even though they didn't know him from Mayor Giuliani, because walking with Valon meant he'd been vetted. Pete still didn't totally understand how he'd passed that test, other than having a God-given aptitude for throwing and taking punches and the constitution of his native blood, but those things seemed to be enough. Pete didn't want to fuck things up by talking too much in front of Valon or his father, Ramadan, who was the only person Valon lost some of his swagger around. The raki and the Heineken chasers always loosened up Pete's jaw, though, and he would flap his mouth until even his own drunken ears would tune in to the crazy Albanian pop streaming from the speakers just to not have to listen to himself. And yet Valon still let Pete hang around, still let Pete crash on the office cot, still began calling Pete cousin by the end of their third week as a duo, which meant the dude had to be a saint or a sucker, despite not really seeming at all like either.

And now there were more cousins, just like St. Valon had promised. Cousins with breasts and hips, long hair, and dark, dark eyes, which Pete was just beginning to think was maybe his type. Cousins like Ariona. Even if she did speak English, Pete could tell she'd still be quiet. Serene quiet, though, not Shanda's kind of quiet, not quiet like a hunted animal trying to go unnoticed. Ariona communicated exclusively in bashful smiles, like a Disney animal in love. Man, a smile. Pete didn't know if he'd gotten one out of Shanda ever, and here was this Ariona, already smiling by the time Valon introduced them.

"This is my cousin Ariona," Valon said, steering her by the shoulders to Pete. "My cousin Petrit," he told Ariona, pointing at Pete. He said it in English, so Pete knew that it was for his benefit. He added, "Ariona is a good girl," a warning as much as a threat.

A good girl. Yes, she looked like a very, very good girl, and that made it even worse. It was just occurring to Pete how long it had been since he'd been with a girl, good or bad, or, like Shanda, somewhere firmly between the two.

Pete was a couple of Heinekens and one glass of raki in, so he brought Ariona's hand to his mouth and kissed it. "Madam," he said, like some French cartoon lothario, some Pepé fucking Le Pew. Ariona's smile went from bashful to explicit, tight-lipped to open, and even the giggle that leaked out sounded like it was in a foreign language, this girl so off-the-boat Pete was surprised she'd found her land legs already.

"You're a weirdo," Valon said, but he walked away as he shook his head, which meant he'd granted Pete some alone time with this budding Albanian flower.

And suddenly, without Valon, Pete didn't know what to do with her. It wasn't just that there was no translator; it was like there was no power source, no other guy for Pete to have to puff out his chest around. Pete smiled, and it made him realize that Ariona's smile meant about as much as his did. It was a substitute for small talk when two people had zero words in common. In any case, it didn't feel as good to wear one as it did to see one. He had to really concentrate to get one to appear on his face, and that got him thinking about how he had nothing to really smile about, and that made him want to do something closer to crying, and that made him hear Dom's voice saying, You don't stop that crying I'll give you something to cry about. This made Pete acknowledge that he didn't really have anything to cry about, either, seeing as how he'd had the good fortune to end up with a group of Albanian brothers—well, cousins, or dudes that didn't mind being called that—and especially Valon, the most stand-up, un-pussyish guy he'd ever met, who was handing Pete a job and shelter and this dark, shy beauty and another glass of raki.

Goddamn, the raki. Five minutes ago he was laughing and now he was almost crying and he momentarily had enough clarity to blame it on the raki.

"Valon," Pete said to Ariona, nodding his head in Valon's general direction, though he couldn't see where Valon had gotten off to. Probably with his own version of Ariona. Pete gave a thumbs-up, to communicate: that Valon, he's all right, huh? It worked. Ariona understood enough that her face lit up with what appeared to be an actual smile, and she brought both hands to her heart and held them there for a few seconds, saying something that she knew Pete couldn't understand.

"You're in love with Valon," Pete said.

Ariona looked confused.

"And he's a good guy who doesn't want to break your heart so he wants to pass you off to me."

The vague smile again, accompanied by just as vague a shrug.

"You know I'm not good like Valon, right?" Pete took her hand. "You know I walked out on my own son. His mother, too. I mean, they're both better off without me, but still. The options were stop being a fuckup or leave and I chose leave."

Ariona shrugged and laughed a tiny, precious little laugh.

"I'm gonna go back to my son someday, though. He's such a cool kid. He said his first word at ten months and you know what it was? Cock. He had this stuffed cockroach that sang "La Cucaracha," and man, he loved that thing so much it was the first word he said and the only word he ever said for like three months. Me and Shanda never stopped laughing about that. He talks normal and everything now but he never did that baby-babble thing, it's like he only talks when it's worth his time. Such a cool kid. I miss the living shit out of him." Pete took a swig from his bottle. "I'll go back for him someday. Just gotta stop being the kind of fuckup who talks to girls who don't understand a word I'm saying."

Ariona smiled wider, a little wilder, looking now over Pete's shoulder for someone to rescue her from this freak having a conversation with a woman who would've been too good for him even during his prime. And yet she hadn't pulled her hand away, and this little bit of skin-to-skin contact made his prick stiffen into a semi, like he was some nerd at a middle school dance.

"What are you guys talking about?" Valon said. He'd been standing there for who knows how long, and Pete quickly dropped Ariona's hand and made sure his jersey covered the crotch of his jeans. Valon noticed, and said, "I'm not her father, dummy."

"I know," Pete said.

"Whatever you were just yapping your mouth about, she didn't understand it," Valon said.

"No shit."

"Then why bother saying anything?"

"Because you walked off and what were we supposed to do, charades?"

"Petrit, this is not a woman you mess around with," Valon said. He shot back the remainder of the raki in his right hand and followed that with a swig of the Heineken in his left. "Ariona's brother was my best friend back in Kosova. We lived three doors from each other, went to school together, fought over the same girls, everything. Even when we moved here, I still called Flamur my best friend. Flamur," Valon said, nodding to confirm to Ariona that he was talking about her brother, and when he did, that shy, beguiling smile faded from her face, and it made her somehow even hotter.

"You think you're tough?" Valon said. "Flamur could wipe his ass with you. With me, too. He could, but he wouldn't unless you fucked with him, and nobody would fuck with him. Even when we were kids, everybody liked him and everybody was scared of him," he said, as if those two things were inextricably linked. "You know where Flamur is tonight, Petrit?"

"I don't know, White Castle?" Pete said.

"In a shallow grave, motherfucker. At least as far as we know. Couldn't really tell which one was him after they burned up the bodies."

"Jesus, what?" Pete asked. "Who? What bodies?"

"The Serbs," Valon said. He sounded harder with every word he spoke, but still managed to look tenderly at Ariona, who in return stared at her feet, her eyes wet and black as rain-slicked pavement.

"They killed Flamur, they killed his uncles, they killed his neighbors, our neighbors. Ariona and her parents came here because they knew what was about to happen, but Flamur wasn't going to run. He didn't run."

If this was some kind of peacocking, it wasn't a kind Pete had encountered before. And it was effective, because Pete was a little afraid of the anger in Valon's voice. He hadn't heard it before, not even when Valon clocked him outside the pizza joint. That had obviously been just business.

"And now we are obligated to kill them in return," Valon said.

"Who?"

"Us. Albanians."

"And them?"

"Serbs, you dumb shit."

"You know who did it?" Pete asked.

"They all did it."

"You're going to kill all of them?"

"This is a war. That's what happens in a war. You don't even know we're at war, do you?"

"I'm not at war," Pete said. He sounded vaguely like the hippies at the festivals out west that he and Shanda had attended solely for the purpose of getting lit up. Those guys got lit up so good Pete could suffer through their awful hippie smells and endless droning guitar solos so long as they shared their weed and peyote, and they usually did.

"Are you one of us?" Valon asked. "Or did you get the wrong tattoo on your chest?"

"It's the right one," Pete said.

"Then there are people out there who would kill you for having it. And if you think you deserve to wear that eagle, then you should be prepared to fight for it."

Maybe Valon was coked up. Pete got that way when he'd done a few lines, all paranoid, thinking the world was created just to ridicule him. But Ariona was dabbing at her eyes, and then full-on crying, turning to

Valon for comfort when just a little while before it seemed like Valon
was offering her to Pete to do that kind of thing. Pete had already for-
mulated a plan for their life together: get that framing job, get into the
union, move her out to Long Island. Someone like Ariona would probably like it out in the suburbs; this little girl from a little village must
have hated the cement and brick of New York City's nether regions,
hardly a plot of earth to be found outside of the tiny little triangle
parks that peppered the blocks mostly just to remind people like Ariona of the lives they'd left back in the old countries. She could learn
English, at least enough to express gratitude to Pete for the little home
he'd set up for her out in Ronkonkoma, enough to care for Dakota
when Pete started collecting him again for weekend visits.

But no, Ariona was looking to Valon for comfort, and all Pete could
do was stand by and swig from the bottle of Heineken he'd picked up
from the table he was leaning on. It wasn't his bottle to begin with, but
it had been mostly full, and whoever it had belonged to was obviously
too drunk to miss it.

And yet his stomach turned when he pulled next from the bottle.
And yet he found himself dropping the bottle back down to the table
before he took the next swig, walking over to Ariona, and whispering
in her ear, even as she was under the cover of Valon's arm, "Just tell me
what you need me to do to make it right."

"She doesn't understand you, Petrit," Valon said.

"Then you translate."

"What'd you tell her?"

Pete did feel like a dummy when he replayed the words to himself,
but he said them aloud again anyway. "I said, 'Tell me what you need
me to do to make it right.'"

"Why, what are you going to do it about it?"

"I'm going fuck them up."

"Why? What's it matter to you?"

What was Pete supposed to say to that, that he wanted an enemy he
didn't have to look into the mirror to see? He was supposed to say that

in front of two people who knew the kind of loss that Pete knew he himself would be incapable of surviving?

"It matters to her," Pete said, nodding toward Ariona. "And to this," he said, tapping his chest.

"You prepared to back up those words?" Valon asked.

"I wouldn't have said them if I wasn't."

"Yeah, we'll see. We'll see," Valon said, and then he turned toward Ariona and translated. The look she gave, man—the smile again, but this time more. This time it did say something: begging and thanking all at once, the kind of thing a man waits for all his life.

No more raki for Pete that night. Valon offered but Pete didn't take, and he carried around a half-full Heineken bottle for the rest of the night to pretend he was drinking something else. Pete must have been getting old, because when he thought about repeating that morning's hangover the next day, standing under the beating sun in a sea of tar, forgetting to pack the Gatorade and greasy, sweating salami on white bread that would be the only known antidote to his condition, he almost wanted to cry. He almost wanted to cry at the thought of his cot, too, that sacred vessel that would transport him to dreamland, where he could spend almost a full six hours if he landed there in the next twenty minutes or so. But that wasn't going to happen that night, because Valon was accompanying Pete back to the shop to get some work done, another thing that made Pete want to cry.

"I gotta finish up some things," Valon had said. "Stuff I can't get done standing on top a building with a crew of hungover assholes like you."

It seemed Valon's father, Ramadan, had some work to do, too, because he was sitting in the office on an ancient swivel chair that didn't swivel anymore, screeching the frozen casters over the cement floor to reach for a box full of more cash than Pete had ever seen in one place in his life. Pete didn't want to stare, but it looked like some hundreds in those rolls, held together with elastic bands like some little girl's pigtails. Ramadan stared straight at Pete and kept counting, and he didn't seem to worry for a second that a stranger like Pete was seeing that much cash. That kind of casual indifference worked better than any threat to warn Pete that he better not be getting any wise ideas about that money.

Valon greeted his father with a kiss on the cheek. That still surprised Pete about all these hard-asses, how they kissed each other, but Pete knew better than to ever bust Valon's balls about it. Pete himself just nodded at Ramadan, who looked back at Pete as if he were a portrait at a yard sale, trying to decide if it was interesting or pure garbage. At least it was better than the way Dom used to look at him, as if he were a cockroach he couldn't be bothered to get up to smash.

"How much longer this cat going to be here?" Ramadan asked Valon, in English so perfect he could pepper it with fifties slang.

"Little longer. He's getting on his feet."

Ramadan looked down at Pete's feet, then back to his face, clearly unconvinced.

"He's good on the rooftop," Valon said. "Strong as shit. Can haul shit like an ox."

"Watch your mouth," Ramadan said, and Valon nodded his head.

"We have to use this office for work," Ramadan said. "A lot more work coming in. Word is getting out."

"That's good, baba."

"We can't have this guy hanging around when we're doing this kind of work."

"I don't know, he's all right."

"He's not one of us."

"He is. He's Albanian," Valon said.

Ramadan looked at Pete and streamed out a full thirty seconds of the gibberish the rooftop guys called a language. Pete didn't speak Spanish, but he at least understood it as Spanish when he heard it come out of the mouths of the Puerto Ricans in the hallways, but when Albanians spoke Albanian, it seemed impossible that any of the sounds they made could make any sense to anybody. And yet Ramadan kept it coming, and Valon kept his head bowed, taking it all in.

"Well, yes or no?" Ramadan asked Pete at the end of what must have been a question.

Pete looked to Valon, who looked at his shoes. He shrugged.

Ramadan shook his head and went back to the fat knot of cash in the little metal box. The lock on it looked like nothing, like it came from a child's diary, like the one Drita had had when she was a kid. Pete had snapped that diary open with his fingers and found a single entry consisting of lyrics to a Whitney Houston song, and Drita later told him she wasn't stupid enough to write secrets down in pen. Pete didn't bother snooping around in her room after that, just like he wasn't about to go snooping around in that Tristate Roofing office.

"I ain't gonna talk," Pete said. "Just here to shut my eyes and go to sleep."

"What do you think it is that you're not going to talk about?" Valon asked.

What there was to talk about was that cash and where it came from, because it sure as hell wasn't just from roofing. "None of my business," Pete said.

"Maybe it is your business, if what you told Ariona wasn't just you running your mouth for some pussy she's not going to just give away," Valon said.

"You sound stupid when you talk like that. Like a peasant," Ramadan said.

"You want me to go, I'll find somewhere else to stay," Pete said. It wasn't really a threat, because he knew nobody would really care if he left, but it wasn't really something he meant, either. He'd made enough money so far for maybe a few rides on the Metro-North, where he could get off at every stop between 125th and New Haven looking for the van he'd abandoned, but the piece of crap was probably in some impound lot being readied for auction, and even if he found it, it was basically just scrap metal without the keys he'd lost with his wallet and the last shred of his dignity. He didn't even have a driver's license. He didn't even have any of the forms of identification required to replace a lost driver's license, because those either had been lost along with the wallet or were things that existed back at Jackie's place, where he wouldn't have gone even if he could have.

But he didn't need to let Ramadan or Valon know that. People figure out you want something from them, they tend to exploit that. Something else Pete had picked up on back in the days hanging out with the hippies. They shared their shit, yeah, but it wasn't ever really free.

"I don't care what you do," Ramadan said, swatting his hand a few times as if shooing an insect.

"He's a good employee. And he's Albanian. Just grew up with a bunch of Italians after his parents died," Valon said.

Ramadan paused from thumbing through papers and bills. "Your parents are dead," he said, or maybe he asked, Pete couldn't really tell.

"They died when I was a baby," Pete answered.

"How did they die?"

"I don't know about my father, actually. Nobody figured out where he was. My mother, I guess, like, starved or something. We were found with her on a boat."

"We?"

"Me and my sister. Twin sister. Drita."

"She was fleeing," Ramadan said.

"I guess. I don't know why else you'd take two babies on a rowboat."

"So that runs in the family?"

"What?"

"Running away."

Maybe it was supposed to be an insult. And maybe it was the relative sobriety, but it didn't sting. It felt almost good to hear it, like tough love, even if it came from someone with whom he shared no love at all.

"Guess so," Pete said.

Ramadan folded the aluminum box of cash and pushed it to the edge of the desk. "Our people aren't cowards. Our people, we stay and fight. But stupidity also doesn't run in our people. Someone's coming after you with guns and you have only sticks, there's nothing you can do but run. Your mother was from Albania, then?"

"Yeah, I guess."

"We're all Albanians, yeah, but we're not all from there. Us," Ramadan said, pointing at Valon and back to himself, "we're from Kosova. All the guys you been working with, they're all Kosovar. You know what Kosova is?"

"Yeah," Pete said. It was a lie, but he figured it wouldn't help his case to tell the truth, a conclusion he often came to and that often came back to bite him in the ass.

"You know what they're doing to us then?"

"Serbs," Pete said, echoing vaguely what Valon had said earlier that night. "Shooting people."

"Killing us. Killing our mothers and daughters. Not just our fathers and sons. And before they started shooting, they tried to make us believe we weren't who we are, that we were Yugoslavs. There's no such thing as a Yugoslav. That land was our land and they took it, and they expected us to either become one of them or to run. And they got tired of waiting for us to do that, so they took out their guns."

Pete had come for a cot, not a history lesson, but he found himself nodding respectfully, like a soldier to his sergeant.

"And they think we ran. They think we're not going to fight. But we're fighting. Right there," Ramadan said, gesturing at the cashbox, "that's our ammo."

"Well," Valon said. He laughed once, then looked to his father to see if he'd offended him, but Ramadan smiled back, so it was a go. "That's some of our ammo."

"Yes, that's right, some of our ammo," Ramadan said.

Valon looked at Ramadan, and Ramadan shrugged and nodded. Valon turned to Pete.

"You want to see some more?" he asked.

Pete mimicked Ramadan, a shrug and a nod. He was expecting another cashbox, more knots of twenties and fifties and hundreds, not a single one of which he would dare think of peeling off once Ramadan's back was turned, because he sensed that Ramadan's back was never really turned. Instead, Valon pulled Pete's sweatshirt at the shoulder, beckoning him up, and Pete followed him out to a storage closet in a corner of the main warehouse. Valon pulled from his pocket a ring that looked like it held the keys to every door in New York City, and without even looking found the one that unlocked the dead bolt to the closet. Pete could tell the closet went far deeper than he would have thought, but he couldn't see anything until Valon fumbled around and found the string that triggered a single overhead light.

Then Pete saw what they meant by ammo. Boxes and boxes of it, along with the machines the ammo fed. They had to be called machines, because guns was insufficient. Guns were things that fit beneath baggy denim you could cuff up to the knee. They were things that people occasionally shot at squirrels and otherwise sat protected in a dusty oak-and-glass case in a bedroom, or in a little metal box with an insufficient lock, like the one Dom used to keep under the bed. These were machines, bulky and shiny with chambers covering intricate series of mechanisms designed to work in a perfect dance with one another. These were the kinds of machines Pete had seen only in Schwarzenegger movies. These were built to take down creatures not human.

"Dude, the fuck?" Pete said.

Valon said, "I told you, we're at war."

Pete had met guys who could rattle off the makes and models of all kinds of weaponry, which guerrilla group used them in which third-world insurgency, who manufactured them and what kinds they stashed away in their bedrooms in their cinder-block duplexes. These were day laborers that Pete worked alongside in ad hoc construction teams in the Southwest, guys that had seen no more combat than they had UFOs. They were all talk, and they talked a lot, unlike Ramadan, who had not spoken a single word to Pete until that night. But this guy's janitorial closet held what could only be called a cache, the kind that could only be used in a war, the kind that's reported about more in the *Soldier of Fortunes* those construction crews read than in the daily newspapers that ended up shredded in the bottom of their pet iguanas' aquarium tanks.

"How come I never heard about this war?" Pete said.

"You heard about it tonight," Valon said.

"Before that."

"You heard of Abri të Epërme? You heard of Reçakut? Your family vacation there?"

"What? No."

"That's why. People here never heard of those places. The people there didn't exist to Americans. But these are your people, even if you didn't know it."

"So, what, you're going to hop in a boat and join the Kosovo army?"

"It's Kosova, Cousin. Kosovo is what Serbs call it. And yeah, I am."

Pete inhaled deep through his nose, trying to detect bullshit.

"I already been," Valon said. "I go every month, right now just to deliver this stuff to the UÇK. But yeah, all this is going to them, and then I am, too."

"How the hell do you get those guns over there?" Pete said.

"On a plane, dude. On cargo."

"They let you just take machine guns onto a plane?"

"This is America, dude."

Pete shook his head. "Where the hell do you get all this in the first place?"

"I just told you, this is America," Valon said. "My father collects the money to get the shit, and then we get the shit. People from all over the world send money here, because here's where you get the machinery."

"I don't know," Pete said. "This sounds kind of crazy."

Valon turned to face Pete, and for a moment Pete thought he was going to punch him in the face. But his fists, still balled, stayed at his sides. "What's crazy is bodies burned in a ditch and nobody doing anything about it. These are my family, my neighbors. These are your people," Valon said, jabbing Pete in the chest. "Your people. You think that's crazy? You wouldn't fight to protect that? Did you ever fight for anything in your life?"

The question was rhetorical, maybe, but Pete looked at Valon and his rage was so real it made his own feel hollow. He shook his head and waited to be called a coward. Pete could take it because he knew he was. He'd known it his whole life, even when he tried to cover it up with tattoos and baggy sweatshirts and a smile or a sneer, depending on who was watching.

Valon nodded. "You would if you had something to fight for. I know you would."

Pete thought about the last straw before he split, when Dakota got sick, Shanda off working some pointless job, Pete doing exactly what Pete did: being a screwup, watching kung fu movies stoned off his face, just a few drops of Jack and Shasta left in the plastic tumbler he carried around with him like a baby bottle, finally a day off from another construction site with another douchebag foreman telling them they'd be putting in another fourteen-hour day when Monday rolled around. Dakota had had a stomach bug, but his bout of puking and diarrhea seemed to have ended, and the silence afterwards was a gift to Pete, because Pete needed quiet to . . . to what, exactly? What did he ever need to concentrate on, other than to read subtitles to things that didn't mean anything in any language? Pete had checked on Dakota a few hours before and he seemed fine, as tired as a kid who just puked his innards out should be, and it was nice to be alone in the way he was before Dakota was born, which had been exactly the kind of aloneness that had terrified Pete his whole life.

"Pick one up," Valon said.

"Pick what up?" Pete answered.

"A gun. Pick one up. Hold it in your hand."

Pete stepped inside and pulled out the closest machine he could reach. He meant to whip it out and pose with it like a kid playing G.I. Joe, but when he held it he instinctively understood it as something too significant to make a joke of. It was heavy and sleek and ergonomic, a perfect complement to human anatomy.

"You don't feel like a loser now, do you?" Valon asked. "Not gonna lose anything when you got that in your hands."

Pete was a little surprised at how quickly and easily he agreed with that.

A few minutes ago, all Pete had wanted was to lie down and sleep the sleep of the dead, and to see what it was like to wake in the morning feeling reborn, or at least like something other than garbage. But then he realized he wasn't feeling like garbage right then, and that was unexpected enough that he had to stop and wonder what that was about. He was feeling kind of warm, something physical, almost like skin-to-skin contact, maybe something residual from earlier in the night, when he'd taken Ariona's hand and whispered close enough into her ear that his lips were just barely on her flesh.

No, it wasn't that. That was just lust, and an unrequited one. This feeling was good. He settled into it, and it felt right, and that's when it struck him: it was comfort. As alien as the feeling was, he recognized it as sure as he recognized his own reflection in the mirror. He was being invited into a tribe, not pushed from one the way he was back at home, even by Drita, who he once upon a time believed was the only other member of his. He'd tried and failed to create his own with Shanda, but they weren't a tribe, they were just two vagabonds traveling together because they didn't know where else to go.

Pete smiled, feeling like he had finally landed somewhere not by accident but by fate.

9

DRITA TOOK THE SMALL, BLAZING FIGURE SPRINTING TOWARD HER car when she turned the corner to her apartment for a tweaker, and as she pulled closer, she realized she wasn't far off. It was Shanda, slapping her hands onto Drita's driver's side window while the car was still creeping toward her usual street parking space.

"Where's my kid?" she shouted, even as she could clearly see the kid squinting at his mother from the backseat.

Drita had expected Shanda to be pissed—she welcomed it, even, so that she could use Shanda's fire to ignite her own smoldering tinder—but she didn't expect to find herself a little afraid of the woman screaming on the other side of the tempered glass. Before that, Drita had only sensed what must have been simmering beneath that caldera all those years.

"Aunt Drita, Mom's freaking out," Dakota said in his own usual flat voice, but in the rearview mirror she detected fear in the little man's eyes, too.

"Stay in here a sec," Drita told him. She unbuckled herself from her seat, but Shanda hovered so close to the door that Drita couldn't open it. Instead Drita rolled the window down, because even if Shanda's crazed eyes scared her, she figured that, as with the growling dogs who sometimes confronted her at patients' homes, showing fear would just make her more susceptible to attack.

"He's right here," Drita told her, pointing aggressively at Dakota. "Safe and sound, with grown-ups the whole day. The better question is, where were you last night?"

Shanda didn't answer, just dashed around to the rear passenger door to retrieve her son. Drita managed to push the automatic lock just before Shanda pulled the handle to open the door, Dakota's head pivoting from left to right as if he was watching a tennis match on ESPN.

"What are you doing? Open the goddamned door," Shanda yelled.

"I'm not handing my nephew over to you like this," Drita yelled back.

"I'm his mother."

"That doesn't mean shit if you don't come home at night to actually mother him."

"I was working!" Shanda said.

"You were scheduled to get off at nine."

"They asked me to stay and do inventory on the night shift for time and a half. You know I can't afford to say no to that."

"I don't know anything unless you tell me, and you didn't tell me."

"I called a hundred times!"

"I was home all night, Shanda."

"It was busy every time," Shanda said.

Drita readied a retort but then remembered the stupid modem was on all night, and that would have tied up the phone line. It wasn't outside the realm of possibility, then, but Drita wasn't ready to take Shanda at her word. Her eyes were shiny with what could have been anger or fatigue or the stew of all of the things that coming out of a high often brings on, and Drita stared at her, trying to discern which version she was looking at.

"What? You don't believe me?" Shanda asked.

"Why should I?" Drita said.

Shanda's eyes welled over then, and the wetness became actual tears. An option Drita hadn't considered from Shanda was actual sadness, or its cousin, shame.

"I thought I was going to be back before you left for work, but you weren't home. I didn't know what to do," Shanda said.

Drita sighed and hit the unlocking mechanism. Shanda opened the door and pulled Dakota from the backseat before he was unbuckled.

"Mom, that hurts. The belt," he said.

Shanda fumbled while Drita opened her own door and stood. Shanda tried to hug Dakota, who tolerated it for all of two seconds before wiggling down from her hip.

"Seriously, Shanda, do you think I would have stolen him?" Drita asked.

"I don't know what you might do. You were never exactly nice to us," Shanda said.

"What does that mean, I haven't been nice to you? I haven't even seen you for years to be nice to you."

"Exactly, so how do I know how you're going to be?"

"Then why would you leave him with me at all if you don't trust me?"

"What choice do I have?" she said. She shook her head and added, "You told Pete when we had Dakota that you weren't going to help us."

Drita turned her gaze to Dakota, who stared back like a chess master analyzing the possible moves.

"That's missing context," Drita said. "And anyway, I'm helping Dakota, not Pete."

"Are you going to call DCF?" Shanda asked.

"Are you using?"

"I'm not. I swear I'm not."

They continued their staring duel from opposite sides of the Hyundai for another few seconds, and then both reluctantly called off their arms.

"I did take him to Jackie's house, though," Drita said.

"Jesus, Drita," Shanda said.

"Well, I told you, I had to work. Anyway, it's good for Dakota to have some family, don't you think? Like it or not we're the only ones he has."

Shanda looked down at Dakota, holding his new oversized stuffed Furby in his arms.

"Well, what did you think of Grandma Jackie?" Shanda asked him.

"She's funny," he said, which made Drita believe he didn't really know what funny meant, at least not in the ha-ha sense. Regardless, he was triumphant with his new toy, and this gave Drita a sense of triumph by proxy.

"Did she say anything about me?" Shanda asked Drita.

"She said to tell you she was sorry to hear about your mother."

"That's it? She doesn't hate me?"

"Yes, that's it. What makes you think she's going to hate you?"

"Because I ruined her son."

"You didn't ruin Pete," Drita said. "You didn't do anything to him that he wouldn't have done on his own. And anyway, you gave her a grandbaby, so you'll always be one up on me."

"That's not true. You're the good one in the family."

That was exactly the kind of thing Pete used to say to her all the time, the thing that—despite the evidence he presented to her—she always told him to stop insisting on.

"I'm not that great," Drita said, and before Shanda could follow up on that, added, "Come inside. But you can't ever, ever not come home like that again."

"And you can't ever, ever take Dakota anywhere without telling me again," Shanda answered.

Drita wanted to defend herself, but it was freezing, and the fight wasn't worth it, and in the end, Shanda was right: Dakota wasn't hers to take. They were visitors, people Drita was tending to, like her patients, in a moment of acute need amidst a lifetime of chronic need. They couldn't become two more anchors holding her in place. That was Pete's job; her job was finding Pete and making him do it.

Shanda and Dakota mercifully fell into their futon early that night, so Drita wasn't forced to kill time looking busy before getting online. After the alien gurgles and bleeps that always seemed to Drita a little performative, like the modem had been programmed specifically to sound like the future, she heard the words that stopped her heart for a second every time, no matter how hard she tried to brace herself for disappointment: *You've got mail!* What it usually meant was You've got offers for barely legal fuck buddies and a refinance of a mortgage you may never have!, but that night one piece stood out like a life raft amidst a sea of crap, a message with the subject line "Eagle Calling," sent not from the generic email address but from someone by the name of Valon Zaimi.

> My father gave me your email. He said you're interested in learn-
> ing more about volunteer opportunities with our organization. I'm
> very busy most of the time, but if you have specific questions I'll
> try to answer them.
>   Sincerely,
>   Valon

Valon's response was less than robust, but it was a response, and it included a last name, one that Drita immediately searched in con-junction with both Ramadan and Valon. No dice—no matches on the web, including in the white pages, which had been conveniently digi-tized to make prank calling and verbal harassment even easier to achieve than in the analog days. He said he'd answer questions, though, so Drita thought of some that an invented nineteen-year-old might pose.

> I read in the paper that some people are going over from Amer-
> ica to fight with the UCK. My questions are where do I sign up
> and when can I help kick some Serbian ass?

It took two days for Jetmir to receive a response that must have taken no more than forty-five seconds to compose.

> The men who have volunteered to fight for Kosova are committed to protecting the lives and rights of our people. This is a serious war, not a movie about war. I appreciate your desire to help, but your best option might be to organize a food drive.

Drita had figured the language and psychology of young men would be easy enough to hack, but she'd failed to account for one essential component: the instant resentment of other young men whose soaring testosterone levels competed with their own. Maturity and discipline couldn't have been actual prerequisites of KLA recruits or else Pete wouldn't be among them, but she'd obviously played her hand wrong in addressing Valon so directly and aggressively.

Damn. What next.

She had an idea, a flash of inspiration from the unlikely source of the insipid conversations she witnessed in chat rooms. She quickly set up a new email account, toggled back over to Valon's email, and typed,

> Dear Valon,
>
> My idiot little brother left his email open on the computer, and I read the messages he sent you. For the record, he's 17, not 19, and the only person he's ever fought was Scorpion in Mortal Kombat. I'm sorry he wasted your time.
>
> Just so you know, I think what you're doing is awesome. I wish some of the guys I know from around here would go help out over there, but all they care about is cars and stupid videogames.
>
> Anyway, I know you have more important things to do, but if you ever get the chance to tell me more about Eagle Calling or whatever, you can hit me up luv_lindita@aol.com.

Drita silently apologized to her co-worker for borrowing her name to lie to an Albanian guerrilla hero, then told herself the real Lindita would be happy to help the cause any way she could.

Later, Drita was pleased, and not entirely surprised, to find a new message waiting in luv_lindita's virgin mailbox.

Hey Lindita, thanks for letting me know about your brother. I'm used to dealing with kids like that. Everybody wants to think they're a hero, but at least he gives a crap. It's cool that you give a crap, too . . .

Drita poured herself a cup of wine and smiled. She was one lie closer to an actual truth.

10

1972

THE COURTHOUSE WAS DESIGNED FOR CEREMONY, AND THE HIGH-
stakes transaction she was there for called for ceremony. Jackie really
believed that, and knew she was stupid for believing that. Still, the
ending of three lives as they had been known—Antonella's, her own,
and the baby her belly once contained—in exchange for an insurance
payout with that many zeros seemed to Jackie to warrant time in one
of the grand chambers of the courthouse downtown, at least a little bit
of granite and dark-stained oak.

But it turned out those chambers were reserved for people with
stories worthy of the papers, like city employees who drained the local
coffers to finance their secret second families in Kissimmee, Florida, or
murderers who swore they weren't despite motives and fingerprints
smeared all over town. Jackie was a cripple who wasn't pretty enough
for her story to be tragic, so she didn't get a ceremony, just an out-of-
court settlement that was consummated in the reception area of an
artificially lit office. An attorney handed her an envelope, shook her
and Dom's hands, and told them to call again for any future legal
needs, perhaps a will or a real estate matter. Now that she had nothing
worth living for, she was supposed to just get on with her life.

It wasn't just that she wanted to be part of some pointless ritual, because she got enough of that at the church, it was that she thought she'd see Antonella at some point in the negotiation process. What that would've meant she didn't know, but whatever clarity might've come from the occasion was denied her. They hadn't set eyes on each other since the hospital, and Jackie didn't remember anything from those first weeks, until she was moved to a rehabilitation facility forty minutes away from where all her friends and family lived. It was clear, without anyone expressly stating it, that when she was discharged several months later, she was not going back to where her friends lived, not because they'd left but because they were no longer her friends. It wasn't Jackie's idea to file a lawsuit against Antonella or, as Dom's and Jackie's parents insisted, against Antonella's insurance company, and what Antonella's insurance company collected from Antonella and her parents wasn't their concern. But since it was Jackie's name in the court filings, she was the snake, despite not being conscious enough to sign any of the papers. When Jackie's parents pulled up to their house now, ladies in the neighborhood yelled about loyalty, said there'd been no ill intent, said that Antonella was suffering as much as Jackie and the Christian thing to do was forgive. Jackie's parents screamed right back that it looked like Antonella was easing her suffering by walking herself to The Pines for darts and St. Pauli Girl night after night after night, which was a thing their daughter would never get to do again. And anyway, none of it was personal, all of it was just necessary— Jackie and Dom would have to retrofit the house that they suddenly had enough money to buy, they'd have to get a special van, they had all those medical bills, and if there was any money left over for something nice, so what, didn't they deserve it? Married less than a month and already their marital relations as good as over, since Dom wasn't going to make love to a wife who couldn't feel much, never mind the fact that Jackie would've preferred it that way even with her spinal column intact. They'd lost their baby and, with her ruptured uterus, their chance to make more of them. They'd never take that thirty-year anniversary trip to Hawaii, where they were supposed to take pictures standing knee-deep in water they could see through. Instead they were fated to sit beside the opaque muck of the Long Island Sound, where all the camera would capture were algal blooms and jellyfish bobbing on the surface.

Those were the arguments volleyed back and forth on either side, and in the middle was Jackie.

Before the scorn, which she'd only heard secondhand, there was pity, which she hadn't heard at all, only understood. There had to have been talk about her atrophied, useless legs, spoken in the same hushed voices that followed the Ferraro boy, born with cerebral palsy, after his mother wheeled him out of the IGA. Nobody had bothered to tell Jackie that she wouldn't walk again until after her discharge, because it was decided that it would keep her spirits up to not know, to continue to have the same kind of pointless faith that had been programmed into her since birth with no discernible results. At the rehab facility she was ostensibly taught how to dress herself and shit without relying solely on others, which she surely could have learned on her own and saved tens of thousands of the dollars her family demanded from Antonella, but mostly she sat alone with thrice-read *Readers Digest*s and waited for her legs to wake up. When it was finally explained to Jackie that she'd be in that chair for the rest of her life, she didn't feel extraordinary anguish over the loss of her lower limbs. What great use was that kind of mobility to her? She'd understood her trajectory from the time she was a small girl, taking care of her even smaller cousins: she'd live in a small house in her small city and tend to a man who'd have no access to or even curiosity about the contents of her head, the only place she dared live boldly. In time, in that head, she even felt some relief at no longer being obligated to be a wife to Dom in the bedroom, and she could be a lazy one in the other rooms in the house. What she felt grief over was the lost baby, whom Jackie was going to raise to be the probe into the world that she, even prior to the accident, had not had the braveness to penetrate, the way that Antonella and

Denise had. What she felt anguish over was Antonella's and Denise's warm hands on her belly, those afternoons with them the closest to real intimacy she had ever felt and, now, would ever feel, the memory of taking Dom's curved pecker in his uncle's cellar not even a close second. She felt grief over the last words between her and Antonella that night in the car, knowing in retrospect that they amounted to a goodbye.

All day while Dom worked, she sat alone in a house paid for with her settlement money, in rooms she hadn't even gotten to tour before Dom signed the paperwork making them legal lien holders, with furniture she'd paid for but hadn't chosen. They'd settled in the East End, across town from where they'd both grown up and from where they'd since been essentially ejected, but she didn't miss it, because she hadn't chosen the old neighborhood any more than she'd chosen the new one. None of it had ever been hers; it had all just been there when she was born and it continued to be there in her absence. She hadn't chosen her family, hadn't really chosen who she married as much as simply ended up with one of the two or three neighborhood guys in her age range in the same general category of physical plainness. She thought she'd chosen to become a mother, because that was the single thing she'd done in her life that required some amount of will—she'd made herself screw Dom without a rubber and never even considered any of the remedies the old ladies and whores would have offered if she'd asked them how to chase all those eager swimmers away from her fertile young womb. She could admit to herself now that what she had wanted with a baby, even before the accident, was the chance to love a thing of her own choosing. It had been the best option available to her, because the thing she had wanted to love wasn't a possibility. She had wanted to love Antonella, in the way a wife was supposed to love a husband.

She could let herself understand that now, since both were equally impossible. Before the accident she'd let herself stay too stupid to even understand that the desire, never mind acting upon the desire, was a possibility. Now that she had evidence that the God she'd been fearful enough of to defer all humanly appetites to either didn't exist or didn't reward deference, she had no choice but to smarten up. What was left for God to do, strike her dead for wanting things she could never have? As if that wouldn't be a mercy. The little luxuries that populated her isolated little world were just there to remind her what had afforded her those worthless objects. A color TV she kept on to hear voices that would never address her. A teak hutch whose shelves Jackie mostly couldn't reach and were filled with china she wouldn't ever use. A brand-new Oldsmobile Cutlass, which Dom had deigned to buy in the sedan model instead of the coupe to make it easier for him to lift her into it for Sunday drives to Kent Falls, as if either of them took any great pleasure in that.

Jackie would trade in the Cutlass for Denise's Corvair in a heartbeat. Not Denise's Corvair, per se, but the last few minutes of consciousness in it. Antonella at the wheel, that moment of dreadful, thrilling realization when Antonella talked about the baby, talked about the fantasy of their own little family, before everything went dark. She would live that moment over and over again in an endless loop, which others might call purgatory but which she would consider her singular moment of grace.

Jackie's mother thought it was a kindness to purchase, on Jackie's behalf, subscriptions to magazines that Jackie had no intention of ever reading. Jackie preferred to watch television programs that were as inane as the magazines but easier to digest, or else just close her eyes and drift off into what was sometimes sleep and sometimes just the opaque absence of everything. When a storm took out the power in the neighborhood one afternoon, she figured she'd just go lie in bed until she could turn the TV back on, but when the power was restored a few hours later, she discovered the television was a permanent casualty. Meanwhile, the neighborhood kids were screaming and climbing over an elm tree that had fallen across the road, and Jackie's agitation over both was such that she knew closing her eyes would be futile. She picked up a copy of some glossy rag that had arrived courtesy of her mother, the stack of back issues piled high enough in a wicker basket that she didn't have to fold over to reach it. It was some Catholic version of *Good Housekeeping,* of course, something that would serve as kindling once winter rolled around and Dom insisted on heating the house mostly with a woodstove that didn't do the job near as well as the oil furnace. She thumbed through it but retained nothing until the large, bold black font of an advertisement caught her eye, standing out because it used so much white space, and looked ascetic enough to be Baptist.

SAVE A LIFE.
OPEN YOUR HEARTS AND HOMES
TO KOREAN ORPHANS.

At the bottom, in smaller print, was the name and address of an organization to write to for more information. They were based in Washington State, which Jackie thought may as well have been Korea to a wheelchair-bound housewife in Connecticut, and she had no intention of writing to them, both because the lag time between coasts would be unbearable to someone with nothing to do but wait and because Dom would never allow a Korean baby into the family. But it made her wonder if there wasn't another organization that did the same kind of work closer to home, maybe one that dealt in white babies whom she could groom to eventually resent and outgrow their narrow-minded hometowns, ones who would thank her for showing them the way.

Jackie felt a little stupid that adoption hadn't occurred to her before. In her life she'd known only women who got knocked up too easily and ended up with more kids than they wanted, not ones who wanted kids but couldn't make them happen. Also, she'd stopped longing for a baby once hers was taken away, because she'd realized it was a surrogate for her other longings. But Antonella was gone, driven away by Jackie's own greed and apparently off self-destructing somewhere in the city, so it occurred to her that perhaps she could revert to the original plan, somewhat revised to account for her current biological reality.

For the first time since regaining consciousness, Jackie felt a sensation that was neither physical pain nor existential demolition. That she couldn't name it was from either the lingering fog of her brain injury or its unfamiliarity. She pondered it and determined, moments after Dom returned from work and informed her the living room smelled like farts, that it was hope, a feeling that Dom's presence put into stark relief. She might, once again, be able to have something of her very own to prompt her to rise from bed.

In the coming days, while Dom tried and failed to fix the television before giving in and buying a new one, Jackie thumbed through the magazines page by page to see if she could find another ad like the first she'd seen, but they all seemed to come from the same place out west. People besides Joan Crawford had adopted kids before, that side of the country couldn't have been hoarding all the orphans, but Jackie didn't know where to begin her own search, who to call for help. In the immediate days and weeks after the accident, people had sent Dom casseroles and gift baskets and cards that said to call on them for anything they needed, anything at all, but those offers had been rescinded before all of the scraps of stuffed shells had been dumped in the trash. Now the only people who offered assistance were the church folks, despite Jackie not including herself among them anymore, and likely because they couldn't afford to lose any more parishioners, what with all the old folks dying and their hippie kids abandoning the pews like church was the draft. But if the Washington group advertised in a Catholic magazine, then probably the church folks weren't the worst ones to reach out to. It was about time for them to give her a little something for all the time she'd given them over the years.

Father Michael himself was the one to return Jackie's message, which meant they considered a phone call from her important, and that inflated Jackie's sense in the righteousness of her mission.

"How are you, Jacqueline?" he said. "We all miss you here at the church."

"Oh, I'm okay, Father Mike. It's real hard for me to make it down there these days," Jackie said.

"I can imagine, I can imagine. God will wait, as long as you keep your faith," Father Michael said.

"Yes, of course. Listen, I've been curious about something I read in a magazine," Jackie said.

The father was silent while Jackie explained that she'd been thinking about adoption and had heard there were Catholic groups that specialized in that kind of thing. Jackie expected silence from priests—they were used to the confessional booth, and didn't speak until the end, but he remained silent even for a few seconds after Jackie was done speaking, which she didn't expect. She was about to hang up and redial, assuming the connection was lost, until she heard:

"Jacqueline."

The next silence was what she would later, when re-creating the moment, bitterly call a pregnant pause, long enough for Jackie to understand that she was about to be spoken to like a child, not a grown woman looking for a child. Like a child, she became immediately petulant, and chose to not respond to her name. He had not spoken it with a question mark at the end, as if he expected an answer from her; he had spoken it like anything that followed should not have needed an explanation.

Indeed, when he began speaking, Jackie remained on the line only to be able to commit the moment to memory, as she intuited immediately that she'd want to relive it in moments when she was making inventories of the ways the world had scorned her. "The Lord sometimes makes plans for us that are difficult, with the limitations of our human faculties, to understand."

Silence from Jackie.

"We don't understand why the Lord put you in the car that night, or why the truck passed by you on an otherwise empty stretch of highway at the precise moment it did. In the coming years, with prayer and reflection, we may find a suitable answer to that," the father said.

He continued: "But as painful as it is to consider, I think it's clear why He took your baby away at that moment. What kind of hardship would it be for an infant to be in the care of a mother who is herself enduring such hardship? How will a mother who can't walk respond to the sudden cries of her hungry child? How will a mother who can't walk stop her child from running unexpectedly into the street? Do you understand that?"

"No," Jackie said, quite calmly. "Please explain it in such a way that a simple woman like me can understand."

The priest sighed. "Children who have been given up or abandoned by their birth parents require special care. They've already suffered the loss of their mothers, which means their adoptive mothers must compensate with even greater attention, even more love. They'll need community—a community like the church, for example. You've said yourself that it's prohibitively difficult to get to mass these days, and I understand that, I empathize with that. We all do. But it's just not practical for someone in your situation to consider adopting a child. It must be so difficult to hear that, having only recently lost your own unborn baby. My heart does ache for you. I've said prayers about it every night since it happened."

"Oh really?" Jackie asked. "What have your prayers asked for?"

The father seemed taken aback by the question, reverting to the pointed silences he believed he was so skillful at deploying. "These prayers are conversations between myself and God, Jacqueline."

"He's not getting your messages, so why don't you tell me?"

"Not getting the answer you want doesn't mean He doesn't hear."

"Well since you have His direct line," Jackie said, "next time you talk to Him, why don't you tell Him to go fuck Himself? On my behalf, of course, and on behalf of my baby, who's an orphan in purgatory."

"Jacqueline," the priest warned.

"What, those aren't His rules? Then I guess they're your rules, Father, so fuck you, too."

She hung up and thought only afterwards of a line she wished she had added, that she was done listening to rules, God's and God's messengers', who every man that walked the earth believed they were. She quaked with anger but also recognized simultaneously a sense of glee, one that she knew must accompany every first taste of freedom. What a bitch it was, tasting her first freedom while bound to a chair she hadn't yet developed the will or upper-body strength to properly maneuver.

Joan Crawford's kids didn't come from a Catholic organization. They came from something that didn't bother with a virtuous front: money. Jackie wasn't famous and she wasn't rich, but she had money enough, and she'd be damned if it was all going to go to satisfying Dom's whims.

Over dinner that night, she told him exactly that, omitting the part about how she'd come to that conclusion.

"I'm going to adopt a baby," Jackie said.

It was difficult for Jackie to pinpoint any of Dom's charms, but sense of humor, even before they were married, never made it onto the list. She was so unaccustomed to his laughter that at first she believed him to be choking on his sausage, and it dawned on her only later that she didn't make a move to slap his back or Heimlich him. Only after she realized what the sound was did she actively wish his windpipe had been jammed.

"Do you think I'm making a crack?" Jackie asked.

He shook his head and let his wheezy chuckles putter out. The bastard sounded like a sputtering two-stroke engine.

"Well, get your laughs in now, because when the baby comes you're going to have to keep your yap shut."

Dom looked down at his fork like he wanted to slam it on the table, but there was a hunk of meat speared on the tines that he couldn't bear to not bring to his fat mouth.

"I don't want to hear any more of this stupid talk. Nobody's gonna let you get your hands on any baby. You're not even potty-trained yourself, how you gonna do it for a kid?"

It surprised and delighted Jackie that what prevented her from driving the steak knife that Dom didn't bother using to cut his meat into his heart wasn't her inability to navigate quickly toward him; it was that he didn't matter. He had never mattered. He'd only ever been a seed donor, a way to get out of her parents' house, and the least complicated way to get people to not ask questions. She'd chosen Dom to get marriage out of the way as quickly and painlessly as possible, and that held true only if she didn't let him pain her.

"It's called a catheter, and I'm better at using it than you are using your functional pecker." She enjoyed how calm she was remaining, and enjoyed especially how that very feat made Dom grip his silverware like a pitchfork. It made him look like the diminutive, impotent devil he was. "My arms work just fine. I'll have no problem changing a diaper."

Dom looked in contempt at the same meat on his plate he'd been enjoying just moments before. "You can't even make a decent dinner," he said, finally throwing down his fork. "What, you gonna boil a sausage on a hot plate for a kid their whole life?"

"I can figure it out. I just needed the motivation, and now I have it."

"I'm finished talking about this, Jackie," he said. He was quiet about it, adopting the same tactic she was using, but he couldn't hide the swath of splotchy rouge that covered his neck. His temper was so textbook that Jackie almost felt sorry for how easy it was to read him, like a Little Golden Book.

She shrugged. "We don't need to talk about it. I wasn't asking, I was just letting you know."

Dom's arm swept his plate, with a quarter-link of sausage and the entire pile of French-cut green beans, onto the floor.

"I'm not going to clean that," Jackie said.

"Because you can't!" he roared. "You can't do shit, you can't even shit on your own, and you're not bringing anybody else into my house for me to take care of! You're more useless than your old lezzie friend. I got enough to deal with with you alone."

"A couple of things, Dom," Jackie said. She almost added a laugh but thought that might be a little over the top. "Number one, you don't take care of me. Any help I've gotten is from my mother or from a nurse. Number two, this isn't your house. My settlement money made the down payment, and it's my name on the mortgage because you're so bad with money the bank wouldn't let you near the loan. I've got plenty more money left over, and it's all in my name, and I'm going to do what I want with it, and what I want is a child."

Dom was shaking now. She could see it all over him: thinking through what the old neighborhood would say if he strangled to death his wife in a wheelchair. He stood up from the table and kicked the cabinet beneath the sink instead, which responded by meekly opening and spilling a jar of Ajax onto the floor. "I filed that lawsuit, Jackie. That was me, in your name. You owe me for that. You owe me for getting knocked up and making me marry you and now leaving me with a whore for a wife who can't even open her legs up anymore. The best years of my life, all of them wasted on you."

"I don't want to go head-to-head about it, Dom, but we both got a bad deal. Here's the thing, though: I'm going to get me a baby, and it's going to cost me some money. The rest of it, fine, buy yourself another Oldsmobile or five, I don't give a shit. Get yourself another whore or five, I don't give a shit about that, either. What I need from you is a husband on paper, and what you need from me is a wife with paper." She was proud of herself for a pun she'd pulled out of nowhere. "There doesn't have to be a problem, there just has to be an understanding."

"You're a lunatic," Dom said.

"I think I'm being very reasonable," Jackie said. "What's not reasonable about this? I'm not telling you you can't have everything you want. I'm just telling you I'm going to get what I want, too."

For half of a very long minute, Jackie watched Dom consider murder one final time. It wasn't his moral center that stopped it, but it was all that Sunday schooling, his uninspired adherence to the way some book said things should be. When he reached the conclusion, he bent down more slowly and painfully than an able-bodied man of twenty-two should have and began cleaning up the mess he'd made. He said nothing as he did it, but that said it all.

11

To: Lindita Kushta (luv_lindita)
From: Valon Zaimi (valbanian73)
Subject: hey

You're 21? I bet you haven't told your parents you're hitting me
up on here or else you wouldn't have hands to type with. I know
what Albanian parents are like lol. I'm 25 and I'd rather face the
Serb army than my father when he's pissed. Course I'll be facing
the Serb army soon anyway so I guess I'll find out one way or
the other. My sister's married now and our parents keep begging
for grandkids but at the same time I bet if they found out she had
sex with her husband they'd actually kill him hahahahaha.

   Where were your parents from anyway? You still have family
over there? I hope they're not in Kosova but then again I don't
know why your brother would've emailed us if they weren't.

   Anyway, you seem mature for your age. What are you going
to school for? I was taking classes at Hunter for a while but I had
to stop. I might go back once this is all over. I mean if I come
back alive lol.

———

Drita considered giving credit to the random AOL chat rooms she'd occasionally pop into for training her how to a lure stranger on the internet, but the fact was she was chatting with a twenty-five-year-old guy, and twenty-five-year-old guys the world over worked exactly the same way: bat an eyelash in their direction and wait for their inner Soldier of Fortune to emerge. Isaac was never like that, and maybe that's why he was, to date, the only relationship she'd managed to sustain for more than a weekend. And Isaac was an actual soldier, or whatever a peacetime version of a soldier whose only battles were executed inside of college classrooms was called. He didn't even mention that he'd gone to West Point until their third date, and then it was only because he spent his time between bites of molten lava cake eviscerating some militaristic and neoliberal take on the Sudanese Civil War that he'd read about in *The Economist* or some other neoliberal apologist rag. After nodding in agreement during that date and looking up *neoliberalism* in the Columbia library before their next, Drita didn't ask why he still let the military pay for his education, because the answer to that was obvious: because he was no idiot. That she knew before the first date, and it was why she'd agreed to it in the first place. The important thing was that he would've been an avowed pacifist if he were the type to make avowals about himself.

Meanwhile the twenty-five-year-old on the other side of the modem would probably call himself anything he thought a twenty-one-year-old Albanian virgin would want to hear. She would've felt almost bad about that if it didn't also feel so good.

To: Valon Zaimi (valbanian73)
From: Lindita Kushta (luv_lindita)
re: hey

I don't really talk to my parents about my personal life. Not like I have much of one between work and school and stuff. I'm major-

ing in nursing so I'm in classes like alllllll dayyyyyy and then I
work and then I study and then I sleep and then I get up and do
it all over again. I can't wait to graduate and get out of here to be
honest. My parents are fine but they're so old-fashioned. My dad
works all the time and my mom just wants me to have babies
now that her own kids are grown up even though they also expect me to be a virgin forever like your sister ;D They came over
from Struga before I was born, and their parents are dead and
all their brothers and sisters left a long time ago so we don't
really go over there or anything. That's why I don't really speak
Albanian, which every Albanian around here is SHOCKED
about. Sorry to disappoint you lol.

I feel kind of stupid for complaining about all that stuff when I
know you're doing actually real things. What does the group my
brother emailed about actually do, anyway? Like, what do you
mean you're gonna be facing the Serb army soon? That's crazy
if it's literally true. Is it because you still have family in Kosova? I
hope you're not just a wannabe Rambo like my brother.

Sorry if those questions are too personal. You just seem really
interesting. The guys around here are so boring they think I'll go
out with them if they get better rims on their Mitsubishis.

I think you were just making a joke before but I hope you
come back alive if you really are going to fight over there.

To: Lindita Kushta (luv_lindita)
From: Valon Zaimi (valbanian73)
re: re: hey

It's okay for you to complain about school. It's kind of nice to
hear about regular life for a change. I feel like all I ever hear or
talk or think about these days is the war. I mean pretty much
everybody I know around here is a mess about their families
back home so I understand why they can't think about anything
else, but I like that your emails take my mind off it for a while.

To answer your question, yes, I'm going back overseas soon. My parents and me moved to New York when I was a kid but most of my family is still in Peje. At least I hope they're still there. We haven't heard from some of my uncles and aunts and cousins for a couple weeks so we don't really know if they're even alive or in a camp or what. Mostly we raise money to buy things they need over there, and I've already been back a few times to deliver supplies but next time I'm going to stay and fight. My father says he needs me to help with his business and manage our shipments overseas and that kind of thing, but I'm not just gonna send other guys to risk their lives while I sit around and do paperwork and slop tar around. Plus, not to sound like your brother or anything, like I think it's a videogame, but I'm ready to blow some shit up. You were lucky you were born here and that you haven't lost anybody but I've seen shit I can't ever unsee. I wish I could tell you I'm doing it because I'm a good person but the things I want to do to these motherfuckers definitely aren't good.

I hope that doesn't freak you out. I used to be like those dumbasses you know with the rims and shit, but it's hard to know this kind of stuff is happening and keep giving a shit about your Mitsubishis.

Fuck, that got dark. Sorry. I told you I liked hearing from you to take my mind off the war and then I just went right back into it.

Maybe if you send me a pic I can take my mind off things for real for a little while. Hope that's not too forward. I know how Albanian girls are;)

It sounded like a videogame, all the talk about blowing shit up, but the rage behind it was probably genuine. Earned, even, if this guy really had family back in Kosova. She could understand that. Nothing elicited rage so much as family, though in her case it was family itself that stirred the feeling, not the threatened destruction of it. Of course Isaac could talk about what he'd read in the news as calmly as he'd probably notify his future patients about their future cancers. It wasn't like he had family in Sudan. His family was in Michigan, happy and healthy in a house in the Upper Peninsula that Drita had visited each of the three Christmases that they were together. They were so nice, and they raised such a nice son. Not the kind of son who dreamed of blowing shit up, even when he enrolled in the same military school that his father had attended, along with a good number of people who made the decisions about which bombs to drop and where.

Valon didn't seem *not* nice, exactly. He was distressed, understandably. She could be empathetic to that. She could understand it. What wasn't understandable was what Pete had to do with any of it, and she reminded herself that that was her objective here, even if she felt bad for this guy. She had to remember what question she was trying to answer.

To: Valon Zaimi (valbanian73)
From: Lindita Kushta (luv_lindita)
re: re: re: hey

Maybe you know how Albanian girls are, but you don't know how I am. Why would you bother to write to me if I was like every other girl you knew? Not to be a bitch or anything. It's just that I don't want you to think that I can't handle hearing about the war. I'm not saying it's anywhere near as bad as what you've seen, but I've seen some pretty shitty things in my fieldwork, too. I've had to work in some rough neighborhoods, and maybe nobody's trying to actually murder some of these people, but they definitely don't care whether they live or die, and is that much better?

Sorry. I mean I know it's nowhere as bad. I just mean that I already know how crappy humans can be to other humans. I think I understand why you'd want to do something about it.

Are most of the people going over there like you, like it's personal? I heard there's this guy from around here who volunteered. Maybe you know him, Petrit DiMeo? If you do, don't tell him I asked about him because I know his ex-girlfriend and they didn't exactly end on good terms. I don't know if you know this, but he doesn't even know a single person in Kosova or Albania for that matter, so I don't really understand why he'd enlist. I mean, there are horrible things happening all the time all over the world, right? Why is this the thing he's willing to do? Just from what I know about him, he doesn't seem like the kind of person to sacrifice himself for anybody.

Sorry, I'm supposed to be the person who reminds you about regular life. Did you watch Friends this week? I'm totally normal, I swear. Maybe you can tell from my picture ;) Send me yours?

To: Lindita Kushta (luv_lindita)
From: Valon Zaimi (valbanian73)
re: re: re: re: hey

I believe you've seen some shitty things in your work but have you ever seen a ditch full of bodies after they've been shot and set on fire? I mean old men, women, kids? You sound like you have half a brain, but you were born here, you can't really understand that. It's good that you don't understand it. I don't want the girl I see in your picture to be ruined like that. I'm not gonna lie, I look at your pic a lot. A lot. You look older than you are. No offense, you don't look old or anything. But you seem mature, so maybe I'm just imagining you a little older. But you don't look broken and I'd rather you stay that way. You don't have to talk about Friends but I like to think about you doing regular things. I like to think about you dressed in a nurse's uniform and helping people. And I like to think about you in a nurse's uniform for other reasons;)

See, you're taking my mind off things and all I have is one picture and a few emails. I guess you're helping me, too.

That's funny about Petrit. I do know that guy. There aren't that

many of us so I kind of know everybody, but I actually know Petrit pretty well. He's been doing some work for me and my father,
roofing and some other stuff. He's kind of a crazy one. He wasn't
even raised in our culture and he didn't understand shit about
what's happening over there when I first met him, but he's built
like a mule and he wants to help, so I wasn't about to turn him
out. Basically I could tell he was in a rough spot and kind of desperate to be somebody so I didn't have to work real hard to bring
him on board. Plus he's a citizen and doesn't have any accent so
he never raises any eyebrows in a gun shop, so that's convenient. And to be honest we need him because he's a genuine
American, and do you think the U.S. government's going to give
a shit about us if we're just a bunch of Mediterranean guys with
accents? It's not like we have oil anybody wants to get their
hands on. There's no chance in hell we win against the Serbs
without NATO and we're not getting NATO without the U.S. on
board.

　　I like that you're interested in what's happening. I guess I kind
of hoped when we started emailing that you'd be cute and a dis-
traction and you are, but you seem like more than that, too. I feel
like I'd like you in real life.

　　But would Valon like her if she told him how wrong he was: that
Pete's desperation was to be nobody, not even the father he most definitely was? Valon was trying to do something he thought was important. No, something that *was* important; she'd read the news, she'd
listened to the real Lindita; there was a literal genocide under way.
Even Isaac wouldn't have been a pacifist if his family was being hunted.
Or, even worse, maybe he would have been, and would have been content to bystand and clean up after the fact, the way he planned to do
after he finished med school and signed up with something like Doctors Without Borders, which, she was embarrassed now to admit, was
also what she planned to do after finishing her degree, after complet-

ing her fieldwork in a hard-up place that had nothing to do with her, just like Pete had suggested all those years ago. Do-gooders, Isaac and her, but really, how much good did that kind of good do?

God, all this idling was frustrating. That's what she was trying to do emailing Valon in the first place, trying to jump-start something again. It's just that the something was getting fuzzier every time she logged on.

To: Valon Zaimi (valbanian73)
From: Lindita Kushta (luv_lindita)
re: re: re: re: re: hey

Do you think you'd like me in real life? I think some people think I'm too intense and it freaks them out, and I can kind of see their point but I don't know what I'm supposed to do about it. Most of the things people spend their time on make me want to pull my hair out, and I can pretend that I'm into it but that's not exactly going to make me any happier than I'd be just being alone all the time. I think that's kind of a nice thing about talking to people on the computer, it takes too long to type out small talk so you can just get straight to the things that are actually worth the time. You can say things you'd be too embarrassed to say if you had to look someone in the eye. Like, you said the war is personal to you because you lost people, and I don't like that you lost people but I like that you told me that. When you said you wanted to do bad things to people, it didn't scare me like you were afraid it would, it made me want to know more.

I guess I want to know more because I understand how other people's shittiness could make you do things you otherwise wouldn't do. Like I know this person who keeps blowing up other people's lives and walking away scot-free, and it's making me a little crazy, like I'm getting stupid about trying to make this person make it right. I mean, what right do people have to mess up other people's lives? I mean, it's just one guy, but if you multiply that kind of guy times a million it's enough to mess up the whole world, right?

Sorry, I know this is all so petty and not even close to what you're talking about. I guess you can tell that I don't really understand the bigger picture. And I don't understand how you could smell bullshit in my brother's email right away but it's okay to let someone like Petrit DiMeo in. I get that he's useful, but is it good for the cause if he's not even really fighting for the cause?

I wish I could be dumber and not ask so many questions. It'd probably make my life easier and make you look forward to my emails more. I hope this new pic is enticing enough for you to open my next message.

To: Lindita Kushta (luv_lindita)
From: Valon Zaimi (valbanian73)
re: re: re: re: re: re: hey

You are kind of intense. I think I sensed that about you and that's why I wrote you back. I mean I don't know why else I would email with you. I worked tarring roofs for twelve hours today and then I handled all the email shit that my father doesn't really know how to deal with and now I should be sleeping so I can get up tomorrow and tar more roofs and buy out a bunch of Army-Navy stores in New Jersey like some weirdo who lives in a basement in Queens or some shit. I won't lie, the pictures help, but not to sound like a douchebag, I don't really need pictures. I know a lot of girls, my mother's always trying to fix me up with girls, you know Albanian mothers think you're supposed to be married with four kids by the time you're 25. But I feel like I know all the girls around here too well, like I either grew up with them or else they all act exactly the same, they all wear exactly the same clothes and have the same hair and say the exact same things. But I bet they'd say I look and sound like every other guy they know, because it's not like I'm getting too deep with them, I'm acting like the same tough guy they see on every corner around here. Nobody's asking me the kind of questions you do. I like your questions as much as I like your pictures, to tell you the truth.

You're right, Petrit wasn't in it for the cause at first because he didn't have one. He didn't have shit when I met him. No money, no friends, nowhere to stay. We gave him some work and a place to sleep and we schooled him on what was happening. He thought he was nobody and we reminded him who he was, and suddenly it's like he understood his role or something. Trust me, he's a thousand times better off than when I met him. I don't know what he was like before but you can tell his ex-girlfriend he's actually doing something worthwhile now. If he comes back he'll come back respectable. No offense, but your brother's just a kid from Connecticut who heard a story he liked at the mosque. Don't get me wrong, there are young people signing up for us, too, like high school kids, but they're not kids like your brother, they understand they're not playing a videogame. They don't want to fight for points, they need to fight. Me and most of the guys, we need to fight because we lost something. Petrit needs to fight so he can get something. Jetmir wants to fight be-cause he thinks he's gonna get a girlfriend out of it. That's not somebody we need representing us, you know? You're Albanian, you must understand besa. It's allegiance to your people, honor above everything else. That's why selfishness makes you feel sick, because besa's in your blood. You can't see it, but it's there.

I can see it in your picture, too. Not gonna lie, I'm looking at it a lot.

Drita had sent a real photo. That part wasn't a lie. She scanned a snapshot of herself taken on a day too unimportant to have captured on film, based on the zero recollection she had of the moment, and emailed it to Valon because she thought it showed just enough décolleté to entice a twenty-five-year-old man to wonder what existed just a little under the frame. She didn't expect him to imagine anything beyond that, never mind see something that Isaac never had. Even if he was wrong about what he was seeing, he was looking, and it was humbling how it made her fingers tremble.

To: Valon Zaimi (valbanian73)
From: Lindita Kushta (luv_lindita)
re: re: re: re: re: re: re: hey

I hope you don't look at my picture when you read this. It feels so weird to write it. I've never really written or said any of this before.

Does it make you lose respect for me that I don't know that word, besa? I told you I don't really speak Albanian. I'm a spoiled American brat.

But something I don't really get about besa is what you're supposed to do if being honorable means you can't be loyal to your people, like if your brother is up to something stupid so you rat him out. Isn't that what I did with Jetmir? Or say one of your people wants something and another one of your people wants something else, and they can't all get what they want. How are you supposed to have allegiance to them all? Somebody's going to get wronged, aren't they?

Remember that guy I talked about in my last email, the asshole? He has a little boy. Five years old. It's kind of a long story how it happened, but he's staying with me because he has nowhere else to go, and he has nowhere else to go because his father walked out on him. I guess I'm not as smart as you think I am, because I'm too dense to figure out how somebody could do something like that, force somebody to exist and then make sure their existence is as hard as possible.

You probably think it's none of my business, but I've been try-ing to track him down because I can't live with the idea that this kid has to bear the consequences of somebody else's mistakes. I'm not Mother Teresa. I just don't know how to keep living in a world with people who don't give shits.

I know that must seem ridiculous to you. You probably know dozens of kids worse off than this one. You probably know some that have been killed. It's actually selfish of me, I guess, because really I'm probably doing this because I want to feel like I'm actu-ally capable of doing something in the world. And to feel like I belong in it.

It's so embarrassing to write that.

It's crazy how I feel like I can tell you these things and I don't even really know who you are. What do you even look like? You never sent that picture I asked for. It'd be nice to be able to imagine you actually talking back to me in real life.

To: Lindita Kushta (luv_lindita)
From: Valon Zaimi (valbanian73)
re: re: re: re: re: re: re: re: hey

You shouldn't be embarrassed. Actually I think I get you even more than I did before.

It's two totally different worlds but I feel like we want the same thing. Like we can't rest until we fix something. For you it's this kid and for me it's a country. Except if you want to know the truth, for me the war didn't start because of a bunch of dead strangers and people fleeing in caravans, for me this war started when someone I loved got killed. I guess I'm selfish like that, too. By now I don't even know who else is gone, but I don't need anything more to tell me what I have to do. My father thinks we should do things the American way, with money and guns that other people shoot for us, but that's not the kind of doing that's gonna let me rest at night.

Was that intense enough for you?

This got realer than I thought it would when I first wrote you back. I kinda wish I hadn't started, because now I want to meet you for real and I can't really do that now.

To: Valon Zaimi (valbanian73)
From: Lindita Kushta (luv_lindita)
re: re: re: re: re: re: re: re: re: hey

Why can't you meet me? I'd get on the Metro-North tomorrow.

To: Lindita Kushta (luv_lindita)
From: Valon Zaimi (valbanian73)
re: re: re: re: re: re: re: re: re: re: hey

I don't know when I'm coming back or if I'm coming back and that would be shitty to do to you. You have that kid to take care of, I don't want you worrying about me.

I never sent you a picture. Here you go. If you like what you see you can wait a little while for it, right?

To: Valon Zaimi (valbanian73)
From: Lindita Kushta (luv_lindita)
re: re: re: re: re: re: re: re: re: re: hey

I like what I see. I just hate waiting.

"Aunt Drita, do you want to play motocross?" Dakota asked.

The kid looked like a birch tree, skinny trunked, all the weight balanced on top. Pete had been like that, too, until he filled out at puberty.

"Not really, dude. How about you play and I just watch you?"

He nodded. His stiff curls didn't move when his head did. That feature had come from his mother, ringlets that were dark at the roots but somehow almost golden at the tips, sun-kissed despite his having spent distressingly little time in the sun, especially now that he'd discovered the computer. The hazel eyes he stared intently at the screen with came from who knows where—not from Shanda, not from Pete, not from Nadia. Dakota's eye shape, too, was distinctly his, a little hooded but still enormous, something it didn't seem like he'd outgrow. His existence seemed half inevitable and half cosmic mystery. It made Drita wonder if there was any chance it might lead to something other than more tragedy.

And then her mind wandered to Valon. How the scale of any of the tragedies in her living room didn't even register next to his. How she admired that Valon wanted to correct tragedies, not create them. How she pitied him that he was so invested in the idea of besa that he thought he saw some in Pete. Valon didn't deserve to put his faith into someone who would desert a cause as surely as he would desert a son.

Drita wished Dakota would quit playing his game and go to bed so that she could log on herself and look at Valon's photo again in private. It embarrassed her to acknowledge that, like it embarrassed her that her confessions had woven themselves in with her lies until finally they overtook them, including the part where she liked what she saw.

"Aunt Drita, it's stuck," Dakota said.

"What's stuck, Dakota?"

"The computer screen. The motorcycle isn't moving."

"I don't know what to tell you, kid. Computers are finicky. You sure you don't want to go outside for a while? We can take that bike Grandma Jackie got for you," Drita said.

He didn't answer.

"Dakota?" she asked louder.

"Huh?" he answered. He was close to drooling, so transfixed was he on the screen.

"You want to ride your real bike outside?"

"No," he said. "It's fixed. It's moving again."

"Why would you rather play with a fake bike on the computer than a real bike on the street?"

"I don't know how to ride the real bike."

"It's got training wheels. That's how you learn."

"I can't concentrate, Aunt Drita," he huffed.

He was getting some attitude. That could've come from Shanda or from Pete. But Pete had gotten ahold of Dom's pliers and detached his own training wheels almost as soon as he'd gotten his first bike. His physical grace was infuriating to Drita as a kid because it was completely unearned. He could hit any window with any rock, while Drita couldn't get a softball to home plate whether she threw underhanded or over. He could do back flips through will alone, while two years of gymnastics classes at the Y and all Drita ever managed was a one-handed cartwheel. He never wanted to watch television, or if he did, it was something like *Enter the Dragon*, some karate flick he could emulate, while his son only wanted to steer a cartoon machine within another machine in 2D.

It seemed that she and Dakota had more in common with each other than with their respective brother and father, in that they were doing most of their living in a world that was missing its final dimension. The difference was that Drita resented it, and Dakota came most alive in it.

She wondered if Valon had messaged her while Dakota tied up the computer. She hated that she wondered that, and she hated that he probably hadn't. He'd said he was going to be busy. He'd said he was leaving soon. He hadn't said where he was now, other than in a folder in the half-real world of the internet. As close as she'd come, she hadn't triangulated exactly where he and, by proxy, Pete, actually were. All the doing of the past couple of weeks, and still nothing had changed except for a few feelings.

"Okay, kiddo, you gotta wrap it up," Drita said.

"But why?" Dakota whined.

"Because all this computer time's not good for you."

"But there's nothing else to do here."

"There's nothing else to do on there, either," Drita said. "It's just the same picture over and over again. Maybe try to make something in real life."

"Like what kind of something?"

"I don't know, Dakota, like maybe draw something? Or make a fort again out of your sleeping bag and some pillows."

"You said I made a mess last time."

"I know I did, but I don't care anymore. Go ahead, make a mess. I'd rather you make a mess in real life than make nothing on the computer," Drita said.

Dakota sighed and slid dramatically from the chair.

"Hey," he whined when he saw her take his place on the seat. "That's not fair! You said not to use the computer anymore."

"I'm not playing on the computer, Dakota, I'm working," Drita said, but she doubted her own words when she heard them. She wanted to be doing something in real life, not to keep using pixels as a surrogate for it. And what would happen when she found Pete, if she did find Pete? She'd be back to looking at websites for possible Plan Bs and Cs and Ds. That didn't constitute—what was the word that Valon used?— besa. Besa wasn't a website, it wasn't a feeling, it was doing something, like Valon was doing something. She could be doing something.

Drita swiveled in her seat and turned to Dakota.

"Hey, kid, let's make a mess," she said.

12

FROM THE LIVING ROOM WINDOW, SHANDA WATCHED A GUY IN A puffer coat and what looked to be a Miami Dolphins beanie roll his bike between two buildings, one boarded up and one still decorated with Christmas lights that had been strung up six years before and had burned out six months later. Her mother had given her money to buy some custard cups at the Portuguese bakery and ribs and rice at the Puerto Rican place, but she didn't want to mess with either social workers or dudes sniffing around for drugs, and the young white guys who ended up on her street were always one of the two.

"Shanda, why haven't you left yet?" her mother, Nadia, yelled from the love seat.

"There's a guy out there," Shanda said.

"So what, you think this street belongs to us? There's guys allowed to be out there. He ain't gonna bother you," Nadia said.

"He doesn't look right," Shanda said.

"What's he look like?"

"Just . . . dumb. He's just walking back and forth like he doesn't know where he is."

"So maybe he's lost."

"He's going to ask me directions. I don't want to talk to him."

"Please, Shanda! I asked you to go out a half an hour ago. I'm starving, baby, just ignore the damn guy."

Shanda breathed in deep. The neighbors didn't talk to her, but they didn't bother her, either. It was the weirdos who showed up from out of nowhere who always seemed to sniff her out like dog shit. She told her mother a few years back about the dad-looking guy who rolled up slowly beside her in a dark-tinted minivan and demanded she get in, and since Nadia had just told her to stop wagging her ass so much when she walked, Shanda didn't bother to mention the other guys who whistled or grabbed or followed, even when she was in a knee-length winter coat, even when she looked even younger than the twelve she was when it all started. Instead, she pulled a Patriots cap over her head low enough that her eyes wouldn't be visible to anyone over five-foot-three and shoved her fists deep into her coat pockets, along with the brass knuckles she'd stolen from the bookbag of some girl at school dumb enough to let her backpack gape open through a whole lunch period.

Just as she knew he would, the guy called out to her as she headed down the block, yelling from the other side of the street.

"Miss," he said, "miss, excuse me."

She ignored him, but he trotted over, and when he blocked her way with his bike on the sidewalk, she pulled the knuckles from her pocket without bothering to ask what the fuck he wanted.

"Whoa, I'm not trying to fight you, I'm just trying to get to Roller Magic."

Just as she thought, the dude was lost, or at least claiming to be. But what he claimed he was looking for took her by surprise.

"Roller Magic?" she said. "What you want with Roller Magic?"

"I'm supposed to meet somebody there," he said.

"Aren't you a grown-ass man?"

"I'm nineteen," he said. Whether that was to affirm or deny that he was a grown-ass man wasn't clear. Shanda finally stopped and took a good look at his face. He could've been nineteen. He didn't look like a schoolkid, definitely not anyone at her school, but he also didn't look old enough to be a full-on pervert for hanging out at a roller-skating rink.

"You're too old for Roller Magic," she said anyway, because he was old enough to be a loser, if not a pervert, for hanging out at a roller-skating rink. But she realized she wasn't trying to fully shake him anymore, either, which alarmed her, and made her begin walking again. He was kind of cute, dark eyes, not all tweaky like she expected him to be, but that was no reason to think he wasn't up to something.

"I'm not trying to skate, I'm supposed to have an interview there. For a job," he said.

"You're interviewing for a job at a place you never even been? How'd you fill out the application?"

"I mean, I went when I was a kid, like everybody else," he said. "And I didn't fill out an application, I got sent there by—"

He stopped midsentence.

"By your PO?"

"I don't have a PO," he said.

She kept walking.

"But I am on probation and I am supposed to find a job," he said.

"What'd you do to get on probation?"

He put his thumb and index finger together and brought it to his lips. It looked like he was making the sign for okay until he took a deep, exaggerated drag.

"Buying or selling?"

"Pfft," he said. "What you think? Selling."

"That supposed to impress me?"

"I wasn't trying to impress you, I was just trying to get some directions," he said. "You don't trust me, I'll go ahead and peace out."

"You're gonna get your ass kicked and that bike stolen rolling around here on that thing," she called out as he hopped on his wheels and began pedaling away. It was some BMX-looking machine that seemed way too small for him, maybe something he'd stolen himself from some poor little kid more pathetic than him.

He popped a wheelie that he rode down the street, then dropped the front wheel and lifted the back. The bike spun around like a planet on an axis, and he pedaled back toward her.

"Endo," he told her.

"But you're not trying to impress me."

He shrugged. "I wasn't at first."

"And now?"

He pedaled a few feet, stood up on the pedals, moved over to the two pegs that jutted out from the front wheel, and swung the bike in a full orbit around him.

"Whiplash," he said.

She shrugged so imperceptibly under her giant coat that the guy would've had to have been looking hard to notice it.

He jumped the bike onto the sidewalk, rode it to the end of the block, then jumped off again while spinning the bike around in a circle.

"Bunny hop 360," he yelled to her.

"Don't you have a job interview?" she asked when he circled around again.

"I don't want that stupid job," he said.

She didn't know why she was entertaining the guy. Usually the white boys around there were the ones with the biggest chips on their shoulders, the most to prove. All this kid was proving was that he was an idiot, like an overgrown and kind of hot middle schooler. That might've explained why she hadn't booked it out of there, actually. He was playing with her. No kids had ever wanted to play with her, and now that she'd long ago made herself not give a shit, some idiot comes around with a toy and some kind of implied invitation.

"How old are you?" the guy asked.

"Seventeen," Shanda replied.

He considered this for a minute, craning his neck to get a better look under the brim of her hat. "You lying?"

"Why would I lie about being seventeen? Being seventeen doesn't get me anything."

He shrugged. "Just want to make sure I'm not getting into illegal territory."

"Talking isn't illegal."

"Do you want to do something else?"

"I gotta go," she said.

"Where are you going?"

"None of your business."

"You want a ride?"

"On your bike?"

"You can get on the pegs." He pointed to the two metal knobs attached to the hub of his back wheel.

"I'm not a hooker," she said.

The guy flinched at first, as if he thought she were about to smack him, even as she stood a good eight feet away. Then he shook his head as if she had actually smacked him and jutted out his lower lip in a cartoonish simulation of a frown. Then he laughed at his own foolishness and looked at her like he expected her to join in.

"Come on," he said, when she didn't. "What's a hooker going to do on the back of a bike? Anyway, I don't have any money, so I couldn't pay you for anything anyway."

"You're not getting anything," she said.

"I'm not asking you for anything. I'm just offering a ride. You just looked kinda sad."

That made Shanda pause. She hadn't had a feeling she'd bothered to name since before DCF had plucked her away the first time, years before. "What's that supposed to mean?"

"That you don't look happy."

"What's happy look like?"

The guy pointed to his face and broadened his mouth into a wide, slack-jawed smile.

"You look dumb," she said. "Does that make you happy?"

"I'm clowning with you," the guy said. "To make you smile."

Shanda had had this stuffed clown once, a present that had come from Toys for Tots. The thing was a horror prop, corpse-white with blood-red stains around its mouth and the eyes of a demon. She never bothered asking for presents again after that, because she'd rather have nothing for Christmas than nightmares.

"I don't like clowns," Shanda said.

"But do you like me?"

The guy didn't look like that demon clown. He looked like the kind of guy who'd work at the mall, selling shit from a kiosk in the hallway. Gold-plated jewelry, stuffed robotic puppies that did flips, coffee mugs printed with photos of dozens of World's Best Moms and World's Best Dads. All the kinds of things so out of reach to Shanda she'd never bothered to learn to want them, which meant she didn't know if she'd like them or not.

She shrugged.

"Seriously, when was the last time you had some fun?" he asked.

Once again, it was something she had to consider before she could answer. On TV she'd seen people run hand in hand, laughing, or ride in bumper cars or go to parties or go roller-skating, and that was what she understood of fun. The closest to Roller Magic she'd ever gotten was the parking lot, where she threw rocks at kids in her class on their way to birthday parties inside, but even when they didn't turn around to beat the shit out of her for doing so, she understood what she did on those Saturdays wasn't even in the realm of fun.

"I never had fun before," Shanda told the guy.

"Never in your whole life?" the guy said, and he smiled like she'd told a joke.

"Nope," she said. She didn't smile, because she hadn't told a joke.

For the first time the guy's features flattened out to match hers. "That sucks," he said. "What's your name?"

She realized when he asked that she had never actually introduced herself to anyone before. Teachers knew her name from rosters and social workers from case files, and the grown men she'd learned to navigate around weren't ever interested in her name.

"Shanda," she told him.

"Pete," he said.

Shanda released the brass knuckles into her pocket and felt the ten-dollar bill her mom had given her. It was meant to feed both of them, but Shanda was never really hungry for food, and she always only ever got the scraps anyway. Her mom could live another couple hours without eating, or she could get her ass off the couch and make herself something from the boxes and bags Shanda was sent out to buy when Nadia's disability checks came in, if she even remembered how to heat up water to make her own damn ramen.

"I got ten dollars," she said. "Is that enough to have any fun?"

"That's enough to have fun and go home with change. Hop on," Pete said.

Shanda stepped up onto the pegs mounted to the bike's back wheels. She'd seen other kids ride around this way, but she'd never even been on a bike before, and when it flexed and bobbled before Pete adjusted the bike to her weight, she was terrified. But still, terror was a feeling. The feeling wasn't fun, but it was at least something. She clutched his shoulders, and that was another first: reaching out to another of her own volition. If the guy was out to kill her, at least he was letting her live a little first.

Fun that day came in a bottle labeled Wild Irish Rose, and a fifth of it left Shanda with enough to buy the ribs and rice Nadia had sent her out for, only Pete had made Shanda herself eat it in order to sober her up a little before dropping her back off at home later that night. By then Nadia had called the cops, who took down Shanda's name and description as a courtesy before telling her she'd probably just run away and would probably just come back. The cops were wrong on both counts: she hadn't really run away and she also never really came back. From that day on she was with Pete, most of the time in body and all of the time in spirit. When he brought her home to his house she realized she could never bring him back to hers, because she knew where she slept at night would offend anyone who'd grown up like a civilized human. And since being in Jackie's house with all those crocheted afghans and Air Wick air freshener jellies made her feel inferior, they found other places to go: parks when it was warm enough, the mall when it wasn't, couches or floors in Pete's friends' apartments, which were almost as disgusting as the one that she'd come from. Shanda stopped going to school a few months shy of finishing the academic year, and yet somehow she still ended up on the roster of graduates. Pete took a job doing maintenance at a motel, which mostly meant unclogging the toilets the nastiest customers destroyed, and then he got her a job cleaning the rooms, which wasn't a much better gig than cleaning the toilets, but as part of their compensation they got to stay in their own unit with a minifridge and a functional hot plate. Even in their own place Pete wouldn't have sex with Shanda until she turned eighteen, not because he respected the law but because he respected her, at least that's what he told her after she told him she'd never done it before. He seemed to think that was noble of her, and she didn't correct him by telling him it was because pricks repulsed her.

But when she turned eighteen and she still didn't want it and Pete began to take that personally, she felt she had no choice but to come clean. She told him he wasn't her first, only the first she'd had any real say about. She told him about the landlord, and Pete turned so red and quaked so palpably she thought when he stormed out the door that he was disgusted enough with her to leave forever. It turned out what he really did was find the landlord, drag him down his own concrete landing to the street outside, and kick him in the mouth so hard he wouldn't have been able to talk to the police if he had the balls to go to them, and he wouldn't have after Pete made it clear what and who he was avenging. After that she still didn't really desire sex but believed she owed him hers, and after she learned to tolerate it and because she did actually love him, she told him about the lawsuit payout she'd be getting soon, twenty thousand dollars from a Rottweiler attack when she was a kid, minus lawyers' fees, held in escrow until she was what the state determined was adult enough to manage that kind of cash. She handled it by throwing a couple thousand Nadia's way and with a couple years of some really good times with Pete. He kept on building on the kind of fun he offered her on that very first afternoon, and she was at such a deficit of fun that nothing could fill her up. He turned her on to some hippie shit, big fat buds and acid and shrooms they took at clubs that played drum-and-bass tracks that would've made her lose her mind if she wasn't tripping her face off. They tried out some raves in Brooklyn and Long Island, and it was there that Shanda discovered something even better than fun, which was the absence of everything that she felt after snorting a fat rail of ketamine. Nothing in her entire life mattered down there in that K-hole—not that she'd somehow have to get herself to work tomorrow, or make up some good reason why she couldn't get to work despite living on the premises; not her fear that every time Pete was out of her sight he was taking up with some ugly girls rolling on the purest E their Fairfield County money could buy; not the handsy dads of foster care or the landlord who made giving Pete a blow job impossible without loading up first on shit wine and enough weed to knock a girl her size onto her back for hours. When she woke up the next afternoon, she crawled past Pete into the bathroom and sobbed at the memory of briefly existing in that space of nothing: first in gratitude at having discovered it, then in anger at having taken so long to discover it, then in sadness at not being in it at that very moment.

It wasn't something they could get their hands on easily outside of the New York party scene, and the New York party scene wasn't something they could access as often as Shanda wanted. Locally they had their own parties with Pete's friends and whatever they could get their hands on. They tried coke, but it just made them fight each other, and after they'd split up because of the fight, Shanda would have to fight whatever other girls tried to make a move on Pete in her absence. Pete drew a hard line against crack, and she didn't argue against his arbitrary limits because she wasn't in search of the moreness of cocaine, the way it made things and people seem to come at her even harder. She craved the opposite of more, the opposite of anything at all, the thing she'd found in that hole.

Then, one day at the motel, she walked into a room she was assigned to clean and screamed when she found a woman in the bathroom, a pile of limbs and torso on the floor instead of the usual wet towels. The woman's eyes fluttered briefly open and Shanda recognized something in them: the utter Elysium of nothing. She also recognized the plastic baggie responsible for the woman's pleasure resting against the woman's foot and shoved it into her pocket. She called the EMTs on the way out the door and left with three more bags she found in the room, two of which were untouched and one of which contained residue that Shanda instinctively understood was precious.

After her shift she returned to their room and hid the full bags. She knew that Pete wouldn't approve, but more than that she already felt protective of them, positive that they were going to change things for her in a way she didn't want Pete to interfere with. She carefully emptied the contents of the last little baggie onto the back of her left hand. The pale brown powder almost disappeared into her skin, so perfectly matched it was to her, like the whole thing was a matter of fate. There was so little of it left, which was good, because Shanda didn't know how much was too much and it had obviously been potent enough to knock that lady in room 14 on her ass. She sniffed it and waited to feel that nothing she'd been looking for since that early morning in North Babylon, but what she felt at the rave wasn't what she felt when this stuff kicked in. This stuff didn't really kick in, in fact. It didn't buck like a horse trying to get her off its back. What it did was gently caress her, first one shoulder, then the other, much like Pete did that first night on the stoop after he dropped her back off at her apartment and told her to call him, unaware that her phone had been out of service for months. But unlike the low-grade agitation that Pete's touch set off in her even after she'd grown used to it, this stuff made her feel okay. Okay was a thing Shanda had never felt in her life, which made that moment a miracle. The same old world with the same old shit was all around her, but finally it was okay. She felt a gratitude that she knew would make her cry later, but at the moment she didn't feel like crying, either. She just wanted to be.

If Pete recognized the shift in Shanda's entire experience of the world, he didn't mention it. He might've been high himself, because weed alone seemed capable of getting him to where he needed to be, or he might've just been gracious enough to accept that Shanda's existence had been elevated to a place she assumed was closer to what regular people felt all the time. Regular people, the very idea of whom up until that day used to torment Shanda. Regular people, like Pete's sister, who was pretty, who was in college, who they were supposed to have dinner with later that week while she was home from UConn. Pete told his parents he wouldn't go if he couldn't bring Shanda, and Shanda had panicked that they agreed to those terms because she didn't want to go, but that was before she discovered the secret to being okay around regular awful people.

When the day came she held off on being okay while she showered and dressed and tried to make herself look like someone who could be at a dinner table with a middle-aged Italian couple and their perfect Italian-adjacent kids, but she couldn't make her hair not puff out in the wrong places no matter how much Dep she applied, which made her hair not only puffy but greasy and flaking off white gobs of gel onto her shoulders. She couldn't remove the eyebrow piercing Pete had gotten her for her birthday a few weeks before or it would close up, and she wondered then if Pete had done it for her as a way to piss off his parents, knowing they'd have to stare at the thing over dinner all night. Her cheap Rainbow clothes didn't fit right, because clothes didn't ever fit her right—the smallest women's sizes were too baggy and the biggest kids' sizes were too short. The panic was rising, but it never flooded, because she knew that she could dam it anytime, and the time to do so was ten minutes before they left, with the last remaining tiny bits of the original bags she'd taken from room 14. The brand-new bag, which she'd secured off a kid on her old street who used to spray himself down with skank shield when they crossed paths but was more than happy to meet her face-to-face for a transaction, was tucked into her sock just in case she needed a re-up before dessert.

She thought it might've been overkill at first, or too risky, or not worth blowing something so precious at a place that didn't deserve the filter of the exquisite, but within seconds of walking into the restaurant, she felt proud of herself for having so much foresight. She'd seen this kind of thing on TV before—a host in a suit, tablecloths and candles, framed artwork of boats and fruit and other things that were to Shanda too boring to have committed to paint—but she'd only stepped foot into take-out joints decorated with flypaper and handwritten specials for things like the chicken gizzards her mother couldn't get enough of. Jackie half nodded at her when they sat down while Dom openly scowled, just as Pete said he would. Pete's sister, Drita, said, "Nice to meet you," but Shanda was suspicious of that because Pete had told her his sister didn't actually like people so much as need to be superior to them. Shanda was intrigued by the breadsticks on every table in the place, but she realized that there was no way she'd be able to get them down without choking. She didn't understand why she didn't feel okay; she'd taken the same amount of the same stuff that had been making everything okay for several weeks. Clearly she'd walked into a situation that was so potently awful it would require a little extra dosage for her to become level with it.

Everyone got wine, which nobody was carded for, and instead of taking that last little edge off, it made Shanda sloppier after the first sip. She dropped her fork and then hit the little plate that was next to her right hand onto the floor when she reached down to pick up the fork. She placed the fork back onto the table, where a waiter swooped in like a cop to remove it and set down a new one. She had enough sense to be embarrassed about it. She had enough sense to be embarrassed for being there at all, which meant she knew that she was going to have to make a trip to the bathroom soon.

But first, she decided, she had to earn it. The more she had to endure, the sweeter the reward would be. She endured Jackie's endless talking about things that nobody in the world, including anyone at their table, cared even a little about, like someone Pete and Drita had gone to high school with holding up a liquor store, and another one getting killed in an Army Jeep accident at boot camp in North Carolina, and how Bill Clinton was handsome enough but couldn't he keep it in his pants for a few years? Dom mentioned the bomb those Muslims had detonated in the World Trade Center, and said, "It's a good thing we snatched you up from those kinda people, huh?" the only words he spoke all evening. Jackie told them all to change the subject, and so Drita asked Pete how his classes at the community college were going. By the time Shanda realized what that question implied, he was lying easily and fluently about an English class he had never taken, then pivoting the same question back to Drita.

She shrugged and said classes were fine. "It's boring, you don't want to hear about it."

Shanda did kind of want to hear about it, because the more other people talked the less it mattered that she was there, and because she was curious about what it was like to go to college, an actual one with dorms and people from other places, not the local one that Pete obviously fake-attended to impress his fake-parents. UConn, to Shanda, was a basketball team people advertised on their sweatshirts, and the rest of it, like any other college, might as well have been Pluto, something that supposedly existed but had no bearing on the world she walked around in. That made Drita the equivalent of an astronaut to Shanda, which made Shanda vacillate between admiring and resenting her, which she acknowledged was an attitude she might have just adopted from Pete.

"What're you going to get?" Drita asked Shanda. The direct address instantly opened her pores. She felt her skin get slick and her hands dampen the napkin she clutched in her lap. The napkin was made of fabric, which felt like a thing of value, so it made no sense that they would give it to someone to spit and sweat and smear food into, and she felt guilty for doing just that and let it go. She replaced it with the hem of her own dress, which felt flimsy by comparison.

Shanda said, "Spaghetti."

"Why do you want to get just spaghetti? Jackie could make you spaghetti," Pete said.

He knew damn well why she was getting spaghetti: because it was the only thing on the menu she recognized.

"Even you guys can boil your own water, can't you?" Jackie said.

"We do boil our own water. Even people who don't go to college can do that much," Pete said.

"But you do go to college," Jackie said.

"Not for that," Pete said.

"Did you decide what you are going to go for?" Drita asked.

"It's not even really college," Pete said. "I'm doing the tech stuff."

"Like what?"

Pete snapped a breadstick in half and nibbled on one of the broken ends like some rodent. "Machinery."

"Machinery? Like to work in a factory? Pete, you know there's no work in the factories anymore. Scovill moved down south last year and nobody's coming to take their place," Jackie said.

"Dad could've taught you welding, if you want to work in a shop," Drita said.

"I don't want to be a welder," Pete said.

"Then what do you want to do?" Jackie asked.

"I don't know yet, Ma. I'm fine doing what I'm doing for now. Why don't you ask Drita what she's going to be if you want to hear about a kid who's not a loser."

"I don't think you're a loser, Pete," Jackie said.

"Dad does," Pete said, to which Dom nibbled on a breadstick.

"I'm paying my own way," Pete said anyway. "Just 'cause I didn't get to do what Drita got to do doesn't mean I'm gonna be knocking over liquor stores like Bobby Sawicki."

"Get to do?" Drita said.

A waiter walked over, pad in hand, then looked at Drita and retreated.

"Get to do?" she repeated.

"Like, get to go off to school," Pete said, but quieter than he was with Jackie.

"You think someone invited me? I applied. I filled out an application, that was it. It's not like it's some great privilege."

"You know what they would've done with my application," Pete said.

"They would've looked at all the shit grades and suspensions you got and said no," Drita said. "But that's on you. Not fucking up all the time wasn't something I 'got' to do, it was just something I did."

"Kids, enough," Jackie said.

"Trust me, I'll be getting farther away from here than UConn when I'm done," Drita said.

"Why don't you just go now? It's not like you really give a shit about anybody at this table."

"You think I don't give a shit about you because I stopped cleaning up your messes? How about I stopped cleaning up your messes *because* I give a shit about you?"

"You never gave enough of a shit to step in when Dad basically implied I want to blow up the World Trade Center."

"That's not what he said."

"You're supposed to be the smart one, and you can't read between the lines?"

"You just want to outsource all your problems to other people, Pete. Stop being such a victim. You didn't grow up in an orphanage. You had a good home, which is more than a lot of people around here can say."

Shanda didn't raise her eyes to check if Drita was looking at her. If she was, she didn't want to know whether it was in pity or in contempt.

"Drita and Pete, stop it. People are looking. We're here for a nice dinner, let's just have a nice dinner," Jackie said. "Where'd that waiter go?"

"I have to use the lav," Shanda said to no one in particular, in a language she hadn't used since elementary school.

"I'll order the spaghetti for you," Drita said.

Shanda was about to thank her when Pete said, "Don't be a bitch, Drita."

"You're the one who started this whole thing by calling her out for wanting spaghetti," Drita said.

It was the last thing Shanda heard before she sped into the bathroom, wondering first whether it was Pete or Drita who'd just insulted her and then understanding it was Pete *and* Drita who'd just insulted her. That was obviously the whole reason Pete had wanted her to come along, just so he could look superior to someone at dinner. At least he knew what the hell veal scallopini was. At least Drita saw her brother wasn't the biggest piece of shit at the table. Her stomach ached with the kind of pang she knew from experience wasn't from hunger, despite the days that she would sometimes go without real food, and she made herself sit with it on the toilet for a good two minutes before she flopped off her shoe and reached for the baggie in her sock. The release was better the tighter the hard knot in her belly was to begin with. When the knot threatened to rise up to her throat, she opened the bag and poured a little bump onto her fist, then remembered that the little bump she took before they left the motel room hadn't done much and so poured a little more. She sniffed it, shoved her foot back into the shoe, flushed the toilet, and walked back to her seat before the effects fully kicked in, just to ensure she'd make it there cleanly without arousing suspicion.

And then it did what she was afraid it wouldn't do: it made whatever suspicion she aroused irrelevant. Drita told Shanda she'd ordered her meatballs with the spaghetti and hoped that was okay, and Shanda found she couldn't form the words to say it was fine, so she nodded slowly instead and smiled the broadest smile she'd ever managed to bring to her face. Bobbing her head up and down felt incredible, and she understood then why babies love being swaddled and rocked, and since she was certain she'd never been swaddled and rocked as a baby she continued doing it for herself at the table to make up for all that lost time. All that lost time! She couldn't be sad about it, but she'd never been more aware of it. All the joy she'd missed out on while Nadia feasted herself into stupors, while scurrying roaches kept her from sleep, while kids in her neighborhood found answers to their own wrecked homes with each other and by taking their rage out on her—the joy had been simply delayed, not stolen. It had been put in safes in some hidden corner of Shanda's mind, and she'd finally found the key to accessing it. The treasure that the key in her sock unlocked was even better than the ones that had come before, and her heart surged with the possibility that there might be even greater treasures in store for her. She scanned the room and for the first time was the giver and not the receiver of pity, because nobody in that space understood what pure joy was. Nobody at the table understood. They all looked at her as if they had questions, and they perhaps even asked the questions, but they weren't the right questions. She listened, but nobody asked: How? She listened harder, and all she heard was: Is she all right? The poor people, she thought. Poor Pete. Poor Drita, who'd leaned over to Shanda and felt her forehead. Shanda watched Drita do it and waited to feel her make contact, but the sensation never came, and Shanda realized it was because she was no longer with them. She was in a warm glass box safe from their voices and their touch, and she was sorry for Pete, who waved his hand with what her old, broken mind would have understood as panic. She was sorry for not being able to free him with her but found that if she closed her eyes she didn't have to be sorry, because he was no longer there. In the gray of her new warm space, she could be selfish with her happiness, she could ingest it all herself, and she was famished, and she took it all.

13

DRITA SAT AT A PATIO SET ACROSS FROM JACKIE, WHO COULDN'T look away from Dakota long enough to see her daughter staring at her.

"So I've been thinking about, you know, maybe making a change," Drita said.

"Oh yeah, honey? Tough day at work?"

Drita slumped on the cushioned seat, still damp from an afternoon shower that reminded her it was too cold, even in April, to be sitting outside. But outside was where Dakota sat on his bicycle, too terrified to lift his feet from the ground even with training wheels to keep him upright, and wherever Dakota was, Jackie wanted to be.

"A regular day at work. Just, I don't know, a weird couple of weeks outside of it."

"It's a lot having a kid around if you're not used to it. It's so great you were able to take him in, though," Jackie said. "I think it's gonna be so good for Dakota to be around family again."

"Yeah, well, I'm not really the family who's supposed to be with him. Anyway, I don't know how much longer I'll be here."

"Oh?" Jackie said, taking her eyes off Dakota at last to look at her daughter. "What are you thinking about doing?"

"I'm not sure yet," Drita said. "I'm thinking maybe some volunteer work. Like with some aid group or something. I've been researching some options." Her emails with Valon felt adjacent enough to research for it to not be a wholesale lie, even if "aid work" was stretching the limits of truth. The work Valon was doing wasn't exactly the Key Club. It wasn't the Peace Corps. It was the opposite of that. It was a war, and not the metaphorical wars of the NGOs that tacked informational flyers to the corkboards back at Columbia: wars on malaria, wars on poverty, wars on people shitting into ditches that leached into potable water sources, even if the color photographs of babies wading in those tainted rivers generated the most zeros on the checks the guilty faraway others wrote to the cause. Those were the things she and Isaac used to talk about getting involved with, in a way she now thought of as naïve. Those were all selfish objectives, ways for them to feel necessary to an otherwise indifferent world.

Jackie smacked her hands on the glass tabletop, and the snap of it brought Drita's attention fully back to the dreary moment. "That's fantastic, honey," Jackie said. "That's exactly the kind of thing you wanted to do before you ended up back here. I wish you would've seen that through."

"It's not like I chose not to go, Ma. Pa died and you got sick."

"And Dom's still dead and I'm not sick anymore."

"You don't know, it might happen again. Blood clots can happen to people with spinal injuries, you know that."

"Yes, and you know that because you're a nurse, which means that you know there are other professional people who can step in if it happens again. I never asked you to put everything on hold for me."

The headache that had started with her first patient's blaring of *The Price Is Right* at max volume and followed her through every subsequent stop compacted and moved into the space behind Drita's right eye. She pressed on it until she saw white, and used the split second of relief she found to answer Jackie without losing her composure.

"You didn't have to ask. People who need help shouldn't have to ask."

"I'm not saying I haven't appreciated you being around, Drita. You know I love the company. It's just that, I don't know, you should've maybe asked about my needs before you assumed anything. I'm a grown woman, you know."

Drita looked at Jackie with a disbelief that Jackie didn't catch, her eyes still trained on her grandson.

Jackie sighed. "I just don't want you to get stuck, you know? If there's one thing I wanted you to learn from me, it was how to not get stuck."

"That was what you wanted us to learn from you? You and Pa were miserable together, and you stayed put until he was dead. You're still stuck in this house. How was that showing us how not to get stuck?"

"I hoped you'd see why you shouldn't let it happen to you," Jackie said, with a hard edge Drita rarely heard from her. "Me and Dom, it might not have been the Cleavers, but there was an agreement, there was some mutual benefit. It's not like I could get up and run off toward what I wanted."

"I know it wouldn't have been easy for you, Ma, but I never saw being in a wheelchair stop you from doing what other people did," Drita said.

"It wasn't just the wheelchair. Things were different in my day. And yes, I did exactly what other people did and that was the problem. That's the thing I didn't want for you. I didn't want you to turn out like this."

Drita had been close to apologizing for pushing whatever button triggered the rise in Jackie's volume. But that last sentence had a meanness to it that Drita almost missed, until it landed hard and replayed itself in her head.

"Turn out like what? What's wrong with how I turned out?" Drita asked.

"Nothing, Drita, you're fine. I'm sorry."

"No, really, I'd love to hear your take on this."

Jackie kept silent.

"Come on. I'd love to learn what's making me miserable, other than being stuck in this place where I have no friends and no future and now a small child living in my small apartment."

"That's exactly it, Drita. It's nice you want to help, but you can't fix everything."

"Oh my god, Ma, you were literally dying in the hospital. Shanda and Dakota were literally going to be out on the street. Would you rather I just have fuck-offed like Pete? How am I the asshole here?"

"You're not an asshole," Jackie said. "It's just, it's not good for you. And it doesn't really fix anything for anybody else, either. It didn't help Pete. It always just made him feel like he was never good enough for you."

"Oh, I see, so he abandoned his kid because I made him feel bad about himself. Okay, got it."

"That's not what I meant, Drita. Pete's issues are his. It's just, it's more complicated than that. You just can't understand everything about it. He's not a bad guy, he just . . . I think he feels things a little too much and he doesn't know how to cope with it. It's just his nature."

"His nature? He's my brother, we literally have the same nature."

"No," Jackie said. "You don't. You're very different."

"What if we're not as different as you think?" Drita said. "What if I told you he's actually out trying to fix something that has nothing to do with him instead of the things that have a hundred percent to do with him?"

"All right now, Drita, let's calm down. I didn't mean to get you upset."

"What if I told you I know where he is?"

It was a question Jackie apparently didn't want to answer, because she gave no response even as her jaw hung slack.

"I mean, generally where he is. Or at least what he's up to."

"What are you trying to get at, Drita?" Jackie finally said.

"You watch the news, right? You know about what's happening in Kosovo?"

"Don't try to change the subject now."

"I'm not," Drita insisted. "I'm getting to it. You know that it's Albanians who live in Kosovo, even though it became part of Yugoslavia after World War Two?"

"Why would I know any of that?"

"Well, it is. And you know how the Serbs killed all those Bosnians a couple of years ago? Well, now they're doing it to Albanians in Kosovo."

"I don't understand what this has to do with Pete."

"I'm getting there. Pete's signed himself up to be a hero to those people in Kosovo."

Jackie leaned forward and squinted sideways at Drita, as if her daughter had informed her that her son had recently colonized Mars.

"What do you mean, help the people in Kosovo?" Jackie asked suspiciously. "Did he join the army or something?"

"Not really. I mean, not the U.S. Army."

"I don't understand, Drita. What does that mean?" Jackie said.

"It means what it sounds like it means. He's going to join an army, or a kind-of-army, that Kosovars formed to fight against the Serbs."

"What?" Jackie yelled. She noticed Dakota gawking at her after her outburst, and she lowered her voice to a near-whisper. "What," Jackie said. "It just doesn't make any sense."

"Nope, it doesn't. But I guess I should stop trying to track him down and fix him, right, because that's my fatal flaw."

"No, Drita, no," Jackie said. She stared at Dakota, who stared directly back from the bottom step of the porch.

"Grandma Jackie, what's the matter?" he called, too nervous to approach farther and yet somehow aware it was inappropriate for him to continue playing, if that's what pacing in a driveway with a bicycle could be called.

"You have to talk him out of it. It's stupid and it's dangerous and he has a son," Jackie said.

"I know these things," Drita said, a little less sharply, on account of Dakota's presence and the slickness that glazed Jackie's eyes. "And I'm trying to."

"Someone must have recruited him. They must have talked him into it," Jackie said.

"What does it matter? You were just saying that all the things I ever tried to talk Pete into or out of made no difference at all."

"It matters here," Jackie said. "That isn't who Pete is."

"Wanting to play tough guy and leaving me to take care of his messes while he gets to screw around? I don't know, it kind of tracks."

"No, it's not Pete. I'm saying it's not Pete."

"There's a lot about Pete you never wanted to believe was true," Drita said.

"But no, this isn't true," Jackie said. The glaze that had coated her eyes spilled over. "Oh, god, this is never what I meant to happen. I never would've done it if I knew this could happen."

"Ma, what are you talking about? Nobody could know this would happen."

"It was supposed to make everything easier," she said. She wrapped a tuft of her hair in her hands and pulled so hard that it alarmed Dakota, who they'd both forgotten was watching.

"Grandma?" he called.

"I'm so stupid! So, so stupid!" Jackie wailed.

"Ma?" Drita said, in the same uncertain timbre as Dakota.

"I'm so sorry, Drita," Jackie said.

Drita shook her head, reluctant now to provoke more.

"Pete's not what we told you he is. He's not like you. He's not one of them. I just wanted to make things easier for you two." Jackie ran her sleeve across her nose. "I didn't mean to make more trouble. I was trying to make untrouble."

14

1972

JACKIE CONTINUED HER ADOPTION SEARCH IN THE PLACE SHE
should have began it: in the yellow pages. She didn't bother calling
two of the three listings—the Catholic Hope Charities and the Connecticut State Welfare Department, assuming the former would be as
dismissive of Jackie's condition as Father Michael had been, and knowing that the latter would likely only offer older kids snatched up by the
state and already ravaged by whatever life had thrown at them. It's not
that she didn't feel bad for those kids, but she felt bad for herself, too,
and she couldn't manage a house full of pitiable souls. The third one
was called Family Match of New Haven County, a name that sounded
promising by being both secular and not obviously bureaucratic.
Jackie later wished she'd remembered the name of the woman who
she spoke with there, because without her nothing that happened afterwards would've happened, and for that the woman deserved a card
at the very least, and perhaps even the middle name of the daughter
Jackie would eventually land.

The conversation went well at the beginning, as Jackie fished for
information that the woman fed to her. They worked mostly with
unwed mothers, placing newborns that the young women had already

chosen to give up. The babies were delivered, the documents signed, the paperwork made official in the courts, and a family was made. There were fees to the agency, of course, and adoptive parents were responsible for the medical and living expenses of the birth mother, which could add up to quite a lot. Jackie told the woman she understood and had the money, and though the woman did not articulate relief, Jackie sensed it in her breath, the quick exhalation before she moved on to the next bit of information.

"The birth mother generally meets with prospective parents during her pregnancy and decides on the best fit," the woman said.

"Ah," Jackie said, doing her best to not convey deflation. She knew that most women wouldn't choose a paraplegic for their baby if there was a line queuing up for it, and that gave her some pause. It would be an uphill battle, maybe, but a battle that could be won. There were other things that might win a young lady over—the girl's desperation, for instance, perhaps the most powerful tool at Jackie's disposal, though not necessarily the one she should go for first. The girl could be Italian, and want her baby to end up with other Italians. A knocked-up, hard-up girl probably didn't come from money, and Jackie didn't come from money, either, but now had it, which might make her inspirational. In any case, she could practice and turn on the charm, or whatever it was she'd have to turn on to get what she wanted.

But then the woman interrupted Jackie's strategizing. "We also do extensive interviews with applicants and home visits to ensure we're placing children with stable, loving families."

A knocked-up fifteen-year-old might not know from stable, loving families, but adults who made their living from them certainly would.

"Of course," Jackie said. "Of course you would do that. I mean you should do that."

"I take it you're married?" the woman asked.

"Oh yes, of course. Love of my life," Jackie said.

"How long have you been married?"

"Oh, let me think," Jackie said. She sensed things going off course, all because of the idiot, irrelevant facts that she couldn't do anything about. "It's been about a year now."

"A year. Newlyweds, then," the woman said. Her tone gave away nothing.

"No, not really. We grew up together and always knew we'd end up together." She told herself it wasn't technically a lie, because it was essentially fate that she'd ended up with Dom, or if not him, just another version of him.

"And you've already decided that adoption is the path you want to pursue?"

Jackie inhaled deeply, straight into the receiver. She knew people adored tragedies, and if these people would be doing a home visit and would see her wheelchair with their own eyes, then she'd have to appeal to their sense of guilt instead of reason. "Well," Jackie said sadly, "I'm afraid we have no other choice. We . . . we can't have our own children. And we so desperately want them."

"I understand, and I'm very sorry to hear that, though adoption is such a wonderful alternative. Believe me, the parents we work with are so grateful to have found their family matches that I truly believe it makes them love their children even more."

"I would, oh, I really would," Jackie said.

"I can hear that in your voice," the woman said. "And I'd love for you and your husband to come in and meet with us so that you can see if you think we're the right fit for you as well."

The woman had to know that they were the only possible fit of the three entries in the yellow pages, and Jackie would bet that was as true for everyone else who contacted them as it was for her. But everyone else probably wasn't in a wheelchair, one that Jackie was doubtful she'd even be able to convince Dom to push her into the Family Match office in. The woman seemed so nice, though, so earnest, so willing to help, that Jackie almost felt sorry for putting her in a position to face her impending wrath.

"We would love to do that," Jackie said. "But I should tell you that the reason I can't have children is because I was in a terrible accident a year ago. I'm lucky to be alive, and I thank God every day that I am." It wasn't an obviously religious agency, but it seemed strategic to adopt piety when attempting to convince strangers of your decency in as short a time as possible. She sighed again, just short of what an actor might get away with on a stage. "I lost my baby in the accident."

"Oh goodness, I'm so very sorry," the woman gasped.

"Thank you," Jackie said. "And I lost my ability to have more children. And I lost my ability to walk. My spine was broken and it means that I now get around in a wheelchair."

"Oh my," the woman said, just barely, as if on the verge of tears.

"But I've gone through months of rehabilitation. I've gotten very good at navigating in my chair." She figured she could make that true before a home visit. "And I'm as good as ever from the waist up. In fact, I often care for my cousins' children, and they don't even seem to notice that I'm in a wheelchair. And my husband is one hundred percent normal, just as healthy as can be."

Jackie was keen enough to be troubled by the woman's silence.

"So shall we schedule an appointment?" Jackie asked.

"It's just," the woman began. "I have no doubt that you'd be a wonderful mother. My sister is in a wheelchair, and I know that she's as whole a person as she could be."

"That's wonderful," Jackie said.

"And it breaks my heart to think that she could be denied the opportunity for motherhood. It really does. But to be honest—and this is not a policy I agree with, it's just because we're subject to state regulations and oversight and so forth—I just don't think our caseworkers would find your family suitable for caring for a newborn."

"Oh," Jackie said. It was just a syllable meant to be a placeholder for the anger and disappointment she had every intention of conveying bluntly to the woman, but before she could form the words, the woman interrupted.

"It's unfair. I think it's truly— Well, it's discrimination, if you ask me. But nobody's asked me. But," the woman said, in a register up from the sad, low tone she'd been using in the previous few moments, which gave Jackie a bit of hope.

"But?" Jackie said.

"I have the names of some people who deal in private adoptions." The woman was speaking lower now, almost whispering. "We're not supposed to refer people to these kinds of individuals, because they're not necessarily licensed in the same way we are. But it's not necessarily illegal, either, technically, so don't worry about that."

"Oh?" Jackie said.

"They're just kind of . . . brokers, I guess. They have more flexibility in who they place with. They also cost a lot more money," the woman said.

"I have money," Jackie responded.

"Would you like some names?"

"I would," Jackie said.

After Jackie took down the information, she found herself saying something to the woman that she was surprised to hear, especially as honestly as it came out.

"God bless you," Jackie told the woman.

"God bless you, too," the woman said.

The attorney didn't ask where Jackie's husband was, so she didn't have to explain that Dom was waiting in the car, wasting gas keeping the engine and heater running so that he wouldn't have to pay for a parking garage. That was Dom's story, though the real one was that he didn't want anything to do with this whole baby business, which was all the same to Jackie. A baby grown from another seed was a bit of a genetic crapshoot, but at least it would have a chance to not inherit Dom's weak chin or his family's predisposition to heart problems or his slack-jawed mouth breathing when he watched crappy Westerns all Saturday afternoon.

The attorney wouldn't be able to guarantee a baby that would grow up to breathe with its mouth closed, but at least he asked about preferences. Race, gender, age, that kind of thing. Jackie told him boy or girl, under a year, white.

"How white?" the attorney asked.

"What do you mean?" Jackie asked.

"Do you mean not Black, or do you mean European?" he asked.

Jackie hesitated. "We want a baby who, you know, looks like us."

"I understand," the attorney said. "You're Italian, correct?"

"Yes," Jackie said.

"And you're darker-complexioned."

"I suppose."

"I'm just wondering if you might be open to a child from Latin America, say, or a child perhaps more racially ambiguous."

Jackie took a sip from the water the attorney's secretary had brought in. She hoped in that time that he might read between the lines, but after a few more swallows he seemed to be still awaiting her reply, the tip of his pen resting on his legal pad, ready to record her answer.

"Well, I'm not a bigot," Jackie said.

"Of course not," he said.

"I suppose," Jackie started.

He nodded. The prick was going to make her come out and say it.

"My husband wouldn't be comfortable raising a child of another race."

The attorney nodded. "Of course. I understand. I assume you'll be telling the child, eventually, that it's adopted? On account of your— your condition."

"Well actually, paraplegia doesn't make a woman incapable of getting pregnant," Jackie said, more defensively than she meant to.

"I see," said the attorney, though he clearly didn't.

"But in my particular case, because I was with child when I had the accident, there was a lot of—" She felt her cheeks begin to redden. It felt imprudent to talk biology with this stranger, particularly her own personal biology. "The doctor just said that I wouldn't be able to carry to term." She didn't add that both she and Dom seemed horrified by the prospect of intercourse with each other, a condition that they were almost certainly heading toward before the wreck and that her injuries only accelerated.

"I'm so very sorry to hear that. I certainly hope you received some compensation for your suffering," the attorney said.

Fishing for clients, even as he had one in the office. No wonder there were so many jokes about lawyers at her family dinners—it wasn't just about them being jealous of the lawyer Cadillacs they all drove.

"I did," Jackie said. "Thank you for your concern."

"I'm glad to hear that. Listen, I'll be honest with you: matching potential adoptive parents with a child outside of the typical channels can be very expensive."

"I understand that," Jackie said.

"And it can also take a very long time. And the more narrow your search criteria, the longer and more expensive it can be. The days of young girls being sent off to homes for unwed mothers are ending, what with the rise of birth control. To be blunt, there are more Americans who want to adopt than there are children to be adopted."

"I can wait," Jackie said. If she had to wait, she would, but she could feel the knot of anticipation forming in her stomach already, just above where sensation stopped altogether.

"That's good, because in time, I'm confident we'll be able to find just the right match for you."

Jackie nodded. "Thank you."

"I would just urge you to be open-minded, and open-hearted," he continued.

"I have plenty of money," Jackie said.

"Mrs. DiMeo," the attorney said. He rounded the desk to take the seat next to Jackie's, pulling her hand from her lap and holding it in his own as he talked down at her. Not since she was a schoolgirl had she been in such a position, and like when she was a schoolgirl, she

tolerated it because this man had some authority that she could benefit from, whether or not he deserved the respect. "We don't have to talk
numbers just yet. Let's begin with what I like to call the 'matchmaking
process' first and see if we can't find you a baby you'll love just as much
as your very own."

The repugnance of this man was what made Jackie believe that he
would be the one to come through for her. She understood that someone so clearly interested in his own bottom line, unlike the priest or
the kind of agency that advertised in the yellow pages, would ensure
that he met it one way or another.

"I do so appreciate you taking the time to meet with me today, and
for being so compassionate about my situation," Jackie said. She smiled
a smile that, before the accident, might have been read as flirting,
though she wasn't convinced that the attorney even saw her as a
woman.

"The pleasure has been all mine," he said. "I look forward to working with you in these coming days."

When the attorney said days, what he meant was months. Jackie would
call and he would avoid the call, or he would return it with some leads
on exactly the kind of baby she had explicitly told him she wasn't interested in.

"The mother is a very pretty girl, clean, healthy, has a good head on
her shoulders," he'd say.

"What's her background?"

"Oh, the typical story. Young, underprivileged. Her parents were
from Haiti. She speaks fluent French."

She managed some patience in the first two months, and sprinkled
in some anxiety and uncertainty in the next three, and after that gave
herself over to the same utter despair she'd felt in her first months out
of rehab, before the settlement money had come and the ramps and
support bars had been installed in the house and she'd convinced her-

self to replace thoughts of Antonella with the plan to become the dot-
ing mother to a newborn foundling that needed her as much as she
needed it. Without one of the two, what on earth did she have?

She became convinced hope was a thing installed in her just so that
God could have a good laugh snatching it away. God had told everyone exactly who He was in the Old Testament, and still people tried so
desperately to please Him? She was no Job, she wasn't going to keep
praising a God who'd taken everything from her just to prove His own
stupid point. Honestly, the God she'd been instructed to worship since
she could mouth the word *amen* was just like half the boys in the
neighborhood—He needed constant reassurance of His greatness,
when if He was actually great He wouldn't need to puff Himself up
with so much praise, like a second grader starved for attention.

If He was all-knowing, He could just go right into Jackie's mind and
know how she cursed at Him. But since she no longer believed He was,
she wheeled herself to the living room, where a cross Jackie's mother
had embroidered for her while she was in the ICU hung above the
sofa, and screamed: "You want my praise, you sonofabitch? Do something to earn it, why doncha?"

The cross dropped from the wall, bounced off the back of the sofa,
and landed on the coffee table, where it nudged off a *Redbook* that
Jackie had been lazily flipping through. The magazine spilled to the
floor, open and facedown, and when Jackie picked it up, a perfect, serene infant stared back at her, along with a coupon for twenty-five
cents off baby-shaped Kimbies diapers.

Instinctively, Jackie very nearly enacted the sign of the cross. She'd
been trained to never ignore signs, and signs could be anything from
the first robin of spring shitting on a car windshield to the visage of
Mary appearing in a tub of Country Crock. This one was so overt that
she looked over her shoulder to check if a camera had been planted,
because it could just be that she'd been set up on *Candid Camera*. She
was alone, though, and for a moment that made her afraid: she was
alone with an angry God, and not even in a position to run away. That

realization reminded her that she need not fear an angry God, because what more was He going to do to her, smite a husband she didn't care that much to see? Kill her, as if she hadn't considered taking care of that herself?

"Big whoop, an advertisement. All-powerful enough to send me a coupon for some diapers I don't need. Try a little harder next time," she said and wheeled herself away.

There were no more messages as obnoxious as that first one, but in the following days Jackie took notice of a few more celestial winks. The batteries on the clicker Dom bought when he replaced the TV with a bigger, more expensive one died just as he tried to steer the channel away from news of the Yankees losing, for example. A neighbor's cat giving birth under their porch to five little kittens, which Jackie wouldn't let Dom shoo away.

Every little sign convinced Jackie that God was actually with her, and that He was pathetically impotent, pulling off these sad little magic tricks like a third-rate act at a lunchtime show at the Ramada. She still despaired about what she didn't have, but she felt a little satisfied knowing her conclusions about God had been spot-on, meaning she knew something that millions of people the world over didn't.

"Sad," Jackie said aloud to the cross that Dom had rehung. "Just sad."

When the phone rang minutes later, she half expected it to be God Himself, sniveling that she shouldn't talk to Him like that. Instead it was the attorney.

"There's a case I think you might be interested in learning about," he said. He barely bothered with a greeting, which was normally what he spent the first six minutes of a phone call on—catching up, well-wishing, excuse-making, all the things meant to soften the blow of the coming disappointment.

Immediately Jackie's hand began trembling. "Oh?" she said, not daring to say more.

"There's an expectant young woman a social worker just brought to our attention. Local case, very sad situation. First kid, no money, husband was killed in a hold-up. Absolutely desperate. Speaks no English," he said.

"Oh," Jackie said. Another Dominican baby, maybe Chinese.

"But listen, no, she's from one of those hard-up countries in the Balkans, one of those closed-off Communist places. Albania, you heard of it?"

"Sure," Jackie said, though she wasn't sure if she had. She'd heard of countries that started with *A* and ended in *-ia,* but it didn't matter, she could look it up in an encyclopedia later. What she cared about was: local, Europe, desperate.

"Anyway, she came over here with her husband, brought over by some of his cousins—there's a little community of them starting up here—but she's got no prospects, no money, no paperwork, not even a visa. She's going to get sent back soon as she delivers this kid, and she's got no kind of life in Albania for a kid to go back to. That's what the translator says she says."

"That sounds . . . that sounds wonderful," Jackie said. She looked at the cross, fearing it might fall again.

"So one little thing is, it's close to Italy, Albania, but it's— Well, it's not like Italy. It's more, uh, let's say less advanced. It's fairly third-world, I'd say. And it's more, well, Mediterranean, more Turkish than Italian, let's say."

"I don't know what that means," Jackie said.

"The woman's going to look a little different. The family was Moslem, and she wears, you know, a scarf and that kind of thing. But take off the scarf, put her in some clothes from JCPenney, you'd swear she was Italian."

The cross stayed where it was. Not a flutter.

"Anyway, if you're interested, I'll need you to come by and we can continue our discussion in person. Can you come tomorrow, say three o'clock?"

Dom would be working, and her mother didn't approve of Jackie's work with the lawyer and vowed to not lift a finger to help her. But

she'd get there, one way or another. She had what she might call faith
that it would happen.

"Of course," Jackie said. "Absolutely."

She didn't have time to get to the encyclopedia to look up Albania
before a knock came at the door. She thought it'd somehow be the attorney, who zoomed up in his attorney Cadillac to tell her something
too sensitive to mention on the phone, maybe about some deformity
the Albanian had or a further increase in his fees.

But when she opened the door it wasn't the attorney. It was a face
she knew by heart, one she still conjured in her most self-pitying moments, despite not having seen it in upwards of a year.

"Antonella?" Jackie said.

"Hi, Jackie," Antonella said.

Then Jackie drew her head down to her eye level and found that the
body Antonella had brought herself here on wasn't at all familiar. It
was brand-new, at least eight months of baby filling up that belly.

Jackie turned to her mother's ugly cross-stitched cross. "You son of a
bitch, you did it," she said.

15

DRITA LOOKED IN THE REARVIEW MIRROR AS DAKOTA STARED DOWN at his Game Boy in the backseat. Somehow he ended up with her even after she turned him away that day back in New York, and she wasn't going to repeat that mistake. Maybe if she hadn't literally closed the door on people when they showed up, she wouldn't have had to spend so much time alone. Maybe she just had to be more flexible in what she expected from people.

"Aunt Drita, where are we going?" Dakota asked, when he finally looked up and realized he was on unfamiliar streets.

"Roller Magic, kiddo," Drita said.

"What's Roller Magic?"

"It's a roller-skating rink. We're going to go roller-skating."

"Why?"

"Because it's fun." Dakota's face suggested he had no idea how that answered his question, but Drita had already shifted the car into park and unbuckled her seatbelt and motioned at Dakota to do the same.

"Aunt Drita, I don't know how to roller-skate," Dakota said. He still hadn't unbuckled himself, so Drita opened the back door and did it for him, a little too aggressively, based on the grimace on his little scrunched-up face.

"Ow," he said.

"Nobody knows how to roller-skate until they learn. Except your father. Your father could do anything on wheels, almost better than he could use his feet alone. It was kind of weird. It's not like an instinct anybody should have, you know? It's not like wheels exist in nature. No, don't take the Game Boy. Leave it in here."

Dakota's huge eyes scanned the perimeter of the chain link as if doubtful he were in a place where fun could be had, but he let Drita lead him toward the concrete pillars that Drita remembered as the portal to another land.

"But it's not like nature always nails it. Nature messes a lot of things up, and sometimes humans make it better and sometimes we make it worse. Wheels are probably an improvement over nature most of the time, at least if you're trying to outrun something, right? I mean you go way faster. But you know, I was never that good on skates, not like your father. Of course now that makes total sense."

Drita looked down at Dakota. Nothing she was saying made sense to him, that was clear. She knew that if one of her patients were raving to a child the way she was at that moment she'd likely attribute it to a manic episode, despite not having the credentials to diagnose anyone with anything, only to distribute the meds that other people pre-scribed. Since she realized with such clarity at that moment how little she'd really understood about most things most of her life, she figured there was no point in stopping herself from behaving madly. Maybe it was cathartic. Maybe her patients were onto something instead of just on something.

"One adult and one child, please," Drita told the ticket guy sitting inside the booth, as if he couldn't see with his own eyes the adult and the child in front of him. But what did he really see? A mother and her child? A babysitter and her keep? Surely he didn't see the truth, be-cause even Drita didn't see before that afternoon that they were simply two entities briefly existing parallel to each other. They were nothing. She was not his aunt, because his father was not her brother.

No, of course the ticket guy didn't see that. The ticket guy, like everyone else, didn't care anyway.

So why did she? Nothing materially had changed about her life since learning that she and Pete weren't twins, weren't even kin, weren't anything but abandoned souls made to board together. They shared nothing except for parents who also weren't their parents. She should have felt relief, knowing now that Pete's nature was inscrutable to her because they didn't actually share one. She shared her nature with no living thing she'd ever met, in fact, which explained why everyone seemed as inscrutable to her as Pete did. She should have been feeling better than ever, since knowledge was supposed to lead to peace or something like that. She could not nail down why she felt more acutely sad than at any previous moment she could recall.

She also couldn't recall walking herself and Dakota to the skate rental counter, but there they were, and that snapped her attention back to the task at hand. Fun. She was going to travel back to a time when she was still capable of having fun, when she had a brother who could lead the way. Maybe Pete was onto something, and feeling good was a better short-term goal than a long-term one. She used to enjoy roller-skating, even if she never managed to learn to go backwards or use the stoppers properly. She even got asked to slow-skate on Michael Jackson Day, to the song "Human Nature," which now struck her as ironic, given how little she understood of human nature then or now. She got felt up beneath her bra for the first time squeezed in tight beside the Galaga machine, and when Pete found out about it, despite Drita insisting that she had been okay with it, he dragged the guy to the bathroom and punched him in the mouth, all while on rental skates with laces so old they'd disintegrated when he tried to tie them. They never got the chance to enter their final pushcart race, which they'd been practicing for on the abandoned tennis courts in the park, but it was still one of the most thrilling days of Drita's life, which she knew was sad but that still obviously inclined her to return to this place, which hadn't changed at all in fifteen years. There'd be no one to make out with today, since the only options were preadolescents or the dads who dropped them off before fleeing to Mr. Happy's for a few hours, and Pete wasn't around to defend an honor she'd let go of long ago, but she was seeking comfort from something she rarely let herself feel, never mind get pleasure from: nostalgia. A time and a place where she was part of a family, in a community, mouthing every word to whatever Debbie Deb track was blaring through the speakers that Saturday afternoon, back when she imagined having to warn every weekend to look out for her.

"What size?" the girl behind the counter asked.

"Eight," Drita said.

"What about him?"

"Him? Oh, him. Dakota, what size skate do you wear?"

Dakota's giant eyes lolled toward the floor. "I don't know. I told you I don't know how to skate."

"And I told you you're not supposed to know how to skate yet. I'm going to show you. And your skate size is just the same size as your shoe. What size are your shoes?"

"Aunt Drita, I don't know," he whined.

Drita sighed and knelt down. "Take off your shoes."

Dakota looked panicked. It was like he thought he should be prepared to run at all times.

"It's okay, dude, they're going to hang on to them while we have their skates. They're not going to steal them."

He dropped down to his butt but didn't move to take off his shoes, so Drita unvelcroed them herself. She tried to pull the sneakers from his feet, but he kept his toes flexed and rigid and though he avoided her gaze, Drita swore she recognized defiance in his eyes.

"Dakota, why are you fighting me? We're here to have fun," Drita said.

"Why?" he asked.

"Why are we going to have fun?"

"Yes, why are we going to have fun?"

Drita finally wrested the kicks off his feet, pulling with them both of his socks. "Because little boys and girls halfway across the world don't get to roller-skate and have fun. Little boys and girls halfway across the world are fleeing armies in the back of donkey carts. That's if they're lucky. If they're not lucky, I won't tell you what happens to them."

Dakota turned toward the rental counter girl, who cared little for the drama playing out on ground level and began assisting some pre-teens who wouldn't waste her time.

"Is that not a good answer? How about because I want you to have some memories you can look back on when life gets crappy and you need something to convince you to keep going."

She pulled his socks back on, checked the soles of his sneakers, and yelled "Five" to the counter girl.

"Or how about because having fun is the fun aunt's job. You re-member going to the mall, getting that Happy Meal? Wasn't that fun? Have you ever not had fun with me?"

Finally Dakota looked at her as if he pitied her.

"What is it, Dakota?"

He shook his head.

"No what?"

"No, I'm not having fun. I don't want to roller-skate. I want to play my game."

"You haven't even tried roller-skating. You can play your game any day of the week."

"I like my game best," he said.

"How do you know you won't like roller-skating if you haven't tried it?"

"Because I do."

"Do you not think I want to do what's best for you? Do you not trust me, Dakota?"

Dakota shook his head slowly, letting big fat drops spill down his face like it broke his heart to tell her so. "No," he said.

Drita dropped her ass to the ground and her head into her hands, because it broke her heart to hear it. She was no better than Jackie, making up stories and trying to fit other people into them. Look at the outcome of that: three generations of people who shared nothing except for feeling sorrow in tandem.

Dakota stopped crying in a few minutes, and Drita followed, not because she felt ready to but because it signaled to her that he was ready to move on, and she'd already kept him against his will long enough to register as endangerment. She scooted closer to him and asked the girl at the counter for their shoes back. The counter girl, obviously embarrassed for her, pulled them out of their cubbies without making eye contact.

"I was just trying to do something nice for you," Drita said to Dakota, once they were soled and on their feet again. "It was stupid. I'm sorry I made you come here."

Dakota didn't answer, dazzled by the lights and bleeps of the arcade games lined up against the wall, the Galaga unattended right where it had always stood.

"Do you want to go see them?" Drita asked him.

He looked up at her, unsure if she was to be trusted.

"We can walk there. No skates."

He took her hand and bobbed his head up and down. He wouldn't be able to see the screens or reach the controllers, but they walked over to the periphery of the rink together and strolled slowly around the machines, and Dakota seemed to take this as a sufficient act of reconciliation to eventually smile up at Drita. She smiled back and her lips stayed curled after he looked away, though the gesture had shifted to a grimace at the odor of urinal cakes leaking out from the men's restroom. She remembered the boy who'd felt her up smelling of that and a fresh application of Jōvan musk, and she was flattered that he'd made the effort before their slow skate together. She had no recollection of his name or his face, likely because she'd never seen him again after they'd gotten booted from Roller Magic permanently, or at least until their faces had been made unrecognizable by puberty, at which point they were too old to want to return. She'd been furious at Pete after it happened, though she forgave him in time because he really did think he was helping. He just had some messed-up ideas about how to do that, some mixed-up ideas about right and wrong.

"You want to try playing?" Drita asked Dakota. The boy nodded furiously in return. She slipped a couple of dollar bills into the coin exchange machine, a transaction that Dakota perceived to be as magical as the videogame itself, and she hoisted and held him on her hip as he quickly lost one round after another. As small as he seemed to her most of the time, his weight quickly became painful to bear, but she held him until the last quarter was gone, afraid that she might screw things up with him again, too. Maybe she somehow shared Pete's moral dyslexia. Maybe that condition didn't come strictly from nature.

16

EVEN IF HE DIDN'T ALREADY KNOW WHAT THE GUY LOOKED LIKE, even if he didn't live three doors down from the shithole Pete helped Shanda escape from, Pete would've been able to track Shanda's dealer down by his car. Toyota Supra, of course, an '86 or '87, Maaco-red because the dude obviously believed he got initiated into the Bloods after learning a couple of Cypress Hill songs by heart. The guy was nothing but another nobody scumbag on an extended audition for the role of walk-on gangster number one, and even if he wasn't a wannabe but an actual be, it didn't matter because now Pete had a gun too. Pete didn't know how to load the gun, he wouldn't have even known it was a 9mm if it wasn't engraved on the barrel, but that didn't mean he didn't know how to use it. Firing a gun was just one way, and maybe not even the best way. If Pete shot the dude, the dude wouldn't be able to think twice about selling junk to a mother, and he wouldn't be able to spread the good word.

That was how Pete later rationalized what, in retrospect, was not only not rational but indescribably stupid. He wasn't thinking straight when he burst into Jackie and Dom's place, grabbed the gun Dom kept stashed in an aluminum box under his bed, and left without saying goodbye. He was thinking straighter when he made it to Shanda's old street, but what he was thinking about wasn't what might happen the next day or the day after that but what he'd found the day before, which was Shanda in an oblivion so deep that he wouldn't have let her pick up Dakota from daycare even if she had remembered it was her turn that day. She had promised him she was done with that shit for good, but it was obvious that as long as number one existed, he and Dakota were always going to be a distant two and even more distant three in her world.

"Yo, I gotta talk to you a sec," Pete said, addressing the dude as he sat alone on a porch that needed a paint job twenty years before. Before the guy could so much as nod, Pete lifted the hem of his Starter sweatshirt to reveal that he wasn't actually there to talk. He put his palm to the grip both to let the guy know that he was prepared to draw and to steady his hand, which was quivering like he'd had too much caffeine on an empty stomach. It worked, though. The guy scooted back so fast that Pete could almost feel the slivers that must've punctured the guy's ass, and it gave Pete the confidence to keep moving toward him.

"Hands up," Pete said, realizing as he said it that he sounded more like a cop than a gangster.

"What you want, dude?" the guy asked. He was scared but spoke clearly, like he had practice at this.

"You know Shanda? Used to live down the street from you?"

The guy nodded.

"I want you to leave her the fuck alone. Stop selling to her. She had her shit together and you fucked it all up."

"Man, she came to me," the guy said.

"Don't fucking talk to me unless I tell you to," Pete said. He was getting the hang of it now, he thought. If he was all talk, he was at least getting better at that part. "I don't care if she comes to you on a fucking Pegasus. I don't care how much she begs you. We got a kid, a two-year-old. She doesn't need your shit. We don't need your shit."

"She don't come to me, she's just going to go somewhere else," the guy said.

"I said don't talk unless I tell you to," Pete said and rammed his fist into the guy's face, the metal of the Glock or whatever it was now shiny with blood. He hadn't planned to do that, but he also didn't expect the guy to keep talking after he told him to shut up. When the guy's eyes went sideways Pete figured he was counting the birds circling his head, but then Pete saw a couple more figures approaching from the end of the block, still a good minute away. Pete wasn't a betting guy, but he knew two or three on one wasn't good odds, even if he had a piece, because chances were they had them, too, and actually knew what to do with them.

Pete spit on the ground and put the gun back in his waistband. "Remember what I said. Don't fuck with her anymore," he said. He wanted to believe he walked coolly back to his car, or rather Drita's car that she'd left behind when she moved away for grad school, but more likely he half ran, the adrenaline too concentrated in his veins for his limbs to move slowly, a feeling he used to be able to get from bikes or skateboards and that now he only got, it seemed, from digging deeper and deeper holes.

1999

That had been Pete's first and only experience with a gun, and he promised himself and Shanda that it would be his last. Turned out the guy wasn't a wannabe Blood but an actual Los Solido, and Pete was still just a white boy from Town Plot once he dropped the 9mm back in Dom's lockbox.

But Shanda broke her promises first, because no matter where they went, she always managed to find the parts of towns that most mirrored the very streets they just fled. He figured that meant he was off the hook with his end of that bargain, and anyway, the job he was on that day wasn't a fool's errand like trying to keep Shanda straight; it was a righteous one, helping Valon and his father help their people, and Valon and Ramadan had, in between shifts coating the tops of buildings with tar and in the back office before leaving him to his cot, let Pete know what their people needed was guns. Not that he understood guns any more than he understood the geopolitics that made them necessary. He still called the small ones gats and the big ones AK-47s, but he knew better than to make a fool of himself by using those names out loud. It wasn't his job to be an expert, just to pay attention to the shopping list Ramadan had written on the back of a blank Tristate Roofing invoice.

"What do I say to these people if they ask what I want with this stuff?" Pete had asked Valon before they each set off down I-95 in their own work vans, Valon's emblazoned with the Tristate logo and Pete's a rusted white that had never stopped reeking of the cigars its previous owner must have smoked before it ended up in the impound lot. That was likely because Pete himself had half-assedly detailed it after Ramadan bought it at auction, ostensibly for construction gear but also, apparently, as transport for this burgeoning military operation.

"Why would they ask you that?" Valon answered.

"I don't know, because I'm going in there to buy enough guns and ammo to stock an army?"

"Yes, that's exactly what you're doing," Valon said.

"But they're not supposed to know that, are they?"

"Cuz, aren't you the American one here? Why would he ask you what you want with this stuff?"

"Because it's not, like, a normal amount of stuff," Pete said.

Valon laughed and smacked Pete's cheek lightly. It was meant to be playful, and Pete hated it but didn't react because he'd seen all the other roofers do the same to each other. He learned quickly that Albanian was as physical a language as it was verbal, and he thought some primal part of him might recognize it as native even if he knew he'd never pick up the tongue, but he still clenched his fists every time.

"Cuz, there is no normal amount. One gun has the same job as fifty. And anyway, trust me, all they'll want to know about you is how much more money you have to buy more of their shit. You're American, how do you not know this already?"

"I'm not American, remember?" Pete said.

"Whatever, American. Here, take this," he said, handing Pete a knot of bills that would barely fit in any of his pockets, along with the same model Nokia that Pete had seen attached to Valon's ear when they were up on the roofs, Valon still somehow managing to out-tar the rest of the crew. "Call me when you're done and we'll meet up afterwards."

The cash in Pete's hand would have been enough to get him to Long Island and set him up in a decent condo for months. He could send a wad to Dakota in an envelope with no return address and feel like he'd done enough to get him through the next year guilt-free, or if not free, guilt-reduced, until he got his life together for real and could swoop him up from Shanda in person. Even the cellphone he could cash in for a month's worth of Happy Meals, and once he was rid of it, nobody would have any way to trace him.

Pete thought about these things and was proud that they were only thoughts. Valon would almost certainly literally kill Pete if Pete drove off with his money, true, but that wasn't what stopped him from doing it. What stopped him was that Valon trusted him with it in the first place, didn't even hesitate before sending him off unsupervised. It wasn't like Valon didn't know Pete was a piece of shit. Pete hadn't hidden that from him—how could he have, the way Pete reeked when they first encountered each other—and yet, unlike Dom, Valon must have seen something innate in Pete that Pete didn't even see in himself. He just needed the opportunity to prove himself, and he understood that the day would be full of opportunity.

Pete pulled into the parking lot of what was, from the outside, a regular civic center, like the ones where Jackie used to take him to see monster truck rallies and WWF matches for his birthdays when he was a kid. But when he stepped inside, just past the vacant kiosks that still smelled of the eleven-dollar personal pizzas they'd been slinging at whatever family-friendly event the space had hosted twelve hours before, what he saw was a warehouse for at least a few of the globe's less principled militaries. Inside were enough arms and munition to take down every last Serb in Kosovo, along with another good chunk of the world's population.

"What're you looking for?" the first vendor he passed asked him, likely because Pete had stalled at his table ten steps into the joint.

Pete eyed the vendor. The guy looked like every grizzled middle-aged dude who'd ever given him dirty looks at the VFWs he'd sometimes go to for the cheapest beer in town.

"Guns," Pete said dumbly.

The man laughed, though he didn't much seem like someone with a sense of humor.

"I would've guessed that much. What kind of guns?" the man asked.

Pete crinkled the list in the pocket of his cargo shorts, but he didn't pull it out. The endless folding tables lined up in the aisles all looked more or less the same, some draped in American or POW-MIA flags and some bare, but all stacked high with rifles and handguns that Pete couldn't identify any more specifically than that.

"Just guns," Pete said. "Big guns, for hunting."

"Big game, you talking about?"

"No game. For real," Pete said. He was getting anxious, the list in his pocket going soft with sweat. Just his luck he'd end up at the first undercover fed's booth in the place.

The man's heavy-lidded eyes seemed almost to close, though in fact he was squinting to make Pete out more clearly. "Well, if you ain't playing, then you should check out something like this." He picked up something that resembled a prop from *Predator* and bounced it in his arms, then walked to the other side of his table and handed it to Pete. "This one ain't a toy."

Pete took it and held it the way the guy had. It looked like a toy, or at least he felt like a kid playing war, but it felt surprisingly natural cradled against him. The weight of it steadied his tendency to sway nervously from side to side.

"You recognize this puppy?" the guy asked.

Pete shook his head.

"Steyr AUG, Austrian. Illegal until they made some cosmetic changes a few years back, thanks to that pussy Bush. Selective-fire, can go from semi to full, can take your choice a barrel from 250 to 621, polymer and aluminum body—it's a piece of modern art, you ask me."

Pete hadn't asked him, and he didn't ask the guy what any of that babble meant, but he nodded along the whole time, and pulled the piece of modern art to his eye to look through the viewfinder. Just like when he looked at modern art, he couldn't make out shit.

"You know what any of that means?" the man asked.

Pete lowered the rifle. He didn't want to say no, but he also knew better than to lie to a heavily armed man.

He shook his head.

"What're you in here for really?" the man asked.

"Are you a cop?" Pete asked.

The man laughed again, sounding this time like he meant it.

"What you planning to do, son, shoot up a post office?"

Pete didn't say anything.

"Listen, what you do with your guns is your own business. This is a free country, ain't it?"

The guy sounded like Valon. Pete found himself getting all kinds of civic lessons he never signed up for.

"It is a goddamn free country," Pete said.

"Goddamn right," the man said.

"And in this goddamn free country, I'm gonna help make another country goddamn free," Pete said.

"Sounds like a fine plan, son," the man said and expressed no need to know what the plan was.

That was good enough for Pete. The Steyr AUG wasn't named on the paper that he pulled from his pocket, but when the man donned his reading specs, he nodded at the list, looking not at all disappointed by what was on there. As many as possible AK-47s, a piece of machinery so legendary that even Pete had heard of it. As many as possible Dragunov sniper rifles. Receivers, stock adapters, magazines. Ammo for everything. The man set off almost giddy and said what he didn't have he'd work with other vendors to get. He told Pete to relax, he'd take care of it all, he should go get himself a hot dog, which Pete did. It was disgusting and cost four of Valon's dollars. He watched the man tap a couple of men at other tables on the elbow, whisper to them, gesture back at Pete, and after a first few seconds of disbelief they'd all look back at Pete with what he was beginning to recognize was respect. It was that easy, in and out within forty-five minutes. He even got a little discount for buying in bulk and in cash, and the three vendors who'd pooled their resources to fulfill his shopping list even helped him carry everything out to the van, as if he was an old lady at the grocery store. Before he pulled off, the first vendor stuck his hand out for Pete to shake and offered him a business card.

"Good luck spreading freedom. If you need any more supplies along the way, here's where you can find me," the man said.

The card said "Rick's Smoke and Gun."

"Cigars, too, if you're in the market," said Rick.

"Not today, thanks," Pete said.

Pete lit up a Marlboro instead as he pulled out of the lot. It had taken him more than twice as long to drive to the Delaware shit town he'd already forgotten the name of as it did to fulfill his mission, which was what Valon had called that day's errand. It sounded a hell of a lot better than going shopping, which was what Pete had at first thought of it as, but pulling back onto the I-95 on-ramp in a van loaded with enough firepower to take down some of the world's flimsier governments, he couldn't deny that he felt like a bona fide commando. He felt worthy of those gun dudes' admiration. Valon didn't task one of the off-the-boat Kosovars with this job. And sure, it was true that they didn't possess the right paperwork to buy or transport guns legally, they hadn't yet earned their Second Amendment rights the way Pete had by virtue of citizenship and somehow managing to have never caught a felony rap, but Valon knew plenty of other dudes with their papers, most of the Albanians in a ten-block radius of Arthur Avenue and plenty more beyond that.

And still he'd chosen Pete. It should've made Pete suspicious, but instead it made him prouder than any single moment that he could recall in his entire life.

Pete pulled out the Nokia Valon had given him—a gadget until that day he thought only ER doctors, CEOs, and drug dealers used—and dialed Valon's number.

"Where you at?" Pete asked by way of greeting.

"You know where I'm at," Valon said.

"You're not done yet?"

"Cuz, I just got here. You finished already?"

"What can I say, I'm efficient," Pete said.

"Your dumb ass probably fucked it up, is what happened."

"Nah, it's good. It's all good."

"Come out and meet me here," Valon said.

"I'm already back on Ninety-Five," Pete said.

"Then turn around."

"I don't know where you're at."

"I will tell you, asshole. Get yourself to a gas station, treat yourself to a new road atlas courtesy of your friend Valon, and direct yourself to me."

Pete grunted for Valon's benefit, but in truth, he was more than happy to backtrack west and kill the day in the backwoods of Pennsylvania, free of gridlock and tar and instead full of trees, driving with a cache that made him un-fuck-with-able.

"Go ahead, gimme the coordinates," Pete said.

"The what?" Valon said.

"The address or whatever," Pete said.

Pete held the paper with his shopping list against the steering wheel with one hand and with the other wrote down what Valon said. The horn beeped twice as he did so, and the driver of a passing Buick glared at him. Pete flipped him off, dared the old man to mess with him.

"K, see you in however long it takes to get there," Pete said. He took a deep pull off his cigarette and smiled a little, posing for the camera that should've been capturing that glorious day.

When Pete arrived he wondered why they had bothered to separate. Aside from the license plates, the insides and outsides of the joints were exactly the same. Even the vendors were exactly the same, like someone had decided there was some reason to make replicants of a bunch of old paranoid militiamen to populate gun shows up and down the Eastern Corridor.

But Valon's shopping list had been different. Shorter. Inside Valon's van were only two cases, hard-shell rectangles that Pete at first thought held electric guitars, and Pete was ready to bust some balls about that. Then Valon opened one, and Pete saw that this was no electric guitar. It was a series of metal barrels and pins and rods that Valon, like a magician, assembled into a single unit in under a minute flat.

"Jesus fucking Christ," Pete said.

"Whoever you want to pray for, it's not going to save you from this," Valon said.

It looked like a Hollywood prop. A long gray skeletal body propped up on legs that didn't look capable of supporting it, like an enormous, horrifying praying mantis. It was straight-up science fiction.

"Barrett M82. This thing can shoot right through a concrete wall, through armored vehicles, it can shoot down airplanes. Look," Valon said and pulled a silver projectile from one of the cardboard boxes that lined the bed of the van. "This is the bullet."

It spanned beyond the width of Valon's palm, six inches long at least. Inside the cardboard boxes were hundreds more. The guns must've weighed thirty pounds at least. They weren't things to be toted around by young men playing dress-up in discarded American military uniforms. They were things that had to be transported, set up, thought about before firing. Pete felt a little nauseous standing there. It must have been that hot dog he'd eaten, all that salt and no fluids.

"Pretty fucking awesome, right?" Valon said.

Pete nodded. In the most literal way, it was awesome. "These are no joke," he said.

"None of this is a joke," Valon said. "This is a war. Come on, let me see what you got."

At Pete's van, Valon had to agree: Pete had not fucked it up.

"Nice job, cuz," Valon said, patting Pete's back like a Boy Scout troop leader.

Pete was getting his stomach back. He just needed a little walk was all, and the reassurance that he'd done his job well didn't hurt. He shrugged his shoulders beneath Valon's hand.

"No big deal," Pete said.

"It is, though. It's a very big deal. This is what liberates our people, cuz. They don't win without us. Without us, they die. With us, they live, and the people who want us dead die. We didn't ask for this shit, but we have to answer it, you know?"

Pete nodded. He was only learning, but even a dumbass like him understood that was the first step to knowing.

"You ever shoot anything like this?" Valon asked.

"No," Pete said.

"You ever shoot anything at all? Water pistols don't count."

"No," Pete said. He didn't even know if he was supposed to be embarrassed about that.

Valon closed the doors to Pete's work van. "Wait for me and then follow me out of here. Don't get lost, stay right behind me."

"I've got the atlas," Pete said.

"We're not going back yet, we've got a couple stops to make. Stay right behind me, you understand?"

Pete nodded. He preferred not having to map his own route anyway.

The vans drove deeper into nowhere, Pete tailing so close he very nearly clipped Valon's tow hitch at every stop sign and traffic light that existed for no apparent reason. Their little caravan would've been conspicuous to anyone watching, but seventy miles west of Philadelphia was about the same as a thousand miles from anywhere, until Valon banged a right on a dirt road that brought them to a clearing where a few vintages of F-250s were parked in a diagonal row. Valon pulled in a respectful distance from them, and Pete a less respectful distance from Valon.

Valon opened the rear doors to Pete's van, pulled two of the AKs out, and handed them both to Pete, along with a box of ammo. He walked to a wooden box mounted to a post on a half-rotted gazebo, wrote something on an envelope, stuffed it with a couple of bills, and slid it into a slot in the box. Then he turned back to Pete, still standing twenty yards away, and yelled, "The fuck you doing over there? Come on, let's get a few rounds in."

Whoever was off in the clearing must have heard Valon, because as if on cue, the unmistakable sound of gunfire at close range popped off, recognizable even to Pete, who'd only ever heard dudes talk shit about gats and sawed-offs, and they were probably just repeating stuff they heard from N.W.A. songs. He was glad Valon's back was turned so he didn't see him jump, and he braced himself against the next rounds so that it wouldn't happen again. He followed Valon to a booth that was closer than comfortable to the ones beside it, which were occupied by what must have been the drivers of the pickups. To their left was a lone guy with a shotgun, aiming at a paper silhouette of a buck; to their right were two others taking turns with a handgun, giggling to themselves like schoolgirls. The man with the shotgun turned briefly toward them and nodded, and both he and Valon gave the same greeting back.

"Here, set them down so we can load them," Valon told Pete.

"Are we allowed to do this here?" Pete asked.

"It's a firing range, this is exactly where we're supposed to do it," Valon answered.

Pete didn't want to argue, but he was skeptical. As easy as it had been to buy all the stuff in the van, it seemed impossible to him that a regular nobody human like him could be allowed to actually use it. And as long as they were in this country, they were civilians—he'd bet a dollar ninety-nine people out of a hundred couldn't point out Kosovo on a map, never mind give a shit about some villages they could never pronounce the names of going up in flames. Christ, he was one of those people a month before, and yet here he was, as of that day one of the primary suppliers of the KLA's front line.

"Come down, watch how this is done," Valon told Pete.

"Okay, Rambo," Pete said.

Valon looked at Pete in a way that made Pete want to walk off onto the range, in the line of the hunter's target.

"This is not a joke, Petrit. These will kill you just as easily as they'll kill an enemy," Valon said. Nobody ever used Pete's full name, not ever. It was messed up that his own name sounded so foreign to his own ears, and though he wanted to die a little to hear Valon lecture him like a child, he liked how serious it sounded. It was starting to sink in, Valon's message: what they were doing was serious. It was life-changing, life-ending, serious-as-fuck business.

Valon tilted one of the guns to its side. "This is the safety," he said, pointing to a lever. "Anytime you're not actively firing, the safety stays on. You got that? Go ahead and do that to the other gun."

Pete did as he was told.

"Now you see this other lever? Push that in, and then pull the magazine out."

"This is where the bullets go?" Pete asked.

"Yes, but not yet. First you still assume the gun is already loaded."

"But the magazine is empty."

"There can still be ammo in the chamber. See this slide? Pull this all the way back. If there's a round in there, it will fall out."

"These are brand-new, why would there be ammo in there?" Pete asked.

"I don't care if you watched them put this fucker together on the assembly line, you always assume the chamber is loaded. The one time you're too lazy to do that is the one time you kill somebody you don't mean to," Valon said.

Pete nodded and pulled the slide back as Valon had instructed. Nothing, as he would've guessed.

"Now we load," Valon said. He began stacking bullets into the magazine one at a time, seemingly endlessly.

"How many is that?" Pete asked.

"This cartridge holds thirty," Valon said. "Better in combat to use the drums you picked up. Those take seventy-five, less time wasted reloading."

Valon waited for Pete to finish with his magazine. He didn't even seem too annoyed at Pete's fumbles, when his big, dumb sweaty fingers lost their grip on the bullets.

"Okay, attach the magazine back on like this," he said. He checked Pete's work and nodded. "Now stand up, bring the sight up to your eye. Line up the bull's-eye with the target. Look good? Good. We're going to go one at a time. Lower your rifle, just watch me first."

Pete watched as Valon checked his sight, lowered the gun, unlocked the safety, and pulled back and released the lever on the chamber. He raised the gun back up.

"You want the butt against your shoulder, like this, to steady it and to control the kickback. It's a smooth shooter, the kickback's not too bad considering the power, but if you're not prepared for it it'll knock you on your ass," Valon said. Then he brought the sight back up to his eye and fired. Pete was braced for it this time, didn't jump at all, even though the sound was horrible, like pressing an ear right up against a backfiring muffler. The hunter on the other side of them wore ear protection, which made him appear to Pete to be either wiser than them or a total pussy.

"You ready?" Valon said.

Pete nodded. He tried to mimic what Valon had done: look, lower, slide, slide, look again, fire. He got it almost right: he managed to look through the sight but not at anything, so when he fired, his shot went nowhere near the paper target he was supposed to aim at, but he checked around and it didn't look like anybody nearby was accidentally dead, so he considered that a success.

"Not so hard, right?" Valon said.

Pete raised the gun and tried again, this time looking at and hitting the target. It wasn't so hard at all. It was shockingly easy, actually, something that momentarily made the madness of what he'd been able to do that day acutely clear. It made Pete suddenly a little more aware of the danger in the world around him, despite now being literally armed against it.

"Are you enjoying playing soldier?" Valon asked.

"You said we're not playing," Pete said.

"We're not, you're right. I just thought all Americans dreamed of being soldiers."

Pete shot again, and again, and again. His aim was fine, close enough—did that count with AKs, too, or was it only hand grenades?

"Dom tried to convince me to join the Marines," Pete said. "When he got sick of trying to straighten me out himself."

"You didn't want to go?"

"Fuck no. Why did I want to get up at the butt crack of dawn and get yelled at by a bunch of assholes?"

"To serve your country?"

Pete thought about that, then shrugged. "I didn't see them doing anything for me," he said.

"My father had to serve for Yugoslavia," Valon said. "Every man did, no matter if they wanted to be a part of Yugoslavia or not. He served his time, and they thanked him by shutting down our Albanian schools. If I wanted to learn math, I had to learn Serbian. Here, let me get back in there."

Valon pulled the sight back to his eye and fired again. His aim was, not surprisingly to Pete, dead-on.

"I've seen you do addition, so I guess you learned Serbian," Pete said.

Valon fired again. "I did. I had no choice, but what did I care? I was a kid, I didn't understand anything. I even had friends who were Serbs. My father was fine with it. All the trouble we thought was with the government, not with regular people. Everybody over there has hated each other forever, but that was in books, not on the streets. And then."

Bang, bang.

"What changed?" Pete asked.

"I don't really know," Valon said. "We moved here for money, because the government fired all the Albanians from their posts. I was fifteen when we got here, I didn't care about that place anymore, I was just trying to figure out how to be American. I was a shit, I didn't even want to visit my gjyshe in the summers. Now she's dead, thank fucking god from cancer and not from being burned alive."

Valon laid the rifle down, pulled in the paper target, and swapped it out with a clean one.

"Remember I told you about Ariona's brother, how we assumed he was one of the burned bodies in a ditch?"

"Yeah," Pete said.

"It wasn't just him. His son, too. Three years old, shot through the eye like a deer. I couldn't tell Ariona that. She thinks he's missing, that there's a chance he fled. There's no chance."

Valon lowered the gun again and turned to Pete. He didn't bother to hide that he was using his sleeves to wipe away tears, even in front of Pete, even in front of the handgun kids beside them, who'd been trying not to stare as Pete and Valon fired their rounds.

"Last year I was taking classes at Hunter, a couple at a time on the side. Economics, can you believe it? And now." He shrugged. "Now this is what I do."

He wiped his eyes again and brought the sight back to the bridge of his nose. In seconds, Pete learned what an empty chamber sounds like.

"Twenty or thirty of these in a row and your shoulder starts to feel it," Valon said. He rubbed at a knot before laying his gun down and sliding on the safety. "Hurry up, get your shots in and let's get back to New York."

Pete nodded but couldn't bear to look at Valon. He looked instead at the target on the line, a silhouette of what was supposed to be a man but that seemed too frail to be one. It was like a child, or it had been until their bullets had tattered the form into an abstraction, like looking at a child through a kaleidoscope. He thought of Flamur's kid, but that kid didn't have a face. He couldn't help it; he thought of Dakota, lying helpless on the ground as Pete stood by and idly screamed into the morning. He'd already gotten a glimpse of what his son would look like dead, and Pete hadn't run toward the danger, the way Valon ran toward danger; he ran away and found Valon, whom he now followed into something that hadn't felt like danger until that afternoon, because it had nothing to do with him. Holding an AK at a shooting range, pointing it even at an imaginary enemy, made it have something to do with him, and yet he somehow didn't feel as powerful as he had hours, even minutes, before. Even the illustrated version of a corpse that Valon pulled from the line made Pete's knees buckle the way they had that day back in Waterbury when he ran to his car and never looked back at the guy he'd just pointed a barrel at. Now he was inching closer to a literal war, convincing himself he was standing beside Valon and not behind him, using him as some kind of shield.

"I'm good, dude," Pete said, standing up and rubbing an imaginary knot out of his shoulder. "Gotta save something for up on the roof tomorrow."

17

1996

IN 1947 BERNARD BARUCH TOLD THE SENATE, *WE ARE IN THE MIDST of* one of these, *which is getting warmer.*

"Really, Alex? That's all you got? The fricking cold war," Drita said. She kept the television on mute so that Isaac could sleep off his last sixteen-hour shift at Presbyterian, but you didn't get cosmic credit for correct Final Jeopardy! responses unless they were said into the ether, and anyway, nothing would wake Isaac after one of his sixteen-hour shifts at Presbyterian: not the car alarms that sounded every three minutes, not the guys yelling at the other guys setting off the car alarms, not Drita stirring the stainless steel pot of semi-homemade minestrone on the stovetop with a stainless steel ladle, doing her best to hold out on getting seconds so that they could maybe finally eat a meal together for the first time in three weeks. Their Morningside Heights apartment was geographically incapable of receiving sunlight, so what it lacked in quiet it made up for with a darkness so chronic that circadian rhythms weren't rhythms at all, just one long sustained note that put a body straight to sleep.

At least it put Isaac's straight to sleep. That and his rotations. She didn't resent that. She wasn't allowed to resent that. He'd put in too much work to ask him to sacrifice a couple of hours of his increasingly precious slumber to, say, watch a movie with her. Not even a movie—an episode of *Jeopardy!*, preferably one with an easy enough final answer that she could say it out loud and remind him that she was no dummy, even if she wasn't one of the med school blondes who wore strings of pearls under their lab coats and lived in Upper East Side co-ops their dads bought them as presents when they graduated from Vassar. Not that he ever suggested Drita wasn't good enough. He thought the work she was doing at Columbia was cool. He'd tell her that on those rare occasions they were awake in the same room at the same time. It was fine if that wasn't often, because their time was coming. Once he was done with his residency and she was done with her practicum and they were both doing things so important that other couples would find them annoying, which they'd laugh about over whatever kind of wine annoying, important couples toasted over. Not the kind that Jackie drank, surely.

"Fine," she said, also into the ether, when her stomach reminded her that the half portion of soup she'd served herself wasn't enough to compensate for the not-really-lunch she'd had earlier in the day. She stood up from the sofa and at first mistook the knock at the door for her own footsteps, and she was annoyed at herself for not taking off her boots. She placed the bowl on a bookshelf and bent down to untie her laces, and the knocking this time came unmistakably from the door.

Her impulse was to ignore it; nobody ever came to their apartment, New York was not a hanging-in-apartments kind of city even for those with time to hang out, and she assumed it was a lost food delivery guy or, given who her neighbors were, a weed delivery service.

Then a voice called, "Drita?"

She knew the voice but didn't believe it could have come from the person she knew it belonged to, until she opened the door and saw not just its source but another figure standing beside it. Two and a half figures, actually, because one of them was holding a small, sleeping child in their arms.

"Hey, Drita," her brother said. He smiled and held his arms open as if he were there to surprise her on her birthday. It wasn't her birthday, which was also his birthday, and even if it had been, they hadn't bothered with so much as greeting cards for the last couple, not since Pete decided to keep that grudge about Drita's reaction to the child his girlfriend was somehow cradling, despite not appearing like she had the strength to hold her own wet self upright.

"Jesus Christ, Pete, what are you doing here?" she asked.

"Good to see you, too," he said.

She couldn't say that she hadn't thought of him at all, like at the interim Fourth of July gatherings, where he hadn't bothered to show up with black-market fireworks and put on enough of a show that she wouldn't have to try to come up with something to say to Dom, or on their real birthdays, because their birthdays were one occasion where they had at least one significant thing in common. But it wasn't good to see him at that moment. The only explanation for him appearing at her door like that was that he'd screwed up something big, for one. For two, Isaac was sleeping in the next room, and she'd managed to get two years into their relationship without ever finding a reason to introduce Isaac to her brother.

"Listen, I'm sorry I didn't call to let you know ahead of time. We were in a rush," Pete said.

"We don't have any money on our calling card," Shanda offered meekly behind him.

"We were in a rush because"—Pete looked hard at Shanda—"there was some trouble at home."

Drita nodded because it was weirdly satisfying to her for him to so bluntly acknowledge what she already knew, though Pete seemed to take it as an invitation to continue.

"There's this guy in Shanda's old neighborhood who's been messing with her. Like, really, really messing with her in a bad way."

"It was my fault," Shanda said. She shifted the sleeping boy to her other hip, and his eyes briefly fluttered open to look straight at Drita.

Drita hadn't spent much time with the kid. She'd sent the perfunctory gifts at his birth and at Christmas, though Pete and Shanda didn't even really come around for holidays anymore. He was cute enough, maybe even cuter than most babies, who ordinarily didn't do much for Drita. But of course he was cute, because he was Pete's son, and Pete was cute, and that added another degree or two to her rising temperature.

"I didn't want to, but I had to get physical. He didn't give me a choice," he said preemptively. "I had to defend the mother of my son, you know? That's just a family's job, to protect each other."

"What did you do?" Drita asked cautiously.

Pete seemed to be caught up on his last point, though. "It's like when that kid was messing with you at Roller Magic. Like that kind of thing, I had to step in."

"We were making out," Drita said.

"He was laughing with his friends about it."

"We were like twelve, Pete. I know that's not why you ended up at my door unannounced," Drita said.

"I was just protecting my family," Pete repeated.

Drita looked to Shanda. "What did he do?"

Shanda looked at the floor.

"I told you, there was a guy back at home was messing with Shanda, and so I did what I had to do. Except." He exhaled and found the same spot on the floor that Shanda was still looking at. "Except it turns out the guy's in a legit gang and so we can't really show our faces around there for a while."

"Jesus, Pete," Drita said, acting surprised, though it wasn't really surprising at all.

"He's my dealer," Shanda said into her son's winter coat. "Pete didn't want him to sell to me."

"Anyway, we just need somewhere to stay for a night or two to figure things out," Pete said.

"No way," Drita said, and Pete's face suggested that he was truly surprised by her response, though if he'd been paying attention the last twenty-something years he shouldn't have been.

"What?" he said. "Just for a night or two. We're not asking to move in."

"I can't, Pete. Isaac is sleeping, he just finished sixteen hours at the hospital and he's got sixteen more to work tomorrow. And this place is tiny," she said, opening the door wider so he could see for himself.

"You won't even know we're here," Pete said.

"Your two-year-old doesn't cry? Your girlfriend doesn't . . ."

"Doesn't what?"

"Nothing. I'm just saying that three extra humans are going to be pretty obvious. There's not even anywhere for you to sleep."

"We can sleep on the floor."

"There's not even floor space, Pete. And why would you even want to involve us in this? We're professionals, Pete. We can't be harboring someone who's on the run from a drug dealer."

"Drita, please," Pete pleaded. "We don't know anybody else outside of Waterbury. You're all I have."

If Drita had been softening at all, that last line turned her right back into stone. Drita wasn't all Pete had. She wasn't even at all what Pete wanted. He was always looking to anyone besides her for validation, and he always got it no matter what he blew up along the way. He had friends to get him into and out of trouble. He had Jackie cleaning up his messes. So Dom liked to remind him that Pete damn sure didn't spring from his genes; now Pete had his very own offspring to ensure he'd never again live alone on an island of isolated freak DNA. She was the one who'd done everything the right way, who deferred gratification to the point where she wondered if it would ever come, and finally she was on the cusp of collecting the rewards that were supposed to come from living righteously, and Pete sure as hell wasn't going to come in and swipe that from her the way he swiped everything else he wanted from Bradlees.

She looked at the kid sleeping in his mother's arms. Maybe he was a consequence of Pete's decisions, or maybe he was a reward. Either way, he was Pete's, and it was too late for him to claim that Drita was all he had now.

"Sorry, Pete, you're going to have to go somewhere else and be a stranger, the way I always had to be everywhere I went," she told him and closed the door without giving him the chance to talk her into anything.

The radiators in that apartment, that was another whole thing. There was no regulating them, so when they were on it was oppressive. They could've grown tropical plants if not for the lack of natural light. No wonder that Drita was sweating when she walked away from the door, her heart racing like she'd exerted herself having a simple conversation that could not have gone any other way. No wonder Isaac slept like he did in the bedroom, the air around him weighing him down like a lead blanket.

But of course Isaac would choose that night to be noise-sensitive, for the sound of a door closing and a two-minute hushed conversation to rouse him.

"Who was that?" Isaac asked. He patted his afro down as if making himself presentable for company.

"What?" Drita asked. She didn't see him emerge from the bedroom, but she should have expected it. Of course it would be that night. Of course Pete would be the one to rouse him.

"Who were you just talking to at the door?" Isaac asked.

Drita took a pull from the glass of water on the coffee table, which she was pretty certain was left over from the night before. She wondered if she should lie. She told herself Isaac would know if she did.

God, it was too hot in there.

"It was my brother," Drita said.

"Your brother?" Isaac repeated.

"Yes, my brother and his girlfriend and their kid."

"Well," Isaac said. He looked at her as if expecting her to explain more, and when she didn't, he said, "Where'd they go?"

"They couldn't stay," Drita said.

"Why not? Why didn't you tell me he was coming?"

"Because I didn't know," Drita said.

"Why didn't you wake me up? Where did they go? Are they coming back?"

"No," Drita said. "I told you about Pete. I told you what he's like."

"So?" Isaac said. "That means I never get to meet him? After two years?"

"He didn't come to say hello, Isaac. He needed something. Like always."

"What did he need?"

"A place to stay."

Isaac mouthed the words she just spoke to himself, like he was running them through some translation software. "And he's not staying here?"

"No, of course not," Drita said.

"Well, why not?"

"Are you serious, Isaac? Here?"

"I mean, we have an air bed. He has a kid."

"And that's his responsibility. We have different responsibilities."

"Jesus, Drita, he's your brother."

"Yeah, exactly, and I know my brother, and the last thing he needs is more people bailing him out."

"I get it, Drita, but, like, he's got a kid, and it's cold out. Maybe he can figure something else out tomorrow, but it's cold out tonight. You know being out on the street isn't going to make someone make better decisions. I bet you read a whole book on that."

"Maybe he should have thought of that before he beat up a drug dealer," Drita said. "I don't need you telling me how to handle my brother. You never met him, he's not a case file, and you don't understand him."

"I can't understand a person you never let me meet," Isaac said.

Drita could see as Isaac stared at her that he needed more sleep. His eyes were red, his shoulders slouched the way they were when his day had collapsed on him.

"Just go back to bed, Isaac," she said. "I'm not going to be able to explain this all in a night."

"And I bet you won't bother to explain it tomorrow," Isaac said.

"Yeah, so?" Drita said. "What does any of this have to do with tomorrow?"

18

1972

ANTONELLA SAT ON THE SOFA BESIDE JACKIE IN HER CHAIR, BOTH OF them giggling with glasses of Chianti that Jackie wasn't sure Nella should be drinking. It had less to do with her being pregnant, because everybody knew that a glass of wine or two in the last trimester was good for the blood, but because of what Nella had told Jackie she'd been up to over the last year or two, which was nothing good. She'd dropped out of school, dropped lots of LSD, moved on to some other substances that appealed less to hippies than to the kinds of lost souls that slept on the steps of Our Lady between services. It was all so, so sad, but in the third miracle of the day, within an hour of their reunion they were laughing like they'd never been separated, like they'd laughed when Jackie could still walk and Nella could still walk straight.

"Jimmy DelVecchio?" Jackie said. "And you gave me such a hard time about Dom!"

"Well, at least I'm not marrying the guy. I haven't even told him about this," she said, pointing to the enormous bulge beneath her muumuu.

"But I mean, people must be talking," Jackie said. "It's not like you can hide much around here."

"That's why I haven't been around here. I've been staying with some friends out in Queens. I swear, it's exactly like *All in the Family* out there."

"So exactly like here with thicker accents?"

Nella shrugged. "Yeah, that's about right." She grew quiet again and took a hearty pull from her glass. "And listen, I don't want anyone around here to ever know about this. They're so judgmental, Jackie. You know that. Look at how they treated you, and you're the innocent one here. You have to tell people you don't know who the mother was. It was a closed adoption, you don't know a thing about the mother."

That made Jackie quiet, too. She did know things about the mother. The mother knew things about her, more than anyone else ever had. She wanted to keep knowing things, even if they were painful, even if what she knew was what local jamoke had managed to stick it in Nella and what kinds of substances Nella had to swallow or smoke or inject to get herself to forget that she'd let it happen. But Jackie also wanted that baby in Nella's belly, and she would abide by Nella's terms to get it. It didn't feel like that much of a compromise, because whatever happened to Nella after it was done, Jackie would always, in a way, know her. She'd always get to live with her, even, because the baby that Jackie would get to raise would be from Nella's own flesh and blood. And this time they'd do things right. Jackie felt compelled to reassure Nella of that.

"We're gonna do it right this time," Jackie told Nella. "This one's not gonna grow up like us. This baby's gonna see the world and do things for it, I'm going to make sure of it."

"I know, Jackie. That's why I came to you," she said. She grabbed Jackie's hand, and it gave Jackie a physical sensation that she hadn't felt since the accident, and not because of any spinal damage. "But what about the other baby, the one you said the lawyer found for you?"

Jackie shook her head. So many months, so much time and money she'd spent on that one! "I guess I can cancel it," she said. "I'm sure somebody else is always looking for a baby."

"Or maybe you could have two babies?" Nella said. "I mean, if you want this one to have a brother or a sister. I can tell you that I'm not doing this again."

"Two babies?" Jackie said. She meant to sound incredulous, but to her own ears, it sounded like the incantation of another wish she didn't previously dare make aloud. "Me? Look at me. How am I going to follow two toddlers around in this thing?"

"You'll get help. You got your mother, you got all those cousins that owe you some serious childcare," Nella said. "But I bet you won't even need it. You're so strong, Jackie."

Jackie blushed. "I don't know. I mean, I feel like I already know your baby. I don't know this other one."

"This is your baby," Nella said, pointing again at her belly. "And the other one can be. It's all on how you raise it, right?"

"The baby the lawyer found is Albanian. I don't know anything about Albania," Jackie said.

"That's even better! That one's starting out not like us. That's what we want, right? For your kids to be, like, different and exotic? And they'll grow up so close! They'll be like twins. I mean, you can even tell them they're twins."

Jackie smiled. "Twins do have that special connection, right? Like they feel each other's pain and all?" She thought back to the conversation with Father Mike, and while she'd already dismissed and defied almost every word he said, there was something in there that seemed reasonable enough: community. Everybody should have people in their lives who understand them, and it damn sure wasn't going to be the same church and same neighborhood that guaranteed she and Nella would never belong. Better for these babies to have each other, and not have to do all that searching later on.

"Albanian twins. It's so worldly. They'll come out of the womb already having lived lives that are bigger than ours," Nella said.

"Well, I mean, they're still gonna be from Waterbury," Jackie said. "Or Queens, or wherever you go into labor."

"Why?" Nella said, suddenly pink with something Jackie didn't think was a pregnancy-related hot flash. "They don't have to know that. I mean, what's history but a story anyway? They'll inherit any history you tell them."

"But what's the point? They're still going to be raised here, in this frigging city, with me as their mother."

"That's exactly the point," Nella said. "Let them know they came from somewhere else so they know from the day they're born that there's more to life out there. Don't let them get trapped like we did."

"Oh, Nella, you always had such a wild imagination."

"Not really," Nella said. "I never in a million years could've imagined us sitting here like this. Having to sit here like this," she said. She didn't point this time, but Jackie knew Nella was thinking of Jackie's chair. Jackie didn't like the pity, mostly because she liked the smile Nella was wearing a few minutes before better than what she saw on Nella's face now.

Jackie said, "I have everything that I've ever wanted, Antonella. All because of you."

There that pretty smile was. Jackie hoped the baby would inherit that smile, so that Jackie could look at it forever.

Jackie felt a preemptive relief for those babies, because they would never have to share her curse. If she made them into a two, it meant they would always have each other.

19

DAKOTA DOZED OFF IN THE CAR ON THE WAY HOME, AND WHATEVER harm Drita had inflicted on him at the roller-skating rink she partially made up for by not subjecting him to the indignity of a bath when they got to the apartment. The afternoon had been a lot for him, apparently, because all he seemed to be able to do was sleep. The afternoon had been a lot for Drita, too, which meant she likely wouldn't sleep for days. Not like that was new. All those AOL disks advertised hundreds of free hours of access to the World Wide Web, but in the few weeks that Drita had become acquainted with it, she'd paid big, not in dial-up service fees but in all the overnight hours lost to the pursuit of the ungettable. She lost the family that she sometimes resented for very clear reasons, and was left with a mother who felt like a stranger and a brother who wasn't a brother and a nephew who wasn't a nephew and a woman who lived with her for reasons that now just felt like a weird kind of charity, when she already gave $19.23 biweekly to the United Way through automatic payroll deductions.

What she'd gotten in return for her money and time were emails in a folder she'd labeled Eagle Calling. She went out looking for Pete and she'd found Valon instead, like she'd somehow written the world's

most complicated personals ad. It made her miss the simple useless-
ness of the *Advocate*, where the ads asked for nothing and gave it back.
When she logged on to her email and saw nothing from Valon, it felt
like it cost another penny of hope from her diminishing reserves. She
knew she shouldn't have expected anything; he'd told her he wouldn't
have much time in the coming days. He was gearing up for another
trip, this one not as a courier but as a soldier. Maybe Pete was going,
too. She tried to access the fury that had conjured in her that morning,
when she believed Pete had abandoned her to care for their sick
mother and his own son in order to steal her job of correcting the
world. All those same grievances were still justified, plus a new one,
which was Pete defending the honor of people who, it turned out,
were hers and not his.

The fire just wouldn't light. All flint and no spark.

So now what. She could sign up with a traveling nursing agency.
Shanda could take over the lease, once she saved enough. Jackie would
help her out, so long as she still had access to Dakota. That was an easy,
reasonable plan, not like the fool's mission she'd set out on. How stupid of her to think she could have ever intervened in a single other
human's course, never mind the whole world's.

She moved to close out of her email, but her right hand hesitated
over the X. Her eyes lingered on Valon's last message. All she could see
was the subject line, which simply read re: over and over and over
again. Regarding regarding regarding. About about about. What were
all of her messages regarding. What was all of this about.

A new window seemed to open on its own, a new message with a
new subject line into which Drita found herself typing.

Hi Valon. I know you're busy. I'm sorry to bother you. Or probably I'm not bothering you because you won't even see this because you're gearing up to join a war because people are being
killed and the rest of the world is doing nothing to keep them
alive. I'm not doing that. I'm typing letters on a keyboard and
feeling sorry for myself.

You're probably already gone and you're probably not going to read this, which is the only reason I can bear to write any of this out. I'm sorry for that, too, even if I'm not apologizing to you but some robot mailroom delivering sad messages that it can't understand. Can you imagine how many sad confessions this robot has seen? Imagine the kind of blackmail it could do if it were capable of being as awful as humans are. At least I don't have to imagine you reading this because if I thought you would I'd never be able to get it out.

God, that's pathetic.

Anyway, I'm sorry for more than just bothering you. I'm sorry that everything I've told you was bullshit. Well, actually, most of what I've told you is closer to the truth than anything I ever let myself say to anybody else, but it doesn't count because it was built on bullshit so that stink contaminated everything I piled on top of it. Anyway, for the record, I'm not a sweet dumb thing who intervened to keep her brother from doing something stupid, I'm a regular dumb thing with a computer who wanted to blow up my brother's life the way he blew up mine. And for the record, Jetmir isn't my brother, because Jetmir's not even real. Pete DiMeo is my brother, except that's not really real, either. Turns out my twin is actually just a kid my mother's friend gave her, the way normal people give other people housewarming gifts like, I don't know, Tupperware sets? If it makes you feel any better about me, at least I get to keep my tragic third-world story. I actually am an Albanian who can't speak the language or do the dances they do at the Albanian festival. I was found through a shady lawyer and not on a drifting boat in the Adriatic, but I did have a dead Albanian father and an Albanian mom with no options, so it sounds like I might fit right in with my people.

That's not funny. I don't know why I would write that to you. I think just to let you know what kind of person I really am and because you're not really going to read this.

Anyway, I thought you should know the truth. I shouldn't have had to learn this through experience, but now that I realize how much damage untrue stories can do, I thought I should acknowledge the ones I'm responsible for. I don't expect my confession would make you cry any more than it would whatever robot is actually reading this thing. I know sadness is a matter of scale, and this one doesn't register. I guess I'll just say mirupafshim, and be embarrassed that I asked my co-worker how to write that so that I might impress you.

   Oh yeah, one more confession: Lindita is the co-worker's name. I'm Drita.

Drita read over the message and felt weak with embarrassment. She felt like one of those war widows writing letters to husbands they wouldn't find out until too late had already been dead for months, except she was never really betrothed and hers was a story that would never be told on PBS. She hovered over the trash icon and clicked on it before she could reconsider. Because the program was designed to facilitate, not discourage, bad ideas, it asked her, **Are you sure you want to delete this email?**

This time she did consider it. The message wasn't really for Valon. Valon was always just a virtual receptacle for the things she only wished she could tell someone else. He was a receptacle for all her wishes, and the man had more important things to do than be her personal genie. Fight against an actual genocide, for example. Dear god, was she a shit.

   YES, she clicked.

She minimized the window and stared at the screen until it went into its hibernation dance, a psychedelic movement of bright geometric shapes that was the opposite of the way organic living things hibernated, which was in stillness and darkness. Stillness and darkness—that's what she, an organic thing, really needed. She'd almost forgotten there was a room in her apartment dedicated to it. She made her way to it and nestled herself under the covers and didn't expect sleep to come, but it must have, because she felt a sudden fear that always came in the moments after she unexpectedly woke from a slumber.

She tried to find a reason for the fear. Maybe she'd forgotten something important. She waited for some clarity, and in the next seconds it came to her: the modem. Shanda was working late and if she had to call she wouldn't be able to get through, and Drita remembered with even more clarity what the outcome of that was the last time it happened. She roused herself to shut down the computer, but in what had quickly and distressingly become an instinct, she first woke it to check for new messages. Among the spam that collected in her inbox like gnats in a light fixture was a new message from Valon.

Hey, I'm sorry I haven't written. I've been busy, but I haven't forgotten about you. You're giving me something to look forward to besides fucking people up. I've been so fixed on this one thing for so long that I almost forgot that I used to actually like to do things. It was shit that feels dumb now, like videogames and fish tanks, but it just kind of reminds me that what's the point of wanting people to survive if not for all the dumb shit that's there so you can ride out your time until you die in fifty years instead of next week? So thank you for that. It feels like a miracle.

I didn't want to ask you this because I thought it would just make things more complicated, but if you're serious about me and about what we're doing, maybe you can see me off. We're having a ceremony this weekend before the first wave of us flies out. I get it if you can't or you don't want to but I don't know, maybe you can be like my good luck charm.

Drita's hand quivered on the mouse, making the cursor dance some kind of digital jig. She read Valon's email again, then again. A good luck charm, like that disgusting green rabbit's foot Pete had won for her from one of those claw machines at Roller Magic once upon a time. She could be like that thing, an inert, disembodied piece of flesh that someone keeps until it falls apart or stops working, which is to say they stop believing in it.

She thought of her unsent confession, and how acknowledging the truth even to herself felt momentarily like liberation. But that was when Pete still seemed too far away to reach, before she had an address with a date and a time, one of those actual invitations she was always hoping for. There were still larger truths remaining, like her own fate.

Drita sat at the table as the night turned to predawn and Shanda arrived home from her overnight shift, walking through the door of what had, somehow, become their shared apartment.

"Hey," Shanda said wearily.

"I know where Pete is," Drita said. "I'm going to find him on Sunday, if you want to come."

20

THE RADIATOR PUMPED HEAT THAT THE OPEN WINDOW ABOVE IT released freely into the streets of Staten Island. Pete could hear Dom's classic pissing-money-out-the-window speech as he took in the April air, but without the circulation everyone inside that living room would've suffocated. Albanians were freer with their money than Dom was, or at least these Albanians were, and there were enough Albanians crammed into that apartment that he had to assume it was a pretty good cross section of the entire people. Pete watched from his place in the corner as the men shoved dollar bills into the pockets of the little kids that managed to weave through their legs. They stuffed bills into the cushions of a baby carrier before the baby's mother was swifted away to the kitchen, where the rest of the nënës gathered, taking turns making fresh rounds of coffee and not even seeming to resent not earning money for it the way the kids did just for having been born.

Nënë. That was about the only word Pete had figured out in the weeks he'd spent with Valon and the roofing crew, and he figured it out because Pete had taken to sulking silently in the corner when he couldn't understand what was going on, which was most of the time. What, you don't want to be here with us? Valon asked him when he passed by an hour before with the same cigarette he'd arrived with still tucked unlit behind his ear. You rather hang out with the nënës in the kitchen? Pete would not rather do that, not least because he wouldn't understand what the mothers and women were saying, either. It was dumb, but he thought the language might have come to him a little more naturally, like it lived in some kind of gene that might suddenly begin expressing itself when he was in a room with his own people, but he didn't pick up on it any better than he picked up on Spanish after running with those Puerto Rican kids back in high school. Every once in a while a new face would appear before him to shake his hand with a force that surprised him every single time, pointing to Ramadan and saying in very many syllables something that Pete assumed meant Thank you for your service, but it was hard to revel in a glory his ears couldn't make out.

Maybe it wasn't even glory. They could've been talking about the weather. The party wasn't for him, just a celebration for that new baby getting passed around in its carrier like a church collection plate. Pete didn't even really care that they weren't all there to celebrate everything that Valon and Ramadan were doing with his help. They didn't care that he'd probably doubled the number of UÇK members now armed with guns instead of just national pride. Did Valon even include that part of the story when he told his buddies? It didn't matter. Actually, he was glad. Pete was relieved to not be spending his Sunday in a mid-Atlantic gun shop with gun shop people, whom he'd quickly come to understand were Americans who'd spent every day since Vietnam thinking they were on the brink of what was already happening to people they didn't give any shits about over in Yugoslavia. But he felt undeniably annoyed about something, so he tried to figure out what it was, and what he settled on was a retroactive resentment that the birth of his own son had received the opposite of this kind of reception. There were no dollar bills at Dakota's arrival into the world, no coffee, none of the dancing that was definitely going to break out in the apartment later that afternoon. Nothing. Maybe not absolutely nothing, since Jackie kept Dakota in fresh Pampers and onesies for at least the first two years of the kid's life. But nothing from Drita, his only real kin, except for a Kmart gift certificate tucked into a greeting card that said Good Luck! instead of Congratulations! Nothing from friends, because, truth be told, he and Shanda hadn't exactly cultivated the kind of peer group capable of planning a baby shower.

Someone came by and shoved a plate of food in his hand. He picked up some doughy, flaky thing and put it in his mouth instinctively. The gifter was long gone by the time Pete thought to tell them thanks, as if the English word for it were as foreign to him as the Albanian one.

Shit. There he was blaming everybody back home for not doing enough for Dakota, when he was sitting in a room full of people to celebrate a stranger's son instead of doing a damn thing for his own.

He was working on it—becoming a better man, the precursor to becoming a better dad. He was making an honest living, one so honest it didn't even cover proper rent, but he more than paid for Ramadan's cot with the favors he did for him. It was a step. Maybe only a half step, but some kind of movement.

It's just that he still felt as far away from Dakota as he had when he first found himself on that Fordham Road subway platform. He was still standing among a bunch of strangers and not with his son.

Suck it up, Pete, he told himself. It was a party. He used to be okay with people he didn't know, better than he was with the people he did. He took a bite of the flaky thing. The flaky things were undeniably delicious.

And not everybody there was a stranger. Ariona was in the kitchen, taking a turn holding the baby and giving Pete a sneak peek of what kind of nënë she would be. Probably more of a natural than Shanda. Of course Ariona was probably raised with a thousand siblings and cousins while Shanda was barely raised among humans, which wasn't Shanda's fault, but nonetheless, when Pete finally got Dakota back, Dakota would deserve to be around someone who understood something about family. The people in that room cared about nothing but family. Ariona would love Dakota, no doubt. Someone like Ariona could teach Pete how to do family right.

Pete trashed his empty plate and brushed the crumbs from his tee. He would hang out with the nënës if Ariona was among them. He leaned against the doorframe, which made the women quiet down and look at him funny, except for Ariona, who looked away and leaned in closer to the mother of the new baby. So shy, so small-town, these women. Which isn't to say they dressed like peasants in a village, especially not the younger ones, especially not Ariona, who wore a clingy crushed velvet dress he didn't think a good Muslim girl would be allowed to leave the house in. He reminded himself that even if he didn't know most of the people there, they knew him, or at least knew about him, or at least should have known about him, and that he had therefore earned the right to stare at Ariona until she acknowledged him. That was the kind of thing Valon would do. Pete tried it, and lasted all of seven seconds before he felt like a creep and backed away.

Maybe it was just the hair and the makeup that made Ariona anyway. Shanda never wore makeup and didn't seem to know any hairstyles other than gelled-back ponytail. He always liked that about her, though, better than he liked the heavy black eyeliner and cartoonishly lined lips of the girls he'd been with before her.

Pete settled back into his corner. Of course this party was being held in the one borough he couldn't rely on a train to shuttle him away from. Of course he'd probably be there for several more hours. Maybe he could go for a walk and try to find out where Wu-Tang lived, but if their songs were to be taken at their word, he probably wouldn't be too welcome in that neighborhood, either.

Pete noticed another guy in another corner who seemed to be looking at him with a Wu-Tang kind of glare. Pete turned away, and when he turned back the guy was still staring. If this is what he had looked like to Ariona, no wonder she didn't return his gaze. But Pete wasn't Ariona. He wasn't a little woman from a little village in a little country. Pete looked right back at the guy, hoping it'd be enough to send him off, but instead it did the opposite. The guy weaved through the room and stopped right in front of Pete.

"You Valon's friend?" the guy asked, his accent just barely more de-tectable than Valon's.

"Petrit," Pete said.

"The American," the guy said.

Pete didn't answer.

"You know Ariona?" the guy said.

"We met before," Pete said. "Just wanted to say hi."

The guy said something in those words Pete couldn't understand, but his inflection at the end suggested he asked some kind of question.

Pete answered with his own. "She your cousin?"

The guy laughed a little. "No, she's not my cousin."

Pete knew what that meant. It meant this guy had unfamilial de-signs on Ariona, and Pete thought he should call the dude out on it just on principle. But he didn't. Even he knew better than to start a beef at a baby shower.

"She seems nice," Pete said. "I wanted to ask her where she got that dress so I could get something like it for my girlfriend back at home. Maybe you could ask her for me."

The guy shrugged.

"She your girlfriend?" Pete asked.

"Nah, she's just a good girl," the guy said after a few seconds.

I bet she is, Pete thought. The guy probably didn't even know there were other kinds of girls out there.

"What's your name?" Pete asked the guy, still trying to disarm him.

"Arben," he said.

"You Valon's friend, too?"

"I know him from around."

"Him and his dad, they're good people," Pete said.

Arben nodded. "You work for them?"

Pete stood up straighter and talked softer, because Valon told Pete not to be running his mouth about what they'd been doing on the weekends.

"I'm just doing what's got to be done," Pete said.

"Roofing?" Arben said.

"What? No. I mean, I do roofing, too. I'm talking about the other thing."

"Yeah, the other thing," Arben asked. "Why do you even do the other thing?"

Pete looked for signs the guy was messing with him, maybe still pissed about Ariona, but he was deadpan, chewing on a toothpick he'd pulled out of nowhere.

"For our people," Pete said.

"Aren't you from here, though?"

"I'm Albanian," Pete said.

"Albanian from here." Arben shook his head. "Why you want to get involved in something like that? You got family there?"

"I don't got much in the way of family anywhere," Pete said, then thought of Dakota and felt immediately bad for saying it. One son was supposed to be enough, wasn't it, in the way one sister couldn't be? But that was why he was doing it—for Flamur's son, for all the sons out there that had no choice. So when Dakota someday asked him why he took off in the middle of the night he wouldn't have to answer: because I'm a coward.

"You got lucky being from here. Seems kind of stupid to throw that luck away over there," Arben said.

"Bro, you might be too scared to do anything, but that's on you."

"I'm not afraid," Arben said. "I'm alive, and I worked to bring my family here so they can be alive, too. I just know what I can do and what I can't do."

"Does Ariona know what you can't do?" Pete said. "Anyway, somebody's got to take care of business."

"It's not your business, though," Arben said. "That's what I'm saying."

Pete wished this guy would try to say this kind of shit in front of Valon, but then Valon walked by on cue, patting Pete on the shoulder and giving a quick nod to Arben. Arben returned the nod, glared one last glare at Pete, and then walked off to talk more shit to more people he probably thought were trying to mack on a girl he'd never deserve anyway.

"You know that douche?" Pete asked.

"I know everybody. Where you been hiding at?" Valon asked.

"I've been standing in the same place pretty much this whole time," Pete said. "Where did you go?"

"I'm just catching up with some people. There's some people I had to talk to here."

Pete didn't ask why he didn't get to talk to them, too. He knew the answer. It's because he couldn't join any of those conversations, and not speaking the language was only part of the reason.

"Anyway, make sure you eat something. We got a couple stops to make after this," Valon said.

"Jesus, dude, I'm tired," Pete said.

"Have some of that Turkish coffee, you'll never sleep again."

"We gotta do everything tonight?" Pete said.

"The first recruits are leaving next weekend," Valon said. "I'm sure as fuck not going to join them empty-handed."

Pete sighed and looked around for a tray of the coffee that'd been circulating since they walked in, and of course there was none to be found.

"I'll be over by that window when you're ready to leave," Pete said and walked back to his little corner.

That's where Pete stayed when the dancing started, even when Ariona joined in and bounced right past him over and over again in that hand-holdy circle thing these people did every time they celebrated anything. Arben cut into the circle right next to Ariona and took her hand, and Arben could do that because he knew the steps of the dance and Pete didn't. Pete just watched from behind the glass of raki that had somehow ended up in his grip and confirmed when Ariona circled by: it wasn't just the makeup and the hair. The girl was straight-up beautiful. A beautiful, good girl, but he didn't feel the same kind of heat he usually did when looking at her this time around. They'd have nothing to talk about even if they had a language to share. Good girls just weren't his thing. Maybe he should learn to appreciate the things that he had instead of spending his time helping other people get what they wanted.

21

1998

FOUR AND A HALF YEARS AFTER DAKOTA WAS BORN, STANDING OVER
a bed covered in his vomit—a bed that Pete obviously hadn't visited
once during her entire overnight shift at the used car lot where she
laughably worked security on weekends, as if she could stop anyone
from absconding with an air freshener—Shanda suspected that Pete
had convinced her to have the kid mostly to keep her off the junk. It
was the last and most radical of his attempts and, to be fair, the only
one that had stuck for any length of time. Buying the van and getting
the hell out of Dodge slowed her down only in the places where they
didn't stick around long enough for her to find a connection, but that
was rare, because connections tended to show up at the van doors of
those who lived on wheels chasing festivals so they could convince
themselves they were on an adventure and not on the run. Settling
eventually in a duplex in a desert city that wasn't intended for humans
to inhabit was supposed to remind them that they were survivors who
could beat nature at its own game, but it mostly reminded Shanda
why she'd previously never bothered to try all that hard to continue to
exist. But when Pete found the box to the pregnancy test she thought
she'd hidden under enough mounds of styrofoam beverage containers

to deplete whatever little ozone remained intact over their Arizona-in-July hellscape, he proposed something so unexpected that she was taken too off guard to put up the fight he expected.

"Babe," he said, getting on his knees and kissing a belly that as yet showed no signs of life within it, "we have to do this. This is what we're here for."

Shanda was at the point of her usual recovery cycle where she wanted to do things right, when she was past the dope-sickness and not yet back to the world-sickness that drove her right back to the dope, and in retrospect she saw that it was disingenuous of Pete to pitch her any idea in that state. She was vulnerable to bad ideas in those moments, likely to think back on her last time getting stoned as a kind of omen, because she had found herself only a couple of weeks earlier wandering the aisles of the baby department in Walmart cooing over fleece onesies that a child born in Arizona would never need to wear.

"How do we know how to do it right?" she asked him, because despite shocking herself by believing him, in feeling an instant and rare kind of hope, she knew that he'd be expecting a protest.

"It's nature, babe. We just have to trust our instincts. All the bullshit that messes us up is because we don't trust what we really are."

"And what are we?"

"We're animals. Big-ass monkeys, Homo sapiens," he said, like he'd just discovered the cheat sheet for a high school biology test in the pocket of his Dickies. Shanda didn't know anything about animals, aside from the mice back when she was a kid. But she knew from experience that those fuckers were way lower on the food chain than humans, and that felt somewhat empowering.

"But what if I go back to using?" she asked, the momentary hope ebbing as quickly as it had flowed in.

"I won't let you." He brought her tighter, in the kind of grip that she usually instinctively resisted but let him hold on to this time. "It'll be instinct, anyway, to protect our kid with our own lives. That's what animals do, right? You remember that blue jay that attacked us when we tried to save that baby that fell out of the nest?"

She did remember that. She also remembered that she had seen no evidence of these same instincts in the human nest she'd been raised in.

But she also thought she'd seen all the ways to mess it up, which meant any other choice she could make had to be better just through process of elimination. She had a chance to do something different, to walk through door number two.

"Okay," she said, and that was how their son came to be. Even at the time she thought there should have been more to it than that. She loved that little bugger in a way she didn't understand, in a way that felt metaphysical, the subject of a book she'd stolen from a room back in the motel-cleaning days and that she had only pretended to understand prior to having Dakota.

Whatever that kind of love was, it wasn't natural, like Pete had said it would be. It was never easy. Five-plus years on, she understood how wrong Pete had been about their natures. They weren't animals, because animals take care of their young or else they eat them. They sustain them or get sustenance from them. Pete had clearly gotten his sustenance from two bottles of Olde English and the half box of pizza rolls that Shanda had been looking forward to eating after her overnight shift. He didn't seem to be getting much at all out of his own spawn, based on how he seemed to prefer spending all his spare time watching *Enter the Dragon* instead of their child. Meanwhile, it looked like Dakota had gotten his sustenance not from the cheese and tubs of peanut butter that the state provided but from something unidentifiable encrusted over his face, hair, pj's, and the mattress.

"Jesus Christ, Dakota, what did you get into?" Shanda asked him straight-on, full volume, as if he would've answered her even if he were awake. But the kid was in the kind of deep sleep he never seemed to fall into when it was her night with him, when he roused every couple of hours even long past the age where he needed bottles just to stay alive until morning.

She thought about letting him sleep, but the fact was if she didn't clean him up now, he'd wake himself just when she was dozing off herself, and Pete would likely need to clean his own mess off his own self whenever he peeled himself off the sofa. So she cursed Pete aloud and leaned over Dakota to gently nudge his shoulder, which felt heavier than usual, embedded in his comforter.

"Dakota," she whispered, despite not having bothered to be quiet until that point.

She nudged him again, and again a little harder. His little body bounced with the mattress, but he didn't release any annoyed moans or flutter his eyes or perform any of his usual waking-up histrionics.

"Dakota," she repeated, not quietly.

She moved her hand from his shoulder to his forehead, then snatched it quickly away as if scalded, and then it registered that she felt scalded because she had been, and by the skin of her child. He was on fire.

"Dakota." She yelled it this time, afraid to touch him again, not for fear of being burned but for fear of what was happening inside his body to cause that kind of heat. He was a little kid, down with a cold or flu or bug every other week or so, had just gotten over his third round of strep two weeks before, but once enough walk-in clinics had convinced Shanda that children were essentially germ incubators, she'd stopped losing her mind about every round of vomit or diarrhea. It cost a fortune to have a guy in a white coat shake a bottle of baby Tylenol at them, and if she took any lesson away from her own child-hood it was that kids aren't actually that hard to keep alive. So Dakota had been a little quiet and a little green when she left the evening be-fore; she'd shaken that bottle of baby Tylenol at Pete and told him to check on Dakota before he went to bed. Her mistake was thinking Pete would be going to bed instead of passing out and coming to, but that was just the most recent of a long line of mistakes she'd made with Pete. The biggest one dated back to that day when she allowed him to cling to her belly and convince her that sustaining life would be as easy as creating it.

She saw that when she saw the bottle of Tylenol now empty on the floor, a few droplets of the disgusting cherry sap that Dakota inexplicably loved dried on the carpet.

"Dakota," she cried again. "Dakota. Dakota." She snatched him from his bed and felt his fire against her chest, and she felt herself begin to shiver. When it occurred to her that he wasn't breathing right, and she remembered that air came from outside, she ran with him through the living room and out the front door.

"Babe, what the hell?" came a stupid, dull voice from back inside the house.

She laid Dakota down on the patio floor, still cool from the overnight retreat of the sun. His eyes briefly opened when his spine hit the concrete, and Shanda felt a moment of relief, even some pride for her quick thinking. The boy just needed some air, and to get out from under those blankets.

"What's going on?" came the stupid voice again, this time from the doorframe. It was Pete, just making his loud, empty Pete noises.

Dakota's body went stiff at his father's voice, and Shanda was about to yell at Pete to shut up, couldn't he see that the boy needed to sleep? Dakota's muscles released and contracted again, his eyes opened to look straight into Shanda's, and then he began to seize.

Shanda watched her son transform before her eyes from a boy to something she'd only seen in horror movies and in the hallucinations she'd had if she made the stupid decision to watch the horror movies high. His mouth was contorted and agape, but no sound came out, and that was somehow more terrifying than the guttural incantations *The Exorcist* had conditioned her to expect. So she did what her son couldn't do and screamed, a sound she didn't recognize because she realized as she released it that she had never done it before. She'd hoarded every bit of fury, hunger, want, and torment she ever felt, the way her mother did boxes and food wrappers and Band-Aids. She'd incubated a baby in those toxic waters; of course he'd be poisoned by them, of course he'd be writhing on the ground in front of her now. It all seemed so inevitable that she was able to understand it fully even as he fitted and she screamed, even if she couldn't articulate it to the neighbor lady who'd run outside to see what the commotion was, then run back inside once she saw.

When Pete joined them, though, words came.

"What did you do to him? What did you do?" she screamed. She pounded her fists into Pete to reinforce what she screamed, even if she knew she wasn't making sense. "The whole bottle is gone. The whole bottle!"

"The bottle of what, Shanda? What bottle?"

"The medicine! He got the whole bottle. The whole bottle is gone!"

"What medicine? Jesus Christ, what's wrong with him?"

Shanda didn't have to answer that. What was wrong with him was perfectly clear. Pete must have known that, because he didn't ask her again. Instead, he sank to his knees beside Dakota and helped Shanda do what she couldn't do herself, which was land a punch hard enough to hurt. He pounded his own fists into his thighs, and when the flesh proved too soft, he aimed instead for the concrete ground, which was painted with little pink blossoms after his hand pulled back.

"What the fuck? What the fuck? He was fine last night. He was fine when he went to bed," Pete said.

As if to prove his father right, Dakota's body stilled and relaxed, and he closed his eyes like he was back on his mattress the night before.

"What the fuck," said Pete. "Why is he so quiet now? Is he—?"

"Don't touch him!" Shanda screamed. She kicked Pete away. Pete stood for a moment, then bashed his head onto the stucco apartment exterior. He punched through the glass top of the tiny outdoor dining set they'd just picked up from layaway. He uprooted an agave that had always to Shanda looked like some kind of tentacled monster. He was trying to erase the ridiculous props they had acquired to simulate a normal life, and Shanda hated him for letting her think for even a second that any of it had been viable.

The neighbor lady had reemerged, shrieking something that Shanda didn't bother to listen to. Dakota breathed so haltingly and hotly into her neck that she couldn't hear much of anything anyway, even the siren of the ambulance that Shanda only later realized the neighbor lady must have summoned. Still, when the uniformed men pulled Dakota from her arms, she released him with no fight, because she understood that if there was any chance at all for Dakota, it wouldn't come in her arms.

Shanda forbade Pete from following them to the hospital, and she was enraged at him for doing what was asked of him once in his life. It left her alone in a sitting room full of the kinds of people that Shanda didn't want to be so intimately familiar with, waiting on the kinds of people she had no idea how to even exist around. Doctors, nurses. Nurses like Drita, Pete's sister, who almost certainly regretted having saved Shanda's life the first time they met, and who was now—according to Pete, who'd heard it from Jackie the last time they re-upped the calling card to phone home—doing home healthcare visits back in Waterbury, a place she'd once vowed to never live in again. It was a different kind of relief to Shanda to not have to be around Pete's family anymore, because they made her feel so stupid. They never said anything to make her feel stupid to her face. To her face Jackie was always making her sandwiches, while Dom had avoided her face altogether, just like he did with his own kids, and Drita was off doing good and wearing firsthand clothes from Old Navy. It was just their perfect little brick ranch house, their annual school photos framed on the walls, the decorations they put up for every single holiday, even the dumb ones like Flag Day. It all just seemed like a reminder that she came from and belonged to a different place, one a few miles down the road on a map but in a different galaxy in every other way.

They made her feel stupid because she was stupid. She could accept that. She was also insignificant, meaning so little to the world that her stupidity would almost certainly lead to her own doom but couldn't possibly be fatal to others. She lived with that belief for so long that she never bothered to reconsider it after Dakota was born, but now here he was at death's door, and she saw that belief was further evidence of her stupidity. She wasn't harmless. She was worse even than her landlord, than all the guys on her street that would catcall and grab, than the kids in school who would punch and scratch and take the nothing that she had. Those people were all opportunists, just snatching the low-hanging fruit. She was as bad as a god, creating a life just to watch it falter.

"Ms., uh, Zah ... Zah-peeta?" a women in teal called out. She held a clipboard, which meant she was important.

Shanda stood up and walked toward the woman.

"Sorry for butchering the name," the woman said. "Follow me."

Shanda did, ignoring whatever unimportant things the important woman said along the way, until the woman deposited her in another, smaller room to wait for the next important person to show up. She assumed it would be a doctor, but the woman who entered next wore a shapeless floral matching skirt and blouse set, looking more like a kindergarten teacher than a doctor.

"I'm Ms. Mercedes," the woman said, holding out her hand in such a way that Shanda knew she was supposed to shake it, but she couldn't get her fingers to ungrip her own elbows, and eventually the woman pulled her hand away.

"I take it you've spoken to the doctor?" Ms. Mercedes said.

"Not really," Shanda said.

"Well, I'm one of the social workers here on staff," Ms. Mercedes said. That explained the outfit, and why Shanda knew instinctively not to trust her. "I'm here to talk to you about what's next for Dakota, after he's released."

"Released? Like, gets better?"

"Yes, exactly."

"Oh," Shanda said. "Like all the way better?"

Ms. Mercedes nodded. "Dakota's going to be fine. You were smart to bring him here when you did, because it was on the verge of serious, but he's going to bounce right back. But we just want to make sure that something like this doesn't happen again."

She handed Shanda a trifold brochure that absorbed the sweat pooled in Shanda's palms. "Hidden Household Toxicity Dangers." Social workers had handed her brochures after each of the several times the extra doses of her own medicine had landed her in the hospital, and those had mostly served as repositories for her chewed-up Trident. She wouldn't even dare open this one, for fear of learning all the other ways she could accidentally kill her son.

"The doctors told us to keep that medicine in the house," Shanda told her. "He was always getting sick, and they said that would help him."

"Of course. Acetaminophen is perfectly safe with the right dosage, but it can be very dangerous in large doses. That's why it's important to give the dose that's on the label and keep it out of reach."

"He likes the taste. I don't know, he's weird like that. But he likes the taste and he can climb and his father was supposed to be watching him but he fell asleep."

"I understand that it's impossible to have eyes on them all the time. That's probably why it's one of the most common sources of poisoning in children. It's why we have the brochures," she said, pointing at the one in Shanda's hand. She must have helped design it, so eager was she to have Shanda open it.

"Are you going to take him away?" Shanda asked.

"What?" Ms. Mercedes smiled the kindergarten teacher smile. "Of course not. We just want to do everything possible to make sure something like this doesn't happen again."

Shanda knew better than to say too much to a social worker. There was nothing in the intake paperwork that would have let Ms. Mercedes know about her own history of the same affliction. Had Shanda known that it was a hereditary condition, maybe she would've heeded Drita's suggestion five and a half years before when she peed on a stick and spared the little cluster of cells the indignity of becoming a junkie's kid, like all the junkies' kids who'd terrorized her in the neighborhood because they had no idea how to exist without obliteration, either of themselves or of others. Maybe it wasn't a hereditary condition but a contagious one, then. It didn't really matter. Whatever the cause of her condition, she was the cause of Dakota's.

"We all just want to see Dakota get better, just like you," Ms. Mercedes said. "We're just here to help you make that happen."

Shanda didn't need Ms. Mercedes to make that happen. She needed Pete, not for Pete himself but for the people Pete had access to.

"Thank you," Shanda said. She knew from her previous experiences that that was the kind of thing you could say to get a social worker to leave you alone.

Ms. Mercedes beamed and asked, "Would you like to see Dakota now?"

This time Shanda didn't have to bullshit. "Yes," she answered. She did want to see Dakota, more than she wanted all the other things that weren't for the best. She wanted to absorb him back into herself, where her body could take the battering the world would keep handing out. But she couldn't do that, so she wanted to tell him about everything that had led to that moment, from the mice, to Nadia, to his father appearing outside her building like a knight on his BMX bike, to the terrible discovery she'd made on a motel room floor, to the solace the methadone she received each morning from a public health department van never delivered, to how, in the course of that single morning, she'd come to think of him as not something to save her from herself but someone to be saved. But she couldn't do that, because he was sleeping, and a little child, so she took a seat beside his bed and watched him until the nurses took over.

She was still terrified two days later, when Dakota was discharged, but she was learning to use the terror as fuel to get her to the next step, which was getting Dakota to safety. Safety meant getting back East, to the only person she kind of knew who seemed like they kind of understood how to help keep people alive. Drita was a nurse, trying to be some other kind of fancier nurse or something like that. She didn't like Shanda and she never wanted Dakota to be, but anyone could see how seriously she took the very idea of responsibility. Even Pete must have seen this, because he'd left $347 and a note on the table, the former Pete's penance and the latter his explanation for why they were better off without him. Three hundred and forty-seven dollars would probably cover the gas and tolls and garbage food it would take to get Shanda and Dakota back to Connecticut on a Greyhound, and Shanda convinced herself that Pete had planned it to work out just that way. Then Dakota, not just his battered little body but all the invisible stuff inside that made the body a thing of value, could really get better. A thing Shanda valued enough to not let her own hands destroy it.

22

THE ARGUMENTS STARTED BEFORE THEY MADE IT TO THE CAR. Shanda insisted on leaving Dakota with Jackie, and Drita insisted he come with them to Yonkers.

"How does a five-year-old belong at a whatever this is? There's probably going to be guns," Shanda said.

"Yes, probably," Drita said. "It's a military operation."

"No it's not," Shanda scoffed.

"Paramilitary. Whatever. It's legit."

"What does Pete know about the military? What does he know about . . . what's it even called?"

"Kosovo. And nothing. He doesn't know anything."

"And what are we supposed to be doing about it?"

Drita gripped the keys in her palm. She always used to have an answer to that, and it had never once led to what she thought it would.

"I mean, he should be paying child support, at the very least," she said, because it was the easiest thing to say. "To help you get on your feet so you can get your own place. That's why we should bring Dakota. To remind him of what his actual duty is."

Shanda was silent for a moment, then told Dakota to get his sweatshirt. "The blue one, the warm one," she said.

"And my Game Boy?" he asked.

"Sure, whatever," she said. "It's gonna be a long drive to who knows what."

"It's a ceremony, and I want to try to catch him before it starts."

Shanda seemed to not register the urgency. She peed twice before she dressed and once more after, and she brushed her teeth long enough that nine out of ten dentists would've told her it was time to get on with her life. When they finally made it to the car and onto Route 8, she asked Dakota if he wanted to stop at McDonald's, and once that genie was summoned, there was no putting it back in the bottle. Before Dakota had finished his hash browns but not before he'd squeezed at least two ketchup packets onto his lap and all over the Sonata's upholstery, Shanda asked Drita to pull off at the next exit with a Dunkin' Donuts.

"Jesus, Shanda, no. You already got a coffee at McDonald's," she said.

"It's not good," she said.

"What's not good is missing this whole event or whatever it is because we can't make it out of the Naugatuck Valley."

"Well, are they even going to let us in? They don't just let people walk in off the streets to do Army stuff."

"Yes, they actually do, you can literally join the Army at a kiosk at the Brass City Mall. And anyway, it's not that kind of army, and it's not a battle, it's a ceremony. It's for the public, for the news and stuff. They're not trying to be some kind of covert operation. They're trying to get attention."

"Maybe we should just let him go," Shanda said.

Drita snapped her head toward Shanda, a reckless move while nestled between a big rig and a Jersey barrier.

"Aunt Drita, you're freaking my ass out," Dakota called from the backseat.

Drita didn't stop to wonder where he'd learned to talk like that.

"You told me you moved back here to help Dakota," Drita said.

"I did move back here to help Dakota," Shanda said.

"And we're this close to getting him help from the person who's supposed to be doing exactly that."

"Supposed to doesn't mean he will. Pete's a grown man, he made his own decisions."

"But he's made so many shitty ones."

"So? I'm not his mother. And you're not, either."

No shit, Drita thought. I'm not even his sister.

She almost said it out loud. Maybe Drita's new existential solitude would be something only someone as utterly abandoned as Shanda would understand. Shanda had invented a whole biography for her mother in an obituary that ran for Shanda alone—how was that so different from what Jackie did, other than Shanda's lies neither hurting nor benefiting anyone but herself? Maybe it was better than simply accepting a disappointing truth. Maybe Drita was doing the same thing at that moment, trying to steer them all into an outcome that made sense in the kind of world she wished to inhabit.

Drita turned up the radio briefly, then turned it off altogether when she understood that there was no boy-band or pop-punk lyric too corny for it to seem inordinately profound in her state. She didn't want to risk getting emotional, not as close as they were to something that felt like it might be a resolution. "I just think Pete should think about his people before he joins a war for *his people*."

As if on cue, Dakota said, "Is Dad an Army guy now?"

Drita remembered first laying eyes on Dakota those weeks back, when he clutched in his hands a pile of inert plastic soldiers. It was clear from the way he handled them that he didn't know what soldiers were supposed to do, why toys had been made in their image when toys could be any number of more magical things: Furbies, space robots, videogames. It was probably the videogames that had clued him in to what Army guys were, now that she thought about it, and he didn't know that the version of war videogames offered was about as realistic as a mutant space hamster. How convenient it was to always land so firmly on the side of the good guys, for the allegiances to be so clearly defined. But he was five years old, still an age when humans weren't supposed to have learned to distinguish the fantastical from the real. It was the rest of them that were supposed to know better.

"I don't know what Dad is, kiddo," Drita said. "That's what we're going to find out."

"Is that what we're doing?" Shanda asked.

"I think so," Drita said. "Don't you want to know?"

"I do know," Shanda said. "Pete is Pete."

"You don't know everything," Drita said. "We're so close, Shanda. Think about Dakota."

"Why are you talking about me all the time?" Dakota called from the backseat.

"To give you an even bigger head than you already have," Drita told him.

Shanda sighed. "I don't understand any of this."

"Well, that's the point, to figure it out," Drita said.

Shanda closed her eyes and leaned back against the headrest. She couldn't have fallen asleep, but she didn't answer, which meant they were done talking for now. Drita drove this stretch of highway several times a week for her job, had probably done it while scanning paperwork or eating a sandwich so sloppily assembled that it required near-total concentration to get it into her mouth without the insides dropping instantly to her lap, and only now had it occurred to her how close to death she and everyone else who dared to drive their respective hunks of steel at high speed inches from each other were at every turn. She could get them all on the news with one reckless flick of a wrist: Family of Three That Wasn't a Family Killed on Congested Stretch of I-95. That's how easy it was to cease to be, so, so much easier than it was to continue to be, and yet it seemed so important for some reason to do the latter. It's what got them all in that car in the first place.

They rode in silence until the Merritt Parkway became the Hutch at the New York State line, Dakota sound asleep in the back, cradling his

Game Boy as if it was something warm and plush. It was too late to turn back at that point, which Drita understood wasn't really true but just felt like it. They were double-digit minutes away from something, whatever the thing was, and that was better than forever dwelling at the start.

23

PETE DIDN'T REALLY FEEL LIKE PARTYING, BUT THE WAY THE PEOPLE around him found a way to celebrate something almost daily, he was surprised there wasn't some kind of Saturday night going-away blowout for the goers-away. Not even a round of drinks with the Tristate guys, some of whom would be getting on a flight hours after the ceremony thing Valon and Ramadan were staging, not even a little something to celebrate that the pallets of ammunition they'd wrapped in diapers and canned goods got through JFK with not a single raised brow from security. But Ramadan was on call after call on his mobile phone, talking to congressmen and reporters and all kinds of people Pete was shocked he was able to get on the line. Valon was taking the overflow at the desk in the back office, and all the guys leaving on the first charter apparently had families who wanted to toast or plead with or preemptively grieve them in the privacy of their own homes.

Pete had spent these last weeks grateful for the roof over his head and the paycheck and the cot to rest his body on, spine-wrenching as it was, but mostly for the purpose. He thought he understood for a little bit why Drita wanted to do the kind of work she said she wanted to do, and probably would have been doing if not for his negligence.

He thought he was helping, and it had felt good for a while. Only now he felt that old familiar panic creeping back in, a realization that when he wasn't driving box vans full of rifles and ammunition over state lines, his life in a bird's-eye view didn't look very different than it had in months and years past. No, actually, it did look different; now he slept in a warehouse among buckets of tar and rolls of asphalt, whereas once upon a time he only worked with construction supplies and slept next to a son in a bona fide apartment.

He cracked open the first four of his Heinekens all alone from his cot, watching his commanders do their commanding while he didn't have a single order to fulfill. Going to a bar alone was even sadder than drinking in a warehouse in the presence of people working, though, so he stayed put and watched them, partly out of respect and partly in the hopes that they'd shut it down for the night soon so he could at least pass out unobserved. On the fifth Heineken his self-pity turned to boredom, and on the sixth the sentimentality seeped in, which brought with it, as always, the regret he tried to keep ahead of by never staying in place for too long. He tried to remember if it was his intention when he first drove away from the townhouse in Arizona to be gone forever, or just long enough to show Shanda how sorry he was, or to make Dakota forget he ever existed so he could come back a brand-new man and let that version be the dad the kid got to grow up with. He tried to remember his last night with Dakota, the one where he got sick, if he'd sung to him that horrible Barbie Girl song that he loved only because of how stupidly Pete sang it. More likely he'd just dumped him off in his crib so he could take a few rips from the one-hitter and settle in for a night of kung fu on VHS.

He'd never found the wallet he left behind in whatever bar he'd lost it in that first night in New York City. It had taken two trips to Stamford on the Metro-North plus several extended, loud phone calls to the Connecticut DMV to get a replacement, but in the end it was just a rectangle that any stranger in any office of that bureaucratic hellscape could print out and laminate. The pictures that he'd had in there of

Dakota as a newborn, of him holding Dakota as a newborn, were gone forever, the negatives left behind in some storage unit whose contents had no doubt gone to auction or the dump for nonpayment. He couldn't be trusted with a picture of a son, never mind the human form. And yet he had one—no length of highway, no amount of lager had succeeded in making him forget that he was directly responsible for a life in this world.

Pete was at the bottom of his trip down memory lane when Valon finally wrapped up whatever secretarial work his father had him doing and sat himself in an office chair near Pete.

"Get me a beer," Valon said, sighing in harmony with the hydraulics on the seat post.

It was the kind of order expected to provoke pushback, but Pete didn't have the fight in him. He pulled one out and tossed it to Valon. The foam spilled over the lip of the bottle when Valon cracked it open, and Valon glared at Pete and shook his head.

"Dick," Valon said. "You shook it up."

Pete shrugged.

"Shit's warm, too," Valon said after his first sip, though it didn't stop him from taking a second.

"I'm a fuckup," Pete said.

Valon looked into the eye of his bottle, as if the voice were coming from within. "Dude, I was just joking," he said.

"I wasn't," Pete said.

Valon rubbed his eyes. Pete knew he was trying to signal he wasn't up to having this kind of conversation, but Pete also knew he was too many beers in to stop it.

"I don't know what I'm even doing here," he said.

"You're just pissy because you're not shipping out tomorrow with the rest of the guys. You don't even have a passport. Get your shit together and maybe you can go out on the next trip."

"That's not why I'm pissy," Pete said. "I'm not pissy. I'm just, I don't know, sorry."

"Sorry for what? You been a big help to me and my father, on the roof and off it."

"I just haven't been around long enough for me to mess up yet. Ask anybody who really knows me, it's coming. Ask my sister. Ask Shanda."

"Petrit, I'm telling you, you shouldn't think about that now. There's other girls for you out there. There's still good girls, I promise. Remember Ariona?"

"Yeah, I remember Ariona. Doesn't mean I forgot Shanda."

"Why do you even want to mess around with junkies, dude?"

"I don't want to mess around with junkies, I just wanted to mess around with her." Pete shook his head. "She was like an alien when we first met. Everything was new to her. I felt like a magician just, like, showing her how to ride a bike."

"You couldn't have been stupid enough to think that version was coming back. You know that's not how that shit works."

"I was stupid enough. I was stupid enough to not get why she wanted to be on that shit to begin with."

"The only reason someone wants to start doing heroin is because they're a loser, Pete."

"That's not the only reason. You don't know her," Pete said.

"This is the Bronx. I know people like her all over the place."

"You don't know her," Pete repeated. "Her life was fucked. You can't blame someone for losing if you put them in a game that nobody could win."

"Everybody has to deal with shit. Most people don't deal with it by getting strung out. You didn't."

"What does that matter? Look at me now," Pete said, holding his bottle up in salute or disgust. "I'm more messed up than she ever was."

"All you are is drunk, dude."

"You don't even know, Valon. You don't even know me. You know I have a son?"

Valon froze, his hand midway to his lips, a little sea sloshing at the bottom of the green bottle.

"What?" he said.

"I told you, I'm a fuckup."

"You have a son? Where is he?"

"I don't know anymore. I took off when we were living in Arizona, after I almost accidentally killed him. Figured he was better off without me."

"That's fucked up, Petrit," Valon said. The disgust in his voice was gratifying to Pete, because he deserved it, and devastating, because there was still some stupid part of him that believed Valon could make Pete's worst suspicions about himself not true. "How do you leave your own kid? That's something Americans do. That's not what we do."

"A bunch of guys are leaving their kids to get on a plane in a couple days," Pete said.

"To do something their kids will be proud of, Pete, not to abandon them."

Pete shrugged. "Now do you believe me?"

Valon didn't answer, which was an answer in itself.

"We tried, kind of. I tried," Pete went on. "We were working, she wasn't using. Dakota was easy. He wasn't like other babies, he was so easy. I don't know why I thought it was hard, all we had to do was feed him and change his diapers and make stupid faces at him. He didn't cry that much. And Shanda was kind of normal, and I was kind of normal, and everything was pretty good for a while."

It was obvious even to a thoroughly buzzed Pete that this was not a conversation Valon wanted to be having.

"But then I thought I killed him. He got sick, and man, I watched him froth at the mouth like a . . ." Pete inhaled. "We had this neighbor when I was a kid who hated when people's cats went into his yard. They didn't even do anything to his yard, they just annoyed him for being alive in his space. One day he got so sick of it that he put out bowls of antifreeze in the middle of winter 'cause he knew they'd go for it when everything else was all iced up. I saw this one cat just, like, foaming at the mouth, throwing up like crazy, and then it had, like, a seizure or something and I just watched it happen."

"Did you give your son antifreeze?" Valon asked. "Did you poison him?"

"Jesus, dude, no, I didn't give him antifreeze," Pete said.

"Then how is him getting sick your fault?"

"I'm just saying I watched it happen. I didn't do anything. I couldn't get my dumb ass to do anything to help."

"That's normal, dude, that's called being in shock."

"How am I gonna go fight a war if I go into shock watching some-one else die? If I can't even hack my kid having a seizure on the patio?"

Valon pulled a Parliament from his shirt pocket and put it to his lips. "You don't have to worry about that right now." He lit up, and it wasn't the smell but watching the cigarette's burning tip bounce as Valon spoke that forced Pete to turn away.

"Well, when am I supposed to worry about it? What am I even sup-posed to be worrying about? You're leaving in a couple days. Your dad isn't going to want me around."

"You still got a pretty Amerikani face and pretty American papers," Valon said.

"So your dad will still want to use me as, like, a mule?" Pete said.

"What's wrong with doing your part, Petrit?" Valon asked, finally looking back at Pete. "There's sixteen-year-olds signed up to fight. They're kids, and they're already thinking about things bigger than their own sixteen-year-old problems. What are you, twenty-six? A full-grown man, and your little Connecticut-grown ass still can't think about anybody but himself."

Pete wished he'd never said anything at all, which was to say he wished he could delete the last five beers. He could've asked Valon to come along to some strip club, knowing Valon wouldn't, and slipped out into the night without ever having to confess any of this to him.

But even however many Heinekens in as he was, Pete should've known that Valon wasn't a sleeping kid he could walk out on unde-tected.

"I'm just a roofer, dude," Pete said instead.

"Then stay here and be just a roofer, for all I care," Valon said. He stubbed his cigarette on the boot of his Wolverines and dropped the butt in the dregs of Heineken. "I swear, I don't even know what you're doing with that tattoo on your chest."

Pete shrugged. "I thought it was a cool picture," he said, after Valon had already walked out the door and disappeared into Arthur Avenue.

24

THE PARKING LOT HAD BEEN REPURPOSED AS THE STAGING AREA for the main event, which meant Drita had to park the car blocks away, and as they walked back toward the hotel Drita could have almost believed they were en route to the same kinds of festivals that took place every spring and summer at Lakewood Park back in Waterbury: the Greek and the Ponte and the Dominican, with the flags and the food trucks and the fights that inevitably broke out after the teenagers had been left unattended with smuggled six-packs of Zima all afternoon. On closer look, though, the only thing those festivalgoers and this crowd had in common were the miniature flags they clutched like desperate last cigarettes. The older women wore shapeless dresses and headscarves, and the younger women wore shirts that barely covered their rib cages, and in all of them Drita looked for something she might call resemblance, as if she might possess some native trait that would make her feel any sense that she deserved to be among them.

Shanda trailed behind Drita, and Dakota somehow managed to trail behind both of them, even tethered to Shanda's hand. Shanda and Dakota made no attempt to fit in, but to Drita's relief they weren't the only ones who stuck out. Most of the crowd was Albanian—if the flags didn't give them away, their Italian loafers and unfiltered cigarettes did—but there were others who weren't, and it was easy enough to tell because the rest wore press passes printed with names like Amy or Jared, along with dispositions that ranged from official to bored.

"That's actual news," Shanda said, pointing to a video camera that took two people to fully unfurl from its bag. The equipment was branded CNN, and Drita was simultaneously impressed and apprehensive in a way that would probably have been more useful ninety minutes before, when they had started their drive. What seemed to her until then like a niche street fair could turn out to be something Wolf Blitzer weighed in on, and she wondered again what authority she thought she had to be there at all, among the true believers and the aspiring soldiers and devastated left-behinds.

"Hey, Dakota, you might end up on TV. You might be famous," she said instead, as if they were touring a film set. He didn't move his eyes from the people in camouflage, which on blacktop in Yonkers was very much not meant to blend in. Maybe it had been a mistake to bring Dakota after all; he wasn't the only kid there, but he seemed to be the only one not hoisted on a father's shoulders, sitting astride the necks of men in military fatigues adorned with American and UÇK patches. Somehow those men had figured out how to be fathers and fighters both, and here she and Shanda were with their eyes peeled for the man who'd thus far only managed flight. Dakota looked at them the way she'd only seen him look at screens before that, and she felt a momentary pain in her chest that reminded her heartache wasn't an abstraction. She turned back to Dakota to ask if he wanted to sit on her shoulders, but he shook his head and looked at his feet in something very near shame.

"No?" Drita asked. "Why not? Is it because I'm not a soldier? I won't drop you, I promise," she said.

He mumbled something that Drita was going to ask him to repeat, but Shanda interpreted on his behalf.

"He has to pee," she said.

"Oh." Drita knelt down to Dakota's face level, and although she was a little annoyed that he hadn't gone at their last McDonald's stop thirty miles before, she told him, "You don't have to be embarrassed about that."

"You walk so fast," he said, and Drita wasn't sure how that was a response.

"Well," she said, "if you were on my shoulders, you'd be going fast, too."

"If he were on your shoulders, your back would be wet in about three minutes," Shanda said. "I think I saw a porta-potty on the other side of the fence."

Drita's sigh was so slight that the ambient noise swallowed it. "Okay, go ahead. I'm going to stick around here and keep an eye out."

But her eyes wouldn't find what she was looking for outside the lot, where the civilians streamed in and the cops intervened only to direct the prettiest young Balkanistas to the ceremony, where, to the cops' disappointment, the girls' betrotheds would swear allegiance to their homeland and the UÇK. It wasn't like anyone could get lost, even if the young women were as dumb as the cops wished they were, because inside the perimeter of the lot the recruits had already congregated in a formation that appeared vaguely military, at least according to versions of the military that Drita had seen in movies, which is where she assumed these soldiers had also gotten their training. She craned her neck to try to spot Shanda and Dakota, but they'd already been swallowed by a crowd that she told herself wasn't so thick that they wouldn't find each other again if she jumped the gun and entered the fray. So she did, and took advantage of being alone to sidle swiftly toward the front of the crowd, taking in the serious faces of those in fatigues and ball caps with gold-and-red emblems, the double-headed eagle matching the one Pete would always wear on his chest.

She was surprised by the number of volunteers, at least a few hundred ranging from high schoolers to advanced middle age. She was more surprised by the few female faces she saw, dressed in the same ill-fitting fatigues as the men around them and looking at least as tough, a different breed than the girlfriends and wives and mothers, who seemed born mourners, likely because they'd had reasons to mourn long before that chilly Saturday. Drita was no military strategist, but even in their stiff Army-Navy camo and combat boots, it didn't seem like an army that could win a ground war. Still, she could understand how it could win the battle that she knew Valon and his father intended to wage that day: the one to get people with actual power to drop more bombs on this army's behalf, to get them to press a few buttons and detonate a few of the million pounds of munitions Americans made sure the whole world knew they had in their possession. Brave faces, anguished faces, stoic faces, faces of those too old to assimilate when they'd fled their homelands, faces of kids who had been born on American soil and would never be fluent in the language of their parents, if they were fortunate enough to ever know them. All of them European-looking enough to pass on national television, so long as the average Americans watching could convince themselves the headscarves the old women wore were the kind their own great-great-great-grandmothers wore in heirloom photos taken in folksy Bavarian villages, and not because they were Muslim.

The woman to Drita's right turned to her and spoke something that Drita didn't understand.

"I'm sorry?" Drita said.

"Nuk je shqiptar?" the woman said. "You're not Albanian?"

"No, I am," Drita said.

"Oh," the woman said. "Who are you sending to fight?"

The woman had no idea how complicated both of the questions she'd asked were, and Drita understood that the woman was not seeking complicated answers.

"My brother," she answered. "You?"

"My husband, two brothers, three cousins, and my uncle all signed up," the woman said. "Your husband didn't?"

"I'm not married," Drita said.

The woman gasped. "But you're so pretty."

"I can't cook," Drita said. "Why aren't you crying, sending so many people over to fight?"

"Only my two young cousins leave tomorrow," the woman said. "The rest are waiting to be called."

"Aren't you scared for them?"

"I'm too proud to be scared. They're going to fight for our country, our freedom." It sounded like the kind of canned sound bite one of the news reporters could have pulled from archival footage without having to trek all the way to Yonkers, but the woman spoke it so emphatically that she bounced as she said it, for lack of walls around her to pound on. "If we don't fight, they'll do to us what they did to the Bosnians. They've already started. You know this, that's why your brother's going. Aren't you proud of him, too?"

"I'd like to be, but I can't find him. I've gotta go find him. Sorry. Mirupafshim," Drita said, surprising even herself that she remembered enough from Valon's emails to attempt a word aloud.

Drita began to walk the perimeter of crowd, a semicircle closing in on the enlistees and a podium at which a few suited men talked among themselves. She scanned deeper into the rows of volunteer soldiers but didn't see the face she was looking for, though who knew what Pete looked like at that point. In the years since she'd seen him, he might've gone puffy from too much pilsner and Hot Pockets, or he might've gotten concave from not scoring enough shifts from construction foremen who plucked up day laborers in Dunkin' Donuts parking lots, or he might actually be as clean-shaven and handsome as that news article that started this chase a few weeks back suggested. The Pete-less cadets she could make out encompassed that full range, but none of them were familiar in a way that only a brother, or at least a man known to her since infancy, could be. Sometimes a dim face shadowed by the brim of a visor made her take a second look, but each turned out to be someone else's brother to grieve or, as the woman she'd just met was doing, celebrate.

Drita couldn't do either. They'd exited the Sonata only fifteen minutes before, but already Drita feared an impending futility, the sense that her best-laid plans would end no differently than the tiny impulsive ones she'd been enacting on a daily basis. But before she could break away from the crowd and march through the rows, one of the men at the podium tapped on the live microphone and cleared his throat into it, signaling it was time for silence and stillness from the crowd.

"Përshëndetje and mirëseardhje," the man said. "Hello and welcome."

His voice was loud and resonant but not especially polished, a slurry of Albanian and borough, the aural equivalent of what he looked like: thick head of salt-and-pepper hair, off-the-rack dress shirt beneath a worn leather jacket, gold chain polished enough for the glint to reach Drita twenty yards away. He spoke not with the polish of a politician but with the ease and confidence of a man delivering a toast at a wedding. Behind him were mostly variations of the same man—some in wool sweaters instead of button-downs, some in brown slacks instead of gray—except for one, who wore the same military camo as the enlistees the speaker gestured to, on his head an emblazoned beret instead of a cap. He stood several feet behind a cluster of what Drita might call elders, but his proximity to them made it clear that he held some elevated position, something that in the case of an authorized military force might be conveyed with an insignia and not just a general air of authority. And though his attire was entirely different from the Champion sweatshirt and Knicks cap he wore the last time she saw him, or at least a low-resolution photo of him, Drita recognized Valon the moment she saw him.

"Oh," Drita said aloud, though by that time the American national anthem had begun playing and swallowed the sound. She craned her neck to look for Shanda and Dakota, but there was no sign of them, and maybe that was for the best. If she hadn't gleaned it from their emails she would have deduced from his posture alone that Valon was no skittish stray animal, but now she worried that accosting him three-on-one would scare him off, and Drita didn't want to scare him off. She didn't want to scare him off because she needed him to tell them where Pete was, but she understood as she stared at him that it wasn't fear alone that caused the sudden quake in her knees. She felt like she had her first time on roller skates, her legs not fully under her own control.

There, not twenty yards away, stood the human form that machinery could never fully replicate.

The man on the microphone spoke what Drita knew, despite understanding none of the words he spoke, to be slogans and implorations to give their lives, or at least some money, to the cause of their people. That man ceded the mic to another, who delivered in English the thoroughly New Yorker version of what the first man had said. Like when she was watching the Olympics, Drita felt an unexpected surge of patriotism. She clapped when the people around her did. She chanted, "UÇK! Free Kosova!" along with her neighbors. She waited for Valon to speak, and when the speeches and ceremonies were over and he hadn't taken the mic, she found herself even more intrigued, because here was evidence that Valon was a man who acted and not a man who talked about acting.

After the last cries of *Long live Kosova! Long live the Albanian people!,* Drita shouldered her way through the crowd like a groupie eager to get backstage. An older man caught her eye and winked at her, and she was almost grateful for the heat the embarrassment brought to her skin, because the gray April day had turned cooler and she had started to shiver. She worried the incoming rain would disperse the crowd before she found him, but after a few minutes, one of the men whistled and shouted, "Valon!" a sound that raised her pulse and made it impossible to distinguish her sweat from the drizzle. She stepped back a few paces, trying to appear only incidentally close, but she pulled back in when she saw Valon approach the group again. She wasn't there to eavesdrop, and she would need an interpreter for that anyway, but she heard him speak for the first time and it somehow felt familiar.

She watched him kiss the cheeks of a new man who entered the circle—a local politician, she gleaned from his boring suit, overly enthusiastic smile, and the fact that the men around him switched to English when he joined them—and she heard the man who'd winked at her introduce Valon to the suit as his son.

And then Valon looked over.

In the first seconds of eye contact, his face retained the same stony composure he'd been wearing throughout the ceremony, and Drita instantly lost the nerve she'd been building in all the days leading up to that afternoon. Something shifted, though, and his eyes stayed fixed on her even as he continued talking to the men around him, until after an unbearable minute he patted the shoulder of the suit and broke away. He headed straight toward her, and if she could've gotten her legs to move she wasn't sure if they would've moved toward him or run away.

She didn't have to make a decision, because suddenly he was there.

"Lindita?" he asked.

Drita stared at the patch on his chest, a stray black thread hanging from the talon of the double-headed eagle like some prey it was bringing home to its nest.

"What are you doing here? You didn't tell me you were coming here. I wish you would've told me, I could have met you somewhere nicer." He paused, and his smile revealed a row of slightly crowded teeth that he kept hidden in his photo. "Fuck. I'm glad you're here, though."

"You look good," she said. "You're a soldier."

"My god, Lindita." He smiled bigger and stepped back to take her all in. "I can't believe you're really here."

"I'm really here," she said. "I mean, kind of."

Valon grabbed her hand and brought her right index finger to his lips, like he was the star of a pirated version of the most clichéd Western romance imported to the Balkans. It was exquisite and excruciating and Drita wished it didn't feel as good as the movies had always made it seem.

"What do you mean, kind of? Are you a mirage?" he asked, still smiling, still locked in to her eyes.

"No," she said. "I'm just—"

"Just what?" Drita missed Valon's smile as soon as it disappeared. "Did you lie when you said you didn't have a boyfriend?"

"No," she said, "I lied when I said my name was Lindita."

The smile returned, and now Drita wished it would go away again, because it made saying what she had to say even worse.

"What, you don't like your real name? That's fine, I'll call you whatever you want," he said. "I tell people my name is Val sometimes, it doesn't matter."

"My name is Drita," she said.

"Drita's nice."

"Drita's not nice. I mean, the name is fine. I don't mean the name."

He laughed. "I think Drita's nice," he said.

"Listen," she said. "God, this sucks. I want you to know that I really like you."

"You do have a boyfriend, don't you?" he asked.

"No, I have a brother," she said. "His name is Pete, or maybe he goes by Petrit now."

Valon paused, then asked, "Pete? Pete what?"

"Pete DiMeo," she answered.

Valon dropped her hand. "You said Pete was your friend's brother."

"I know I said that, because I was trying to find him and I didn't want you to know that I was trying to find him because I thought you might tell him and you wouldn't write back to me."

"So you lied to me."

She didn't nod that time. "It wasn't because of you," she said. "I just really wanted to find him, and if he knew I was looking for him he'd probably just take off again. You don't know Pete like I do."

"And you don't know me," Valon said. "Because if you did you would know what I think about liars."

"I lied, I did," Drita said. "But I'm not a liar, I swear. The important things I didn't lie about."

"So you're twenty-one? You work at a grocery store?"

Drita paused. "Those weren't the important things," she said.

Valon shook his head slowly and began to walk away, and Drita surprised herself by chasing him and pulling hard on his arm.

"I'm sorry," she said. "Can I make you understand?"

Valon gathered all of Drita's fingers in one firm clasp and pulled them from his biceps, and of all the moments in the past months in which Drita was acutely aware of the absence of another physical body, this was the first to bring tears to her eyes.

"Did you know he has a son?" Drita said.

"He told me that," Valon answered coldly.

"Did you know his son almost died, and that he left him all alone with someone who had nowhere to turn?"

"He told me that, too," Valon said.

"So you know he left his sick son," Drita repeated.

"Yes, he told me that last night."

"And you're okay with that?" Drita asked.

"No, it's fucked up," Valon said. "I just didn't know being fucked up runs in the family."

"I'm not fucked up," Drita said. "At least, not like that."

"You're fucked up in the better way, then?"

Drita didn't answer that.

"I didn't think he should be doing what he was doing with you," she said. "I don't think he even knows what he's doing with you."

"And you do? He was doing the least selfish thing possible," Valon said. "All for people he doesn't even know."

"But he's got a family," Drita said. "You understand that, don't you? You told me Albanians were all about family, about loyalty. Besa and all that."

"Don't talk to me about besa," he said. "You don't know anything about besa."

"I had to lie, I didn't want to. I promise you, it was to help you, too. You need to know that Pete's not cut out for this. He doesn't even know what he's doing."

"And you do?"

"I thought I did. I was just looking for Pete at first, but then I found you, and you made me understand what's happening to people over there, and you—" A tendril of hair had escaped from Valon's beret, and she couldn't reach over and put it back in place. "Things got more complicated than I thought they would."

"Let me simplify things for you," Valon said. "You found your brother, good for you. Go get him and be fucked up together. Go act out your bullshit little American soap opera and let me get back to some real work." He turned away from her and shook his head. "All that time I wasted writing to you, all that sleep I didn't get. All this time you were using me."

"I thought I was using you for a good reason," Drita said. "The way you did with Pete."

Valon's face no longer looked at all the way it did in the square-jawed photo he'd sent, when she imagined trading in the pixelated skin for the kind she could touch. Now that she was so close to the flesh, it was even colder than its digital replica.

"He's probably sleeping off last night's case of beer," Valon said. "He wouldn't last a minute going where I'm going." He handed her a business card, as if they were at a trade show. "I'm just telling you this because of the kid. So you can all get on with your fucked-up lives." Drita looked at the address printed on the card, somewhere in the Bronx, just like that Eagle Calling Fund advertisement in the mosque newsletter that kicked off the whole doomed search in what felt like a different life altogether.

Valon raised his hand in a military salute so poorly executed that it would have been offensive to a patriot, but Drita wasn't a patriot. She didn't know what she was, except for faintly grateful and very sorry. Then he walked away, toward an unknown fate that he nonetheless headed toward without hesitation.

The crowd dispersed as the mist consolidated into heavier, steadier drops of rain. Drita sat on a curb beneath the hotel's portico not to stay dry but to be unseen, and it worked long enough for Shanda to be her version of distressed when she finally stumbled on Drita, almost literally.

"Drita, where the hell were you? We've been looking for you for like an hour," Shanda said. "Dakota was about to have a meltdown."

Drita looked up at Dakota, whose huge cheeks showed evidence of past tears but no suggestion of more on the way. Even if he were to unclench the pencil-thin pole of the cheap polyester flag that he'd somehow acquired, he wouldn't be reaching to wrap his arms around Aunt Drita's neck. It wasn't his way, even at five, in what were supposed to be the waning years of that being a boy's way. But he stared at her gravely and confirmed what his mother had said.

"Aunt Drita, we were looking for you," he said, and Drita had to sit on her hands to keep them from grabbing onto him.

"You found me, kid," Drita said. "Now what?"

He furrowed his little brows and thought seriously about it. "McDonald's?" he proposed.

"You know that stuff's not good for you, right?"

He tilted his head like a puppy at a new command. "But you brought me there," he said, confused.

"Yeah, I guess I did. It was good that day. I mean not the food. I mean that that was a good day. I liked that day."

"Me, too, Aunt Drita," he said, almost consolingly.

"I didn't see him anywhere," Shanda said. "Pete. I looked up and down all the rows and I didn't see him."

"He wasn't here," Drita said.

"Oh," Shanda said. Drita didn't look up at her to detect on Shanda's face the tone that her voice was so bad at conveying. "Well, you tried."

"I know where he is, though. Well, kind of. Maybe. I know I told you that before, but it might be true this time." Drita pushed a curl away from Dakota's forehead just to touch him, and she considered it a small victory that he, unlike Valon, allowed it. "His friend—one of the guys who's behind all of this," she said, motioning to the parking lot, though by then it was largely empty of everything but cars, "he gave me the address of the place Pete's been staying." Drita rose to her feet and scanned the lot. It looked like the same key figures who acted as military commanders and international war financiers were also facilities staff, breaking down the PA system and temporary stage. "It's not that far from here."

"Maybe we're just not supposed to find him," Shanda said.

"It's like ten miles away," Drita said. "It'll take twenty minutes to drive there."

"Dakota's tired. He's hungry. He's not going to make it."

"We can stop at a McDonald's along the way."

"Drita, let's just stop it now. I don't need to find him."

"What?" Drita said. Valon was nowhere to be seen among the lingering crew, which felt like both a reminder of her failures thus far and an imperative to correct them. "We're so close. You came all the way across the country for this."

"No I didn't," Shanda said. "That's not why we came back."

"Then why did you come back?" Drita said.

Shanda squeezed her lips together, as if trying to keep the next words from coming out. They opened again, she drew a deep breath, looked toward the sky, and said, "I was trying to find you."

A nearby car stalled at a light, an advertisement for a regional video store chain blaring from the radio. It was testament to the jingle writer, Drita thought, that she could place the notes immediately, while she could hardly recognize the words coming from Shanda's lips.

"I'm sorry, what?" Drita said.

"We almost killed him. Me and Pete," Shanda said quietly, though Dakota was occupied with finding crevices in the sidewalk into which to plant his flag. "We can't do this. You told us we couldn't do it, and you were right."

Drita shook her head, at first to deny that she'd ever said that, and then as the beginning of an apology.

"Pete said you were going to, like, save babies in South America or whatever. I thought you could save him."

"Shanda," Drita started.

"I didn't want to hurt him, it just happened."

"Shanda," Drita said.

"I'm not trying to just, like, dump him on you. I know you're trying to get out of here, too. I thought I would call you, but I was chicken-shit, and then my mother died and you were there and it was like fate, and you said you would help, and then all this happened. I thought you might know what to do for him. I figured you were somebody who knows how to do things."

"What happened to him was an accident," Drita said.

"You told us from the beginning it would happen. If not that, ex-actly, then something like it."

"That makes me an asshole, Shanda, not a fortune-teller."

"You didn't need to be a fortune-teller. It would've been obvious to anyone with a brain. I'm a junkie, Pete's a fuckup who got a junkie pregnant. You were right."

"Well," Drita said. "You're not a junkie anymore."

"For how long this time?"

"Remember how you freaked out on me when you came home and we weren't there?"

Shanda flushed. "I have issues with impulse control. That's what my counselor says."

"Well, your impulse was to freak out because you were scared some-thing happened to your son. That seems like, I don't know, your in-stincts are working fine."

"It's not like you kidnapped him. You were taking care of him. I was wrong then, too."

"Join the club," Drita said. "I don't have the best track record with people, if you haven't noticed. I haven't been much of a family to him. I haven't been much of an anything to anybody."

"You let us move in with you. You're trying to help us now."

"But I'm not actually helping. I'm never actually helping. And I'm not even—" Drita swallowed. "I'm not even really Dakota's aunt."

"What are you talking about?" Shanda said. "Of course you are."

"No, I'm not. It's a long story, but Jackie just told me that Pete isn't really my brother. She lied to us our whole lives. We're not twins. Our mother didn't wash up dead in Italy."

"What?" Shanda started. "Then what actually are you?"

Drita suspected that Shanda didn't intentionally ask a profound question, and so she ignored it.

"Just people who ended up together," she finally said.

"Well, that's all anybody is to anybody, right?" Shanda said. "Unless they don't get that lucky."

Drita stepped back and took in Shanda. She was looking for cruelty, or mocking, or even something as simple and reassuring as confusion.

"It means I'm not really Dakota's family," Drita said.

"That's just, like, a matter of blood. What does that have to do with anything?"

"Pete always said it was everything. Everybody says it's everything," Drita said. "These people"—Drita pointed to the errant bodies in the distance—"they'll kill and die for it."

"Pete doesn't know shit," Shanda said. "I don't know about all the rest of these people."

"I don't know shit, either," Drita said.

"And I don't, either," Shanda said. "And look at us looking to each other for help, huh?"

Drita's eyes stung, which she blamed on the wafting Marlboro smoke and exhaust fumes that clouded the parking lot. Shanda had been right from the beginning; this was no place for a kid, or at least this kid, no matter what flag he held in his chubby little fist.

"What do you think, Dakota? What are we supposed to do now?" Drita asked.

He screwed his face into his thinking pose and offered, again, "McDonald's?"

Drita closed her eyes and willed the moisture to stay behind her lids. "That doesn't sound so bad, kid," she said. She swallowed and turned back to Shanda. "Listen, you're fine. I think you two are just fine. I think you two— I think you're good."

The sky was too gray for Shanda's eyes to water just from looking at it, but Drita wouldn't make her pretend it was from anything other than that.

"You're right, too. This is too much for Dakota. I'm sorry I kept you out here so long. You guys should head back. I'll give you some money, you can take the train. I'm going to try this last stop."

"You can't make Pete do anything he doesn't want to do," Shanda reminded her again.

"I know. I just." Drita pressed the corner of the business card into the flesh of her index finger. Valon's name wasn't even on it, just a generic business name and address that betrayed nothing about the man's true purpose. "It's more about what I want to do."

25

1982

PETE SPRINTED TOWARD HIS BEDROOM SO THAT HE COULD WHIP UP a card for Drita before she got home from the tap class Jackie made her take. Somehow, even sharing a birthday, Pete was so focused on the handheld Space Invaders game he knew Jackie had gotten him—despite Dom saying it would rot the brain cells that Pete couldn't afford to lose—that he had forgotten to find a present for her. He figured he could make up a coupon to stick inside the card, something like One Free Bike Ride or Get Out of Headlock Free, something he could later decide whether or not to honor. He crashed through his door, which for some reason was ajar, and almost tumbled into the wheel-chair and human body waiting for him there. The scream his throat released sounded exactly like one he would have laughed at Drita for, and even in his momentary panic he was glad she wasn't there to hear it.

"Ma," he cried, mostly to reassure himself that it was, in fact, only Jackie and not a serial killer who put on her clothes and sat in her chair after dismembering her body. Jackie was, in fact, intact. Not only intact, but with company; another lady sat on his bed, her arms wrapped around his pillow as if it were a teddy bear.

"Hi, honey," Jackie said. She sounded funny, like a record on at the wrong speed, a little slowed down and deeper in pitch.

"Hi," Pete said. He assumed he was in trouble and tried to think of what he had done. No notes from his teachers, nothing in the house was broken, he hadn't done anything to Drita so bad that she would've told on him for it. He didn't recognize the lady as one of their neighbors, and definitely not the one whose tree he'd been using for target practice after he'd stolen back the Chinese star Dom had confiscated when he saw what Pete had done to his walls with it. Also, Jackie had called him honey, which wasn't what Jackie called him before he got in trouble, unless it was the kind of trouble that was the result of being so dumb that he couldn't be blamed for it, like when she saw his report card and said, all softly, Oh, honey.

"Come sit with us a minute, will you?" she said. Pete hesitantly stepped closer. She smelled funny, too, kind of like the art teacher did after he came back from retrieving the thing he always said he forgot in his car. "Go on, you can share the bed with Nella."

"I don't bite, sweetie," the lady on the bed said, flashing a row of teeth that looked like they were made from cookie dough. They probably couldn't do much damage if she did bite, which somehow didn't make Pete feel better. She smelled even more like the art teacher than the art teacher himself did, so he dropped down cautiously at the foot of the bed, so far down that he had to brace his feet on the ground to support the weight the edge of the mattress couldn't.

The lady moved closer, though, and there was nowhere left for him to go. She brushed her fingers through his hair, not in the morning way of fixing it but in the weird way that Jackie sometimes did it when he was by himself watching TV or drawing, minding his own business.

"You're getting so big," the lady said. "Nine years old. I can't hardly believe it. It feels like days."

"And a century," Jackie said.

"Yeah, that too," the lady said.

"Pete," Jackie said. "Do you know who this is?"

Without looking at the lady, Pete shook his head. She sounded as weird as she smelled and looked, like her throat had been rubbed down with sandpaper.

"This is your godmother, Pete."

Pete looked at the lady. Even after he stopped believing in the fairy variety, he still never imagined godmothers like this. This lady wasn't plump or winged or jolly, and he didn't think she was Albanian, and that was the only kind of long-lost family he imagined ever tracking him and Drita down someday. "What do you think about that, Pete?" Jackie asked. "Isn't she pretty?"

She looked tired and maybe old, though not old like a grandmother. It was a different kind of old, more like something that had been forgotten about.

"I didn't know we had a godmother," Pete said.

"Well," Jackie said, looking briefly at the woman, at Nella, as Jackie had called her. "She's only your godmother, Pete."

"Drita has a different one?" Pete said.

"Drita has lots of her own things," Jackie said, after a brief pause. "This is a thing just for you."

Pete slid his eyes over to the woman, who must've been smiling at him the whole time. He wasn't sure he wanted a godmother. He wasn't sure what he was supposed to do with a godmother that wasn't there to grant wishes or whisk him away to some better place, like he assumed Albania was.

The woman held out a card to him. "There's some money inside," she said, as if to answer his doubts about her usefulness. "For your birthday. I don't know what you like so I figured you could buy it yourself." Then the lady looked at Jackie and addressed her as if Pete wasn't in the room at all. "I wish I knew what he liked. I wish I knew more about him."

"I never knew where you were, Nella," Jackie said.

"Nowhere I wanted you to know about," the lady said. She started to cry, and not in the quiet, secret way that grown-ups were supposed to cry, hidden in a bathroom or early in the morning, when other people weren't supposed to be awake. This lady cried like kids did, loud and ugly.

"You never need to hide from me," Jackie answered her, crying in the more dignified adult way.

Pete took the opportunity to open the card, some powder-blue cursive thing with a poem he assumed wasn't meant for nine-year-olds and thus ignored, and found a fifty-dollar bill inside.

"Whoa," Pete said, interrupting the crying of the other two points in the room's weird human triangle.

"Oh, Nella, no," Jackie said. "That's too much. You need that."

"It's nothing, Jackie. I never gave him anything at all before," the lady said.

"You gave him everything," Jackie said. "You gave me everything."

Fifty dollars, more than Pete had ever held in his hand at one time, and it was all for him, and only him.

"Say thank you, Pete," Jackie said, trying to get back to sounding like a regular grown-up.

"You don't need to thank me," the lady said, looking straight at Pete, then turning back to Jackie. "Thank you for this. I really needed something good."

"He's here for you if you need him again," Jackie said.

Pete looked back down at the green bill in between his fingers. That money in his hand was supposed to be a present, and presents were things you were supposed to get for nothing or for birthdays, but he apparently had given this lady something without even knowing what it was. It felt like they were doing something behind his back and he didn't like that it made him feel stupid, but he did get fifty bucks out of it, so he decided to keep his mouth shut.

The whole room stayed quiet, in fact, until Jackie sighed heavily and said, "Drita's going to be home soon." Another sigh, and then, "Dom, too."

The godmother's face was moist in all its little crevices, and black grit stuck to her lashes and the hollows underneath her eyes. She looked like she might cry again, but she held it in and Pete was glad for it. He flinched a little when she ran her thumbs down his cheeks, but he tolerated it by thinking of the shopping spree fifty dollars would get him. It was probably enough for a skateboard, a Powell-Peralta, not the cheap Kmart decks that he usually got and broke within weeks.

"It was so good to see you, Petrit," the godmother said.

Pete wasn't used to hearing his full name. He nodded. It didn't make sense to say it was good to see this stranger who showed up out of nowhere with some title that obviously didn't mean what he thought it meant, but if five minutes with her earned him more than taking out the whole neighborhood's trash, he could get himself to fake a little something.

"You too," he said. The godmother's face crumpled once more, but Jackie thankfully ushered her out before it could get weird again.

Pete was still thinking about the board when Jackie let herself back into his room a few minutes later. Black deck with orange wheels. Or red. Maybe electric green. But probably orange.

"Is everything okay with you, sweetie?" Jackie said.

It looked like someone should've been asking that question to Jackie, not the other way around. Her face was all puffy and pink and she was attempting a smile that kept moving the wrong way on her face.

"Yeah," he said.

"How did you feel about meeting your godmother?" she asked.

He shrugged. "It was okay."

"I'm glad, honey," she said. "And it looks like you're rich now."

Pete smiled. "Yeah, that part was awesome."

"Good." Jackie put her hands to her face to assess the damage. "So the thing is, Pete, is we can't tell anybody about that visit."

It might have been a trick. Not telling anybody was kind of like lying, and Jackie usually yelled at Pete for doing that.

"Okay," Pete said slowly.

"It's just, we don't want Drita to feel left out, do we?"

"No," Pete said, although he often felt left out when Drita got things that he didn't, like hearing *good job* when she brought home tests that didn't need to be signed and returned. And having fifty dollars would be less fun if he didn't get to brag about it.

"And your father isn't really a big fan of Nella, and you know how cranky he can get."

"Why doesn't he like her?" Pete asked.

"Oh, you know, she's gotten into some trouble in her life," Jackie said. "She's made some bad choices. But she's really a good person when you look past all that. But you know Dom doesn't like to look past anything."

He did know that. Now, at least Pete wasn't the only one in that camp.

"You know you're good, too, right?" Jackie asked. "Even if you have some trouble sometimes, too?"

Pete nodded, mostly to get Jackie to get on with it. He still had to make Drita's card. He still had time to ride to the park and see if there was anybody there he could show off his cash to, as long as it wasn't so many people that he had to worry about getting jumped.

"Okay," Jackie said. "Between you and me, okay?"

"Okay," Pete said, and to his relief, it was the magic word to get Jackie to smile for real and begin to wheel herself to the door.

Except it wasn't, apparently, because right at the threshold she stopped and dropped her head into her hands.

"I haven't seen her in such a long time," Jackie said. She was talking funny again. "She just went away."

Jackie swiveled her neck to look at him, and Pete's eyes fixed on the doorknob so as not to have to stare back. He didn't think this was the kind of thing he was supposed to know how to respond to, like the things they talked about on the news.

"But I have you," she said. "Right?"

"And Drita," he reminded her.

Jackie turned back in her chair, and he could see the back of her head bob up and down before she rolled down the hall.

Pete looked at the bill in his hand. Jackie was being so funny. Something smelled funny about that whole afternoon, actually, and the money seemed like it was meant to throw him off the scent. As far as he knew, people didn't show up out of thin air to give you money just because it was your birthday. If being good was supposed to be the thing that got you rewards, then it wasn't fair that Drita didn't get a godmother who handed out fifty dollars. It wasn't fair that Drita wasn't even going to get the present she wanted, which was the Parisian Barbie she also hadn't gotten for Christmas. Sometimes it was like Jackie wasn't really paying attention to Drita at all.

But he almost forgot about his own sister's birthday, too, which meant he was no better than Jackie. He had to make that card, this time with a coupon for something he really intended to give her. He went searching for some paper and then remembered that he was already clutching some, and that it was way better than the kind that came from the big pad of construction paper he was looking for. He could buy her something, an actual present that she actually wanted, not a ticket for two hours of her-choice TV.

"Ma, I'm going to ride my bike," Pete called on his way out the door. He didn't pause to listen to her yell back that he had to be home by six or that he should stay within the five-block radius he was supposed to be restricted to, because Bradlees was outside of that radius and that's where he was heading. He rode as hard as he could and regretted wearing his winter coat, because he had sweat almost all the way through it by the time he made it to Bradlees. He was still sweating when he raced through the aisles until he came to the toy section and found the one from the abandoned Christmas list: Parisian Barbie. Drita was right, it was cute. He'd just recently begun having physical responses to other bodies, apparently even ones that weren't real or remotely to scale, and suddenly he was happy he was wearing a winter coat that hit just below his groin. By the time he got home, though, his excitement was no longer from racing his bike or involuntary physical arousal but because he knew that he had done something that would blow Drita away.

He was right.

"Oh my god," Drita said, when he handed it to her.

Pete felt a jolt bigger than when he got his own presents, even the surprise fifty-dollar bill, and it made him wonder if his dumb teacher had been right back in third grade, that giving was better than receiving. He watched her jaw drop and felt a tickle in his belly that he assumed was pride, but before that could be confirmed, he watched with horror as tears slicked her eyes.

"That's the one you said you wanted," he said, not sure if he should have been tacking an apology onto it.

"It is the one I wanted," Drita said. "It's just that I don't have anything for you."

It was Pete's turn for his jaw to unhinge. Drita always had something for him, even on the occasions that didn't call for gifts, like Easter and the Fourth of July. Every time she would point out some defect in it and say it was stupid, but Pete suspected that was just to make him feel better about him not being like her. She doubled down on the presents after he'd been held back by that same dumb third-grade teacher, even sometimes making him something like a suncatcher for no reason at all. It's like she was always trying to gift to Pete some of what she naturally generated just so he could at least briefly hold some of it in his hands, and even though until that moment he would've sworn he was sick of being so inferior to someone who was supposed to be made of the exact same stuff as him, when he saw her tears he felt bad for making her feel bad. It was the opposite of what he was trying to do, which made him feel like maybe he didn't know how to be good after all.

"Pete, how'd you get this?" Drita asked.

He wasn't supposed to tell her about the godmother, which meant he couldn't tell her about the money, which meant he had to lie, which also wasn't good. That wasn't his fault, though; Jackie set him up for that. He tried to think of some stupid answers, and he even offered a few that were too obviously stupid to take seriously, hoping she might let it drop. But she didn't, and so Pete backtracked to the doll aisle at Bradlees, when he clutched the sweaty bill in his hand so that nobody would pickpocket it from him. It was a fear that made no sense, because pickpockets lived in fake places like London, like in that *Oliver Twist* movie they had to watch in school, not in actual places like Waterbury. But Waterbury did have thieves; they knew this because the clothes on their clothesline had once been stolen, along with the old Hot Wheels Pete left out on the porch so he could surf it down the hill. Dom would warn Pete every time he got grounded that he was setting himself up to be the kind of punk who would grow up to do things like that, and that gave Pete the idea:

"I rode my bike to Bradlees and stole it," he told her.

Drita gasped.

"Pete," she said.

"What? I did it for you?" he said.

She stopped crying, but she still looked almost sad, like he'd done something to her instead of for her. He didn't understand it. It was like even when he tried to be good he made trouble, like the way Jackie said the godmother did. Then Drita said something in a foreign language, which he obviously didn't understand, but it made him realize that even when she spoke English Pete didn't always understand. He didn't understand why everything was so hard for him to understand.

1999

It seemed to Pete that in all those years in between childhood and that moment, when other people were figuring things out, Pete had gotten so buried under not-understanding that he couldn't see a way out of it. Seventeen years after that birthday and he still didn't know how to do the *right* right thing. He couldn't save Shanda from herself, he couldn't take care of his own son, he sure as hell couldn't G.I. Joe his way to victory over an army of Serbs in a place he'd never belong even if he'd gotten that tattoo on his forehead instead of his chest. All he really knew how to do was pack a bag, which this time around meant a plastic Duane Reade sack that he stuffed with the four pairs of boxers, two extra T-shirts, and one pair of spare Dickies that he'd managed to acquire with his previous weeks' pay from roofing and, briefly, gunrunning. Maybe Dave was still waiting for him out in Ronkonkoma with his uncle. Maybe he could stay sober long enough to get on the right train this time, long enough to actually think his next step through before walking toward it.

He slipped around the partition that separated the warehouse from the front office, a little space with windows and a front door that existed for essentially no reason, since neither construction nor guerrilla armies were the kinds of businesses that attracted much in the way of walk-in clients. He'd rarely seen anyone in there except the occasional glimpse of Ramadan's wife, Valon's mother, silently stuffing envelopes, but he figured she'd be at the ceremony with her husband and son, so he was surprised to find her outside the door, knocking on it, as if waiting for Pete to turn in his key after vacating the premises.

He was more surprised to find that it wasn't Valon's mother out there at all.

"Drita?" he said.

She couldn't have heard him from behind that security glass, but she nodded anyway, and he unlocked and opened the door for her to step inside.

26

DRITA WAS VAGUELY AWARE OF THE FULL-GROWN ADULTS WITH full-grown adult money who'd pay a price exponentially higher than the one on the sticker for the fully intact original Parisian Barbie she held in her hands. But the fact that she didn't know where to find those kinds of adults, and the fact that she knew better than to interact with them if she did know where to find them, wasn't why she spent so long dumbly looking at the doll she pulled from the corner of her closet, hiding behind a laundry basket of tattered elf-themed flannel sheets that hadn't been washed in three Christmases.

She'd never opened the box, not just because she'd outgrown it seconds after Pete dropped it in her hands, but because it felt like evidence, and she knew enough from the police procedurals that Jackie watched to never mess with evidence. What it served as evidence of depended on the day. If Pete dropped a bowl of spaghetti and Dom told him to him eat it off the floor like the dog they were never allowed to have, it was evidence that they were better off being godless foundlings than inheritors of that man's blood. At least Pete tried to do a good thing, even if he messed it up.

In truth, she mostly she kept it as evidence that she could brandish when the time was right, when she needed to claim some upper hand. When Drita's three-day eighth-grade field trip to D.C. was cut down to a day and a half because Pete ditched the class to buy bootleg VHS tapes and dirty Calvin and Hobbes T-shirts from sketchy vendors on the National Mall, she meant to pull it out to show Jackie and Dom that they didn't even know what kinds of things Pete really got up to when nobody was looking. When Drita's middle school friends quietly slipped from Drita's room to the backyard to watch Pete practice aerials on a tenuous ramp he put together out of plywood and cinder blocks, she meant to pull it out and tell them: Do you know what kinds of things your make-believe boyfriend does? Why is he the one everybody wants to look at?

She never ended up narcing on him, though, because nobody liked a narc and she didn't need help being not liked. The girls at school stopped hanging around when Pete's orbit grew way beyond the backyard. Pete's orbit grew way beyond the backyard because he didn't much like her, either, or at least that's what it felt like when he ran off with his boys while she sat on the sofa alone on Friday nights watching family-friendly sitcoms she would've found corny even if she were their intended demographic. In time she forgot about the Barbie altogether, and now, discovering it again, she saw it as just a dumb relic of a life she was days away from leaving behind.

It seemed too valuable to leave to the Goodwill pile, though. And if anybody knew how to extract value from ridiculous things, it was the person who gifted the ridiculous thing to her in the first place.

Pete was miraculously in his room, not working the night shift at Wendy's or doing post–night shift who-knows-what with his Wendy's buddies. Drita knocked. She felt weirdly embarrassed about it; knocking felt so formal, but they hadn't left their doors open to each other in so long that she wasn't sure what the correct procedure was by then.

"Yeah?" Pete said.

"It's me," Drita said. She began to turn the doorknob, and then paused to ask, "Can I come in?"

Pete didn't answer, just opened the door himself.

"What's up?" he asked. His eyes were red, as usual, but he seemed lucid enough.

"Remember this?" she asked.

His red eyes floated to the box, his brows heading up toward a hairline still impressively low and thick even after buzzing it at the start of the summer.

"Jesus, Drita, you never opened it?"

"Nah," she said. "I preserved it."

"For what?"

She shrugged. "No good reason."

He took the box from her and shook it, as if he thought it contained gunpowder. "I can't believe you never opened it. You never really liked it, did you?"

"No, I did. I actually did. I liked it a lot. It just seemed too special to, like, do anything with," Drita said. "It was stupid. Anyway, you want it back?"

"Want it back? Get the hell outta here," Pete said, but he smiled when he said it, and traced his finger over the cellophane. "Barbie's kind of a skank, huh? Looking like she works on Cherry Street or something."

"She's probably worth some money. Not Cherry Street money, collector's item money."

Pete looked at the box again, at the vocab words printed on the side. "*Maison*," he said. "Home. You're the one getting the hell out of maison. Why don't you sell it? You'll probably need some money at college."

"I'll have a meal plan. I can eat whatever I want at the cafeteria. You should sell it and then you can get the hell out of maison, too."

Pete took a long last look at the box and then tossed it on his bed. "I will. I'm going to move out soon."

"Oh, cool. Where to?"

"Me and Dave'll probably get a place together," Pete said.

"In Waterbury?"

"I'm not like you, Drita," he said, but not in the way he usually said it, not annoyed or sad, just regular, as if he was pointing out that she had a mole on her upper right shoulder that he didn't.

"I'm not saying you have to be like me, I'm just saying—"

"You can check it out when you come home to visit. It'll be cool. We're talking about getting a ball python. There's this place near downtown that sells them," he said.

Drita wondered if she should invite him to visit her at UConn. Maybe it'd be good for him to see something so different from what he was used to.

But she didn't even know what that future held for her own self. Maybe she wouldn't get invited to parties there. Maybe she would and Pete would come along and do a better job at them than she did. Probably better to just make that clean break she'd been waiting for since picking up her first brochure at the guidance counselor's office back in her freshman year of high school.

"Yeah, I'll visit," Drita said. "But I don't want to hang out with the snake."

"I won't make you. I bet you'd end up liking it, though."

"Doubt it," Drita said, and hoped Pete would come up with the next thing to say. But he was quiet for a minute just like her.

"Anyway, I'm about to go out for a while," Pete said. "When are you out of here again?"

"Next Saturday," she said.

"Damn," he said. "You want me to finally smoke you up before you leave? Get you ready for those college parties?"

"I don't think so," Drita said. "I don't know if they're going to, like, drug-test me or something."

Pete shrugged. "Well, let me know. And thanks for the doll."

"You're welcome," Drita said. He was gone by the time she remembered that she was the one who was supposed to have thanked him for the doll, but it was almost ten years too late for that, so she just let it be.

"What are you doing here?" Pete asked.

Drita would never know if she'd end up taking to the snake, because she never went to the first or any of the subsequent places Pete ended up moving into. At some point the snake must have been left to fend for itself in a leafy patch of Fulton Park, another good intention gone bad.

But then, as now, if she'd knocked on the door of any one of the subsidized units he lived in, he would have let her inside. She knew that. He always wanted to claim some kind of family, and she mostly wanted him to not be hers, at least not the way he was. She didn't know how to apologize for that. She moved her gaze to each of the walls around her instead, as if shopping for real estate.

"I saw you in the paper," she said.

"Oh," he said. "Like, the newspaper?"

"On the internet, but yeah, the newspaper part of the internet. It said you were working with, um, with some Kosovars," she said.

"Oh." Pete said. "Well, I'm not really working with them anymore."

"No?"

"Nah, it was just like a short-term thing," he said. The silence between the sentences must have been unbearable to him, too, because he asked again, "What are you doing here?"

Her eyes moved to the ceiling. If she were shopping for real estate, that would've been the deal breaker. The roofers, ironically, had a leak in their own space that they hadn't bothered to patch.

She shrugged, finally, and said, "I just thought you shouldn't go. Overseas, I mean."

"I'm not," he said.

"Okay," she said.

"But why not?" he said after the next silence.

In the days before that moment, maybe even as recently as that morning, she wanted to be cruel enough to lay out the whole story.

She could've told him what he expected to hear from her: Because you're not equipped to help. She could have told him what he didn't know: Because they're not your people to help. She could have told him something that would have answered some things and resolved none: Because, Brother, I am not your sister.

But, seeing Pete after so long, she didn't feel it was right to be cruel, and somehow the story still didn't feel whole at all. What difference did it make that it was two young, desperate women who had brought her and Pete together instead of some fusion of cells whose names she'd learned in a middle school sex ed class and long since forgotten? Nature or nurture—like Shanda had suggested, in her surprising, pragmatic wisdom, she wouldn't have had a say in it one way or the other. She only got a say in what happened afterwards, at moments like this, facing familiar brown eyes in a concrete slab that was not a home to either one of them.

"Because I was scared," she told him.

"Scared? For me?" Pete asked.

"Yeah," Drita said. It was neither a lie nor the whole truth, but Pete didn't need to atone for the fears she had that he wasn't responsible for, so those she kept to herself. "You have a family, remember?"

"I remember," Pete said. "But I fucked that all up. I fucked them over so bad. Even you. Even Ma."

"You don't have to worry about me. Or Ma. But Shanda and Dakota," she said, and paused there. She couldn't say if Shanda and Dakota needed worrying about. But worrying wasn't really the job. Man, it was work, but none of it was really a job.

"Shanda and Dakota are back," is what she settled on.

"Back where, back in Waterbury?" Pete asked incredulously.

"Yeah. They're doing good."

"Jesus fuck," Pete said. He rubbed his palms against his nearly shorn head, his hair still ridiculously thick, even as stubble. "Oh. Good. That's real good." He nodded, as if that had been his plan all along. "It's good they got back home. Damn. Okay."

"They've been staying with me. It's been nice to have the company. But it's just a temporary thing. Shanda's getting on her feet. Ma's really happy to have Dakota around again."

"She was always good with him," Pete said.

"She's a natural," Drita said.

"She's not going take me back," Pete said. "Shanda, I mean. Even if I do right after this."

"Doesn't mean you can't do it anyway," Drita said.

"But what is it? What's the right thing?"

"Pete, I can't answer that for you. I'm sorry," Drita said. The apology wasn't for then but for all the times she thought she knew better. She hoped he understood that.

"Me, too. I'm sorry," Pete said, and she wondered what he hoped she understood about his version of sorry. It seemed like a new kind of generosity between them, that they left each other some room to fill in their own gaps.

"I want to get my shit together," Pete said.

"Okay," she said.

"For Dakota, like," he said.

"Okay," she said.

"I thought this was how I could do it," Pete said, looking at the room around them like it was the portal to another world. "But I couldn't do it."

"Okay," she said.

"Really?" he asked. "It's okay?"

Drita's eyes lifted back to the stain on the ceiling, and then they floated back down and landed on him. She looked for resemblance there, and there was some, whatever it meant. They both had brown hair, brown eyes. She wasn't sure whether or not to take comfort in that. Maybe she wasn't supposed to take anything from it. Maybe it was enough to just see it.

"I guess it depends on what you do now," Drita said.

"I guess I just go home?" Pete said.

"I guess," Drita said. It seemed to her as good an answer as any. "You can use my car to get there, if you want."

"You're not coming?"

Drita pulled the keys from her bag and handed the whole ring over to him, the half dozen metal tabs a little tambourine that played an unfamiliar note. "Soon," she said.

The sun had dropped behind the block by the time the man Drita recognized as Valon's father arrived back at Tristate's offices, the city's artificial horizon keeping the last of the late afternoon daylight from warming her. He slung the duffel bag he held in his hand over his shoulder and smiled at her, as if he expected to find her there.

"Mirëdita," Drita said to him.

"Hello, beautiful," he said, and Drita knew she slaughtered the greeting so brutally that he could only respond in English.

"I was at the ceremony today. It was really something. Really moving," Drita said.

"Yes, yes, I saw you talking to my son. You're friends with Valon?"

"Kind of," Drita said. "I guess not really. I guess we don't know each other very well."

"That's too bad for him," the man said.

"Valon knows my brother. Pete, Petrit, whatever he's going by now."

"That joker's your brother?" the man said. He made a face that suggested laughter, though nothing audibly laugh like came out. "Well," he said, "I guess he's all right."

"He had to leave," Drita said. "He's not here anymore."

The man raised his brows, and Drita saw where Valon's dark eyes had sprung from. "What, no notice? He sent his sister to tell me that he quit?"

"He has things to take care of. Things at home. You understand, besa and all that."

"Ah, besa, yes. I didn't think he knew what that meant. He doesn't even speak the language." The man studied her lips, like he could de-termine just from the shape of them whether she knew what her brother did not. "And you? Do you understand it?"

She couldn't tell him no in the language, and that itself was the an-swer.

The man smiled and extended his hand. "I'm Ramadan," he said.

"I'm Drita," she said. "I'm trying to understand."

ACKNOWLEDGMENTS

JUST LIKE AT THANKSGIVING, I'M SURE MY GRATITUDE AUDIT WILL BE missing a few entries, but here goes:

Thanks to my whole effing sprawling family, including the biological, the married-in-and-outs, the close-enoughs, and the ones Ancestry .com wouldn't know what to do with.

Thanks to all my friends in all the places, with particular shoutouts to Christopher Rhodes and the Tuesday crew.

Thanks to my colleagues and students at UNCG, especially Terry Kennedy, Jessie Van Rheenen, Stuart Dischell, Emilia Phillips, Holly Goddard Jones, and Derek Palacio.

Thanks to the Bread Loaf Writers' Conference (again and again) and the Sewanee Writers' Conference.

Thanks to Ross White and The Grind. Seriously, how many acknowledgments must you be in by now?

Thanks to Luella and Abner for their unwavering emotional support. You're good dogs.

An always-insufficient thanks to Julie Barer and The Book Group, with especially deep gratitude to Nicole Cunningham for helping get this thing from almost-ready to here-goes.

Thanks to Andrea Walker and the team at Random House. (I can't believe I get to do this again with you!)

Thanks to the Wayback Machine for corroborating and supplementing my memories of the nineties. In addition to many news archives, I referred often to Stacy Sullivan's *Be Not Afraid for You Have Sons in America* and Paul Hockenos's *Homeland Calling: Exile Patriotism and the Balkan Wars* for insight and historicity. Thanks to those authors for their robust and objective research, and apologies for mucking up their clarity with audacious imagination and speculation.

ABOUT THE AUTHOR

Xhenet Aliu's debut novel, *Brass,* won both the Townsend Prize and the Georgia Author of the Year First Novel Award. Her debut fiction collection, *Domesticated Wild Things,* won the Prairie Schooner Book Prize in Fiction. Aliu's writing has appeared in *The New York Times, Hobart, LitHub, BuzzFeed,* and elsewhere, and she has received a grant from the Elizabeth George Foundation, a fellowship from the Djerassi Resident Artists Program, and scholarships from the Bread Loaf Writers' Conference and the Sewanee Writers' Conference, among other awards.

xhenetaliu.com

Instagram: @xhennyfromtheblock

ABOUT THE TYPE

This book was set in Sabon, a typeface designed by the well-known German typographer Jan Tschichold (1902–74). Sabon's design is based upon the original letterforms of sixteenth-century French type designer Claude Garamond and was created specifically to be used for three sources: foundry type for hand composition, Linotype, and Monotype. Tschichold named his typeface for the famous Frankfurt typefounder Jacques Sabon (c. 1520–80).